PROCEED DOWN THE CENTRE LINE

a dressage novel

by Charles Blackburn

The Author

'Robbie' (RCB) Robinson graduated from Magdalene College, Cambridge, England in the early 1960s. A professional horseman for nearly 50 years, he has also worked as a landscaping and agricultural contractor, a lathe operator and a copywriter. His novels reflect his love of the English countryside and seek to offer readers engaging, unpretentious, light entertainment. Happy endings are guaranteed!

Flight Lieutenant Charles Blackburn, the author's uncle, whose name is represented in the author's middle initials and on the books' covers, was a Hurricane pilot killed on active service during the Second World War. This name was chosen to perpetuate his memory.

By the same author

Novels:
    Lost and Found
    White Wings Over The Lake
    A Copper For Penny
    No Easy Ride
    Taking Possession
    The Southbrook Inheritance
    The Cottage In The Trees
    Flames in the Wood

Equestrian:
    An Introduction To Riding Instruction
    An Everyday Rider's Guide To Practical Breaking

© 2016 R.C.B. Robinson
ISBN 978-1-326 62799-7

Author's Note

This is a work of fiction. No reference or similarity is intended, nor should any be inferred, to any actual person or occurrence, past or present.

Front Cover: The South Downs from Durford Wood
Back Cover: The author and 'Mahbuba'

Chapter One

The deep, cool blue of the September sky was broken with ragged white clouds, reminders of the wind and rain that had lately ceased. She led the horse through the gate and on to the dimpled sand of the riding school, feeling the freshness of the approaching evening whisper against her cheek. It was Saturday, and late enough for the kids to have gone home at last and the peace and quiet so often lacking when she was schooling to be no problem tonight.

The horse stood still as she swung easily into the saddle and settled her feet in the stirrups. If ever conditions were right for some solid, sensible work, they were just about perfect this evening. With the reins in one hand she nudged the horse to walk towards the fence, raising her head to look with satisfaction over the deserted footpath that ran along one long side of the school, and then out across the huge stubble field that reached to the wood at the foot of the hill, nearly three hundred yards away. Here in the shelter of the valley deep in the South Downs the shadows were already lengthening, although it would not be dark for a couple of hours yet.

Hope died as it always did, along with the resolve to make the best of things, when the horse failed as usual to respond to her quiet aid for trot.

It was impossible not to remember, for at least the five hundredth time, what things used to be like, this time last year. She'd had three horses then, all well schooled and far better bred than Gypsy, horses to whom medium or even advanced medium dressage came easily and who were a real joy to ride. The good resolutions made three months ago, when Gypsy had been all they could afford at a scruffy auction in the middle of nowhere, and she was so desperate for another horse she would have bought a donkey as better than nothing, were easily forgotten when the big, idle gelding was such a contrast to what she was used to.

Gypsy was five years old, a shade over sixteen hands, brown and white, and while he was not a heavy horse he was certainly no thoroughbred. Oh, come *on,* Sophy exclaimed bitterly and out loud, giving him a sharp poke with her spurs and finally achieving a reluctant trot. Surely the old camel could go better than this, on a day like today when everything else was as good as it could be.

Last year, when they'd lived in a lovely big house in the country, before Daddy died and the world fell apart, she'd had a private yard of her own with her own indoor school and even a paid girl groom to help, a smart horsebox with its own living accommodation and nothing much to do except pursue what she wanted; and what she wanted was to ride, all day and every day; but not like this, on a horse who wouldn't do anything in a yard where you had to do everything yourself, and people expected you to do favours for them if you wanted them in return. It was idiotic, to have won what she had and been where she'd been, to be mucking about like this in a no hope do-it-yourself livery yard full of kids with scruffy ponies, who only wanted to jump silly little jumps and play the fool and knew and cared nothing about anything else. There wasn't even anyone to talk to about sensible schooling, and how horses were supposed to go.

Gypsy shuffled reluctantly round the school, managing a lumpy, stuffy sort of rhythm now he had finally got started. She turned on to a circle and the horse fell instantly on to his inside shoulder, poking his nose with the bend all wrong and leaning hard on his rider's inside rein. It probably wasn't true, but she could have sworn he was doing it on purpose. She could have cried with the injustice of life. Couldn't the horse try just a little bit? Her arm began to ache with the effort of holding him on the line she wanted to ride, and finally the frustration boiled over and she snatched at the rein with a sudden, vicious jerk, stabbing the horse in the mouth for leaning on her.

"If you do that again," a man's voice said, "I'll get over this fence and I'll bloody well do it to you."

The voice wasn't loud, but it broke her concentration like a pistol shot. She snapped her head up.

The school was shielded from the footpath by a yard wide strip of waist high nettles and rough grass bounded by another, parallel, fence. The man was leaning on the outer fence, his elbows spread, calmly smoking a pipe in the evening sunshine. There was a flat cap on his head and a grey whippet standing beside him. He might have been fifty, he might have been older. He looked like a lorry driver or a labourer out walking his dog, who naturally knew nothing about horses and in any case had no business talking to her at all.

"What do you know about it?" she retorted angrily. Anger at the interference made her swear in return. "Mind your own bloody business."

The man was quite unmoved. He showed no sign of moving on, either. He tapped his pipe out on the fence and began to refill it, glancing up at her occasionally as he did so. He said nothing, as though having expressed his opinion it was up to her now to either justify what she was doing to the horse or else do something else. In any case, he was standing on a public footpath and perfectly entitled to stay there all night if he wanted to.

Sophy walked away from him across the school. She was nonplussed and agitated. She knew herself she ought not to have done that with the rein, however provoking Gypsy was being at the time. But Gypsy was always provoking, and it wasn't the first time she'd done that to him. Not that it made any difference; nothing she did seemed to make any difference. The horse went the way it did, and that was that. But she did have some pride left.

She turned the horse round with exaggerated care and walked back to him.

"Very well," she said with icy, superior calm, gazing down at him from the horse's back. "Perhaps you'd like to show me how it should be done."

He puffed calmly on his pipe, and looked back at her reflectively. Far from being apologetic, or even surprised at this novel suggestion, he seemed to be considering the question quite seriously.

He took his pipe out of his mouth. "All right," he said at last. "I suppose I could try. You'll have to hold the dog though."

He climbed through one fence and over the other, squashing the nettles and towing the dog behind him. Sophy felt a surge of panic. She stared down at him with rising alarm. What was she thinking, saying something like that? Who was he, anyway? And she was alone on the yard, and the main house was well out of earshot as well as being almost out of sight from here.

He approached the horse and looked up at her, seeming to understand her predicament. A faint smile touched his eyes.

"It's your horse," he observed mildly. "You can change your mind if you like. But it was your suggestion. And I have been on a horse before. Once or twice." Again the smile flickered round his eyes, and then his expression changed to one of irritation at her apparent fear of him. "I've no interest in you, madam, if that's what's bothering you."

"Of course it isn't," she snapped. She dismounted aggressively and thrust the reins into his hands. The thought came to her then that last year no stranger would have ridden one of her horses under any circumstances. Even her instructors had always had to ask her permission. But it didn't much matter who rode Gypsy. She'd already let one of the girls sit on him. The stupid kids even liked him. Whatever he did, this man could hardly do the horse any harm. She'd probably get rid of him soon anyway; surely she could get a better horse than this, even if they didn't have much money.

He stood beside her, the horse's reins in one hand and his dog's lead in the other. He was a little older than she had first thought, and his blue eyes regarded her with quiet composure from beneath the peak of his cap. In spite of her feeling that this could be the silliest thing she had ever done, inviting a total stranger to get on her horse, even if it was only Gypsy, there was something oddly reassuring about him.

"You are quite sure about this," he said, and she nodded dumbly.

"I can't do anything with him," she muttered. "Nobody can. He's completely useless."

"Well, in that case I can't do any harm, can I?" he said. He put the dog's lead in her hand and slipped his coat off, letting it fall in the sand.

He was wearing wellington boots against the mud in the wet footpath, but he vaulted on to the horse without using the stirrup, startling her with his agility. He adjusted the leathers in a few seconds with the ease of what was evidently long practice and rode quietly away to the track. His absolute assurance in what he was doing took her breath away. She felt her mouth open in astonishment, and closed it hurriedly. Was he a jockey or something? But he was much too tall for that, and too old.

She stood in the middle of the arena holding the dog, fascinated now rather than anxious that her impetuous offer might lead to disaster.

He asked Gypsy to trot, and in ten yards and without whip or spur found a stride and a carriage she hadn't found in three months. The horse began to swing his quarters, and rounded into his hand, and when he took him on to a circle he bent willingly into the turn, the image of a novice horse working smoothly through his back, light on his feet and showing proper engagement. Even more astonishing, he had something about him, that indefinable something that comes from a horse with pride in itself, enjoying its work, the presence that catches the eye and makes a good horse even more special.

He rode for about a quarter of an hour without speaking, working the horse in rising and sitting trot, using the whole arena as he circled and turned and changed the rein. He didn't canter or attempt anything fancy, although it seemed to Sophy he easily could have done, the way Gypsy was going now, with a cadence in his step and his ears attentive, and a rhythm unimaginable half an hour ago. He was barely recognisable as the stuffy, ungrateful camel he was when Sophy rode him herself.

And the man could ride, by God could he ride. His hands were irresistibly soft and his seat flowed easily with the pace, and when he sat to the trot it was hard to see where the horse ended and the man began. He brought the horse back to her eventually and dismounted, still without speaking. Incredibly, he was still smoking his pipe.

He looked into her face as he gave her the reins, and winked at her disbelief.

"They know how to fool you," he said then, taking his dog from her and patting him as he jumped up in greeting, "but you mustn't be rough and impatient. It's never right and it doesn't work."

He picked up his jacket, stroked the horse's nose and walked away, bending down to get through the fence.

Sophy recovered herself. He *had* to talk to her, he couldn't just go like that. "But who are you?" she called after him. "Will you come back? What should I do?"

He straightened up on the footpath and turned briefly towards her with a wave of his hand. Then he walked on up the hill without looking back, the whippet running joyfully ahead of him and a wreath of pipe smoke curling round his shoulders.

Chapter Two

The stable yard was attached to a big, square, Georgian country house on the outskirts of the village of Fairgate, about a mile up a well maintained track from the main road. According to local report it belonged to a mysterious Arab who presumably had no present use for either the house or the stables or the adjacent estate, and who by all accounts had never set foot on most of his extensive property.

Everybody dealt with a sharp faced, middle aged woman, Miss Agatha Brown, who acted as the agent for the whole estate and lived in an apartment on the ground floor of the big house, next door to the office converted from what had once been the scullery. The rest of the three storey house was closed up with shutters over the windows.

Usually, no one from the stables saw Miss Brown from one month's end to the next, when they went across the courtyard to pay the rent, although occasionally one of the tenant farmers might be observed going into the office. So far as Sophy knew, no one had ever seen the actual owner.

It was unfortunate that Miss Brown should choose this particular evening to inspect the equestrian part of her empire, when the other DIY tenants had somehow contrived to leave the whole yard strewn with straw and dotted with several piles of fresh horse droppings.

She met Sophy coming in from the school, leading Gypsy on a long, loose rein and lost in her own reflections.

Gypsy hadn't felt the same at all when she'd remounted after that strange man had disappeared. It would be stretching a point to say the horse was keen, but he was willing and paying attention and even showed some signs of accepting the bridle; he was still not going nearly as well as he had for him, she had to acknowledge, reluctantly and ruefully, but perhaps he was worth keeping after all. Perhaps there was something to be made of him. The awful thought was also pressing in on her that maybe, just maybe, she wasn't *quite* as good a rider as she'd always thought she was, or else why.....

"This yard is a mess," Miss Brown announced in a sharp tone. "I hope you're not intending to leave it like this. I've got a man from ADAS coming in first thing tomorrow, soil testing. He'll be using this yard for water. This estate has a reputation to maintain, and so have I."

Sophy came out of her reverie and looked at her.

"It's not my fault," she protested. "They've all gone to a party or something."

"I don't care whose fault it is." Miss Brown was evidently not prepared to discuss it. "Your contract is the same as everybody else's. This yard is not be left in a mess at any time. If there's no one else here you'll have to sweep it before you go. Assuming you want to go on keeping your horse here, that is." She glanced round at the muck heap. Nobody had tidied that either. "And do something with the midden," she said with an irritable gesture. "Good evening, Miss Taylor." She muttered something about checking up more often, and walked away across the courtyard.

Sophy put Gypsy back in his stable and untacked him, furious at the fates that had turned life on its head. Nobody used to speak to her like that, nobody would have dared when Daddy was alive. She was tempted to just go away and leave the yard as it was. For a long minute, she seriously considered it. She only ever swept the tiny piece of yard in front of her own stable, and not an inch in front of anybody else's, and she resented having to do that, having always had a girl to do the stable chores for her in those halcyon days that had apparently vanished forever; and she had never tidied a muck heap in her life. She wasn't even sure she knew how.

She watered and fed the horse, and watching him feed settled her temper just enough for commonsense to reassert itself. It would be hellishly difficult to find somewhere else to keep a horse this close to home, especially somewhere with a school, and mother would look at her with that awful reproach, like a whipped kitten, that she simply couldn't bear, and then later she'd say something about money that she didn't want to hear. Muttering to herself, with wide, inexpert swipes of the broom, she began to sweep the yard.

She was standing on top of the muck heap, fork in hand, sweating freely and still growling under her breath, when she caught sight over the wall of the man who had ridden Gypsy passing on the footpath on his way back to the village. He was too far away to speak, but he acknowledged her with a slight wave before he vanished into the trees behind the house.

She drove the two miles home to the tiny, upstairs flat in the cottage with dirtier jodhpurs than usual and an unaccustomed ache in her shoulders. She was also later than her mother had expected.

She appeared in the kitchen doorway rubbing her hands on a tea towel.

"You're late, darling," she said. "Is everything all right?"

"I suppose," Sophy responded sulkily. "That Brown woman made me sweep the yard before I came home. It wasn't my mess. The kids had just left it. And I had to do the muck heap." She collapsed in an armchair without even taking her boots off.

Her mother turned back into the small kitchen, frowning slightly. Sophy still hadn't learned, as she'd had to do so suddenly, that most of the world did what it had to do, not what it wanted to.

Of course, it wasn't her fault. Almost from the day she was born Derek had spoilt her dreadfully. If it came to that, he'd spoilt the pair of them. It hadn't mattered so much then, when the business was expanding and he was opening a new shop once a week, or so it seemed, when if Sophy wanted a new horse or she wanted a new car they would appear like magic within days of the wish being expressed. In those days it never occurred to either of them to ask where the money came from, or that the bubble could burst, or that for years her husband had been using other people's money to pay for his grandiose schemes, and one day the whole precarious edifice, built like a house of cards out of one paper financial fiction on top of another, would come tumbling down around them in a matter of weeks.

What would have happened to Derek if he hadn't been found hanging from a tree in the paddock early one morning nobody quite knew. Although the coroner had been satisfied no one else was involved, it turned out afterwards the Fraud Squad had been sniffing about for some time, and the house had been under siege in the last days from sombre bankers and angry businessmen demanding back what they said Derek Taylor should never have been allowed near in the first place. It was almost a relief that he'd done what he did. There was never any suggestion that she had been involved in her husband's nefarious business activities, and one or two of his duped former associates, at least those who hadn't attempted to claim even the little she had left of her own, had even expressed some sympathy for her when they found out he'd hanged himself; although their sympathy hadn't extended as far as practical assistance when she and Sophy had needed it most.

Not that she had needed sympathy, particularly. Her husband's death had provoked more shock than regret. In recent years Derek's philandering ways and extended absences from home had effectively snuffed out the last of the affection she had once felt for him. With the benefit of hindsight, she thought nowadays that his extravagance towards her and Sophy was probably just a shallow attempt keep his conscience quiet.

She prodded a fork awkwardly at the sausages with a grimace of distaste. Until lately, learning to cook had never featured as part of her plans for life. It had just become a necessary evil, like so many other things.

It didn't help, going back over it, and Sophy was her real concern now. The house, the horses, everything had been taken to pay back what could be paid back of the vast sums Derek had contrived to use and lose over the years. It hadn't left them with much, and now Sophy was bitter and betrayed and at war with life.

She wasn't quite nineteen, as blonde and slim and tall and pretty as any mother could wish for, but still after all these months not coming to terms with the altered facts of life, that now she would have to work for what she wanted and realise it wouldn't come to her simply because she wanted it. Her husband's death, and not least the manner of it, had hit his daughter much harder than it had her, and so far it had been possible to make allowances, but they couldn't go on forever like this.

Buying Gypsy had been foolish, a squandering of the remnants of her tiny capital in a last gesture to her petulant and distressed daughter to try and pretend that things might one day return to what they had been. They couldn't really afford the horse then, and they certainly couldn't afford to keep it, not now. It was all she could do, on her tiny salary, to pay the rent on this small flat and feed the pair of them. Geoff Davis at the gallery in Steeplehurst had taken her on as his assistant mostly for old times sake. Once upon a time, she'd been his best customer and they'd always got on well, socially. It was lucky he lived in the village, and could take her in to work and bring her home in the evenings. It was luckier still that it was a job she could do, when she wasn't trained for anything.

But Sophy was going to have to get a job herself if she wanted to keep that horse. There was no way round it. Sooner or later she'd have to tell her, and it ought to be sooner. There was already a small overdraft at the Bank, largely caused by paying the insurance for running Sophy's sports car. At least she'd been able to keep that. It was just about the only asset they'd had between them that wasn't in Derek's or their joint names when the crash came.

She carried the supper into the other room and set it on the table.

"Do take your boots off, dear," she said mildly, and Sophy pulled them off and let them drop carelessly on the carpet.

"I let a man ride Gypsy today," she remarked, moodily picking at her supper. The image came back to her of Gypsy working smoothly round the school, bending and going forward properly. Why had he never done it for her? He hadn't even done it like that for her after the man had got off and gone.

"He managed to get him going really well. He looked super, actually."

Her mother looked at her with surprise. Gypsy's shortcomings compared with her daughter's other horses had been paraded before her at great length almost from the day they'd bought him. She put aside her curiosity about the man and took advantage of the first favourable words she'd heard about the horse for some time.

"We have to talk about Gypsy," she said carefully. "You know we can't really afford to keep him. I know you do him yourself, but the gas bill came this morning and you know you're always saying he's not good enough for you. I think you have to decide that if you want a horse you really will have to help pay for it. Get a job, I mean."

Sophy wrinkled her nose. Mother was always saying they couldn't manage, but she always seemed to cope somehow.

On the other hand, she wasn't completely stupid. It had crossed her own mind from time to time that she was bored; she had no friends in the village, there was never any money to spend, and having only one horse to ride wasn't enough to fill in the whole day, even with taking mother to work sometimes when that Davis man didn't.

"I suppose I could," she said grudgingly. "I don't know what I could do, though."

Secretly, her mother agreed with her. Her daughter's attitude to her expensive education had largely consisted of impatience that it interfered with the time she had to ride her precious ponies, and then horses. It wasn't that she was unintelligent; it simply hadn't mattered a great deal to either of her parents, and certainly not to Sophy, whether she passed exams or not, since the question of her working for a living had never arisen.

"Well, we'll have to see what we can find," she said, thankful that at least Sophy was prepared to consider the idea. Maybe Geoff could come up with something. Now that the seed was sown, she changed the subject.

"So who was this man who performed a miracle on Gypsy?" she asked. "You've never done anything but tell me how impossible he is since the day we bought him."

"I don't know," Sophy said. "He was passing with his dog and Gypsy was being a pig as usual and I let him get on and he just did it. He didn't say who he was, he just went off afterwards. He didn't beat him or anything. He just sort of sat there and he, well, he just did it."

"He sounds like that instructor you had once that you didn't like," her mother said, a little too innocently, and Sophy flushed and looked down at the table.

Three years ago a man had come to teach her, not like the usual girls who came to help, who were awed by her magnificent horses and lovely school and didn't really know much more than she did, or so it seemed. This man was older, and forthright, and did wonderful things with one of her horses, things she wanted to do like passage and flying change, things she couldn't do and had always blamed the horse for instead of her own shortcomings. This instructor hadn't minced his words when he'd told her why what she was doing didn't work, and she wasn't going to stand for that from a man with patches on his jacket standing in her yard and telling her she wasn't as good as she thought she was.

The usual ploy of bursting into tears had made Daddy see him off in double quick time, and without his fee, but she'd caught mother's eye a little later and had the feeling that she had one parent who hadn't been completely fooled by her performance. After the instructor had gone, she had a guilty, private feeling that he'd been right, and half wished him back again; then she'd gone out and won an elementary class again the next weekend and it hadn't mattered after that.

Since she and mother had been alone together, she'd had that feeling again, once or twice, that mother wasn't totally taken in by some of the things she said, the way Daddy always had been. Anyway, she consoled herself, she was far too old now to burst into tears, whatever happened.

"I'll definitely get a job," she announced suddenly, "and I'll definitely keep the horse, well, for now anyway. Maybe it's just me that can't ride him properly."

Her mother stared at her. She hadn't much understanding of horses herself, but it was the first time she'd ever heard Sophy suggest out loud that anybody in the world could ride better than she could.

She got up from the table and hugged her tight. "Now that's more like it," she said approvingly. "We've both got to learn to make the best of what we've got."

Sophy was embarrassed and pushed her away. "If that man comes back," she said, " he won't get away next time. I'll make him show me how he did it. It can't be that hard. He was even older than Daddy. If he can do it, then I must be able to."

Chapter Three

It was hard to say which was more aggravating, the silly little jump built on the track or Kitty Fittleworth's thirteen hand pony charging about with its head in the air, barely under control.

Either the pony or the jump got in her way every minute, making it impossible to work Gypsy for ten yards in a straight line or even on a circle. To make matters worse, the child's father was leaning on the gate with a video camera, filming his offspring with as much pride as if she was riding in the Hickstead Derby, and evidently thinking that it was Gypsy who was getting in the way all the time.

The excited black pony cut across her again, only three feet in front of Gypsy's nose. Gypsy was unconcerned, but Sophy snorted with annoyance. The kids knew she always rode at this time; why couldn't they let her have the school as usual, especially today, when she wanted so much to try and do with her horse what that man had done yesterday.

She glanced unconsciously towards the footpath, and with a little start of surprise saw him walking by.

He paused close to where he'd leaned on the fence yesterday, but he wasn't looking at the horses, he was watching his dog standing with a raised forefoot and staring intently out across the stubble field.

A rabbit moved, a good thirty yards away, and the whippet shot after it, a low, grey flash astonishingly quick over the rough corn stalks. The rabbit dodged and weaved and doubled back before it finally escaped into the wood, almost out of sight on the far side of the field, and the man walked on then, watching the dog racing back to him. He was quite clearly not going to stop and talk to her without some indication that she wanted to talk to him.

In another minute, he would be gone. A sense of urgency gripped her. She kicked Gypsy over to the fence and shouted after him, "Hey, you!"

Her attention was distracted by the pony galloping by, and when she looked again he was coming back, and then the dog arrived at his feet, panting hard, eyes sparkling with the joy of stretching his legs across that huge field.

The man put his hand in his pocket and gave the dog a titbit. He looked up at her across the nettles and the double fence, unhurried and frowning.

"You're not very polite, are you?" he said coldly. "Good evening to you too. What do you want?"

"I'm sorry," Sophy said, not very sincerely. She dismounted to talk to him, forgetting that she was right in front to the jump.

"Do you mind," the child's father said from the other side of the arena, and she dragged Gypsy back into the centre of the school. The pony cantered past her, and jumped the pole for what must have been the twentieth time.

Sophy could have exploded with irritation. The man on the other side of the fence shrugged and turned to walk away. For almost the first time in her life, she desperately wanted something and it didn't look as though she was going to get it.

"Please," she called out. "Come and ride him again. Show me what you did."

He climbed slowly into the arena, the dog at his heels. Kitty's father lowered his camera and looked at him curiously. The man acknowledged him with a polite nod before he turned to her

"I'll do this once more," he said, "for the sake of the horse. But if you want me to give you riding lessons, you'll have to pay."

"But I don't even know who you are," Sophy demurred at that.

"Mutual then, isn't it?" he responded. "Hold the dog."

Again he jumped into the saddle. Kitty rode Blackie up beside her, and her father came into the school too.

"Who is that man, Miss Taylor?" he asked her, and she was obliged to admit she had no idea. All three of them turned to watch him.

This time, he was more ambitious. It took him a bare minute to re-establish the stride he had found yesterday, and now he began to develop it, collecting the trot until he could ride a shoulder in, and finally using the exercise to produce a canter which Sophy would have died for, reminding her irresistibly of really good days on the beautifully schooled, expensive horses she used to take for granted. Strangely, the jump on the track never seemed to get in his way at all, not like it had for her.

Gypsy swept past them on a circle, impossibly light on his feet for a big horse, the cadence in his canter almost a dance, and if ever a horse was wearing a smile on his face, Gypsy was wearing one now. For a moment, Sophy thought he would ask for a flying change, but he changed the lead through walk with the horse softly balanced and obedient to the aids, and then at last the poetry was over and he walked him back to her and dismounted.

Kitty was staring at him with her mouth wide open and her father spoke to him before Sophy had a chance.

"Do you give lessons?" he said. "Do you think you could get our Blackie to go like that? Kitty never seems to be able to stop him when she wants. The girl at the Pony Club says he ought to go with his head in too, like you were just then, and we've tried all sorts to make him do it and none of it works." He offered the man his hand. "Joe Fittleworth," he said. "This is my daughter, Kitty. Do you live in the village?"

The stranger shook hands cordially enough, and with Kitty too. "Peter Holt," he said, introducing himself. "I haven't taught for a long time. Or ridden much, if it comes to that. I suppose I could start again. I shouldn't do it for nothing, mind. I've been in the horse business a long time and I know from experience that helping people professionally for nothing doesn't usually work out very well, not in the long run. People start taking things for granted and even good friends can fall out."

"Oh, I don't mind paying," Mr. Fittleworth shrugged away that problem. "I don't know much about horses myself, but Kitty's that keen and I've never been struck with some of the girls we've had teach her in the past. I don't think Kitty has been either, to tell you the truth. Most of them don't seem old enough to know much, if you know what I mean."

The man smiled for the first time and took his pipe out of his pocket. He was still holding Gypsy's reins, and automatically handed them to Sophy in exchange for his dog's lead without really looking at her.

"I expect we can work something out," he said. He glanced at Kitty. "I can be tough, mind. I expect people I teach to work. I'm serious when I take someone on. If you can't be bothered, neither can I."

Sophy could have burst with impatience. The conversation he was having with Mr. Fittleworth was the conversation he should have been having with her.

"Excuse *me*," she said pointedly, and the two men looked at her. Mr. Fittleworth grinned apologetically.

"All right, Miss Taylor, I think Blackie's had about enough and we need to get home for tea or the wife will have something to say. Can I call you, Mr. Holt?"

Mr. Holt scribbled a number on a scrap of paper and gave it to him, and Kitty led her pony away, looking back over her shoulder as Sophy was at last able to have the man to herself.

He regarded her with a trace of amusement. It was evident that he perfectly recognised and at the same time was totally unimpressed by her very expensive anorak, and bespoke breeches and boots.

"It's Miss Taylor, then, is it? And so, Miss Taylor, do you want teaching as well?"

"I might," Sophy said guardedly. "How do you make my horse go like that when I can't? I'm not stupid. I've won quite a lot actually, in dressage."

"Not with this horse, you haven't," Mr. Holt said, and she had to admit that was true.

He grunted with the satisfaction of having his opinion confirmed, and paused for a moment puffing on his pipe.

"All right, Miss Taylor, I'll tell you something. I was a professional horseman twenty years before you were born. You seem to think you can take anything you want from a horse, and it has nothing to do but give it to you. You think about giving this horse something back the next time you ride him. Be softer, let him know you care about him. I do come this way from time to time. If it looks like you're doing it the next time I see you, well, maybe I'll take you on, or maybe I won't."

He again looked at her appraisingly from beneath his cap, apparently considering whether he should say more, and then seemed to make his mind up.

"I'm old enough to say this to a girl your age, Miss Taylor, and not be bothered much whether you like it or not. You've got 'Me first' and 'I want' written all over you and it don't look nice. The horse doesn't like it either. I doubt any horse would."

It took a moment for the words to sink in. Her jaw dropped with anger. She wanted to say something back, but it wasn't there. Nobody had *ever* said anything like that to her before. It was *horrible*.

"I've nothing more to say, Miss Taylor. If you don't understand me now, and you still don't in a week's time, I'd be no good to you anyway. Good evening to you."

He ran his hand gently down the horse's neck before he climbed through the fence and left her, angry and bewildered, standing alone in the middle of the school holding a horse she couldn't ride, staring helplessly after him. She saw him bend down to let the dog off the lead, and he strode away completely unconcerned. Tears welled up in her eyes, and she blinked them back. How could he be so mean, how could anyone?

Chapter Four

The anger and the upset had faded into a feeling of black melancholy by the time she got home. Peter Holt's last words kept coming back to her, and with them the image of Gypsy, elegant and relaxed, cantering smoothly round the school. It had to be right, what he said, or why would he go like that for him and not for her?

Turning the words over and over in her mind, with no one to talk to about it, the bitter, unaccustomed seeds of self doubt took a powerful hold, and strangely they were not just about how well she was able to ride. Faced with the obvious, unpalatable truth that she was not the horsewoman she thought she was, the whisper crept into her mind that perhaps, just maybe, she wasn't quite the sort of person she thought she was in other ways too.

For the first time in her hitherto sheltered life, her self esteem was seriously dented, and there was no one to turn to, no safe place where she could go and be hugged and be told how good she really was.

She had never thought before that Daddy's death and all their troubles might have been partly her fault, and after only a moment she knew that couldn't possibly be true even now, but still....

Moody and depressed, she wandered about the village and the yard for two or three days, hoping each day when she rode him that Gypsy would show some sign of co-operating, but it didn't happen, at least not in any meaningful way. Mr. Holt didn't come by again, either.

Things might have been better if she could have got away, driven into Steeplehurst or down to the coast just for a change, to browse round a saddlers or go shopping for clothes or something, but she had no money, not even enough for a gallon of petrol. When she'd asked, mother had been nearly in tears when she had to refuse her. It was another moment of truth, and for the first time it really dawned on her that they weren't just not rich any more; they were poor, so poor she couldn't even drive her car when she wanted to.

Most of the time, there was nobody at the stables at all. The kids were at school during the day, and even in the mornings and evenings, when they were doing their ponies, and riding and giggling and talking their usual nonsense about horses, they hardly spoke to her. It didn't occur to her that her superior attitude when she'd first arrived, driving an expensive sports car and wearing riding clothes that might have cost more than some of their ponies, and regarding them and their beloved ponies with sublime disdain, had hardly endeared her to them or to their parents. Her mood was not improved by overhearing Kitty announcing proudly to one of her friends that she was going to have a lesson on Sunday from Mr. Holt, the only man in the world who could make Gypsy go properly. She glanced pertly over her shoulder as she spoke, knowing Sophy could hear her, and smirked smugly at her friend.

It poured with rain on Wednesday, steadily and relentlessly. There was barely enough petrol in the car to get to the garage, if she ever did have any money to fill it up again, and she was obliged to walk the two miles to the stables to feed and muck out, and then walk the same two miles back. Even her expensive waterproof jacket proved unequal to the task of keeping her dry in those conditions, and then, shoulders hunched against the wind, she found a forgotten pound coin in one of the pockets and her heart almost sang with content. You're pathetic, she said to herself. What can you do with a pound, for God's sake?

But it was enough to go into the village shop as she passed to buy a bar of chocolate. She stood there dripping in front of the counter, and the elderly woman serving smiled at her.

"My word, you're wet," she said.

Apart from mother, it was the only friendly remark she'd heard for days. It was an effort, but she managed somehow to smile back.

"A bit," she confessed. "I've been doing my horse." She pushed the hood off her face.

"I know you," the woman said. "You're Edith Taylor's daughter. You've taken the flat in the cottage by the church. Not a day for riding, I shouldn't think."

She handed her a few pence change. "I wonder," she said thoughtfully. "I've been trying for months to find someone to help out in the shop. It wouldn't suit you, I suppose? I'm not so young as I used to be, and I really ought not to be on my feet all day, the doctor says. You don't mind me asking, do you?"

Sophy was faintly embarrassed. Whatever else she might have to do in this strange, miserable, altered existence, she had absolutely no intention of working in a shop, and in spite of her brave words to mother the other day the idea of any sort of job had been far in the back of her mind since her last interview with Peter Holt.

She smiled apologetically without saying anything, and turned towards the door.

Outside in the street, the rain continued unabated. It was ten o'clock in the morning, and apart from getting dry when she got home, and home was only that tiny flat, she had nothing whatever to do for the rest of the day except watch television until it was time to go back and do the horse again.

It was not an appealing prospect. Even if it hadn't been raining, she couldn't ride just one horse all day, and it wasn't much fun riding Gypsy at the best of times.

How awful could it be, working in the shop? She could always leave if she didn't like it. And mother would be pleased with her just for trying. And she'd be getting paid something, even if it wasn't much.

A sports car passed her with a young woman driving it, with the hood up and the lights on against the slashing rain. It should have been her. It would have been, if she'd had any money for petrol.

She turned round abruptly and went back into the shop.

Mother was even more pleased than she could have expected. Her face lit up with the kind of smile that banished the last of Sophy's doubts about the wisdom of accepting such a mundane, menial occupation.

"It's only part time and it doesn't pay much," she said, embarrassed at the reaction her news had caused.

"It's a start," her mother said feelingly, and yet knowing as she spoke that Sophy still didn't realise what it meant to her, that her beloved daughter was at last taking a step away from depending on her totally, when she simply hadn't the means to take care of her any more, not in the way she wanted to, the way Sophy had always been taken care of in the past.

There were tears in her eyes when she hugged her, and Sophy was confused and muttered awkwardly, "It's no big deal, mother. Really. If I don't like it, I'll leave."

It occurred to her with a sudden shock of horror that mother might want some of the money to help pay the bills, and she couldn't do that, she really couldn't. There would barely be enough to pay for Gypsy's stable and some petrol every week as it was.

She said defensively, "It's for Gypsy. And for petrol."

Her mother wiped her eyes. "Of course it is," she said. "It'll be your money, so you must use it for whatever you want, sweetheart."

She stepped back and regarded her fondly. "I'm so proud of you," she said. "Coming to terms with things like that. I've always said we'll manage, between us, and now I know we will."

Sophy had never had any doubts about that. Brought up to expect that she only had to wish for something and life, or rather Daddy, would always provide it, the shocks of the last few months had still not broken the habit of mind that she was entitled to whatever she wanted just because she wanted it. In spite of losing her lovely horses and her lovely school, and no petrol, and only Gypsy to ride, she'd always told herself it was all only temporary, things would be normal again soon. To be quite fair, her mother had encouraged the idea at first, partly to help her over her father's death, but partly too because it had taken a few weeks for the true horror of their altered circumstances to hit home to her as well.

She spent the first day in the shop restocking the shelves. It was harder work than she would ever have imagined. The stock room was a big shed at the back of the shop, and everything had to be carried across the little yard where the customers parked and then have a label stuck on it with the price. Mrs. Mullins insisted she wore an overall with the shop's name on it, and when Kitty's mother came in she could have died of shame.

Mrs. Fittleworth said pleasantly enough, "Why, hello, Miss Taylor, are you helping out?", and she muttered something barely polite and hardly audible. Fortunately, Mrs. Fittleworth was in a hurry and paid no attention; equally fortunately, perhaps, Mrs. Mullins was busy behind the counter and didn't notice.

It dawned on Sophy then that in a day or two everyone in the village would know she was working here, and what was more she would have to be at least polite to them or Mrs. Mullins would sack her. She hurried back to the stock room and was a long time returning with the next case of dog food, trying to work out from the sound of the bell when there was no one in the shop. She was gone so long the shopkeeper came to see what was the matter, and she fobbed her off with an excuse about getting the tins in a muddle and dropping something.

Mrs. Mullins looked at her doubtfully and said, "Well, never mind. You can make us a cup of tea in a minute."

She went back to the shop and Sophy could have screamed. She knew how to make a cup of tea of course, but people usually made it for her, not the other way round. She bit her lip. The only thing that could possibly be worse than this was going home and telling mother Mrs. Mullins had sacked her after only a day because she couldn't do it.

Somehow, she got through the next two days. On Friday afternoon Mrs. Mullins introduced her to the mysteries of the till, and finally left her to her own devices while she went to put her feet up for half an hour. Sophy's hours of work were ten until four, and she'd already learnt that the quietest time of day was after lunch, when sometimes there were no customers for ten minutes at a time.

She sat down on the chair behind the counter, feeling thankful that at last she was alone for a minute, and could stop struggling to be polite to her employer and the varied assortment of customers who came in. Better still, it was already after half past three.

A huge tractor pulled up in the road outside, its trailer piled high with straw bales, the rumble of the engine clearly audible even in the back of the shop. Two young men came in in shirtsleeves, despite the chill of mid October, breezily cheerful, with pieces of straw stuck to their shirts and in their hair. One of them opened the cool cabinet and helped himself to two cans of coke, tossed one to his friend and promptly cracked open the other and drank it.

"God, I needed that," he said, approaching the counter. He put his hand in his pocket for money, and then saw Sophy instead of Mrs. Mullins waiting by the till.

"Wheyhey," he said, raising his eyebrows. "You're an improvement on the old girl, you are. Hey, Bert, we'll have to come in more often." He winked at her, a broad, intimate, conspiratorial wink, and eyed her up and down as far as the counter would allow with obvious approval.

"Not bad," Bert agreed, also approaching the counter.

Sophy backed away nervously, and the first man dropped a five pound note on the top of the till.

"Well, come on, gorgeous," he said, "aren't you going to give us some change?" He nudged his mate and they grinned at each other.

Mrs. Mullins appeared from the back of the shop.

"You boys behave yourselves," she said severely. She opened the till and handed the man his change. "And you'd better move that trailer, it's blocking the traffic. I've told you before Harry doesn't like you stopping that big tractor outside the shop."

"Yes, *ma'am,*" the young man said, and nudged his friend again. The pair of them went out, and a moment later the tractor rumbled off.

"Don't let those two bother you," Mrs. Mullins said. "It's the kids you've got to watch out for, putting sweets in their pocket when you're not looking."

Sophy recovered herself. "I suppose it is," she said, although it wasn't something she'd ever thought about.

Mrs. Mullins looked at her keenly.

"You're not really used to this sort of work, are you, my dear? You mustn't let the customers bother you like that. And that pair will always try it on if you let them. They were just the same as schoolboys. High time they grew up and stopped all their nonsense."

Sophy, unaccustomed to anybody 'trying it on' around her, and knowing she would appear even more foolish if she admitted it, managed to change the subject.

"Who's Harry?" she asked, thinking that Mrs. Mullins might have a husband after all.

"The village policeman," Mrs. Mullins said. "There's talk of yellow lines outside the shop, mostly on account of those two and that tractor, I think. Most local people park round the corner in the yard, well, you must have noticed, but you can't get something that big in there. Yellow lines won't do the business any good at all, my dear. The passing trade just won't stop."

Sophy digested this information in silence. It occurred to her there was more to running a village shop than she had first thought. Not that she could care less about the business, one way or the other.

Mrs. Mullins opened the till and paid her. "It's gone four," she said. "You'll not want to stay a minute longer than you must, I'll be bound."

She raised her hand to cut off Sophy's feeble attempt to protest. "I'm not silly, my dear. I can see you're not enjoying yourself here. But I would be grateful if you can stick it out for a bit longer. You will be coming on Monday, won't you?"

Chapter Five

Blackie was quite ridiculously smart that Sunday afternoon. His mane was plaited, his coat was shining and his tack was spotless. Kitty was holding him proudly on the yard surrounded by three of her friends, as well as her father, waiting for Mr. Holt to arrive.

Sophy led Gypsy out of his box and towards the school, although she knew perfectly well that Kitty's lesson was due to start in five minutes. She could hardly fail to know, when Kitty had been getting her pony ready for the last two hours and eagerly talking to everybody about it. Mr. Fittleworth realised she was going into the school as she passed him and frowned, but he didn't say anything.

Theoretically, there was nothing to prevent her riding in the school whenever she wanted to. Equally, there was no need for her to ride just now, when she would be bound to get in the way and she had the rest of the day to do it, but perversely she was ready now and refused to wait on account of one silly little girl and her silly little pony.

She settled herself in the saddle and walked Gypsy rather aimlessly round the school. She wouldn't admit it to herself, but she was partly here because she wanted to see what that man Holt was going to do, and she absolutely refused to hang over the fence with all the others, as though she was nothing but a silly little girl herself.

An ancient Land Rover turned into the courtyard and vanished behind the stables. A minute or two later, Kitty came into the school with her pony and the others trooped after her as far as the gate, and then Peter Holt appeared, tidily turned out in well-worn boots and breeches and wearing a hacking jacket and a trilby hat. He chatted briefly to Mr. Fittleworth and lit his pipe before he came into the school.

If he had any opinion about Sophy's presence he did not express it. He acknowledged her with the slightest inclination of his head, and then turned his attention to his pupil as she mounted her pony.

The quiet assurance so evident in his riding was equally plain in the way he approached his lesson. He spoke privately to Kitty for several minutes before she moved off, but Blackie still set off at his usual breakneck pace, head in the air and generally charging about with Kitty hanging on to the reins and struggling to stay in control.

Ha, thought Sophy smugly, with the malign satisfaction of knowing what the pony was like. Maybe you're not so clever after all, Mr. High and Mighty Holt, going round insulting people. And you can't possibly show off and ride that pony yourself, you're far too big.

Feeling better, and grinning inside, she prodded Gypsy into a trot of her own, and nearly collided with the pony in the corner as Kitty struggled to slow him down.

Mr. Fittleworth made an irritable exclamation, easily audible down the length of the arena, but Peter Holt said nothing. He began to work his pupil in trot on big, steadying circles, and under the calming influence of his voice, and his completely unperturbed manner whatever the pony did or Kitty said, the pony's pace began to settle into an even, regular step, less fraught with speed and far more under control. Then he asked her for a serpentine, and again she nearly bumped into Gypsy, who was walking again now, on the track and on the opposite rein.

This time, the instructor did have something to say to her, and his voice was loud and crisp, and plainly audible to everybody.

"There are commonly accepted rules about more than one horse working in the school, Miss Taylor. You should give way to the horse in the faster pace, and you should also give way to a rider under instruction if you are not. A rider with your experience should know this."

Mr. Fittleworth said impatiently to no one in particular, "I don't know what she's doing here in the first place. Why can't she ride later?"

Blackie was excited again now, after his close encounter with the bigger horse, and Kitty was wrestling with the reins to stop him cantering. The attention of the spectators and the instructor switched back to her and her difficulties, and Sophy sulkily pulled Gypsy into the middle of the school and out of the way. It was true, what he said, and of course she knew the rules of the road in the riding school, but it was the first time she'd ever given way to a snotty little kid on a stupid pony. In her own school back home there was usually only her riding, and even if there was some one else whoever it was got out of her way and didn't argue about rules and stuff. It was different warming up at shows, of course, but then they were serious people, not Kitty Fittleworth and Blackie, who were totally useless and didn't matter anyway.

She sat in the saddle and watched the pony settle again.

It was no good pretending. Whatever she thought of him, and she still wasn't sure what that was, there was no denying that Peter Holt was good, very good in fact. He seemed to know what the pony was going to do next while the pony was still thinking about it, and Kitty too. Kitty's face was puckered in concentration, and Blackie was responding to the sensible, quiet work in a way that Sophy wouldn't have imagined he ever would. The step was relaxed and steady, and every now and then he put his head down and suddenly looked a different pony altogether, much as Gypsy did when this same man had ridden him.

Then he asked Kitty to give the rein away, and she did, fearfully at first and then completely. For nearly a whole circle, Blackie kept the same even stride with no contact at all, and then the instructor smiled and told her to walk and said it was enough for today.

A beaming Mr. Fittleworth opened the gate and the instructor walked beside his pupil out of the school, looking up at her as he answered a question. Nobody paid Sophy any attention at all. Mr. Holt shut the gate behind them without even a backward glance, and she was left alone in the school with Gypsy, who was half asleep by now with standing still for so long, and with the miserable thought that all she'd done was get in the way and make a fool of herself.

A week ago she would have been angry and defiant, determined to show them all she was better than any of them, but today she felt only depressed and lonely, with no one to turn to who would understand. Even mother was useless when it came to horses.

She gave Gypsy a disconsolate smack and ambled off towards the track. Far away across the field a murder of crows was circling over the stubble, as black as she was feeling. The horse still wouldn't go and tomorrow she had to go back to work in the shop, assuming she wanted to keep her car on the road. It simply wasn't fair, any of it.

She persuaded Gypsy to trot again, and he set off with his nose hung out as usual, trudging round the school as bored as ever. The improvement in the his going occasioned by Mr. Holt had faded away after only a day, and he felt just the same now as he always had.

She rode a circle in the middle of the school. At least she had it to herself now. It was a shock as she turned to see the instructor leaning on the gate watching. A wild, unexpected muddle of feelings welled inside her. She rode over to him.

"I couldn't resist coming to see," he said, smiling quite pleasantly. "How are you going on?"

"It's just the same," Sophy said. "I..." She was suddenly tearful. He was so calm and so sure of himself, and she was in such a muddle. "I'm sorry about before. I shouldn't have been here really. I...."

"No, you shouldn't," he said quietly. "But never mind that now. Come on, then."

He came into the school and stood beside her.

"Do this with your hands. Ride stronger with your seat and do less with the rein. Let him stretch. Ask him for less and he'll give you more."

He patted the horse on the shoulder. "Go on then. Go large once and then ride a circle."

He stayed with her for nearly half an hour.

He didn't ride the horse, although he stopped her several times to offer her instruction. When finally he said he thought the horse had done enough, Gypsy was swinging along in a big soft stride, bending a little and paying attention to what he was told. It wasn't the transformation that came when he rode him himself, but still it was a huge difference. Sophy was paying attention too. There was something about the way the man expressed himself that brooked no argument, although he never once raised his voice.

Disappointment flooded over her when he said it was enough. She hadn't enjoyed a ride so much for months, and surely Gypsy wasn't tired already.

Mr. Holt read her mind. "You must always stop before he's tired," he said. "So he wants to work again next time. Do you hack him out?"

"Not much," Sophy said. "It doesn't interest me much."

"Well, you must," he said. "The horse must have a life too, not just the stable and the school. It'll do you both good."

He opened the gate for her. "Will you teach me again?" she said eagerly. "I want..."

He looked up at her and frowned, and she flushed with embarrassment, remembering his earlier, unkind words. She wondered then what had made him change his mind about helping her, but he didn't enlighten her.

"You can have today for nothing," he said. "But next time you'll have to pay, the same as Kitty pays. I learnt long ago that people don't value what they don't have to pay for. I will say one thing. The horse has possibilities, and so do you. Mr. Fittleworth has my number whenever you're ready." His manner softened a little. "I have accidentally found out a little about you, Miss Taylor, but I am only prepared to help you in the same measure that you help yourself." He grinned suddenly. "Something else for you to think about, eh?"

He walked off briskly through the yard, pausing to say goodbye to Kitty, who was standing on a bucket and taking out Blackie's plaits. Sophy dismounted and followed more slowly. She saw him pause again to look at her smart, immaculate car, and he shook his head before he climbed into his old Land Rover and drove away, with the whippet sitting up on the front seat looking out through the windscreen.

Chapter Six

Mrs. Mullins was gossiping over the counter with a customer when she went in to work on Monday. Both women turned to look at her as she came in, hurrying and afraid she was going to be late. She'd overslept this morning, and even with using the car to get to the stables and back it had been a bit of a rush to get here on time.

A look of relief crossed the shopkeeper's face, and Sophy realised she really had been afraid she wouldn't turn up.

"Good morning," she said brightly.

Mrs. Mullins couldn't possibly know that the job had acquired far greater importance over the weekend. It was out of the question not to have Mr. Holt's help again, and he had made it perfectly clear he expected to be paid. Lying in bed last night, after an earnest conversation with mother, she'd let her imagination run riot, with Gypsy and Mr. Holt figuring together in a gloriously unlikely dream that turned her into the champion rider she knew she had to be one day.

In the meantime, there was another grinding day at work to get through. Strangely, it wasn't quite so bad with something to look forward to, the thought of riding Gypsy this evening and trying to find that smooth, swinging step again. She might even take Mr. Holt's advice and go out for a hack, although that idea didn't appeal quite so much.

Still, it was easier to admit the truth of what he'd said, now he'd been pleasant and really helped her. All she wanted to do was practise and compete, and if you stopped to think about it the horse must get awfully bored with going round in circles all the time.

There was a van in the little car park at the back delivering biscuits and chocolate, and Mrs. Mullins sent her out to help unload and stack it in the storeroom. The driver was a stout, cheerful, middle aged man, chatty and puffing with the exertion of moving three or four boxes at a time.

"Got a daughter your age," he remarked, leaning against the side of the van and getting his breath back. "Just gone to college, she has. Dunno what she's going to make of that, being away from home the first time. The wife's not sure, either." He winked at her. "I dare say you could tell us what she'll get up to. Things are a bit different now from when I was your age."

He was breezily familiar, plainly talking to her as he would to any one who was helping him with a delivery, casually assuming their places in the scheme of life were roughly parallel, and she didn't know what to say to him. Van drivers weren't the sort of people she usually met, certainly not the sort of people she talked to about life or their children going to college, or anything else for that matter.

She muttered uncomfortably, "I suppose so," and fled into the stock room. It wasn't that she didn't want to talk to him. Anything that broke up the day was a bit of a bonus, really. It was just that she didn't know how to talk to him. The odd thought came to her that Mr. Holt would know how to talk to him. He'd know how to talk to a prince or a street sweeper, and in the same breath.

She steeled herself and went back into the yard. "Would you like a cup of tea?" she asked him, and his grin widened.

"Now you're talking," he said. "Be alright with the boss, will it?" He jerked his head towards the shopkeeper who had appeared in the back doorway.

"That'll be alright," Mrs. Mullins said. "I'm going upstairs for a minute. You'd better stay in the shop while I'm gone."

The van driver had drunk his tea and departed, and her own cup was empty on the counter when Peter Holt came into the shop with his dog on a lead.

"Thought I'd find you here," he said in friendly tone. He glanced round the empty shop and lowered his voice. "Does like to chat, our Mrs. Mullins. Tells all the world everybody's business. How she finds it all out I've no idea. I've brought you this to look at. I want it back mind. And I'll have two ounces of my tobacco." He put a plastic bag on the counter and reached for his wallet.

His tobacco was in a box under the counter, where Mrs. Mullins kept the orders she got in specially. He was still in the shop when the lady herself came back.

"I've told you over and over," she said to him. "You mustn't bring that dog in here. It says so on the door."

"Sorry," he said. "But he is a whippet. Whippets are more than half people, you know."

He left hurriedly before the exasperated shopkeeper could say any more. It seemed to Sophy it was an exchange the two of them had had many times before.

"That man," Mrs. Mullins said. "He will *not* leave the dog outside. And I've got hooks in the wall specially put there for dogs. Everybody else uses them."

"Perhaps you should refuse to serve him," Sophy said doubtfully.

"Oh, I couldn't do that," Mrs. Mullins was horrified at the idea. "He's always so polite, he's such a nice man, everybody says so. I just wish he'd cooperate a bit. It's against the regulations." She sniffed despairingly.

"Do you know anything about him?" Sophy asked curiously. Quite apart from what Mr. Holt had just said, from her own observation Mrs. Mullins seemed to know all about everybody who lived in the village.

It seemed likely that she was the source of Mr. Holt's information about her, and the reason for his cryptic remark the other day about finding out something about her by accident. She wasn't at all sure that she wanted people feeling sorry for her, even if it was to her advantage, so she might as well get her own back if she could. And there was no denying she was very curious indeed about the talented and enigmatic Mr. Holt.

She picked up the plastic bag he'd left for her and peeped in. It was a book of some sort, but she couldn't possibly look at it now. She stuffed it into her bag on the chair behind the counter.

"Oh, it is nice to have someone to chat to," Mrs. Mullins positively beamed at her as she turned round. "He's helping you with your horse, isn't he?"

"A bit," Sophy confessed, wondering how the woman could possibly know that.

"He's lived in the village for about two years," Mrs. Mullins said. "He's got that little cottage at the end of Rosemary Lane. Came down from Yorkshire, I believe. I think he's more or less retired – at least nobody's ever heard him say anything about working. He had some sort of horse business I think. Lives all by himself, he does, except for that dog." She frowned. "It's funny really, I don't think anyone knows a lot about him but everybody likes him. I remember he helped out at the fete last year."

"He's a terrific rider," Sophy said, thinking that Mrs. Mullins knew everything about everybody she didn't care about and not much about the one person in the village she was interested in.

"Is he now? I wouldn't know much about that sort of thing." Mrs. Mullins was still pursuing her own reflections. "I wouldn't have thought he was old enough to be retired myself, but I suppose these days things are different. I suppose it's nice if you can afford it. I think he goes fishing a lot in the summer, or so Mrs. Watson says."

Sophy didn't know who Mrs. Watson was, and didn't care much either. Mrs. Mullins let her have a bread roll and a doughnut for lunch out of the stock, and somehow the afternoon wore on until four o'clock and she escaped to the stables with a feeling of anticipation she hadn't had for some time.

She passed Kitty's mother as she drove in and found Kitty on the yard fiddling about with Blackie. She didn't usually talk to Kitty, but for some reason today she said 'hello' almost cheerfully. It was evident Kitty was sulking.

"I want to go for a ride," she said. "Mr. Holt says I should hack him out one day and ride in the school the next. So he should go out today. And I'm not allowed out by myself, and Jennifer's not coming. She's gone to Steeplehurst. Mother just doesn't understand."

"I'm sure I've seen you go out by yourself," Sophy said without much interest.

"Only when Mum and Dad don't know," Kitty confessed. "Mum knows Jennifer's not coming today." She pouted disagreeably.

"Well," Sophy said doubtfully. It was the mention of Mr. Holt that put the idea in her head. "I suppose *I* could go out with you." It wasn't what she'd had planned at all, but on the other hand she didn't know where the rides were round here and Kitty almost certainly knew all of them, and anyway she'd have to hack out a bit some time or Mr. Holt would be sure to find out she wasn't taking his advice and he wouldn't like that.

Kitty's face lit up, and then she too looked doubtful. "Would you?" she said, frowning, and Sophy was piqued. Kitty obviously didn't think she'd be very good company. Or else she thought she would try and boss her about all the time.

As if she could care less what the kid got up to on her stupid pony. But it meant she could find out where to ride without the indignity of having to ask.

"Why not?" she responded carelessly. "I'll tack up. Just don't keep me waiting, that's all."

Chapter Seven

They rode side by side to the gate on the other side of the courtyard, which opened directly on to the bridle path. Blackie eyed his large companion a little warily as he towered over him, but Gypsy paid him no attention.

The gate was shut, just as it was supposed to be, and Sophy realised with a jolt she'd never opened a gate mounted on Gypsy, and precious few off any other horse, if it came to it. Spending most of her time schooling, the question never arose. It was equally out of the question to admit to Kitty she might have a problem, and to make things worse the child's mother was watching them from beside her car. She deliberately hung back and Kitty reached the gate first.

She reached down nonchalantly, pushed it open and led the way through. Gypsy followed calmly enough, and Kitty waited, clearly expecting Sophy to shut the gate after them. She started to turn Gypsy awkwardly in the narrow track, and then the woman by the car called across, "It's OK, I'll close it," and she followed the black pony and his pert, competent rider up the hill with more than a little relief.

Kitty led the way confidently, but in spite of Blackie's evident enthusiasm she had to keep hold of Gypsy, with his longer stride, to prevent him getting too close to the pony's tail Then the path widened and they were riding side by side. Kitty glanced up at her, and kicked on briskly into trot and then canter. Gypsy threw his head up, catching Sophy by surprise, and leapt forward into a vigorous, energetic stride which bore no resemblance to his reluctant, stodgy steps in the school. He left Blackie behind in just a few strides and when he fell into canter it was as much as Sophy could do to hold him. Fortunately, the track led uphill and steepened quickly, and it was relatively easy to pull him up at the top and look back to see the pony scampering up to her. Kitty was grinning from ear to ear.

"I thought you were going to be a slow dressage person," she said.

It was unexpectedly exhilarating to see the track ahead crossing a wide open field, and to feel the horse beneath her taking a keen interest in his surroundings and showing a desire to go forward that was completely alien to his usual attitude in the school.

It would be stretching a point to say that she and Kitty became friends over the next forty five minutes, but relations between them had thawed considerably by the time they came out on the lane that led into the village and back to the stables. A couple of cars went by, behaving themselves politely as they passed the horses, and then they turned into the main road for a hundred yards before crossing the Down to come back to the stables from the other direction. There was a wide verge, and they were ambling along side by side when a motor bike shot into view, in seconds was right beside them, and then gone.

Gypsy spun like a top, half reared and tore off along the verge back the way they had come. What Blackie did Sophy never knew; half unseated, it took her several strides to recover her balance and seventy yards to regain control of the startled horse, and just then Kitty and her pony were the last things on her mind.

When she finally succeeded in stopping, wildly out of breath, she rode the still agitated Gypsy back to find them.

Kitty was sitting casually on her pony on the verge, exactly where she'd left her, with Blackie grazing on a long rein and indifferent to the Land Rover pulled up beside him and the man in a cloth cap standing talking to his rider. All three of them turned to look at her as she approached.

"Are you alright?" Peter Holt said. "When I suggested you should hack out I didn't suppose you'd be galloping down the main road." His face was suddenly grim. "I know how dangerous it can be, with the traffic."

In spite of still feeling flustered, Sophy was struck by the change in his expression.

"I'm fine," she said. She certainly wouldn't admit to Kitty that for a long moment she'd been quite frightened, not now everything was back under control. Peter Holt looked at her with that wise way she was getting used to, and she realised he knew exactly what she was feeling.

"So long as there's no harm done," he said.

In a moment of perception, Sophy said suddenly, "It must be because he's not been out much. Or maybe he just doesn't like motorbikes." She grimaced ruefully. "He was fine up to then."

"You were good," Kitty said, grudgingly admiring. "I'd have fallen off if Blackie did that."

It was quite ridiculous to feel quite so pleased with the artless praise of a silly child. Sophy blushed a little. Peter Holt regarded her quizzically.

"You be careful," he said. "I don't want my two best pupils getting hurt following my advice." Sophy wasn't too happy about being placed in the same bracket as Kitty, but she realised then that they were almost certainly his only pupils.

"We should be getting back," she said, and Kitty gathered up her reins and the man turned to get back into the Land Rover. The whippet stood up on the passenger seat as he opened the door.

"Why don't you come to dinner tonight? Mother likes to meet all my teachers," she said on a whim, thinking that was something Kitty certainly couldn't ask him.

He stopped in surprise, and frowned. "I've met your mother in the village," he remarked. "It's Edith, isn't it? Maybe I'll come another day, when she might have a bit more notice." He frowned again, and closed the door.

In another five minutes they were back in the yard, and Kitty's mother was thanking her for riding out with her daughter.

"We met Mr. Holt," Kitty said enthusiastically. "Sophy had just been run away with."

Sophy's irritation at this announcement, with its adverse reflections on both her riding ability and suitability as an escort, was quickly tempered by the woman remarking indifferently, "Well, at least it wasn't you this time."

Sophy led Gypsy into his stable with mixed feelings. Buoyed by her competition successes on expensive, largely already made horses, her lack of experience of riding in the real world, outside the disciplined safety of an arena, had never mattered before, or even seemed relevant to someone only interested in dressage. And yet Gypsy's transformation, from an idle plodder to what had felt more like an express train with boundless energy, had made him seem like a different horse altogether. No wonder the man Holt thought he had possibilities. After all, it wasn't that he didn't have attractive paces; it was just that usually he was too idle to use them.

Over the following fortnight, with Mr. Holt's advice fresh in her mind and also partly in response to Kitty's frequent badgering, she got into the habit of riding out at least every third day. Sometimes Jennifer came too on her rather larger chestnut pony, and although the other members of the yard still kept their distance Sophy was beginning to realise, with more than a little surprise, that what she had always thought of as just 'ordinary' people who didn't matter could be really friendly if you gave them a chance. Even the grumpy Mr. Fittleworth began to smile at her when they met, especially after she gave Kitty a lift home one night when her mother's car had broken down.

Mr. Holt's mysterious book turned out to be a technical riding manual written by a retired Hungarian cavalry officer in the 1920s and translated soon afterwards. It was as dry as dust and was solely concerned with the balance and shifting centre of gravity as the horse performed different movements under a rider, from jumping a drop fence to piaffe. Fortunately it was liberally endowed with equally ancient photographs and diagrams, which underlined its antiquity but did help to make sense of some of the more convoluted language.

Her first impulse, to politely hand it back to its owner after a cursory glance, gradually gave way, after reading a few lines describing how a shift in the balance could encourage "the reluctant, or barely obedient trot," to a determination to make some sense of it. She also reasoned that if Peter Holt ever did condescend to teach her, he would expect that she had at least looked at the pictures. It was mostly hard going, but every now and then she suddenly had a little flash of understanding, and could relate the page to how Gypsy felt when he was, or more usually wasn't, going properly.

Chapter Eight

Gypsy's livery was due in the middle of the month. The formidable Miss Agatha Brown, accustomed to receiving a neat and tidy cheque signed by her mother, regarded the assortment of notes and coins Sophy presented with a slight frown and counted them carefully.

"Very good, Miss Taylor," she said at last. Then she added, "Will you be buying hay from the estate this winter? You do know that your turnout agreement will end at the end of the month, and the box rent will also rise accordingly."

Sophy was nonplussed. When her mother had made the original arrangements just after they'd bought the horse in the summer, she had paid little or no attention, only concerned with being able to use the school whenever she wanted and assuming any other details, as usual, would be taken care of for her as they always had been. She muttered something non-commital and left quickly.

Half way across the paved courtyard between the house and the stables it hit her like a thunderbolt that even if she gave Miss Brown every penny she earned at the shop, it probably wouldn't be enough. And now that she'd hacked out a few times, although Gypsy, unlike some coloured horses, had good strong feet they were wearing down and he would have to be shod, and soon.

She fingered the two pound coins in her anorak pocket. After buying half a tank of petrol yesterday and just paying the livery bill, it was all she had left.

Kitty and Jennifer, just escaped from school, were brushing the field mud off their ponies tied up outside their respective, adjacent stables and chatting happily with each other and one of the other girls; clearly all three were about to go out riding together in the last light of the autumn evening.

Kitty said something about her next lesson with Mr. Holt, and then Jennifer asked if she could join in one day. Sophy managed a thin smile and said hello, but then her mood darkened. It seemed everybody could afford to do what *she* wanted to do except her.

It was two days since she'd ridden in the school, but at least she had it to herself this evening. It was fitted with floodlights, not quite needed yet, but she already knew that would be another expense if she wanted to school after work in the winter months.

Gloomy and preoccupied, she put the horse into trot expecting the usual struggle to achieve anything sensible, and was astonished when Gypsy responded quickly and set off down the fence with something of the stride and vigour he showed when she was out with Blackie and they were heading to the Down. She rode on to a circle, and then turned to change the rein across the diagonal.

Gypsy was leaning hard on her hand, and momentarily she was tempted to jerk the rein in punishment, and then a tiny, remembered voice in her head whispered 'less is more,' and with a reckless disregard for the risk of losing the balance completely, she opened her fingers just a fraction instead.

The big horse dropped into her hand like an apple off a tree, and suddenly that powerful back was softly swinging and they crossed the school in a dozen glorious, breathtaking strides of medium trot. It was astounding beyond words, and then Gypsy came to the track and fell on his inside shoulder just as he always did.

Sophy eased him to walk, elated and distraught both at once. How *could* he be so fantastic and so difficult in the space of ten metres? But that trot was quite wonderful…..For almost the first time in her life, she was moved to lean forward on her horse's neck to embrace it, and felt the warm hair against her cheek. On a whim, she stroked Gypsy's ear, and he seemed to respond by turning it back towards her. It occurred to her then that this was exactly what she scoffed at the kids for doing with their ponies every five minutes, and she sat up hurriedly with a furtive glance towards the stables, thankful that there was no one to see.

She offered him a long rein and a familiar voice remarked casually, "Now that was a step in the right direction."

The apparently ubiquitous Peter Holt was puffing contentedly on his pipe, leaning on the outer arena fence beside the path in the last of the evening sun, his ever-present canine companion staring intently out over the huge field, clearly poised to hurtle joyfully in pursuit of a real or imagined rabbit at the slightest excuse. The man and the dog were a picture of contentment, wildly at odds with the desperate muddle of her own existence.

Almost of his own volition, Gypsy ambled over to him. He reached across the gap between the fences and stroked his nose.

"That was better," he said. "Having the odd hack always freshens up the school work. After all, God didn't make horses to spend all their lives going round in circles. That fall on the inside shoulder, it's covered in the book I lent you."

His encouragement contrasted sharply with the unhappiness of her expression.

"You needn't look so glum about it," he added, knocking out his pipe on the fence post.

When he looked up again she was staring down at him, and the kindly expression in his eye made her want to cry as the full understanding of the consequences of what that Brown woman had just said swept over her; no matter how well Gypsy went, if he ever did, or how well she rode, there was simply no money to do *anything*. Just keeping the stuffy animal was beginning to look impossible. She felt the tears begin to trickle down her cheeks as the total unfairness of everything life offered her, from living in a tiny box room in a tiny flat with no money, no friends, a boring job, and soon not even Gypsy to ride, came crashing down on her.

The man regarded her for a moment without speaking. When their eyes met again, he seemed to know what she was thinking without asking.

He spoke quietly. "Do you have a good ride," he said. "I've a feeling he might surprise you tonight. Then meet me in the pub in about an hour. We'll have a drink and a conversation." He added cryptically, "I think it's about time for both of us."

He took an old fashioned mobile phone out of his pocket. "What's your home number? I'll call your mother and tell her you're going to be late."

As she gave it him, a little doubtfully, and wondering about his last comment, he added as a seeming afterthought, "Don't panic, I'll pay." His grin was suddenly mischievous and conspiratorial, and in spite of her tears she found herself grinning back.

The whippet barked suddenly, once, a keen sharp sound that took them both unawares. A moment later he shot off across the field, a grey dart travelling at nearly thirty miles an hour seemingly suspended a foot above the ground. Peter Holt's grin widened as he watched. There didn't appear to be anything to chase, but the dog swung in a wide arc across the far edge of the field and returned, panting ecstatically, for a treat from his master's pocket.

"They do that," he remarked conversationally. "Run for the sheer joy of running. Perhaps there's a lesson in that for all of us. Make the most of whatever you can do just because you *can* do it. I'll see you later then." He turned away from her towards the village.

Chapter Nine

He was right about the horse, at least. Gypsy was more energetic than he'd ever been in the school, and Sophy was beginning to understand, in spite of the frequent frustrations, that maybe he did have more to offer if you started to meet him half way and didn't just demand and expect the right answer whenever you wanted something. She thought grudgingly that hacking out had probably helped, too.

It was odd, but she almost began to like the horse just a little bit, feeling as though the clumsy animal was actually trying to please her instead of simply going his own way out of perversity. Every now and then, and more often as the hour passed, he worked lower and softer and Sophy had enough experience to know she was making a foundation for better work to come.

The expensive and talented horses and ponies she'd ridden for the last six or seven years had all been produced by someone else, but since she'd always been the one who'd won the prizes and the praise, it was easy to conclude that she could have done all the schooling and preparation if she'd wanted to. She remembered Dad saying once, "Why would you do all that work if you don't have to bother? And it's chancy. The horse might be no good even when you've finished, and then what? You can't get your money and time back, can you? I won't buy a company that's not well on the way already, and I won't have my best girl riding a horse that's not ready to win either." It was the point of view she'd grown up with, but now Dad was gone and so were all her lovely horses.

And she had to admit Dad had never been a horseman. His various enterprises had dealt with a wide range of products and pursuits, but horses of any sort had never featured in any of them.

Gypsy was sweating with his unaccustomed effort, and that was something else she had to do for herself now - walk the horse to cool off after work. Another thought struck her. Horses like Gypsy had to be clipped to work through the winter, and even if she'd possessed a set of clippers she didn't know how to do it and that was sure to cost money too. She walked him sombrely round the school, vainly trying to feel positive after a better ride than usual, in spite of everything. Half of her was eagerly anticipating meeting Mr. Holt, but partly too she had a feeling of trepidation that he was again going to tell her things about herself she would rather not know. For a wild moment she thought of not going, but deep inside she knew that wasn't really an option; he was a wonderful horseman and she'd seen how he made Blackie go even when he wasn't riding him, as though he knew what the pony was thinking and could change its mind from a dozen metres away. If he could do that with Gypsy....

Although she was eighteen now, almost nineteen in fact, she wasn't very familiar with the inside of public houses. As she turned her smart car into the car park of the 'Shepherd and Flock' in the centre of the village, nervousness at the slightly odd nature of her appointment prompted a sudden realisation that actually there were a lot of things that most girls her age knew all about that she wasn't very familiar with; and not the least of them was men, or to be more specific, boyfriends. She'd had admirers in the past, of course, especially when Dad was doing well before….. that happened, but none of them had caught her interest much, or mattered as much as the horses. Or mattered much at all, if the truth was told, although she had allowed one or two to kiss her at parties sometimes.

She locked the car carefully; at least that was still hers, even if she couldn't drive it as often as she wanted.

The bar door was half open and a subdued hubbub of chatter greeted her as she stepped into the low-ceilinged, spacious, oak-panelled room. Her riding clothes attracted a few brief, curious glances, and then she saw Peter Holt standing by the bar with a beer glass in his hand, the whippet safely shielded from the other patrons behind his long legs.

He came over to her at once and shepherded her to a table in the corner. He put his beer on a beer mat on the table and the dog's lead in her hand as she sat down and he asked her what she would like to drink. She was nonplussed at the strangeness of the situation, stared up at him and didn't reply.

"Orange juice?" he said. "Glass of wine?" He seemed a little nonplussed himself. "I'm afraid I'm not familiar with what young ladies drink these days."

"I'll have orange juice," she said at last. It sounded safe, and then she added in her most grown up voice, "I'll have to drive home later," and was gratified to see the approval in his face as he turned to fetch it for her.

There was an awkward moment as he sat down on his return. He twisted his glass round twice on its beer mat, seemingly searching for the right opening.

"I don't want you or your mother to think I'm intruding," he said at last. "I have my own motives for wanting to help you with your horse, and I suppose first in these hypersensitive times I should make it clear that I'm not going to flirt with you or try to get you into bed." He grinned suddenly, and the atmosphere changed in an instant. "Thirty years ago I might," he said. The grin became a chuckle. "In fact, you could almost have bet on it. You're certainly pretty enough."

He took a pull at his beer, and the atmosphere changed again. "Now let's get serious. You've got a horse, you've got ambition, and without going overboard you've both got a little ability. In your case, probably not – yet – as much as you think you have. What you don't have is any money. At all." He looked straight at her. "Am I right, or am I right?"

Sophy met his gaze and nodded without speaking. As a statement of the facts it was brutal, but it was true.

His tone softened. "I told you I know a little about your circumstances," he went on. "Mrs. Mullins' gossip," he made a sympathetic grimace, "first excited my curiosity and with time on my hands and the germ of an idea I took the trouble to look up some old newspapers in the Chichester library.

The first time I spoke to you wasn't the first time I'd watched you riding in that school, you know. I've been a horseman all my life and no horseman can pass a rider without looking, even if it's only a glance. I bet you can't either, and I've been using that path for over a year.

"You want me to give you lessons, but what you really want is to be the best rider in the world and ride the best horses and win everything there is to win, whatever it costs. When I was your age, so did I. I can't make it happen, but I can make you as good as you can be, for now at least, and neither you nor I know how good that might be, not yet. But if you can't pay me, I won't start. I've said it before, when people don't pay for a valuable service, to them it has no value. I've been caught like that before, and it won't happen again. You get used, and you lose friends. It's one thing to do someone a favour now and again, but for long term training it simply doesn't work." He looked at her keenly. "I bet your Dad didn't expect his gardener or his chauffeur to turn up for work week after week without wages, did he?"

Sophy shifted uncomfortably on her chair. She sipped her orange juice and looked down at the table. Why had he asked her to come if he was just going to humiliate her and say he wouldn't do anything? When she raised her eyes he was sipping his beer and regarding her thoughtfully over the rim of the glass.

"Well, don't be so glum," he said. "The question is, just how keen are you? Because there might be a way, if you really want it enough."

"I want it enough," she responded automatically, and then realised that in all her life she had never wanted anything more than for this man to agree to help her, to make her the rider she had to be, and to break out of this limbo of useless helplessness that her life had turned into. She tentatively met his gaze, but with undisguised eagerness too.

"What way?" she said breathlessly.

"Sell your car," he said at once. "I know nothing about cars, they don't have legs so they don't interest me at all, but a nearly new Italian sports car must be worth thousands, maybe tens of thousands. Buy a cheap runabout instead. The difference will keep your horse for months, years I shouldn't wonder if you're careful, and it'll pay for whatever else you need to do horsewise for at least the time being. And if you go on working at the shop, that will help too. In fact, I'd be disappointed if you gave that up. Even if we do start working together, you can't ride one horse all day, and however much your car is worth the money won't last forever."

He paused, lifted and emptied his glass. Her own was still untouched, and she followed his glance towards it. When she sipped it, the orange juice was ice cold, different, refreshing and jangled her thoughts together. She was proud of her car, it was the very last thing Daddy had given her, and it was the very last tangible proof she had left that she really was somebody different, important, somebody better than ordinary; the idea of selling it had never entered her head.

He was watching her closely, and her confusion was evident. Even with his horseman's instinct, he could not guess at the emotional attachment she had for what to him was simply a very expensive, inanimate metal object doing a job which was performed equally effectively, and with far less ostentation, by his own ancient Landrover.

Sophy realised he was waiting for her to answer. She opened her mouth to say something, and closed it again.

"It was the last thing my Dad ever gave me," she said at last. Her voice was wobbly, uncertain. He could see now she was on the verge of tears. "I never thought of selling it. I just never did. I…." Her voice faded away.

There was a brief silence. Then the man said quietly, "I did not know that. Of course it's a decision only you can make. Perhaps you should talk it over with your mother. In any case, if I took you on as a pupil I would want her to be aware of all the circumstances from the very beginning. You must take some time if you need to."

It wasn't the conclusion to their meeting he'd been expecting. He finished his beer and their eyes met for a moment. It was the first time in their short acquaintance that Sophy had noticed any sympathy for her situation in his expression.

"I'll be back at the stables for Kitty at the weekend," he said "Why don't we talk again then? You can let me know what you decide." He smiled the cryptic smile she remembered. "Talk to the horse about it too."

He stood up and the dog stood up with him. "This is a perfectly respectable pub," he said, "but I promised your mother I wouldn't leave you here on your own. I'll see you to your car."

He stood beside the door as she settled into the driving seat. He'd never been this close to the vehicle before, and for the first time he began to appreciate the quality of the engineering, the luxurious leather upholstery, the wide, smooth sweep of the bonnet.

The engine started with a deep, low murmur, redolent with discreet power and massive potential speed. It came to him then with added force that for anyone with Sophy's recent history, finally parting with the last such potent symbol of what life had once been, even without its close association with her father, represented very much more than merely exchanging one means of transport for another.

He watched her drive away into the gathering dusk before beginning his own short walk home, feeling rather more sympathy for her plight than he would have expected when the idea first came to him.

Chapter Ten

Her mother greeted her with relief although she wasn't especially late. Sophy looked at her without speaking, deeply preoccupied, and fell into a chair, as usual without taking off her riding boots.

"Don't you want any supper?" her mother said. "What did this man say to you anyway?"

"He thinks I should sell my car to pay him for lessons," Sophy responded, not realising how manipulative this bald statement would sound to her mother.

"Does he indeed?" Edith bridled angrily. "And what else does he want? Or perhaps I shouldn't ask." In recent months her daughter's naivety in the ways of the world had given her cause for concern more than once.

The implied accusation instantly brought back Peter Holt's first declaration as he brought her drink, and Sophy said hurriedly, "It's really not like that. Not like that at all."

"I know that car means a lot to you," her mother said. "Would you really sell it just to have riding lessons? And why is this man so important? I met him in the village once. He looks like a perfectly ordinary man to me. Is he famous in the horsey world or something?"

"I don't know," Sophy muttered. "But he's good and he's all there is. Anyway, he says he won't even begin to help me unless you know all about it, so you needn't worry about *me*, not like that at least."

Her mother turned to go into the kitchen. "You really must eat something, dear," she said. "And take those boots off. I do keep telling you. We have to look after the carpet. You know the agent said it counts as part of the furnishings and we can't possibly afford a new one if it gets all scuffed."

The line of anxiety crossing her forehead deepened momentarily; it hadn't been there a year ago and whenever she noticed it Sophy felt guilty, although reason told her its appearance couldn't possibly have been entirely her fault.

The boots were lying akimbo in the corner and Sophy was sprawled equally carelessly across the small sofa when her supper arrived. Still deeply preoccupied, she sat up to put the plate on her knee before she looked up at her mother.

"It's not just lessons. Gypsy will need shoeing and clipping and hay and the livery is going up too. I simply must have some money from somewhere. Mr. Holt said he'd see me at the weekend when he comes to teach Kitty again. On Sunday. I think he meant I should decide by then."

Edith Taylor looked down at her daughter's pretty, troubled face framed by her untidy blonde hair and her own worries faded a little as her heart went out to her. However little of the blame for their predicament was hers, even less could be ascribed to Sophy. Eighteen years of being given just about everything she wanted as soon as she wanted it was no preparation for this sort of life, where the absolute priority was paying the rent and it was already proving a struggle after only the first few months.

For a moment her sympathy switched into frustration at her own weakness in the face of her daughter's insistence; this situation was mostly her fault for giving in and buying the animal when it made no financial sense, but now her daughter's obsession with riding looked as though it might completely ruin the pair of them. The fear of debt, knowing she had no collateral, had haunted her ever since the crash; in the back of her mind, Sophy's expensive car had sometimes lingered as a last resort, but she'd never been able to bring herself to mention it. It was the last thing Derek had given his darling daughter, the day after she'd passed her driving test, and she had been inordinately proud and protective of it ever since, naturally enough even more so just recently. But trading their security for the sake of a horse, and a horse even Sophy said was not much good, made no sense of any kind at all.

Sophy was pushing the last few baked beans around her plate, still thinking her own thoughts and not paying her mother much attention. She looked up suddenly.

"I can't stop riding," she said determinedly. "I simply can't. And Gypsy *is* going a bit better. And it's already because of him, some things he said to me. And he said I could get another car, a cheaper one, so I'll still be independent. It's just……well, I keep thinking about Dad and …." her voice faded into quiet.

Her mother took the plate with its unfinished supper from her, careful not to spill tomato sauce on the carpet.

"I'll come with you to the stables on Sunday," she said. "I need to meet this man at least as much as he says he wants to see me. That gives us both three days to think it all over. I'll always help you as much as I can with the money, you know I will, but just now you know as well as me there just isn't any. If it wasn't for Geoff we wouldn't even have this flat. And if this horse does get good enough, you'll be wanting to go to shows and all that stuff you used to do, and God knows where the money for that will come from. You've really got to think hard about this, sweetheart. I suppose it's my fault, really, for letting you persuade me to buy the horse in the first place."

She stepped into the kitchen, put the plate in the sink and came back with a mug of tea in each hand. The two women sat facing each other across the small room, sipping tea, each thinking very different thoughts and yet each taking comfort from the presence of the other. Finally, the older woman spoke.

"I never in my life thought I'd ever say this," she remarked ruefully, "but first you have to do that horse and then we both have to go to work in the morning." Sophy raised her eyes to meet her mother's, and the moment of shared bewilderment at their common, only recently unimaginable predicament, provoked them both into a small, involuntary smile which rapidly grew into a conspiratorial giggle.

"We're both alive and well," Edith said stoutly. "We will get through this, horse and car or no horse and car."

"We'll get through it with a horse, at any rate," Sophy said, meeting her mother's gaze with a powerful determination which surprised her. "Even if it is only Gypsy."

She had to share the manège with Kitty and Blackie the following evening, as Kitty practised for her Sunday lesson with Jennifer watching over the gate. Gypsy was being fairly amenable, for him, and he actually achieved a complete twenty metre circle in canter without collapsing on his inside shoulder, although the return transition into trot was a near disaster from the point of view of anyone with any knowledge of how it should have been performed. Nevertheless, Kitty was impressed.

"Are you going to start jumping him?" she asked, and then without waiting for a reply added, "how do you keep the circle round like that? I can't stop Blackie cutting the corners all the time."

Sophy looked down into Kitty's eager face from Gypsy's broad back and tried to explain what she'd been reading in Mr. Holt's book about supporting the shoulder with the inside rein, but it was immediately clear that Kitty had no idea what she was talking about.

"Just hold your inside leg on," she said at last, and Kitty understood that at once. "That's what Mr. Holt says," she agreed. "But it's so hard."

Sophy was amused in spite of herself.

"Let's both try it in trot," she said. "Follow me round so he has a lead to keep him out a bit."

It wasn't the first time in her life another rider had asked her for help, but it wasn't until they were riding in Indian file on to the circle that she realised, with a subconscious twinge of guilt, it was pretty well the first time she'd ever offered it. And there was a real sense of satisfaction, almost of pride, when Blackie condescended to follow Gypsy more less where Kitty wanted him to go.

A few minutes later Kitty's father appeared at the gate beside Jennifer, ready to take both the girls home, and Kitty rode over eagerly to tell him how much better Blackie was going on the circle, and how Sophy had *sooo* helped to make it happen. Knowing very little about horses himself he said non-committally, "Well, there you are then," but still he looked at Sophy with surprise as well as gratitude as she dismounted beside them. For a moment Sophy thought he was going to say something about the last time they'd been riding in the school together, during Kitty's lesson, but he didn't.

It was extraordinarily pleasant to feel important and included as they made their way back to the yard. Kitty untacked quickly, dropping the saddle carelessly on the nearest stable door and Jennifer went with her to put Blackie in the field along with her own pony. Sophy untacked more slowly, and tied up Gypsy ready for a small feed before he too would be turned out in a separate paddock.

The man said tentatively, "It's good there's someone a bit older keeping an eye on these kids when there's no one else here. The wife says you ride out with Kitty too sometimes when there's no one else to go with her. Thanks for that."

He turned to go then as the two girls came back from the field, giggling together like sister elves in jodhpurs. They scrambled into the back of his car, and she heard him say severely, "You two behave on the way home, or else."

Left alone as the daylight faded and Gypsy finished his feed, the idea of losing him and never belonging again on a stableyard, even one like this populated only by silly children, struck her more forcibly than ever as a horror to be avoided at all costs. *At all costs,* she repeated to herself, with a wry smile at the aptness of the word 'costs.'

Chapter Eleven

Her mother had not broached the subject of the car again, and the pair of them seemed to be deliberately avoiding it. It seemed likely that her mother was reserving her opinion until after she'd met Mr. Holt on Sunday.

On the other hand, the question of next month's livery, now due in only a few days, was becoming urgent as were a number of other equine expenses. Tentative enquiries of one of the other, slightly older girls, whose pony lived in and needed to be clipped as well as shod, had given her a rough idea of what might be needed, and there was simply no way to make her meagre wages from Mrs. Mullins stretch even half that far.

The days were shortening as the winter came nearer, and for over a week now she'd been driving to the stables to ride after work after changing in the store room to avoid going home first, seeking to maximise the daylight and save the expense of the school floodlights, not to mention a few miles worth of petrol. She only worked till twelve on alternate Saturdays, allowing plenty of time to return to the flat for lunch first, but this time on an impulse she phoned her mother from the shop and went to ride straightaway. It was galling to have to ask to use the phone when a year ago, like everybody else she knew, she'd had her own, state of the art mobile with all the trimmings on a more or less infinite contract, but truth to tell she hardly missed it now. Except when you want it, like today, she thought bitterly.

The yard was deserted when she arrived, and she remembered then that Kitty and Jennifer's school had some sort of fête that day and by chance the other two young clients must also have been engaged elsewhere. Even the formidable Miss Brown's car was not in its usual space.

Not that it mattered. A morose feeling of despair crept over her as she led Gypsy into the school and threw her leg over the saddle. Even if she sold her car, the man Holt was quite right; Sophy had no idea what her car might be worth, but whatever it was the money wouldn't last forever. And then what?

It was a cloudless autumn day, fresh without being cold, with a tiny breeze off the Down stirring the tall, browning nettles beside the footpath. As if to confound her pessimism, Gypsy seemed to feel sharper than ever before, and came into her hand more willingly than he had ever done. They worked around the school together feeling more of a partnership than Sophy would ever have imagined only a month ago, and when she paused after twenty minutes to give them both a breather she patted his broad neck with genuine affection, and briefly her despair lifted.

Gypsy stretched gratefully into a long rein as she rode off the track and on to a circle. Of course, Sophy reasoned, the horse was fitter now, and what Peter Holt had said about hacking him out for a change of scene was definitely helping. Even when he was out in the field or just standing in the stable he seemed to be taking a keener interest in life. She wondered vaguely if she herself was riding any better, but she didn't really believe that, in spite of Kitty's occasional, flattering comments.

One of the other young clients appeared at the gate leading a brown pony. She saw Sophy walking on a long rein and called out cheerfully, "Have you finished, Miss Taylor? I specially wanted to practise bending. My Dad's coming in a minute." The girl looked towards a neat stack of road cones in one corner of the school.

Sophy's tiny bubble of feeling more positive burst with the interruption. "Might as well," she said gloomily, and rode out as the girl opened the gate.

She rode into the yard. A man she didn't know, presumably the girl's father, nodded to her on his way to the school, and then she was alone again.

It was still only half past one, the sun was shining and there was absolutely nothing to go home for. She rode Gypsy idly out of the yard and ambled towards the track to the Down, feeling the horse step out more vigorously still now he was freed from the confines of the school. Under the influence of a fine autumn day, and with a horse she was beginning to know better, and perhaps appreciate more with the real possibility of losing him just as he was starting to work properly, a determination came over her to at least enjoy herself while she could. The image of her much-cherished car tried to intrude, and with a supreme mental effort she forced it to the back of her mind. Although it was many hours now since Peter Holt had made the suggestion, still she was see-sawing about making the final decision, wondering and hoping that something, anything, might suddenly turn up from somewhere or nowhere and solve the problem for her.

She pushed the willing horse into trot, and was gratified to feel him maintaining something of a correct outline even now he was only out hacking. The track widened and stretched far ahead, more or less straight and rising steadily towards the summit of the Down. It wasn't the way she usually went and she'd only been this way once before with Kitty, and that day they'd turned off the main track to go home through the trees about here.

Gypsy had his ears pricked and was beginning to take a stronger hold, clearly anticipating a brisk and exhilarating canter up the hill ahead of him.

"Oh, go on then," Sophy said out loud, more to get the horse off her hand than for any other reason, and he set sail up the track with a gaiety in his stride unthinkable compared with his stuffy, reluctant canter steps in the school only a few weeks ago.

Taken by surprise, it took his rider a dozen yards to get forward and into balance with the unaccustomed feel of a powerful horse genuinely enjoying itself, exulting in the freedom of its own strength and capability. She felt the wind in her face as Gypsy lengthened his canter almost to gallop and surged rapidly towards the top of the hill, and then for a moment was afraid that she was actually being run away with and would not be able to stop. Experimentally, she tightened the rein and was relieved to feel the horse respond before she let him run on again, to sweep round a broad, left hand curve on a huge, ground-eating stride, over the breast of the hill and into unknown territory beyond the summit.

They saw it together, the massive trunk of a fallen pine tree lying diagonally across the track just as it swung downhill, not twenty yards ahead. Sophy gasped, and then froze in the saddle. It was over a metre high, she had practically no jumping experience and had never jumped a cross country fence in all her life.

There was no time to pull up the horse even if she had been in control of herself, and with no instructions from the saddle Gypsy naturally took the simplest option.

It would have been a huge effort to break his momentum and stop; instead, he measured the distance, shortened his stride to meet the obstruction comfortably, and jumped it cleanly in spite of his rider being hopelessly behind the balance.

A half stride after the shock of the landing Sophy pitched over the horse's right shoulder and fell awkwardly on to the rutted, unforgiving turf, vaguely aware that Gypsy was careering riderless down the hill without her, reins flying and stirrups flapping wildly on both flanks.

The galloping footfalls faded into silence. She sat up slowly, bruised, shocked and winded but gradually realising she was still in one piece, nothing was broken, she was just about OK.

Propped on both hands behind her back, she started to recover herself and breath more easily. The quiet of the woods and the vast expanse of blue sky overhead, broken only by a solitary hawk riding the breeze high above her, suddenly emphasised the loneliness and the inevitable risk inherent in riding out unaccompanied. She thought of Kitty's mother then, and her insistence that her cheeky, overconfident daughter never left the yard by herself; Kitty's cheek might be endearing, but in effect it was camouflaging a real danger, especially for a child.

She roused herself to take stock of the situation. Her shoulder was sore, but otherwise she felt well enough. Presumably somebody would eventually find the horse, but it must be a good hour's walk back to the stables from here, and her bespoke riding boots were hardly the ideal footwear for such a trek. And the embarrassment in front of those kids of returning without her horse would be extreme. She cringed inside at the thought of it.

She hugged her knees to her chest, hid her head between them and closed her eyes; there was no help for it; looking for Gypsy would almost certainly be futile; he could be anywhere by now, and if she left the track after ten minutes she would be lost herself; the only thing to do was to start walking back.

Something warm and soft nuzzled her neck, and she looked up sharply into Gypsy's big, limpid eyes regarding her reproachfully. For a moment they stared at each other, and then Sophy burst into tears, scrambled to her feet and hugged her horse with unashamed passion.

"Oh, you big, beautiful, wonderful horse," she sobbed. "You came back, You came back for me." She leaned on his shoulder, untangling the reins and stroking his ears, and the tears ran unheeded down her cheeks and she hugged him all over again.

She led him round the fallen tree and the horse stood quietly beside it while she climbed awkwardly on to that massive trunk to remount. As she pushed her feet back into the stirrups, it was suddenly, and absolutely, unthinkable to ever part with him.

They headed back down the track, and it seemed to Sophy that Gypsy was picking his steps with special care to look after the still slightly unsteady cargo on his back. She rested one hand on the pommel of the saddle, and found herself talking to the horse out loud, about her car, and her mother, and her father, and how on earth were they ever going to get out of the muddle life had dropped her in.

Gypsy didn't actually reply, but his ears flicked back and forth and Sophy, in spite of knowing all the time it was quite ridiculous to think the horse understood her and was sympathising, began to feel she was not entirely alone on the hill, and to feel less and less foolish for falling off.

They came at last to the foot of the Down and she managed a short trot up the drive towards the yard, feeling better now with every moment although her shoulder was still sore.

Kitty and her mother watched her dismount, rather more gingerly than usual, and Kitty, sharp as ever, said promptly, "You've fallen off!"

A month ago, even yesterday, she would have been cross and embarrassed to be so accosted by a child, even one she knew, and sought for an excuse, but today she felt older, and wiser, and simply told the truth.

"There's a huge tree across the track at the top of the hill," she said. "It's on a corner and we were cantering and I didn't see it until too late. He jumped me off." She added with a wry grin, "I'm not into jumping. Never have been, but we're OK. No harm done."

Kitty said, "Didn't he run off? Whenever I fall off Blackie I can't catch him for ages afterwards."

Sophy grinned. "Perhaps you shouldn't fall off so often," she remarked.

"I don't," Kitty protested. "Well, not so much now I'm older. Do I?" She turned to her mother for confirmation.

"He came back after a minute," Sophy said then. "I'd never have found him if he hadn't. Those woods are huge and I've never been that way before."

Kitty was impressed, and even her mother looked interested.

"Gypsy must like you awfully," Kitty said wonderingly.

Sophy was lifting the saddle off Gypsy's broad back and not looking at them. They didn't see the flash of emotion cross her face and her eyes blink as she answered, "I think he does, a bit."

Chapter Twelve

It wasn't much of a Sunday morning for a life changing meeting. The heavy rain of the early hours had yielded to a grey, heavily overcast sky and a persistent, cold, soaking drizzle that made voluntary outdoor activity of any kind a genuine labour of love.

Nevertheless, Mr. Holt's Land Rover appeared at the yard on time, and safely clad in waterproofs he taught Kitty and Jennifer for half an hour before despatching them and their ponies back to their respective stables to dry off and then report to him in the tack room for a demonstration of rein aids.

He was answering the last of their questions, in between exchanging amused glances with Joe Fittleworth, who was their chauffeur in chief this morning and was leaning on the door post hoping to get home soon, when Sophy and her mother arrived.

In spite of last night's long hot bath Sophy was stiffer than she wanted to admit this morning and there was a large, multi-coloured bruise covering half her right shoulder. They were also late. She had meant to attend to Gypsy before Kitty's lesson finished, and now she would have to keep Mr. Holt waiting while she fetched him in from the paddock, dried him off and fed him. She said a quick 'Good morning' to the two other girls chatting out of the rain under the overhang, interrupted Mr. Holt's tackroom lecture to snatch her head collar, and gestured to her mother to stay in the car for a minute.

With the perversity common to all grey, or even only partially white, horses, Gypsy appeared to have spent most of a wet night rolling in the muddiest places he could find. His rug was plastered, and his white neck was even browner than his broad brown rump.

She tied him up in the box and pulled off the heavy wet rug. Gypsy regarded her indifferently, accustomed to the routine and waiting for his breakfast. Even so, Sophy was remembering yesterday and gave him an enthusiastic pat and then stroked his wet cheek. The stable door opened behind her, and she turned to see Mr. Holt coming in.

"I know all about it," he said with a smile. "Kitty is a good match for Mrs. Mullins when it comes to gossip. How are you feeling?"

"Not too bad, considering," Sophy said. It was irritating, to have her fall broadcast to everybody on the yard, but a moment's reflection persuaded her it was probably inevitable. She thought gratefully that at least she hadn't come back on foot with the horse loose somewhere on the hill. She stroked Gypsy's face again, and the horse turned towards her.

The man Holt said quietly, "It's taken you a little while, but it's good to see you're talking to each other. I didn't think I was wrong about you, but it's good to know for sure."

Sophy blushed slightly, although she wasn't quite sure herself what he meant. His manner changed then.

"I see you've brought your mother," he said. "That's good. But we can't talk here in this weather. I'm sure Mrs. Mullins has told you where I live. Come and see me when you've finished here. I'll put the kettle on. You deserve a cup of tea whatever you've decided." He smiled again. "Although I'm pretty sure I know already."

Rosemary Lane was a dead end, single track road about half a mile long which led from the junction at the centre of the village to Peter Holt's tiny cottage at the foot of Fairgate Down. They passed two or three other houses, and then Sophy saw the old Land Rover parked in the small square driveway beside the front door and drew in beside it. It was exactly where Mrs. Mullins had said it was, but somehow it wasn't the sort of house she would have expected; he'd loomed so large in her life lately it seemed too small for him, not important enough for a man with so much advice and expertise to offer which she wanted so badly.

He welcomed them in the cramped porch and shook hands with her mother before leading them into his kitchen, a surprisingly large room at the back of the house which was plainly an addition to the original structure. The whippet sat up in his basket in the corner and eyed them warily. A wide, modern, double-glazed window above the sink looked out at the foot of the Down and a few damp sheep were visible through the drizzle grazing in the grey middle distance.

The three of them sat down at a broad, rectangular pine table and he poured tea into three large, white china mugs from a huge, blue-enamelled tin teapot which would have been more at home in a works canteen.

Sophy sensed her mother was looking about her with more curiosity than was quite polite, but she herself was too eager to get down to the proper business of the occasion to pay her surroundings much attention. She met their host's frank smile with a nervous, impatient flutter and cradled her tea mug in both hands to steady herself for what she had to say.

Sensing her embarrassment, Holt took the initiative himself and began by addressing her mother.

"I'm so glad you came," he said. "I told Sophy I had found out something about her…background….and so I suppose yours too, I'm afraid. I hope you don't think it was impertinent. It was from the best of intentions, I do assure you, and I hope you'll see that when I explain."

He paused, gathering his thoughts and wanting to express himself without causing offence to a woman he did not in fact know, but whose support for the plans he had for both Sophy and himself was very important, if not actually vital.

Sophy interrupted impatiently. "I am going to sell my car," she said. "I decided yesterday. Actually, I probably decided before but Gypsy was so good yesterday I….well, I can't possibly sell *him* and so that's it, really."

"Quite so," Mr. Holt said quietly. He smiled at her. "I'm proud of your decision, and I say it who shouldn't perhaps but I'm also proud of my own judgement."

He turned to her mother, who was looking a little bemused. "Edith," he said. "May I call you Edith? I've had my eye on Sophy for some weeks, purely professionally you understand, even before I first spoke to her, and her horse too of course. I saw potential in the pair of them, and when I started to find out about how things were for you both, well I had an idea and as soon as I had it I knew it was the right time for me as well."

He paused again, realising that this last remark would make no sense to either of them, but not yet ready to explain it further. He went on steadily, focusing his gaze on Sophy.

"If you have a passion for horses and riding and you don't have any money, you have to do it for a living, become professional. It's not too difficult to become a groom, or even an instructor if you work hard enough, but it doesn't pay much, you get all the grind and none of the glamour, and you have to do what you're told, make no mistake." He grinned ruefully. "I should know. When I started, apart from racing, those were the only options, or else going into hunt service and I never fancied that myself. But today, if you have determination, guts and talent, and most important a decent slice of luck, there's other ways, and one of them is to ride other people's horses. I somehow can't see you working as a groom when you once had one of your own, can you?

"It might sound exciting, riding competition horses for a living, but the downside, especially when you're still at the beginning, is you can't pick and choose. You'll get asked to ride horses you'd rather not, or which might frighten you, but if you want to get paid you just have to get on with it, and believe me there will be times when you'll be desperate to be asked to ride anything or teach anybody. For over twenty years, after I stopped working in riding schools, I was a freelance journeyman, and I never did have that slice of luck to be in the right place at the right time and find a good horse and get noticed or sponsored. I know only too well you don't generally get paid to ride hugely talented or nice quiet horses. There's usually a damn good reason why the owner doesn't want to ride their own horse, and some of them don't play fair – they don't tell you what it is and you might find it out the hard way.

"If you decide you want to do this, with my help and using Gypsy and the cash from your car to get you started, you might just make it. Or," he looked grim for a moment, "you might not. There can't be any guarantees.

"When I first saw you, and the way you were treating your horse, I had my doubts about your temperament, but knowing what I know now," he shot a glance at her mother, who was listening silently with her own mind in a turmoil about where all this might lead her darling, horse-besotted daughter, "I can understand it. And whatever happens from here on in, you've already learned the most important lesson – horses are not machines, they have feelings and responses and if they think you don't care about them they won't care for you either, or try to please you. I am more thrilled for you about Gypsy coming back to you after your fall yesterday than if you rode a perfect passage down the centre line at the national finals." He looked at her intently, and she blushed slightly when he added. "You know what I mean today, and a month ago you wouldn't have.

"There's just one more thing I should explain. There's more to me insisting on being paid when I don't need the money than me just being mean or worried about being exploited. I've had experience if this before, not directly but through another pupil's misfortune. If I enter into a professional relationship with you as your instructor, if you don't pay me properly the question of insurance gets very complicated if there's an accident. My pupil was doing her boyfriend a favour and giving him a lesson when the horse he was riding kicked another one working in the school and broke its leg. It was a valuable show jumper, and because it was a freebie her professional liability didn't apply and her parents were stuck with a huge bill for compensation. It took them years to pay back the bank."

He paused again, and they thought he'd finished. Then he added, very quietly and looking at the pair of them, "There is a huge gulf between paying to ride for pleasure, at whatever level, and being paid to ride for other people, It's not necessarily about ability – a top amateur can be better that many professionals, but it is about attitude and commitment."

There was a brief silence. Almost as though it had been rehearsed, all three of them raised their mugs thoughtfully and took a mouthful of tea.

Sophy put down her mug and was about to speak when her mother put her hand on her arm.

"No," she said, and Sophy rounded on her furiously. Her mother was unmoved. "No decisions now," she said. "At least you will sleep on it." She brushed aside her daughter's protestations.

Mr. Holt poured himself another cup of tea and regarded the pair of them thoughtfully. "I feel like a school careers master," he said. "It is a career choice we're talking about, and you've only got me to tell you about it. Or to trust, I suppose," he added wryly.

Edith Taylor frowned as he offered her more tea. He seemed to be honest and straightforward enough, and she was better placed than anyone to know that Sophy's qualifications and career choices were virtually non-existent at present, and that trying to persuade her to return to college with any kind of horse option open to her would always be a non-starter. But the man had said something odd earlier on which had caught her attention, and she remembered it now.

"What did you mean when you said it was 'the right time for you as well?'" she asked. "I don't understand that." She glared at Sophy, who was bursting to interrupt. "And we don't really know anything about you." She paused herself then, anxious that Sophy wouldn't think she was going to try and block everything simply because she didn't know horses as well as she did.

"I know Sophy's old enough to make up her own mind," she added hurriedly, "but she hasn't much experience of ….things generally….so I have to worry whatever she says. And riding all sorts of strange horses sounds quite dangerous."

They looked at one another across the table, and for the first time the horseman did not include his potential protégé in his response. The woman's face, still attractive but lined and careworn now after these last months of anxiety and deprivation, excited his sympathy as well as a desire to offer what reassurance. he could.

"I will not pretend there are not risks," he said to her, "but for Sophy the satisfaction of achieving her ambition will far outweigh them. At least, it did for me. Still does, if I tell the truth." He smiled slightly. "I doubt if a non-rider can understand the glow of pure pleasure when a horse agrees to come to you when no one else has been able to reach him. Over the years, horses have offered me that joy so many, many times, and I still hope to feel it again."

He wasn't even looking at her as he spoke to her mother, but Sophy remembered then that wonderful medium trot Gypsy had shown her, and knew in a flash exactly what he was talking about. But her mother would never understand that. She tried again to interrupt, but without turning his head he checked her with a slight move of his hand.

"You're right to ask about me," he said, "and much as I would rather not, I must answer." He stood up and went to the window, staring out at the wet, grey morning for what seemed like an age, apparently gathering his thoughts and clearly discomfited, but knowing that both the girl and her mother needed to be told the story that had brought him so far from his native north country, to live alone with only a dog for company in a tiny cottage at the foot of Fairgate Down.

He came back to his chair and faced them with a worried frown.

Chapter Thirteen

"I'll start at the beginning.

"When my career began, of course, dressage in this country was nowhere near as popular as it is now, and when I went independent my stock in trade was mostly jumpers and hunters, breaking and qualifying pointers, for example. I wasn't ever famous, but eventually enough people knew me in my home patch to keep me going, financially.

"Ten or eleven years ago I was riding in a working hunter class at the Great Yorkshire Show and that day my luck changed, or so it seemed at the time. I had dismounted after being placed about fourth I think and I was talking to the owner, a regular client, when a girl I didn't know tugged at my elbow and said could I come straightaway and see this French person. My client recognised the name, apparently, although I didn't, and he looked rather impressed and grinned and said I'd better go then."

He paused in his narration, clearly remembering that time more fully with putting it into words. Sophy was intrigued, but she caught her mother's reproving eye and held her tongue.

"It turned out he was a multi-millionaire factory owner on the Continent with a string of show jumpers at different levels, all ridden for him by an international rider who by some unexpected quirk of scheduling was that day due to ride in two different classes in two different rings on a novice and a well known Grade A horse at more or less the same time. It was obviously impossible, and somebody had suggested me as a last minute, competent local alternative to ride the novice horse. The horse was called Rasputin, I remember, a big bay warmblood, or hunter type as we used to call them back in those days.

"I had time to walk the course, but that was about all. It was a huge field, like novice jumping classes usually are, and the collecting ring was seriously crowded. I jumped the practice fence twice, Rasputin bucked a few times and was getting more and more upset with the horses all round him, and so I decided to jump as early as possible.

"To cut a long story short, there were two jumps off and we made it to the last one, against the clock, along with half a dozen others. As luck would have it, I was drawn to go first. By now the fences were quite big enough for a five year old, and of course I hardly knew the horse under me, so I opted to go steadily and try to get round clear. I should have discussed it with the owner, but he was watching his international horse in the other ring and the girl helping me didn't speak English. Anyway, we might have won because Rasputin seemed to jump better the bigger the jumps got, but we came third because I didn't push him.

"Monsieur the millionaire heard all about it from the groom, he wasn't pleased and only paid me half my fee."

"That's not fair," Sophy interrupted, and he frowned again as her mother insisted she be quiet and let him go on.

"No, it wasn't," he agreed with her. "But that's life. But we're getting closer to the point of the story now.

"An elderly woman overheard the conversation – you know what it's like on a showground, the only private place is in your own lorry – and she'd seen me ride as well. Anyway, a little later I was in the tea tent and she came up to me and offered me a partnership in her business if I agreed to manage it and teach her students. She said her top girl instructress had just left to get married and it was getting to be a bit too much for her but she didn't want to give it up entirely. She said she'd seen me around in other places, with pupils as well as riding, and she must have done some other homework too because I shouldn't think it was just a spur of the moment decision. I think she'd probably been waiting for an opportunity to approach me, and must have thought if I'd just had a row with a man about a riding fee I'd be more agreeable to settling down.

"Of course I accepted like a shot when I knew something about it. Being local I'd heard of her place although I'd never been there. It was a livery yard and there were half a dozen staff who were all students training to become instructors, exactly the sort of yard where a freelance like me would never be needed. It was about thirty acres and fifteen boxes and a good quality outdoor school, with a big old house where everybody lived. As usual," he added with a wry grin, remembering, "the students were all female." He paused a moment, and the grin became a frown.

"So why did you leave?" Edith Taylor knew nothing about the equestrian world apart from watching Sophy occasionally ride a dressage test, but a single man in charge of a house full of girls, several of whom probably worshipped the ground he walked on, would give any mother cause to express disquiet when that same man was showing a pronounced interest in her daughter.

The suspicion in her voice annoyed him, and the frown deepened. "They were mostly teenagers," he said tartly, "and I was at least twice the age of the oldest of them. Please don't compare me with what you read in the papers. You asked me to explain why I'm here and....well, I've not talked about it before and it's not so easy now I've come to it.

"Me and the old lady, we got on pretty well, and the students mostly did OK in their exams. After a while we even had a waiting list. Then just over two years ago, at exactly ten fifteen on the morning of the 17th. of July, there was an accident."

His face changed, he rubbed his forehead with his left hand to hide his eyes, and then he got up quickly and went to the window to stare into the grey autumn morning and the steady drizzle still falling on the patient sheep grazing below the Down.

"It was a lovely day and we were exercising the horses. There was me in front and four of the girls riding in single file behind me walking along a wide roadside verge. It wasn't a busy road and we'd all of us been there many times before, and none of the horses was difficult with traffic. On the other side of the verge was a bank ten or twelve feet high with a tall, thick hedge on the top. It ran for about half a mile, and then it was cut into by a gate with a steep slope up into the field.

"All of a sudden there was a violent crashing noise from the top of the hedge, just at the back of the ride. It was a hedge cutter on a tractor, one of those flail things, the driver couldn't possibly see us and it came closer and passed us, showering everyone with sticks and bits of twig and stuff. It turned out later that a bigger piece of branch might have hit the last horse on the rump, but anyway it leaped forward like a lunatic and set off the others."

He turned abruptly away from the window, sat down and hid his face in his hands.

"It all happened in about a minute, although now it seems like forever. It took me thirty yards to check my horse. One the of the girls screamed. The horses stared to come past me, fast. I grabbed one on the left, and then another on the right, but we were ahead of the tractor again and it kept coming and the horses would not stop. I had some sort of control over my horse and the two I was holding, and the third horse had jumped forward and was trapped behind between mine and the horse on my left. But the fourth was away and gone. The three girls with me started to get a grip, then a horse bucked and one fell off. The tractor at last was leaving us behind but the girl who had fallen was almost under the feet of four prancing horses. I had to let go the two I was holding to give her some space, and thank God the others didn't see what I saw, looking the other way.

"The runaway was still on the verge, eighty yards on and going a full gallop, although it looked as though Ellen was beginning to get some control, and then a deer came running down the verge straight at her and leapt up the bank to run through the hedge. The horse shied into the road and smashed broadside into the front of a white Transit van coming round the corner at fifty miles an hour."

Sophy gasped; her mother involuntarily gripped her wrist and the silence was more dreadful than the words they'd just heard. The quiet was unbearable, and the man Holt did not break it or even look up.

Half a minute passed, and then a small whimpering sound, unnaturally loud in that pregnant stillness, drew their attention to the dog, sensitive to his master's distress and standing beside him resting his chin on his thigh. The man reached down and scooped up his small companion on to his lap. He went on slowly, evidently making an effort to be as matter of fact as possible while he stroked the dog continuously all the time he spoke, his strong hand wandering gently over its face in a constant, tender caress wildly at odds with his brutal narrative.

"I told Jackie to hold the three horses and I took off down the road. My horse shied off the verge as we passed that bloody tractor still working and nearly fell on the tarmac, but by guess and by God he stayed on his feet and we got back on the grass.

"The van was stopped sideways across the road and I jumped off and ran to the front." He stopped speaking; he was looking straight at them from three feet across his kitchen table, but both women knew that he was alone again now with the terrible things he had seen on that far distant, sunny summer morning.

"It was all bits," he said at last, in a voice barely audible, "bits and pieces. All over the road and under the van.

"There was lots of blood and there were….. bits. Just …. bits of a person and bits of the mare Philomena. I couldn't move." There were tears running down his cheeks now, but still his hand moved gently across the whippet's face, with its eyes half closed in comfort and contentment.

He blinked, wiped his own eyes with a handkerchief and then went on with dogged determination to finish the tale he had started with reluctance but which now had to be told to the end.

"The front of the van was crushed against the driver's legs. It was a woman. I heard her moaning, and then that bloody tractor went by, still smashing bits off the hedge. I think I'll hear that noise in my sleep for the rest of my life. The van door was bent and I had to wrench it open. The woman's face was cut and her arm was pouring blood. I took off my tie and wrapped it round for a tourniquet.

"Then a car stopped behind the van, and another one came in front, and then another and there were people everywhere and a man in a suit on a mobile phone. In just a few minutes there was an ambulance and the police and a fire engine came and I was only in the way and although I don't remember doing it I got back on my horse and rode back to the other girls, and we were all just numb with shock all the way back to the yard."

Chapter Fourteen

It was a natural pause, and he stuffed his handkerchief back in his pocket and lifted the dog down from his lap. Automatically, he poured himself another cup of tea, and then went to the fridge in the corner for more milk. Edith and Sophy were staring transfixed at his every movement, struggling to comprehend the horror of the story he'd just told and his own helplessness to prevent it.

It was almost a relief when he was ready to go on, after replacing his incongruously large teapot back on its stand. A thought interrupted him.

"Sorry," he said, picking it up again. "Would you....?"

Their heads shook in unison.

"The business was destroyed in a week," he went on quietly. "It was all over the local media and no one connected with horses or riding would touch us with a bargepole. Not that any of us cared much at the time, certainly not me. And then there was the inquest.

"It took two days, the coroner went to see the site of the accident and we were all witnesses. Unbelievably, the tractor driver had seen nothing; he remembered a deer coming through the hedge fifty yards ahead of him that morning, but that was hardly unusual in that country and the first he knew of the accident he'd unwittingly caused was when a policeman knocked on his door the next day.

"The van driver was still in a wheel chair with her arm in a sling. She was in tears and none of it was her fault. All she could remember was the horse appearing out of nowhere. She was an experienced professional driver, she hadn't been drinking, she wasn't on the phone, she wasn't speeding on that country road and she'd had no chance to do anything.

"And that left me." He paused again. "I had to go through it all, every detail over and over. And over. Ellen's family had a solicitor, the insurance company had a solicitor, and the van driver and her employer had one each. And the place was packed with the press. I did manage to keep the other three girls out of it, they just each made a written statement, and of course my business partner hadn't been there and so had nothing to say at all.

"In the end the coroner said it was accidental death. I'm sure Ellen's family blamed me. They were – are – good people and I don't think they wanted to but I suppose you have to blame somebody for something like that. I still don't know what else I could have done, but I sometimes think they're right. I can't help it.

"The business was sold to a property developer for a huge amount of money He'd been sniffing around before it happened, and there was no point in my old lady holding out any more. He was going to turn the house into flats and he'd already asked the Council in principle about building houses on the fields. I didn't realise until then that I wasn't just a partner in the management, she'd made me a shareholder in the whole thing when I signed on. I mean, I was so pleased at the time I didn't read the small print, who does? That's why Mrs. Mullins thinks I'm too young to be retired and she wonders where my money comes from."

It was the first time since he'd started to explain himself that a hint of looking forward, of hope in the future, showed in his eyes.

"I couldn't look at a horse for months," he said. "I came down here because I couldn't bear to stay where everyone knew who I was and sometimes I found myself thinking people were staring at me when they weren't. And then one fine day last spring I was up on the hill with Teddy, and he was chasing a rabbit and I was watching a hawk high above the village, and something just moved inside me and I thought I can't spend the rest of my life regretting what I couldn't have changed and wasn't my fault. That was when I started to take some interest in horses again." He tried to smile. "I told you I'd watched you ride before that day when you invited me to get on Gypsy."

He turned to her mother then. "I haven't spoken of this since the inquest," he said. "I wasn't sure I could, but it's done now. It's all in the public domain, in the Yorkshire papers of that time, and so it's probably on the internet as well, but I would still be very grateful if you didn't mention it in the village." He looked meaningfully at Sophy. "Or in the shop especially. I don't know what people would make of it now, after all this time, but it can't help anyone to make a fuss."

Another thought struck him. "I guess you know as much about me now as I do about you," he remarked a little ruefully. "So we're even, you might say." He looked again at Sophy particularly. "We both have to start again, from the beginning."

Chapter Fifteen

It was impossible to concentrate on schooling that afternoon when she returned to the stables after taking her mother home, and Gypsy found himself out on the soaking Downs for most of the afternoon while her rider pondered and dreamed about where she might be in a year or two's time if…..

There was never any question about the decision, of course, and it wasn't just that riding and horses were all she'd ever wanted.

Sophy was quite smart enough to have figured out why her mother was so worried about her future. If she didn't do horses, what else could she do that wasn't a job going nowhere and which she would hate every minute?

Actually, she had to admit, that wasn't totally true. There were times in the shop, now that the regular customers were beginning to know her and chat about themselves and the village, when working there was actually quite bearable. And Mrs. Mullins was quite human once she trusted you to turn up every day. There was even a certain satisfaction in the responsibility of being left in charge occasionally.

There was no need for Peter Holt to call at the yard the next morning, but the rain had stopped at last and he made the slight detour from the path as he pursued his Sunday morning walk, persuaded that it was only polite to enquire after his potential pupil following their meeting the previous day. It had in fact not occurred to him until after she and her mother left, as distressed as he had been himself at reliving that dreadful day, that they too might have been more upset by his story than they seemed.

Sophy saw him from Gypsy's stable knocking out his pipe on the gatepost, with the whippet safely on a shortened lead, and hurried across the yard to meet him. He smiled at her.

"It's all settled," she said eagerly. His smile widened.

"I though it might be," he said. His smile faded a little. "I hope you weren't too upset yesterday. Or your mother. I thought it right you should know, but...." His face was suddenly serious. "Let us not speak of it again."

Kitty was coming towards them with a bridle in her hand, and he forced a change of expression. "Now what's all this?" he said to her.

"I'm cleaning all my tack," Kitty said importantly. "Like you said. But I can't undo the rein studs."

His smile returned. He took the bridle from her and expertly released the reins. Kitty retrieved the bridle without speaking and ran happily back across the yard to rejoin Jennifer in the tack room. Holt returned his attention to Sophy.

"We must talk practicalities," he said. "I should tell you your mother phoned me this morning. She's concerned about all sorts of things, but she knows well enough you were always going only one way. I gave her all the reassurance I could, but it's up to you to keep her onside by being responsible and working hard. Now then. When is your next livery due?"

"Friday," Sophy said. "And what about clipping, and shoeing, and....?"

He interrupted her. "Now that we're agreed," he said quietly, "I'm going to help you as much as I can because it'll help me too, to get, well, going again. Get on the internet and find out how much your car is worth, and phone some garages in Chichester tomorrow and see if you can get an offer." It occurred to him then that hard bitten motor traders might try to take advantage of a teenage girl selling an expensive sports car; they might even query if she really owned it. "I'll come with you if you like," he added as an afterthought. "If you do sell it you'll need a lift home anyway."

"But how will I manage without a car?" Sophy said anxiously. "I can walk to work but it's two miles from home to the stables, and I sometimes have to carry tack and stuff."

This time, he really did smile broadly. "There's two young lads come into your shop," he said. "I know them. Bert somebody and Terry Godwin. I know he's a bit full of himself, but that young Terry is a car freak, loves old cars and engines and all that. His father's a tenant farmer on the estate and when he's not working for his Dad he's always got his head under a bonnet somewhere. He was seriously impressed when your car first appeared in the village. He looks after the Landrover for me and…," he grinned and tapped his nose conspiratorially, "I also happen to know he's rather keen on getting to know you better. Next time he comes into the shop you tell him you're selling your car and you're looking for a cheap runabout."

Sophy reddened a little. Those two boys were constantly ribbing each other whenever they came into the shop, and lately had been trying to include her in their ribald remarks. Mind you, if she was honest, she sometimes rather enjoyed it, and her increasing confidence behind the counter as she became familiar with the work was enabling her to hold her own when she needed to. It was also true that she'd had her own suspicions on occasion about Terry Godwin's intentions, without the remotest intention on her part of responding in any way at all.

"I'd better get on," he said then, pretending not to notice her blushes. "And you'll be wanting to ride I expect before it rains again. Give me a call when you're ready and we'll talk soon. There's plans to be made, and business to attend to. It's not just riding all day, being a professional horseperson, and I promised your mother I'd make sure you did the rest of it properly."

He didn't mention that Edith, with her husband's criminally cavalier attitude to financial proprieties all too fresh in her mind, albeit on a wholly different scale, was worried not only about the physical risks but also that Sophy might not pay proper attention to accounting for any money she might earn or otherwise acquire. And both she and Sophy, as she knew only too well, had never had to take responsibility for money matters of any sort, or indeed anything else much, until very recently.

Miss Brown inspected the signature on her livery cheque on Friday morning with rather more care than Sophy thought was quite necessary; after all, she couldn't know it was the first cheque her young client had ever written. Mindful of her last meeting with Peter Holt, two days ago, when he had stressed the importance of keeping accurate records of anything professional to do with money, she carefully put the receipt into her purse and snapped it shut.

It had been a hectic, emotional and rather bewildering few days, and Gypsy had been ridden only perfunctorily on most of them. Selling her car had proved straightforward enough, and reactivating a long dormant bank account, opened for her by her father a dozen years ago in better days when she was still a child, after coping with the bank manager's doubt and surprise at the several thousands of pounds she was suddenly depositing, had not been a problem either.

Having made the decision, the actual act of parting with her lovely car was less upsetting than she had expected. It was while making sure she had left nothing in it before she took it to the garage that she made the discovery which had stopped her dead in her tracks and very nearly changed everything.

Scouring the glove box for a missing mane comb, she encountered the service manual. It was not an item she had ever looked at before, nor in all honesty was ever likely to, and since the car had only ever been serviced pre-delivery, with the next service not yet due since her mileage had been so curtailed, it had probably never been opened since by anyone.

Her attention was caught by something lumpy in the folder, and it was astonishing to pull out an envelope addressed to her in her father's handwriting with something hard and round inside it.

The note was brief. 'My lovely Sophy,' her father had written, 'I hope this will keep you safe wherever you drive. All my love, Dad.'

Tucked in the envelope was an elegant, silver, St. Christopher medallion with a detachable chain to allow it also to be mounted on a small plinth on the dashboard.

It was a thunderbolt. After a minute she ran upstairs to show her mother.

Edith took it from her and turned it over in her hands.

"I'd forgotten this," she said slowly. "I only saw it once, just for a second. He hid it on purpose where you wouldn't find it for a while. He was a little afraid it would be too much car for you to manage. He said he knew it was a silly superstition but he just wanted you to be safe. I wonder now if he knew even then which way the wind was blowing for him, and that's why he bought you such an expensive car, but you know he never talked about money to me." She added a little bitterly, "I could have been much more than just a trophy wife, if he'd let me."

Sophy tearfully took it back from her and put it round her neck. "I'll never take it off," she said, fiercely emotional. *"Never."*

It was the one moment of genuine doubt in that whole week of unaccustomed activity when she wondered if she was really doing the right thing, if it wasn't all just a glamorous self delusion, a pipe dream. The idea of a pipe dream instantly conjured an image of Mr. Holt, with his steady confidence and quiet manner despite what had happened to him, and the doubt faded as quickly as it had come.

One thing was she was sure of; doubt and Terry Godwin were total strangers. He'd come into the shop yesterday, unusually without his friend Bert, but no less forward for being without his accustomed partner in crime.

"How d'you do, my lovely?" he said, grinning broadly.

"Don't speak to Mrs. Mullins like that," Sophy retorted, sensing that her boss was about to say something severe when she urgently wanted to ask him about finding her a cheap car. Although he didn't seem to mind, she couldn't go on asking Geoff to drop her at the stables as he took mother to work with him in the mornings, and Mr. Holt to run her back to the shop after she'd attended to the horse. And the afternoons were even more difficult. It wasn't that she minded walking particularly, if it wasn't raining – it just took so long.

Fortunately Mrs. Mullins was turning to serve the only other customer and didn't hear. Even so, she felt suddenly reluctant to approach a boy she only knew as a shamelessly cocky customer about something so important. His next sally didn't help much.

"Not just gorgeous, sharp as a pin," he remarked. "Razor blades on toast for breakfast, was it?"

It was impossible to talk to him in this mood. In desperation, she said abruptly, "Meet me in the 'Shepherd and Flock' tonight. Eight o'clock. I want to talk to you. Now what do you want?"

His jaw dropped and his face was a picture. He named his purchase, paid and left, turning at the door to look back at her with a confused, crooked grin on his face.

*

As she closed the door to Miss Brown's office a recollection of that meeting last night came back to her, and she smiled to herself. In the absence of his friend and in the private presence of a girl he obviously rather fancied, Terry Godwin was very much less bumptious and very much less sure of himself.

"So what's this all about?" he asked her as they sat down together at a table by the heavily curtained window with two glasses in front of them. The old pub was warmly lit and there was a small fire burning against the evening chill.

"I need your help," Sophy said. "Mr. Holt said to ask you."

He paid attention then. Mr. Holt and his ancient Landrover were, in his own words to Bert, 'a nice little earner.'

Sophy explained she had sold her car and wanted to invest in a cheap alternative, and it seemed he was the one in the village to ask.

He took the opportunity to look at her across the table and she reddened as their eyes met.

"Don't you go getting ideas," she said hurriedly, and he was embarrassed and looked away. He took refuge in the offer of a little hatchback he knew about.

"Do you know an old lady called Miss Burkett?" he asked her. "Walks with a stick. She must come into the shop sometimes. She's got to be ninety at least." Sophy looked blank. The name meant nothing to her. He went on more confidently. "She gave up driving six months ago when the clutch went in her car and she couldn't afford to have it fixed. She's still got the car though. I'd have bought it myself if I had the money. I did try. It's twelve years old so it's not worth much but she hardly ever went anywhere so there nothing on the clock to speak of. I serviced it for the last three years. Why don't I call her and we'll look at it on Sunday? I have to work tomorrow."

"It's no good to me if it doesn't go," Sophy said. "I need something straightaway."

"Oh, I'll soon fix that," Terry said, some of his cockiness returning, "You pay for the parts and I'll have it on the road before you know it. Just watch me."

"Well, OK," Sophy said doubtfully. Unexpectedly, he reached over the table and took her hand. "Let me take you out and I'll do it for nothing," he said.

Sophy demurely removed her hand. "We'll see," she said, nonplussed at the suggestion although after a second she realised she should have seen it coming.

For the first time she looked at him as a prospective date and not as a nuisance customer or potential assistant in her search for a car. Actually, she mused, if you ignored all that idiot banter he wasn't bad looking, with his bushy black hair and brown eyes and lean and muscular figure. He might have been two years older than her, and he was a couple of inches taller, which must make him about six feet. The thought came to her then that this time last year she would no more have considered going out with him, a village farm hand, than jumping off a bridge.

The uncomfortable reminder of her changed situation stayed with her as she crossed the yard to groom Gypsy, and it was several minutes before optimism returned. If that car was anything like what she wanted, she'd buy it tomorrow, he could fix it, and she'd be properly getting to grips with her new career at last.

Chapter Sixteen

Miss Burkett's car was a bright red, small, two door hatchback with no obvious dents or scratches, and the interior was like new. Terry was able to start the engine using jump leads from his van battery, but it couldn't be driven. Miss Burkett was happy enough to sell it, and Terry briskly undertook to fetch it on one of his Dad's trailers the following evening.

"I can't mend it here," he told Sophy. "I'll have to take it to the farm. There's a barn my Dad lets me use. I've got all my kit there."

She asked him about paying for the parts, and he shrugged carelessly.

"Got an account with a factor in Chichester," he said. "They'll deliver 'em when I know what I want. I'll just bring you the bill. Won't be huge."

It was evident he was working his way towards inviting her to the pub for another drink with him, but she was anxious now to get to the stables and ride before the light faded. Peter Holt had been at great pains to warn her about how quickly money ran out if you had more going out than coming in, and it was plainly silly to pay for the school lights when she didn't have to. And she'd been so busy lately Gypsy was overdue for a proper schooling session. It was only a short walk from the flat to Miss Burkett's and she'd come in her boots and jodhpurs on purpose, but the problem now was how to get to the stables. And back again afterwards.

They were standing together outside Miss Burkett's gate, and she debated whether to ask him for a lift. His van, one of the farm vehicles his father habitually let him use for his own off duty purposes, was seriously scruffy but it was clearly the only chance she had.

"I need a favour," she said at last, and he turned towards her with alacrity. He was markedly less enthusiastic when she explained what she wanted, and could he please wait while she rode and bring her back to the village afterwards, but he struck his own bargain then.

"So long as you have a drink with me on the way back," he said. Sophy grimaced internally, but she had no real choice but to agree. Being asked for a lift was clearly not a matter of any great significance to him, and he couldn't know that she felt humiliated by her situation, much more so for some reason than when she accepted Mr. Holt's help, or even when Joe Fittleworth ran her home in the evening when he picked up Kitty, as he had done once or twice.

The yard was usually quiet on Sunday afternoons after about two, as most of the young clients were generally claimed by their families for social activities which did not involve their four hoofed friends. She gave Gypsy a quick brush over, tacked up and led him to the school with Terry in close attendance, although he made no offer or attempt to help beyond opening the manège gate for her. It was perfectly evident that while he was not afraid of the horse, he had no equine knowledge or experience at all.

She tightened the girth and mounted without speaking, and suddenly had an overpowering sense of superiority as she looked down on him. He was actually standing right in the way, just as she would have expected a non-horsey person to do, and she had literally to bite her lip to check a scathing and insulting remark which would alienate someone she very much needed just at this minute.

Already feeling she was getting into a relationship with this boy that she couldn't altogether control and certainly didn't want, it was a huge effort to be polite when she asked him to stand on the other side of the gate. Nevertheless, as he turned away from her she had the disconcerting feeling that she hadn't entirely succeeded in hiding her annoyance at being in such a dependent position on someone who was no match for her in anything really important.

She felt a little self conscious riding in front of him, which she also knew instantly was ridiculous for someone with all her competition experience, and of course he knew absolutely nothing about what she was trying to do.

Even so, it was a relief when Gypsy softened and came into her hand and began to show some of the better quality work she was beginning to expect now. She worked for about half an hour, cantering on both reins and then with great daring essayed a medium trot, feeling it might happen and perversely wanting to show off in front of her audience. Gypsy responded to a degree, although without the enthusiasm he could have shown, but still a quick glance sideways showed that Terry was impressed nonetheless.

"Aren't you going to jump?" he asked her, looking at the small upright fence set inside the track which Kitty should have put away but hadn't.

"That's not what I do," she said haughtily. Then a little devil inside her remembered Gypsy making nothing of that big log on the Down the day she fell off; he'd fly that two foot pole if she asked him. Did she dare do it? Tentatively, she eased into the unfamiliar jumping position. Her stirrups were too long for this, but still she turned into the jump, felt the horse's momentary surprise at being asked the question, then Gypsy jumped it, smoothly and economically, barely breaking his stride, and she sat up again, comfortably in control of herself and the horse. Relief flooded over her, and then she was asking herself angrily why she'd done it. Just suppose…..and she didn't have to prove anything to this stupid boy.

She gave Gypsy a long rein, walked him to the far end of the school to compose herself, and dismounted.

Terry opened the gate.

"You're good," he said admiringly.

Sophy was irritated. He knew nothing about it, and was just trying to get her to go out with him. Still, there was no doubting his usefulness. He even volunteered to sweep the yard for her while she untacked and rubbed down her sweating horse. Getting Gypsy clipped was now becoming urgent. Fortunately Peter Holt said he had some clippers of his own and would show her how to do it as soon she got herself properly sorted out. It didn't look as though that would happen until this boy Terry had fixed the car for her.

He very deliberately put his hand on her knee as they pulled into the pub car park, and she was startled and snatched it off. He was quite unperturbed, and grinned.

"Come on," he said. "It's my part of the bargain now."

"It's not that kind of bargain," Sophy retorted angrily, but with a trace of alarm in her voice.

The boy checked himself. "Alright, alright," he said. "What sort of a person do you think I am anyway? We'll just have a drink and you can tell me about riding. You can't blame me for trying."

They went into the pub. As luck would have it, Bert was leaning on the bar with a pint glass in his hand.

"'Allo, 'allo, 'allo," he said as they entered. He winked and grinned at them, obviously aware, as Peter Holt had been, of his friend's latent interest in his jodhpur-clad companion. It was plain that Terry had made no secret of it among his acquaintance.

Sophy was disconcerted all over again, but common sense dictated she get a grip of the situation without delay.

"Now look here," she said, unnecessarily loudly and several other patrons' heads turned towards her. She blushed and moderated her tone. She took Terry's arm and led him away from the bar.

"I need you to help me with my new car," she said awkwardly. "And," in spite of not wanting to alienate him entirely, it was an effort for her to say this, "I suppose we can be friends, if you like. But I'll pay you properly. I don't want any….misunderstandings. I don't do that sort of thing." She was blushing furiously by this time. Her heavily protected existence up to this point in her life had given her no preparation for dealing with shameless young men who might regard sex as a casual quid pro quo for other services rendered.

Bert came over to them. "I'll get you pair a drink," he said. He looked at Sophy. "What'll it be?"

Terry intervened then. Well aware of the various rumours circulating in the village about her and her mother's recent past, and having spent the last two hours in her company, and also respecting the fact that he'd been soundly rebuffed on the car park, he was beginning to feel some sympathy for her.

"It's OK," he said to his friend. "We're alright. You go and play darts or something. I'll catch you later."

He escorted her to the table she had lately shared with Peter Holt, ascertained that she drank orange juice, and returned from the bar with a glass in each hand to sit down facing her.

"I'd very much like not to get off on the wrong foot with you," he said earnestly. Sophy took refuge in her orange juice. It was necessary to find a neutral subject to talk about.

"How long do you think it will it take to fix the car?" she asked him. "I think I can sort out the tax and stuff quite quickly online."

It was a disappointing response from Terry's point of view, but still he reasoned they would have to meet again very soon and there would be other opportunities to try and reach out to her. He knew she wouldn't understand, but still he briefly described what was involved in replacing the clutch in her recently acquired car and then gallantly insisted on escorting her the few yards home on foot in the gathering darkness, in spite of her protestations.

She was afraid he would try and kiss her at the door, and was preparing to indignantly resist, but he just said a mild good night, glanced at her a little regretfully and walked back towards the pub, presumably to drown his sorrows and rejoin his friend.

Chapter Seventeen

It wasn't particularly late, but her mother was distinctly relieved when she heard her daughter's key in the lock. She switched off the muted television and hurriedly composed her features to greet her with a smile.

"You're later than I thought you would be," she said. "Did you buy the car?"

Sophy flopped down exhausted on the sofa, then guiltily got up again to take off her boots, still muddy from the stables.

"Yeah, it was OK," she said. "Then the boy Terry took me to the yard to ride. And then we went for a drink." She frowned, a change of expression not lost on her mother. Careful not to appear intrusive, she waited for Sophy to say more.

"He's a bit pushy, that Terry" Sophy said. "He does seem to know about cars, though. I wish...." She paused. She didn't want to tell her mother how much she hated depending on favours, especially from people she felt were, well, not really her sort of people. Her mother, however, with her own experience of suddenly having to accept a dependency on those who once upon a time she would never have even met, not on equal terms anyway, and certainly not socially, was not deceived.

"I know I've said it before," she said quietly, "but we have to realise it's never going to be like it was. Actually, most people are just ordinary and kind and sensible and will help when they can, if they think we'd help them too if they needed it." She added even more quietly, "It's no good looking down on people, whoever they are. Did this boy try it on with you?"

"He put his hand on my knee in his van," Sophy said. "I soon stopped all that."

Her mother regarded her thoughtfully. Sophy was fingering the medallion round her neck, a gesture which was rapidly becoming a habit whenever she was troubled about something.

"He's not bad looking, actually," she said suddenly.

"He must think you are too," her mother responded. She smiled. "And so you are, darling. Lots of boys – well, young men now I suppose, are going to think so too. It's a bit of teenage growing up you missed most of, going to a girls' school and being with horses the whole time. I.... well, just be sensible and take care. It's what your father would have said." A mischievous thought struck her.

"Is he better looking than Gypsy?" she asked.

Sophy frowned, caught her mother's eye, and grinned.

"I don't know about that," she said, and they both burst out laughing.

Somehow, another week went by. The weather was fitfully wet, the evenings were chilly and drawing in fast, and getting to the yard and back twice a day for morning and evening stables was becoming a nightmare. Twice she had to walk from the shop to the yard in the late afternoon dusk, and once she found herself walking all the way home in the dark, when Kitty had asked Jennifer to look after Blackie for her and so her father did not come to collect her, and Jennifer lived in the opposite direction. Just working, getting to and from the stables and looking after Gypsy, never mind riding him, seemed to be taking every available minute.

Kitty was at school now and so her weekday lessons with Peter Holt, when she and Gypsy might tag on for a few minutes at the end, were not on the menu. She thought, now she had the money, of asking him for a lesson herself, but even when they were both at the yard together in the mornings, when he was generously waiting to take her to work, really there was no time; getting her new car on the road was fast becoming an absolute necessity. It was taxed and insured, it just wasn't on the road.

A telephone call to Terry's farm had elicited his mobile number from his father, but when she eventually spoke to him he just said it was going well and he'd see her at the end of the week.

It was five to four on Friday when his massive tractor drew up outside the shop, blocking the last of the feeble November sun trickling through the window display. There was a hugely wide folding harrow hung on the back, but even turned inwards it more or less completely blocked the road. He jumped down and hurried into the shop to a furious tirade from Mrs. Mullins, but he somehow managed to ignore the worst of it and spoke quickly to Sophy behind the counter.

"The car'll be ready Sunday," he said. "Meet me by the church about ten and I'll run you over to the farm to fetch it." As an afterthought, he added, "Bring your chequebook."

The shop was sharply flooded with blue light from the police car which had pulled up behind the tractor.

"Oh, hell*fire*," he said and fled even faster than he'd come.

Mrs. Mullins observed his chagrin through the glass door with evident satisfaction as Harry very deliberately presented him with a fixed penalty notice.

"Serves him right," she remarked. "He's been warned often enough. Coming in here to see his girlfriend and blocking the road like that. Too cocky, by half, that boy is."

"I'm not his girlfriend," Sophy objected. "He's just mending my car."

Mrs. Mullins, who had been by her own lights the epitome of restraint towards her assistant since early Monday morning when intelligence had reached her of Sophy and Terry drinking together in the 'Shepherd and Flock,' after being seen arriving in his van, did not believe her.

"Harrumph," she said, regarding Sophy with her head on one side. "If you say so," and in the face of such conviction, and with a two mile walk to the yard in front of her and no guarantee of a ride back after dark, Sophy had neither the will nor the time to argue with her.

The tiredness which had been accumulating over the previous four or five days finally caught up with her the following morning. It was Saturday, and her mother did not have the heart to wake her when she slept through her alarm, reasoning that it was the odd Saturday when she didn't have to go in to work and the horse would survive her being late just one morning. She was still asleep when Peter Holt called for her at half past eight. Unusually, he was wearing boots and breeches himself that day. He was invited in for a cup of tea while Sophy rushed about getting washed and dressed in a state of extreme embarrassment. He was mildly amused, but not unsympathetic, well aware as he was of the difficulties she'd been experiencing. As he drove her to the stables he spoke to her seriously.

"If the school is free," he tapped his breeches with meaning, "I'll give you your first proper session this morning. And we'll get the horse clipped this week. And we need to discuss a competition programme. I know what I'd like you to do, but it's your money and you must want to do it too. Realistically speaking, Gypsy has good potential to at least Elementary level, possibly Medium one day, but I think he'll struggle to go higher. He has his own charisma and personality – " he glanced at her briefly – "as I think you do when you're riding, and as a professional, you have to be seen to be making the absolute most of the horse you're riding, whatever it is, and Gypsy is just about ideal for that, People won't expect him to go as well he's going to, and that's what's going to get you noticed."

Sophy was embarrassed and pleased both at once. It was the first time since that meeting in his house, it seemed like a year ago now, and then mother had been there too, that he'd spoken to her seriously about the next steps in her career.

As he turned the Landrover into the yard car park, he added, "Imagine your career starts today. Get an account book and get some insurance. They're both priorities. You're eighteen, not a child anymore. The taxman will want to know who you are, where you are and what you're doing to earn a living. I bet Mrs. Mullins knows what she's paid you over these last weeks down to the last penny even if you don't. And if you get asked to ride someone else's horse and it puts its foot in a hole, or you're helping someone and they fall off, you'll be liable. I know it's boring, but do it. Accidents happen." His face clouded momentarily.

Sophy was abruptly reminded of the reason for her mentor's presence in Fairgate, and was moved to put a consoling hand on his arm as he stopped the truck beside Joe Fittleworth's car. He checked her with a glance, and returned to more immediate matters.

"I'm going to teach Kitty and Jennifer first this morning," he said. "You be ready about eleven. Alright? And mind. When we're at work, professional standards will apply for you and me from now on. No mud stains on the horse, clean tack and," his slightly crooked grin took the edge off his severity although there was no mistaking he meant what he said,

"No arguments in the school. I know more that I want to know about student tantrums. When things are tough, remember the harder you work the better the rider you will be. It's all about talent, temperament and training. And the last two are the ones that really matter. Any damn fool can have talent, and a lot of them do, believe me, and never get anywhere. It's what you do with it that counts."

They got out together. He spoke briefly to the whippet, lifted a shooting stick off the back seat and strode over to his two pupils holding their smartly brushed ponies.

Sophy made her own way thoughtfully towards Gypsy, looking out at her over his stable door. She had the whimsical notion then that her horse was reproaching her for being late with his morning feed. It made no sense to feel guilty because of a horse, but still she wasted no time providing it; faintly in the distance she could hear Peter Holt's voice carrying in from the school as he called to Joe Fittleworth to help him with some trotting poles.

At *last* it's going to be my turn next, she said to herself, half out loud, and Gypsy briefly raised his head from the feed bucket to turn towards her.

Chapter Eighteen

She never forgot her first 'proper' lesson with Peter Holt that damp, Saturday, November morning.

It was almost exactly eleven o'clock when she and Gypsy passed the two girls leading their ponies back to the yard, chattering happily about what they'd just been doing. The instructor was sitting on his shooting stick by the gate just inside the school, smoking his pipe and exchanging a few words with Joe Fittleworth as he paid him. Both men turned to watch her mount and walk Gypsy over to the track before Joe went out, closing the gate behind him.

The instructor stood up and she turned towards him. There was something different about the way he was looking at her, although she couldn't define it that first time.

"You have ten minutes," he said in a neutral tone. "Work the horse as though I wasn't here so I can see where you are with him, and see how you sit. Do anything you like."

It was as though he'd never seen her ride before. It was highly disconcerting. She was about to say something, but he just waved her away and retreated to a corner of the school where he sat down on his shooting stick and relit his pipe.

Well, damn you, Mr. Holt she thought. It wasn't the start she'd been expecting at all.

She pulled herself together. Gypsy was patiently waiting for instructions. An urgent desire came over her to show the man what she could really do;

after all, she knew she was a far better rider, and Gypsy was going far better now, than when he'd first seen them all those weeks ago. And the odd few minutes he'd given her at the end of Kitty's lessons had hardly given her the opportunity to demonstrate how far she felt they'd both progressed.

She picked up a trot, and Gypsy was keen with lack of work and swung forward with real enthusiasm. For the next few minutes she circled and serpentined all over the school in sitting and rising trot, finally completing two accurate canter figures of eight with really smooth changes of leg through trot. She felt quite pleased with herself, although at the last minute she bottled out of asking for a medium trot. Gypsy didn't always answer and it might have spoilt the whole effect just when she really wanted to impress him.

She halted a few yards in front of him. He leaned his shooting stick against the fence, tapped out his pipe and put it in his jacket pocket.

"You're not sitting deep enough," he said. "Straighten up. I'm going to move your legs. Take your feet out of the stirrups. Stop me if you're getting cramp."

She stared down at him. He took hold of her right leg above the ankle and pulled it firmly at right angles away from the horse. It hurt. Without speaking, he rounded the horse and did the same with her other leg. It hurt. He grabbed her knee, jammed her leg behind the thigh roll on the saddle with one hand and held the bridle with the other. He looked up at her.

"Let go the reins and lean back," he commanded. "As far as you can. See if your hat will touch the croup."

The whole of the front of her body stretched as though it would break. He held her leg there for several seconds. It hurt. Again, he did the same with her other leg. Incredibly, she felt her hat touch Gypsy's back.

"Very old fashioned, these methods," he said. "Nowadays, people are afraid to touch each other. Health and safety, I suppose. It's good you got all the way back. Now, sit up and tell me how you feel, turn your toes up and check your stirrup lengths."

It was astonishing. She had never felt so close to a horse in all her life. She looked down. Her stirrups were two inches above her feet.

He grinned then. "People talk about sitting on a horse," he said. "Good riders sit *in* the horse, not on it, as you're now going to find out. Just let your stirrups down one hole to start with, and walk round the school for me. Get used to it, and then we're going to work in sitting trot for a while."

She walked away from him. Even the lengthened stirrups felt too short. After one circuit of the school he called her over to him.

"I think we'll dispense with stirrups for the rest of the day," he said. "If you let them down any more you'll be reaching for them when we trot, and I know they feel too short now. Take them off."

It was awkward. She'd rarely ridden without stirrups in the past, and certainly never removed them from the saddle while she was sitting in it. He waited as she fumbled with the buckles. It was particularly annoying, not to mention distracting, to see Kitty and Jennifer leaning on the gate behind him and giggling, presumably at her. He saw them too as she handed him the second stirrup, and she thought for a moment he was going to send them away, but he merely shrugged.

"Get used to it," he said. "This is your office and you're at work now. If people watch, they watch. I'm going to work you in sitting trot. I want you to do exactly what I tell you, with no ifs or buts. I want a quality working pace, strong but not hurried, and I want it maintained at all times. *At all times.* And if it's not, believe me, you will be the first to know. Walk to B, adjust your position and transition to trot. Here's a tip. Don't think about keeping your heels down, think about turning your toes up. Go."

She stared at him. His face was implacable, indifferent. It didn't even look like him. Feeling a little numbed, she approached B and asked Gypsy to trot. The aid was half hearted and the horse did not respond.

His voice was as hard as a steel bar.

"Which part of 'trot' did you not understand?" he said. Faintly through her angry disappointment she could hear Kitty and Jennifer giggling again. Half in panic, she kicked Gypsy hard and he started forward abruptly, making her lean back and she hurriedly caught hold of the saddle to steady herself. With no stirrups for support she felt vulnerable and insecure, but then that voice came again, penetrating, commanding and absolutely irresistible.

"Turn your toes up, head up, chin in, bend him in the turn, more impulsion, don't grip up, twenty metre circle at A, then go large, change the rein, more impulsion, you're collapsing the hip, *impulsion*, change the rein, *and* the bend, toes up, longer leg, the quarters are drifting, don't grip up, left hip forward, ten metre circle and keep the energy, come *on,* more impulsion. Your shoulders are tense let me see them drop, let the horse move you a little more, sit *softer* to flow in the waist, im-pulsion!"

She had never been taught with such intensity in all her riding life, and she had never before ridden without stirrups for more than a minute or two.

And yet...undoubtedly, she knew was sitting better and deeper than she had ever done. In a flash of understanding, she realised that without the stirrups under her feet to offer the support which had inevitably lifted her a little away from the saddle, and with his nagging insistence on turning up her toes to stretch the back of her legs, she was closer to Gypsy now than she had ever been to any horse. Ten minutes passed, and she had no time now to glance at those two silly little girls by the gate. Her seat was beginning to feel as though it belonged to Gypsy and not to her at all, and the rein was softer than ever and yet Gypsy was willingly keeping his shape and moving as though he was taking as much satisfaction from the work as his rider was. Not that Mr. Holt was satisfied as she trotted past him for what seemed like the hundredth time.

"I need more energy in the step," he ordered. "And you must shift your weight as you cross over the centre line in the serpentine. Do it again. And keep the horse tracking and tracking up," his voice rose a semitone in apparent desperation. "The horse's back end is in another county for all you know about it. Now go large. Concentrate."

It was the first time he'd used that word in the whole session, and a moment later she realised why. She was sweeping round the short side of the school when the order came to change the rein on the diagonal. As she left the track, her eyes seeking the distant opposing quarter marker, his voice came again.

"Half halt, ease your weight a little back, open your hand and *push*."

It was *electric*. Gypsy gathered himself proudly and surged across the school in a huge, ground-eating extended trot, another world from the few medium steps his rider had been so chary of asking for only forty minutes ago. The big, powerful horse seemed to be airborne a foot above the sand, covering a stupendous distance with every step, and yet somehow, unbalanced as his rider was without her stirrups, she stayed in control and was able to steady the pace as they returned to the track. She steadied herself as the pace steadied, right in front of him.

Incredibly, or so she thought at that moment, he was smiling. "Good," he said. "Go forward to walk and relax. Let him walk on a long rein, but keep the walk *active*."

The instructor's measured response was a marked contrast to Kitty's.

"*Wow*," she said with her eyes and her mouth wide open. Jennifer was staring at the horse and rider as though they came from another planet, and Joe Fittleworth, approaching from the stableyard to take his young charges home for lunch, appeared equally impressed.

Sophy was beginning to realise that she was panting hard and absolutely exhausted, and her seat bones were sore and her thighs were aching where they had never ached before. And yet……that trot! My *God*, that trot! At that moment she would have killed to do it again. It was another minute before she realised she'd done it all without stirrups; maybe that was why she'd done it. She moved her feet. Already it felt natural to turn up her toes and feel the back of her leg deepen, pulling her seat closer to the saddle.

She looked back over her shoulder at her instructor, calmly re-seated now on his shooting stick behind a wreath of pipe smoke. He was still watching her, but Kitty was asking him something and her father was also trying to attract his attention. He deflected their approaches with a polite gesture and came across the school to speak to her.

"It's enough for today." he said, looking up to meet her gaze. "You both did well." He smiled more broadly. "And no tantrums. Even better."

He gave the horse a pat on the shoulder, where the hair was matted and dark with sweat. "Any questions?" he asked her, and she was too dazed and tired to think and shook her head.

He was turning to walk away when a thought struck him and he came back. "I suppose now's as good a time as any," he said. "You'll be half an hour getting this horse cooled down and dried off to leave in the stable. Don't worry, we'll get him clipped this week and then it won't be such a problem. I'm going to take the dog for a walk. When I come back we'll have a strategy meeting in the tack room. And then I'll run you home if you like."

He retrieved his shooting stick, gave her a wave and closed the gate behind him, leaving her alone walking a hot and tired horse around the empty school, her aching legs dangling still without stirrups, and her mind possessed by elation, trepidation and hope, each contending, all at once and by turns, to be uppermost.

Chapter Nineteen

The saddle and bridle were hung on her arm and she was watching Gypsy over the stable door, rolling luxuriously on his fresh straw bed, when she heard the Landrover door close behind her and turned to see Mr. Holt, now minus the whippet, coming towards her. He too regarded the relaxing horse over the half door with evident approval. Gypsy rolled right over, as though he was playing to his audience, stood up with a grunt and shook himself vigorously, every inch of him expressing equine satisfaction.

"Well, he's alright," the man said. "How are you?"

"I'm stiff," Sophy said. "I haven't been so stiff like that from riding for.....well, years." She looked at him with trace of reproach. "I was always told I had a good seat," she said.

"It's all relative," he said then, professional ethics making him naturally reluctant to offer an opinion on her previous instructors. "There's a good seat which is adequate for a determined amateur riding a reasonably well-mannered horse, and there's a good seat for a highly skilled professional who has to get an instant tune out of a horse other people can't even sit on. And that, I hope, is where you're going. We made a start this morning. And his lordship's medium trot," he jerked his head towards the stable, "will have taught you more than I did by the time you've got home and thought about it."

It was a point of view she had never considered before. As he led the way into the tack room, she had the feeling that there might soon be other aspects of being a professional rider where her preconceptions would need revising.

The tack room was in fact a large, L-shaped stable making up one corner of the yard, well appointed with a sink, a kettle and tea mugs and several chairs as well as a cupboard. a small table and the usual saddle and bridle racks. The clients each had a key, and Miss Brown's ever present eagle eye made sure it was always locked and secure when the yard was unattended.

Sophy replaced her saddle on its rack, intercepted her instructor's disapproving glance and guiltily retrieved it. It had needed cleaning even before she rode in it this morning, and now Gypsy's sweat had left a distinct tide mark as well as a number of white hairs clearly visible on the underside. Having to clean her own tack was something else she still hadn't entirely come to terms with. And it seemed to need cleaning every five minutes. She turned it upside down on the table and went over to the sink.

"Your life could depend on your tack one day," Holt said quietly. He sat down on a chair by the door and consulted a diary from his jacket pocket.

"Now then. You must have heard of Downside Equestrian Centre, it's only three miles away on the Steeplehurst road. They run a series of indoor unaffiliated dressage shows fortnightly through the winter. I want you to be ready to ride Prelim. classes after Christmas. Starting unaffiliated means you and the horse will get some experience without the expense of registering with British Dressage, and we have got to minimise outgoings until there's some money coming in. And that's not likely to happen for a while yet."

He saw her about to protest, and forestalled her.

"It's no good you thinking it's beneath your dignity to start again at the bottom," he said. "Frankly, from a professional point of view, it's where you are with this horse. It won't impress any one if you turn up at a top venue in an affiliated novice or elementary class and come half way down the list. And you've no transport either. You can hack to Downside in less than half an hour, ride a class, and then hack home. Your cash won't last a year if we're not sensible with it. If I teach you twice a week, you can school or hack on the other days, and the horse should have one day off a week turned out in the paddock for an hour or two. I'm sure you know that. Make sure he's warm enough after we've clipped him."

It was a lot to take in. She moved stiffly round the table as she sponged her saddle clean. He said more gently, "I do know this is hard for you. It's a question of how much you want it. I'll back you up, and so will your mother, but it's down to you in the end. Do you want to be a rider, or do you want to work for Mrs. Mullins for ever?"

There was only one answer to that.

She was late home for lunch, and it hardly seemed she'd sat down before it was time to set off on foot back to the stables to give Gypsy his evening feed and put him to bed. As luck would have it, she was picked up half way there by Joe Fittleworth and Kitty, returning on the same errand.

Kitty was remembering that trot this morning.

"How did you do that?" she said eagerly. "Do you think Blackie could do it? What are the aids?"

Her father had something else on his mind.

"Mr. Holt tells me you're going to do this horse business for a living," he remarked over his shoulder as she sat in the back seat, "and that's why you sold your car, to give yourself a start. I take it you are going to get another one? We could come to some arrangement if you agreed to feed Blackie and fetch him in and out sometimes, especially during the week in term time. It's not always convenient for me or the missus to be running Kitty backwards and forwards everyday, and school mornings are always a big rush. And tonight we're doing Jennifer's pony as well – I think the family's gone to the pictures. You could get that job too. What do you think?"

Kitty interrupted. "But I like going to see Blackie," she said. Her father ignored her. "What do you think?" he said again.

Sophy was taken aback and for a moment did not reply. The mere idea of being paid to look after kids' ponies was so far beyond her accustomed understanding of her place in the horse world as to be not so much incongruous as ridiculous.

She stared out of the window at the grey November dusk and the steadily increasing drizzle heralding yet another wet night. Gradually, her annoyance at the approach subsided. It was all of a piece with what would have been unthinkable a year ago, like working in a shop, having no car, having only one horse to ride and living in a tiny two bedroom flat with no money to spend.

Logic told her it was a reasonable enough suggestion, but still a huge part of her baulked at the humiliation. On the other hand, even just a few extra pounds a week might mean she could pay mother some housekeeping. Mother hadn't said anything of course, but her own conscience was beginning to make itself felt, when she was contributing nothing and her mother quite clearly had no money at all to spend on anything except food and the household bills. But in spite of everything, she simply couldn't bring herself to agree, not just like that.

"I'll have to see," she said at last. "I've got such a lot of training to do, and with the shop and everything."

They drew into the stable yard and all three of them got out. Joe Fittleworth looked at her keenly and noticed she seemed a little upset. He had only a slight knowledge of her circumstances, and paid little attention to his wife's gossip or that of the village, but she had been helpful to Kitty once or twice lately, and it was also evident that his daughter was in awe of her equestrian prowess. It was also not lost on him that she would not have sold her magnificent car without good cause.

"Well, you let me know when you're ready," he said kindly. "Would you like a lift back later?"

She nodded then. "I….., thank you," she said. "I hope to have my own car tomorrow."

Edith listened to her daughter debating Mr. Fittleworth's proposal late into the evening with rather more sympathy than perhaps she should have.

Her own situation at the Gallery, as dogsbody to someone from whom she had once made expensive purchases rather than taken orders, had months ago dismantled the last vestiges of her pretence to a status she no longer possessed, and probably never would again.

She thought of the extra money – a pittance at best, but still it would make a difference – but she thought too of the potential damage to Sophy's presently fragile self esteem. She looked at her now, fingering the medallion round her neck, still adjusting to the sudden, terrible way her doting father had died, the revelation that she wasn't quite the rider she'd imagined herself to be, that her lovely car was gone and that nothing she had ever known would ever be as it once had been. Knowing her daughter as well as she did, it was easy to imagine her desperation at the shame of being offered payment for a menial horse chore executed for a twelve year old.

She had an idea then which surprised them both.

"Do you like Kitty?" she asked her.

"I suppose so," Sophy responded glumly. "She's alright, for a kid."

"And her father's been very kind to you lately," Edith went on. "All these lifts backwards and forwards."

"So," Sophy was unconvinced. "Doesn't mean I have to say 'yes,' though, does it?"

Edith took a deep breath.

"Why don't you offer to do it for nothing? After all, it won't cost you anything, and if it's a favour you could ask for one back if you ever needed it. And you might, one day. I mean, suppose you got the flu or something. Who would look after Gypsy? You know I wouldn't have time even if I knew how."

Sophy was silent. It had already crossed her mind once or twice, especially lately since she'd had no car, that there might be a day when she just couldn't get to the yard to see to Gypsy.

Her mother said, "I don't suppose you'd have to do it everyday. I don't know the Fittleworths well, I've only met them in the village once or twice, but they seem like nice people." She smiled a thin, weary smile. "It's what people do when they haven't got very much, they help each other. I know you want to give me some housekeeping, but we can manage for a bit longer and you never know what might happen."

She added stoutly, "And you're just starting an exciting new career. We must buck up and all pull together. That man Holt seems to think you're going places one of these days if you work hard enough."

It was the right thing to say at the right time. Sophy looked up with hope in her eyes.

"I don't mind working hard," she said. "Not for that. I suppose....." she paused. "I never really thought about other people's horses much." She frowned. "I suppose I don't mind fiddling about with Blackie if I'm on the yard anyway."

"That's my girl," her mother said approvingly. "See how it works out once you've got a car again."

Chapter Twenty

Late November is not often regarded as a time of promise, but just occasionally the eleventh month brings a day to the South Downs which seems to have fallen too early or too late from the solar calendar to present a brief reminder of a brighter time of year.

Sunday morning heralded such a rare, blue and brilliant winter day. A dazzling early sun sparkled on the soaked village roofs, near-naked trees and patient hills, reflecting shimmering shafts of gold from the puddles puckering the roads and the shallow places where the rivulets gathered at the end of garden paths.

The shining dawn woke Sophy early, and with the zeal of expectation she rose quickly to dress and leave for the stables without waking her mother.

The two mile walk to the yard fled by as the sun climbed higher, and Gypsy, dozing over his stable door in the unaccustomed, pale winter warmth, was roused unexpectedly soon to be brushed, saddled and schooled before another human soul appeared.

Sophy was walking him dry about the yard before feeding him when Kitty and Mrs. Fittleworth arrived. Kitty's face fell when she saw that Sophy had ridden already, but she brightened when Sophy said she might go for a hack later, after lunch, when she'd done the business she had to do that day.

Mrs. Fittleworth, not unnaturally, was interested in whether she had thought about her husband's suggestion the previous evening, but had to be content with a noncommittal reply.

"I'm still working it out," Sophy said. "I've never done horses for anyone else before." Then she suddenly added, without knowing why, and surprising herself with her own words, "I probably will though."

"You're awfully early today," Kitty said, emerging from the tack room with Blackie's head collar. "I though I could watch you for a bit."

Her mother smiled indulgently. "I think she's your number one fan," she said to Sophy, who reddened slightly. She was rescued from replying by the arrival of Jennifer and one of the other girls, both alighting from the same car and arguing about the relative merits of two pop bands.

"I am in a bit of a rush," she said finally. "I have to meet someone."

She changed quickly in the tack room and stuffed her jodhpurs, boots and half chaps into her blue duffle bag, exchanging her riding clothes for trainers and jeans. It was an established routine for her now; after only the first couple of days without her car, it had become apparent that walking four miles in riding boots to and from the yard was neither practical nor comfortable, and had an alarming tendency to raise blisters in awkward places.

She was just thinking rather grumpily that Terry could easily have picked her up at the yard instead of the church and saved her at least one walk when his van appeared coming towards her.

He pulled up alongside.

"There you are," he said cheerfully. "Knocked on your door and your mother said you'd be here. Thought I'd save you the walk." He grinned cheekily. "Hop in." He reached over to open the passenger's door.

The seat was filthy. He wiped it ineffectually with a rag from the glove box, and she had to settle for that. Clumsily, with her bag on her knee, she fitted the seat belt with fastidious care. He grinned again.

"Sorry about the mess," he said. "Accident with a sheep this morning. Got caught in some wire and cut itself. Had to use the van to bring it off the hill first thing. No room in the back, as you can see."

He jerked his head towards the rear, and she saw at a glance it was stuffed with hay and feed bags.

He drove rapidly through the village and two miles towards Chichester before turning off the road into an unmade track winding its way deep into the hills. In spite of her insalubrious perch, the beauty of the morning and the exquisite, broad sweep of the unfamiliar countryside, and the knowledge that in just a few minutes she would be properly mobile again, lifted Sophy's spirits into a feeling of real optimism; surely, with some money in the bank, a 'new' car, with Peter Holt on her side and Gypsy starting to show real promise, life could only get better.

He drove through an open gate into a small square farmyard, bordered on three sides by a long, low, old farmhouse, a line of what looked as though they had once been pigsties, and a smart, modern, steel and cement roofed barn occupied by a tractor she recognised, another smaller tractor with some sort of lifting apparatus on the front, some big round straw bales and various agricultural implements whose uses she could only guess at.

"Home," he announced laconically as he opened the van door, to be greeted enthusiastically by a black and white collie dog. "Come on, let's get this car of yours."

He patted the dog and led the way through the barn to a brick built building a little larger than a double garage fronted by padlocked double wooden doors.

He let them in, and there was her new car, brightly polished and gleaming in the late morning sunlight as it streamed in behind them. It was plain that he hadn't just repaired whatever was wrong with it, he'd also taken the trouble to thoroughly clean it for her; he really needn't have done that, she thought.

It occurred to her then that perhaps he didn't so much fancy her as feel sorry for her, and she had to suppress a brief surge of anger at that idea. He was opening the car door for her to get in, and she took refuge in the obvious question.

"How much do I owe you?" she asked, and as he hesitated she had an opportunity to look about her.

She naturally knew nothing whatever about garages or workshops, or mechanical maintenance equipment, but even she could see that this shed reflected more than a just a car enthusiast indulging his hobby. The walls were lined with tool racks filled with shiny spanners, and shelves supporting a wide assortment of mysterious metal shapes, presumably engine parts; there were oil drums and a big pit in the middle of the floor where a man could stand to do things to the underneath of a vehicle, and a system of rubber pipes ran around the walls. There was a computer on a bench in the far corner, and a long line of manuals in the names of different car marques and models on a shelf above it.

He noticed she was inspecting the premises with barely concealed curiosity, and instead of replying he said, "Welcome to my empire. Do you like it?"

Briefly, she was confused. "It's....not what I expected," she said. For Terry, her confusion was an opportunity to explain himself and he took it.

"I did car mechanics at college," he said, "I got keen and got top grades, and I've been on one or two special industry courses since I left. 'Course I didn't know it at first, but,.....well, it's my thing, I suppose, like horses is yours."

"I thought you worked on the farm, for your father," Sophy said.

"Not all the time. We do sheep and barley, and there's quiet times every now and then. When I started wanting to do cars Dad took Bert on to fill in, and it seems to work out OK." A look of pride came over him. "I'm building my own business," he added. "One of these days....."

He was gratified that she was looking at him with a little more respect, and he was also slightly embarrassed at giving away so much about himself. He changed the subject back to the reason she was here,

"The MoT is on the front seat. I had to take it to Chichester for that. It drives pretty good though I say it myself. It's all serviced and ready." He was already enough of a car man to want to warn her that it wouldn't feel the same as that hugely powerful motor she'd just sold, but he looked at her coolly walking round it as though she bought new cars every day of the week and changed his mind.

She said again, "How much do I owe you?"

He went over to the computer bench and came back with a printed invoice headed 'Terry Godwin Motor Care' in smart red lettering.

She took it from him and stared at a list of parts and numbers, all individually priced, which might as well have been written in Greek for all she understood. But she noticed instantly that the space on the form marked 'Labour' was empty.

"Why is this blank?" she said, putting her finger on it, and this time he was seriously embarrassed.

"I......just don't want to charge you for doing it," he said awkwardly. He could have said that he'd heard something about her and her mother's reasons for coming to Fairgate from village gossip and his own parents talking, but when he looked at her and their eyes met they both knew that that had nothing to do with it.

"I like to do favours for people sometimes," he said lamely. "After all, my time doesn't cost me anything, does it? Why don't you let me take you out instead. I'll promise to behave – Dad would kill me if I didn't anyway, and we only need to go to the pub if you'd rather not go further."

Sophy had got used to the idea by now that he fancied her, and if she was honest with herself she was sometimes aware of a faint stirring of interest on her own side, but she refused to allow that to influence her determination to pay what was due. Next to the space marked 'Labour' was another blank labelled 'Hours' and she was about to demand to know how many hours it had taken and his hourly rate when another thought struck her. What was it mother had said last night about favours? Here was this boy saying the same thing.

She surprised him then by walking to the workshop door and looking out into the bright day, through the big barn and to the yard and the old farmhouse beyond, where the dog was sitting on guard beside the front door; the whole scene was seemingly smiling in the benign, unseasonal sunshine.

It was a critical moment. Doing and accepting favours had never figured much in the past, not about anything that mattered anyway. She'd certainly never thought about it. You just paid for what you wanted, and people just did it. It occurred to her then that Peter Holt, for all his protestations about not helping her for nothing, had in fact done exactly that, and she hadn't felt compromised or patronised by his interest in her.

She turned back towards Terry.

"OK," she said, "meet me in the pub tonight," adding as an afterthought, "but don't go jumping to conclusions."

She took her cheque book out of her bag and wrote out the cheque for the parts on the bonnet of her new car.

There was a huge feeling of relief and satisfaction as she drove carefully down the track towards the road with her duffel bag on the seat beside her. It seemed as though she had at last taken a real step towards a brand new life with exciting, if perhaps slightly daunting, opportunities ahead of her.

Chapter Twenty One

A nineteenth birthday is not much fun when the only person who knows about it cannot possibly afford a present, and the demands and expense of Christmas are looming ever closer.

Sophy unwrapped the parcel from her mother the following Saturday morning with a faint sense of wonder that she had been able to buy her anything at all. She slipped on the padded, high-visibility gilet and hugged her hard. Edith had tears in her eyes, but steadfastly refused to apologise or make comparisons with this time last year. Even so, it was impossible for both of them not to share the thought. They looked at each other and Sophy hugged her again.

"I asked Mr. Holt for something you might need and he said it would be useful in the dark evenings," her mother said.

"Next year will be better," Sophy said with unusual determination. "Once I get out with Gypsy things will start happening. I know they will. And I'm going to start paying rent. From next week. I don't care if I can't afford it. It's just not fair."

Her mother sighed. "We'll see," she said. "I know you're doing your best. You've spent an awful lot of money lately."

Sophy was well aware that her bank balance had suffered considerably since that heady day a month ago when she'd made her one and only deposit. Peter Holt's cautionary words about frugality sounded in her head a dozen times a day. Already a big chunk of her money was gone; there was buying the car, Terry's cheque, the instructor's own fees, a new, albeit cheap, pay-as-you-go mobile phone, Gypsy's shoes and a new rug now he was clipped, as well as the higher livery and feed charges since the winter had set in in earnest. Her earnings at the shop, paltry as they were, had become seriously important, and she wondered sometimes whether it had been quite such a good idea agreeing to help out with Blackie without accepting some recompense.

Her mother said quietly, "Will you run me into Chichester before you go to the horse this morning? The shopping is so much cheaper, and there's a bus back around one."

She couldn't refuse, in spite of being due to have a lesson at ten that morning, right after Kitty and Jennifer had had theirs. Jennifer had only lately become a regular sharer of Kitty's class, and her pony, a chestnut called Rufus, was famously lazy and nappy by turns, and was actually for sale, although whether anyone would ever buy him was another question altogether. It seemed likely Jennifer's parents had decided that a little schooling might make him more amenable. He was strong enough for Sophy to ride, although she would be hopelessly long in the leg on him, but so far she had managed to avoid getting involved when Jennifer's mother had hinted at it.

There was plenty of time to drive to Chichester and back before ten, but Gypsy really ought to be fed at least an hour before then. Edith saw her daughter hesitate before agreeing, and guessed there must be something more urgent in prospect with the horse than just going for a hack this morning. Sophy's explanation prompted her to smile a little wryly.

"If Kitty's having a lesson," she said, "her father must be there. You said he always likes to watch. Ring him on your new phone and ask him to do it. Her smile widened. "What did I tell you about favours?" she said. "I know you're fussy about what you give him, but you can tell him exactly, and you know Kitty's watched you feed him often enough."

Sophy frowned, but still she picked up her new phone. Apart from the flat, Joe Fittleworth, Peter Holt and Terry Godwin's numbers were still the only ones in her call list, another far cry from this time last year.

As she passed the end of the track up to Terry's farm on the way back from the City, without the distraction of her mother's company it was natural enough for that interesting young man to inveigle his way into her thoughts.

He'd taken her to the 'Shepherd and Flock' twice now, and she was promised to meet him there again tomorrow evening, but although they usually had plenty to say to each other and relations were cordial enough, still there were times when a brief silence betrayed a lack of both intimacy and openness between them.

Terry seemed to regard her with a mild awe, as somehow superior and untouchable, although he was often as brightly cheeky as ever while clearly becoming more and more besotted. On her side, Sophy could acknowledge he was not without charm but could not decide whether she really liked him enough to take their relationship further, or even whether he was her sort of boy at all.

The recent past still cast a long shadow of doubt and vulnerability whenever she felt the impulse to offer more of herself to someone than was absolutely necessary, especially,......well, to someone like Terry, someone who whichever way you looked at it, just wasn't the kind of young man she was used to. Absently, she fingered the medallion around her neck, and for the ten thousandth time the thought of her father and what had been filled her with grief and regret. Unusually, today her emotion was tinged with anger, with blame almost. How could he have done that……..She released the medallion, placed her hand back on the steering wheel and gripped it hard.

It was her nineteenth birthday, but a vital part of life was not there. It wasn't her father, it wasn't even her horses, and then with a glimmer of self-insight she knew what it was. It was trust. Nothing in her life had any bottom to it. The last few months, as well as taking everything else, had inexorably dissolved her belief in people, in life even. In a flash of unselfishness, she realised her mother must be suffering the same thing.

She was already driving down the hill into the village, and the yard, and Gypsy, and Peter Holt, and other people, were literally just a few minutes away. Brutally, she wrenched her mind out of its gloomy introspection and forced herself to pay attention to the narrow road and the imminent prospect of making polite conversation. After all, she said to herself out loud, I *do* have a new career, I *do* have a half decent horse and best of all I've got some proper help. It *will* work out, it just has to.

It was a shock to find a large blue horsebox parked in the middle of the yard as she turned in at five to ten, and a man in dungarees was lowering the side ramp.

She had to brake quickly and then parked out of the way between Peter Holt's Landrover and Joe Fittleworth's car. The man in dungarees left the ramp down, glanced indifferently around the yard and disappeared towards the office without giving her even a moment's attention.

Kitty and Jennifer appeared leading their ponies from the school, with the instructor and Kitty's father chatting behind them. Sophy went over to Gypsy and picked up the empty feed bucket outside his stable door.

She went over to Kitty's stable then where her father was now leaning on the door, elbows akimbo, as he watched his offspring untack. He glanced over his shoulder, saw the bucket and waved away her thanks.

"No problem," he said with a smile. "You know what they say, you scratch my back ………." He gestured toward the huge lorry occupying half the yard "What's all this then? Bought another one, have you?"

Peter Holt appeared beside them,

"I hope not," he said. "The idea is to ride other people's, eventually."

"I wonder if she'll remember us when she's rich and famous," Joe Fittleworth said, grinning.

"Prob'ly not," Holt rejoined and Sophy was confused as the two men laughed at her. Having her leg pulled by anyone except her Dad was a novel and unexpected experience. Suddenly, she realised that if they didn't like her they wouldn't do it. After her gloomy preoccupation driving back from Chichester, it was a huge confidence boost.

At that moment a magnificent Bentley slipped silently in through the gate and drew up beside the horsebox. An elderly man in a lounge suit stepped out of the driver's door carefully replacing a chauffeur's cap on his head, rounded the bonnet and opened the door on the passenger's side.

The middle aged woman who emerged was hatless but sensibly and expensively dressed for out of town in a tweed suit and low heeled brown brogues. She looked about her with interest, but seemed perfectly at ease with her surroundings. It was evident that she was well aware of the attention she was attracting, accepted it as inevitable, and did not care.

Miss Agatha Brown and the lorry driver came out of the office. The two women stared at each other, stepped quickly together and embraced warmly. As they parted to look at one another, snatches of their conversation could be heard across the intervening cobbles.

"It's been so long…………..it must be ten years since the last reunion,………..I was so sorry when I heard……..Are you coping?……Have you lived here long?……..Is Tony well? Is he still working abroad?….."

The two drivers were standing a little apart. Suddenly Miss Brown's friend turned to the man in dungarees and said , "Will you get her off?" She turned back to the estate manager with a half apologetic smile.

"Gerald always insisted the horses had to be comfortable before we were," she said.

"Quite right," Miss Brown responded. "We'll get her settled and then we'll have a proper catch up." She spoke to the lorry driver. "It's that box over there," she said. "It's all ready, I did the bed this morning." She indicated a stable in the far corner which had been empty ever since Sophy and Gypsy had arrived at the yard, a full sized box flanked by two smaller ones occupied only intermittently by the ponies who generally lived out.

Sophy was mildly surprised that the usually office–bound, efficient Miss Brown had actually bedded down a stable herself, and even the imperturbable Peter Holt, who barely knew the estate manager, exchanged a glance with Joe Fittleworth as they digested this information.

The driver walked up the ramp and disappeared into the lorry. The two women, along with everyone else, waited to see what would emerge.

They were not to be disappointed.

A grey mare, more white than grey, stepped confidently down the steep slope and on to the cobbled yard. She was a magnificent, pure bred Arabian, big for that ancient breed at more than 15.2hands high, and hugely possessed of that proud, intangible, equine quality which cannot be bred, produced or bought, the charisma of a high quality horse aware of its own spectacular presence and beauty. She raised her elegant head, pricked her ears and looked about her as though the yard, the stables, the house, even the hills, belonged only to her.

Kitty, standing on tiptoe to see over the stable door, gasped. It was an emotion shared, if not perhaps expressed in the same way, by the rest of her audience.

The man led the horse to its stable and came out carrying the head collar. He spoke briefly to Miss Brown's friend and gave it to her before he raised the ramp, climbed into his seat and expertly reversed his massive vehicle through the gate and out into the lane.

His departure broke the spell. Miss Brown and her friend briefly inspected the new arrival in her stable and went into the office.

Peter Holt turned to his next pupil and said, "Come to the school when you're ready. The girls have been jumping this morning and I've got some poles to put away before you start. I'll see you down there."

Chapter Twenty Two

He worked her hard on canter transitions that morning, and the concentration he demanded soon banished any thoughts of anything else.

Gypsy was responding well in the upward movement, becoming increasingly sensitive to the aid in fact, but still demonstrating an aggravating tendency to crash on to his forehand and run at the slightest opportunity when asked to trot again. That unbalanced stride was very unseating, and being ordered to work without stirrups just as Kitty and Jennifer arrived to watch put Sophy even more on her mettle.

She was about to demur, but he read her mind before she was able to say anything, something he often did these days. He tapped out his pipe on the palm of his hand as he spoke.

"I wouldn't ask if I wasn't confident your seat was good enough to keep you safe," he said as she gazed down at him. "A fortnight ago it wasn't, today it is. Trot large once, then canter before A, trot before C, canter again at B and trot at A. Then go forward to walk and rest for a minute. Let's see how it goes."

It was no good arguing. It was also pleasing to be told in front of other people that she was riding better all the time. As she crossed her leathers she caught sight of Joe Fittleworth also coming to spectate, and was vain enough to hope he'd heard it too.

She set off round the school, feeling her seat settle deeper into the familiar swing of the step, consciously carrying the rhythm and bringing the horse more together, just as the instructor had known she would. The contact softened as the quarters became more engaged, and she rode the exercise with rising confidence as the improved balance helped the horse to steady in the downward transitions.

He took her through the same pattern on the other rein, and then called her over to him to analyse and discuss what she had achieved. It was a part of every class he gave her now, and she was beginning to understand how important it was to know why something worked or didn't, and also to appreciate that just giving the same aid each time didn't necessarily mean achieving the same response.

"The horse is not a machine," he would say, "And neither are you. Whatever they say about robots, a robot will never be a good rider because it can't feel the horse or get into its head as all good riders do."

He relit his pipe and winked at her, something she knew he only did when he was pleased with her. "Now take the irons back," he said. "Ride the whole exercise again, both reins, and see how much easier it is. But don't," a warning tone came into his voice, "take anything for granted. The minute you get sloppy he'll fall about." He puffed on his pipe and moved over to the fence in the corner to watch.

Greatly daring, she lengthened her stirrups a hole before she started; usually, she would have waited to be told or asked first, but it was a sign of her increasing confidence that while she was aware he was watching her she did not even glance towards him. When she looked up, comfortably ready to begin, there were six spectators watching by the gate instead of the usual three.

Kitty, Jennifer and Joe Fittleworth had been joined by Miss Brown, her well dressed friend and the chauffeur, standing respectfully a little behind. Taken aback by this sudden surge of interest in her – Miss Brown never came to the school, so far as she knew – she paused, and walked Gypsy along the fence.

She should have known that Peter Holt would make no allowances whoever might be watching.

"If you're quite sure you're ready," he said acidly, in that quiet, penetrating voice of his when he was making a point, and she flushed with irritation.

Feeling more nervous than she had for some time, she put the horse into trot.

Although it rode more easily with her feet in the stirrups, the demanding nature of the exercise quickly eliminated any distractions, and then, as she finished, instead of allowing her to relax, Holt put her again into trot and drilled her in a complex pattern of turns and circles all over the school, rising and sitting to the trot, for nearly twenty minutes. He seemed to have something to say, usually a biting correction but just occasionally a word of praise or encouragement, almost every stride.

It was exhausting, but Sophy was not only becoming accustomed to his methods she was, without ever having consciously thought about it, and due in large part to the rigour of his instruction, fitter that she had ever been. Although every bone in her body was aching to stop, still she maintained her position and control and was even able to respond when suddenly, from nowhere, he demanded another canter, and then for her to lengthen it along the long side.

He'd never asked for that before. Gypsy leapt joyfully forward, but was instantly on the forehand, and she was unable to make any sense at all of the following transitions to a working canter, and then through trot to a relaxing walk on a long rein.

After a few minutes silence, intermittently broken by the murmur of voices from the other side of the fence, finally he called her over to him.

"Tell me your thoughts," he said.

She looked blankly down at him, still out of breath, opened her mouth and couldn't think of anything to say.

"Excuse me," a woman's voice called suddenly from outside the arena, "may I speak with you, Mr. Holt? And you too, Miss Taylor?"

The interruption startled the pair of them. The instructor frowned. Sophy knew he hated being disturbed when he was teaching her.

Miss Brown and her friend were gazing expectantly across the few yards of sand, presumably under the impression that the lesson was over.

Mr, Holt looked up at her.

"You keep cooling off," he said. "I'll see what they want." Unexpectedly, he smiled at her. "You did OK," he said. "Medium to working canter is always a pig to ride on a novice when the horse isn't quite balanced and your canter seat isn't quite strong enough to shorten the stride first. Just ask any show jumper."

He walked over to the fence.

"Good morning," he said. He looked at Miss Brown. "Are we in breach of a regulation?" he asked, manufacturing a wry grin. "If so, I do apologise. I know that you and I have never really spoken, but your rod-of-iron rule is famous."

The strait-laced Miss Brown was nonplussed by his bantering approach and humorously raised eyebrow and did not reply. The other woman rescued her.

"It's nothing like that at all," she said, nevertheless casting a quick, knowing glance at her friend. A small smile of her own was not lost on the waiting Peter Holt. It seemed likely that these two women knew each other rather well, or at least had done once, a suspicion soon confirmed by what followed.

"I'm Mrs. Jenny Anne Kenley," she said, shaking hands with him over the fence. "You saw my horse arrive a little while ago."

"I did," he agreed. "And magnificent she is too."

"Well," Mrs. Kenley continued. "I'd like you to take her on. You and Miss Taylor. Agatha says you're very experienced, and your protégé is training to be a dressage rider. That's exactly what I want for Annie-May, now she's finished racing. What do you think?"

"It takes work and time to produce a racehorse for dressage," the man said guardedly. "To be quite candid, I don't think Sophy has the knowledge to do it."

"No," Agatha Brown interrupted. "But you do." She looked at him meaningfully. "Your history is all over the internet," she said, and it was impossible not to understand her.

He was shocked by her casual, almost accusatory manner. She could only possibly be talking about one thing and there was an awkward pause before the other woman spoke.

"Agatha always did call a spade a shovel," she said in a placatory tone. "Even at College it sometimes got her into trouble. Personally, I was most impressed by the coroner's final words."

Peter Holt had recovered himself. "I don't know or care what the coroner said at the end," he rejoined flatly, with a deep frown, "I was there but I wasn't, if you know what I mean, and I don't care if you don't. I certainly haven't wanted to revisit any of that time since, and I haven't."

It was evident he was becoming not so much upset as very annoyed at this unexpected introduction into the conversation of something he had tried so hard to banish into the past.

He was turning away when Mrs. Kenley touched his arm and said softly, "Then perhaps it's time you did know what the man said. He said that only the escort's extraordinary courage, horsemanship and presence of mind prevented the accident from being very much worse, and it was highly probable the van driver would have died without your makeshift tourniquet.

"When Agatha told me there was someone on her yard who might be right for what I want, she told me all about it and....well. Annie-May is very important to me, so I did a little research myself. Long before that accident you had a fine reputation among horsey folk in Yorkshire for getting the best out of people as well as horses. I know. They do race Arabs in Yorkshire too, as I'm sure you're aware, and I have connections of my own up there."

She paused.

"My husband was a very successful businessman with a string of companies to his name," she said then. "He died last year, but I still sit on the board of the parent company. He made money by delegating, by persuading people they could do more than they thought they could, and now I've seen you teach I can tell you have the same gift. My husband's hobby was Arab racing – he always said it was less expensive and more fun than with Thoroughbreds – and Annie-May is the last he bred. She won twice this last summer, makes eleven wins altogether, and she owes me nothing, but she's ten now and me and the trainer, we think she deserves a quieter life. She wanted me to put her in foal, but as my husband's last horse I want to see her out and about enjoying herself, and who knows, maybe winning again at something else."

Unexpectedly, she put her hand on his where it was resting on the fence rail.

"It's sentiment," she said very quietly. "Seeing her doing something out in public, it'll make me feel my husband is still, well, close. Anyway, the breeding option will still be there in a year or two if it doesn't work out, and perhaps I'll feel better about it then."

Peter Holt's usual even temper was resurfacing.

"You'd better meet Sophy," he said, and turned to beckon her over to them.

Gypsy was tired now from his earlier exertions and ambled towards them as though it was almost too much trouble to put one foot in front of the other.

Holt grinned. He said to Mrs. Kenley, "I have a feeling your Annie-May doesn't walk like that very often." He gestured to Sophy to dismount, and she led the horse the last few yards.

She shook hands with Mrs. Kenley as the older woman introduced herself, and Gypsy took advantage of the moment to rest his chin on her shoulder, a habit he had lately developed in the stable sometimes. Automatically, Sophy reached up to stroke his nose.

Mrs. Kenley exchanged a private glance with Miss Brown.

"I really should put him away before I do anything else," Sophy said.

Unprompted and almost in unison, Mrs. Kenley and Peter Holt said, "Yes, you should."

There was moment of surprised silence, and then all four of them smiled. Sophy led Gypsy back to the yard and the others followed. Joe Fittleworth could be heard marshalling his charges and talking about getting home for lunch, although Kitty particularly, having overheard part of the conversation, was all ears for more and angling to stay within earshot.

Miss Brown, sharp and prim as ever, caught sight of her from the corner of her eye and led the way towards the privacy of the office. Mrs. Kenley paused for a moment to watch approvingly as Sophy vigorously rubbed down her sweating horse, tethered now outside his box.

"Join us when you're ready, Sophy," she said. "I think we've lots to talk about."

Chapter Twenty Three

When she knocked a little nervously on the office door, instead of hearing the usual command to 'come in' Miss Brown opened it for her. She frowned slightly at her young client's none-too-clean boots, but still she said, "Come through. I've made some tea."

She led the way through the office to a spacious, rather less formal, adjoining meeting room with refreshment facilities in one corner. Comfortably ensconced in armchairs, Peter Holt and Mrs. Kenley looked up at her with a smile. The chauffeur had tactfully withdrawn, along with his cup of tea, to the window looking out into the yard, presumably to keep watch over the Bentley.

Miss Brown gestured to the chair between her other two guests and Sophy sat down. She'd never been this far into the house before and looked about her curiously. Miss Brown poured her some tea, offered her sugar and milk, and then sat down herself on an upright chair facing the three of them, as though she was determined to keep a close eye on all of them at all costs.

Peter Holt and Mrs. Kenley, in spite of the brevity of their acquaintance, clearly shared a similar appreciation of the estate manager's character and exchanged a faintly amused glance at her apparent insistence on acting as a *de facto* chairwoman over the conversation, the gist of which was already clear to everyone except Sophy.

It was chiefly for her benefit that Mrs. Kenley repeated the terms of her proposal.

"I'd like Annie-May to become a dressage horse," she said again. "I do know Arabs are not well known for it, and I don't expect miracles, but I'd still like to see how far we can go with her. I'll pay all the expenses, of course, and I'll pay you, Sophy, to ride her and look after her and Mr. Holt here to train the pair of you." She paused. "I should add that I used to ride a bit myself, and so did Agatha, once upon a time, so don't think we won't be keeping an eye on things between us. I dare say there will sometimes be shared expenses, such as maybe going to shows together now and again, but I'm not going to pay for your horse as well. So what do you think? When Agatha told me about you I wasn't sure I didn't want someone more experienced, but with Mr. Holt in charge," she shot him a glance, "I'm sure you'll manage fine."

"Do call me Peter," he said mildly. He smiled at Sophy then. "Must be your birthday," he remarked. "You could wait years for an opportunity like this. I know I did."

"Actually," Sophy said, awkwardly embarrassed, "It is my birthday."

"Well, I'm blessed," Mrs. Kenley said, smiling broadly.

"Well, there you go," said Peter Holt, raising a surprised eyebrow. "Perhaps it's an omen." Even Miss Brown condescended to look more interested.

Finding herself even more the centre of attention, Sophy blushed.

"It's a lovely name, Annie-May," she said, trying to divert their interest back to the horse and give herself a moment to let the full meaning of this bolt-from-the-blue chance sink in. A sudden fear gripped her. Could she ride an Arab? She never had before. People said they were different, clever and moody and with different feeling strides.

"She was named after me," Mrs. Kenley said. She smiled a little sadly and turned to Miss Brown. "She was a leggy creature when she was born, even for a foal, and Derek said so was I when he first met me. I said we couldn't possibly have a horse just named Annie after me, especially since she might not win anything, so he said, well, she may win a race or she may not, so we called her Annie-May. The stable just called her May, mostly." Another thought struck her. "And so now she may win at dressage too," she said, and the sadness was gone from her smile now.

"If she moves half as well as she looks," Peter Holt said, "she'll be odds on." He glanced at Sophy, and realised she was feeling a little overwhelmed and not entirely sure of what to say next. With characteristic firmness, he spoke for both of them.

"We'll take it on," he said, momentarily gripping Sophy's hand as she sat beside him. "Now we need to be practical. She'll likely want long-reining to help with the outline, and I'll bet a pound you ladies don't have breaking tack or a dressage saddle between you." He flashed a glance at Miss Brown, still silent but not missing a word. "I've got breaking tack of my own, but bare back's not allowed in the dressage arena." He chuckled at the idea.

Mrs. Kenley was unperturbed. "Whatever you need," she said, getting to her feet. She took a card out of her purse and handed it to him. "Any problems, just give me a call. I'll be back in a week to see how you're getting on and if you need anything special you can tell me then. Or I'll maybe come sooner and catch you out."

"You won't catch me out, madam," Peter Holt said, not quite under his breath as he stood up with her, and she stopped sharply and looked at him.

"No," she said then. "I'm sure I won't. I'm sorry I said that. It's what Gerald always said when he was delegating a responsible job to a person he didn't know, and since he died I seem to have got into the same habit. I, well, I have been caught out myself once or twice in the business since I've been on my own. It makes you careful about trusting people."

Miss Brown was on her feet too and seemed about to say something, but again her friend forestalled her.

"We must shake hands on the arrangement," she said to him, and the physical contact eased away the brief moment of tension. She shook hands with Sophy too, as well as giving her a broad smile of encouragement.

The chauffeur held the door open for all four of then to pass back outside on to the yard. Mrs. Kenley looked for a moment at her horse, her ears pricked as she inspected her new surroundings, and then turned to her friend.

"Why don't we have lunch in that pub down the road?" she said. "Give ourselves a chance to catch up properly. We'll go in the Bentley then Eddy can bring us back to drop you off. Unless you fancy the theatre in Chichester tonight. Come back with me. You used to love the theatre. Gerald had a standing booking with them for his business associates, and I've never cancelled it."

Miss Brown said a little huffily, "I can't possibly go to the theatre without changing."

Mrs. Kenley grinned engagingly. Again, apropos of nothing in particular, she exchanged a glance with Peter Holt.

"Still the same politically correct Aggie," she remarked, and Miss Brown had the grace to grin herself.

"Well, you'll be alright for the village pub at least," Mrs. Kenley said, gesturing a final farewell to her new horse trainer and rider as Eddy stepped ahead of them to hold open the rear door of the Bentley.

The yard felt empty as the car slipped smoothly out of the gate, the silence broken only by the shuffle of a horse's feet in the straw.

Sophy felt as though she'd been picked up, spun round, and then put back on her feet in another dimension. Everything she'd spent the last few weeks wishing for, in spite of Peter Holt's cautions about exaggerated expectations, had suddenly materialised; she turned to look at Annie-May's elegant head, peering over her stable door, and realised the horse was actually watching her too, probably out of curiosity at her new surroundings. The thought of riding her, fresh off the racetrack, was terrifying as well as thrilling.

The instructor was watching her too, and spoke first.

"I don't believe your luck," he said with a smile. "Who'd have thought Miss Brown the dragon lady would come up trumps like that? She must have been watching you, or you and me both I suppose, for quite a while."

"But she's an Arab and a racehorse," Sophy said. "Can I really do it? I…" her voice tailed off."

His smile widened even further. "I can teach you long reining," he said. "We'll get her going nicely from the ground first, and maybe I'll sit on her once or twice myself and boost your confidence a bit. Remember, she's not a youngster, she'll be well experienced with different riders even though she'll have to get used to much longer legs on her and a new way of going. It's going to be great good fun and we'll both be getting paid, too. What more could you want?"

Still she looked anxious, and he laughed at her then.

"Go and talk to her," he said. "Then go home and tell your mother all about it. And you'll have two to feed and bed down tonight so you'd better come back a bit earlier this afternoon. And talk to Gypsy too before you go," he added suddenly. "He mustn't feel neglected in favour of the new kid on the block. And one more thing," he winked at her. "Now that we're business partners you'd better start calling me Peter instead of Mr. Holt. I'll see you tomorrow morning about ten."

He left her then and walked over towards his Landrover, where Teddy the whippet was watching them both through the driver's window. Even from behind. it was evident from the agitation of his shoulders that he was chuckling again.

As he drove past the 'Shepherd and Flock' it was impossible to miss the Bentley gracing the small, crowded car park, with Eddy leaning on the wing consuming a bread roll, and on a whim he decided to lunch at the pub himself to celebrate after the morning's momentous meeting rather than return to an empty cottage and just a sandwich. He squeezed the truck into the last empty space, realised the place must be packed, and gave Teddy a reluctant valedictory pat before leaving him behind and making his way into the bar.

The bar was as busy as he expected. A brief exchange with Terry Godwin and his friend Bert, partaking of a ploughman's lunch while jammed against the wall at one end of the counter, elicited the information that as well as the regulars a party of ramblers had descended on the village and were soon to depart en masse for the car park at the top of the Down to commence rambling.

"Not so busy in there," Terry said with a jerk of his head towards the pukka dining room next door, where white table cloths and waiter service held sway. It wasn't what he'd had in mind, especially in view of the fact that he was still wearing boots, half chaps and breeches, but it was clear it would take an age to be served here in the bar.

He pushed open the glass panelled door with a slight grimace, and was instantly aware of Miss Brown and Mrs. Kenley sitting at a central table, although they were chatting intently and did not notice him as he was escorted to a table for one a few feet away in the far corner.

He was well enough known at the 'Shepherd and Flock' for the girl to call him by his name as she handed him the menu, and Mrs. Kenley immediately turned round to smile at him. She glanced at her companion and in another moment she was on her feet and came over to him.

"Please join us," she said. "I'll brook no refusal. It'll be good to talk some more. Agatha says you've done wonders for that girl already." She looked at him a little slyly. "And not just with her riding, Agatha tells me."

He changed tables and sat down a little awkwardly, the menu still in his hand. The waitress had followed him and waited for his order. It was an excuse not to begin a conversation he had not foreseen and wasn't prepared for. The two women waited as he made his choice, and finally he was obliged to meet their gaze.

Mrs. Kenley sensed his slight discomfort and spoke first. "Your Sophy was a bit of a madam, apparently, when she first came to the stables," she remarked, and when he didn't respond Miss Brown interposed.

"I keep a close eye on that yard," she said. "Closer than people think. Horse livery people are not like farmers, they don't have to think long term and if you're not careful they're up to something or they don't take proper care of things. Two years ago I had to throw someone out for stealing hay, and last winter I had words with Mrs. Fittleworth at least twice for leaving young Katie waiting on the yard until well after dark. I think that's why we see more of her father now. There's a window at the top of the house where you can see everything, even the school. Of course, I don't watch all the time, some days I don't go up there at all, but I do like to know what new clients are doing especially. I have to say, if you hadn't come along when you did I would have spoken myself with that girl about the way she was treating her horse. And she was walking about the yard in a sulk as if even being there was beneath her dignity, and that flash car she had then...." She paused, bridling indignantly at the recollection. "Well, anyway," she finished, "You took her in hand at just the right time."

"She's not my Sophy," Holt replied at last. "On the other hand, I can't help feeling some responsibility for any pupil." He frowned. "I suppose I should admit I did see some talent in her right off, but I won't stand for any horse being misused, not by anyone. I'm actually quite proud she came to her senses so quickly. They don't always. It's the horses that do it, usually. You just point the way, so to speak. Most people don't realise that being a good rider is not about what you know or even what you can do, but it's about who you are. The way anybody rides is a reflection of their personality, and that's why some horses go better than others for different people." He made a wry face. "Unfortunates like me have to get on with all of them, makes me wonder who I really am, sometimes, after riding so many in all these years.."

"I don't believe that for a moment," Mrs. Kenley said. "I know who you are and we only met this morning."

Their eyes met and again a flash of connection flew between them.

The waitress appeared with the women's lunches then, and the conversation paused before Mrs. Kenley began to express her hopes for Annie-May and to ask him about how the sport of dressage was organised.

"Gerald used to sponsor some of the Arab races," she said. "Can you do that for dressage competitions? I'd like to make a contribution and get involved and not just stand on the sidelines."

It wasn't a question Peter Holt had ever considered.

"I'm sure they'll take your money," Miss Brown said with a knowing smile. "I never knew any organisation yet that wouldn't."

"You always were a cynic," her friend said. She turned again to Peter Holt, whose omelette had arrived. "I wonder why you don't want to still compete yourself?" she asked him.

"I suppose I could," he responded. "I could afford a horse or even several nowadays, instead of always having to be paid to ride for other people. I never did have a horse of my own back then, it was simply not a financial option. Then at the school when I concentrated on teaching there was the same satisfaction and it was better for the business if a pupil did well."

His face darkened then. "I'm sorry, that's not really true," he said "I've just rediscovered that I still love to ride and I have thought about competing again lately, but you both know what happened. I've had so long out of everything, but I still can't bear the idea of being the centre of attention again, even down here someone might remember and bring it all back. And it wouldn't be fair if my name suddenly appeared in the horse press as riding a horse somewhere – what would that girl's parents think? And with the internet and all this social media stuff now, which I freely admit I don't remotely understand someone would be sure to notice and say something, even if all I won was a small class at the South Pole.

"Besides," he added with a wry grin as an afterthought and obviously trying to lift the mood, "dressage is all about elegance. I'm not so young or so pretty as Sophy. I must remind her to smile when she comes down the centre line. Judges like that."

"With ordinary luck," Jenny Kenley said, raising her glass and inviting her companions to join her, "we'll all have something to smile about soon."

Chapter Twenty Four

The uneven combination of excitement and anxiety had kept Sophy awake most of the night.

Annie-May had been a perfect lady when she'd tidied her bed and fed her last evening, after attending to Gypsy, but that was no guarantee she'd be equally amenable to ride. And talking to mother had been no help; Edith was thrilled at her daughter's sudden change of fortune, but for all practical purposes could only offer vague reassurances which it was evident she herself didn't entirely believe, and which only poorly concealed her natural apprehension at this unexpected expedition into the unknown.

Sophy's nerves refused to subside even after she'd mucked them both out the following morning and was waiting for Peter Holt to arrive. It didn't help that the yard was busy; Annie-May as a new arrival was attracting everybody's attention, and her own revised status as a freshly fledged professional horseperson seemed to be the principal topic of conversation. At least it was the weekend and she didn't have Blackie to fetch in from the field and feed too.

The old Landrover arrived punctually, and Peter Holt stepped out and immediately vanished to the rear, reappearing after a moment with his arms full of a seemingly random, bewildering variety of straps and buckles and a strange looking bit and a broad leather roller. Sophy had absolutely no experience or knowledge of breaking or breaking tack, and his smile of greeting did nothing to allay her agitation.

With his usual perception he realised she was desperately unsure of herself and equally desperate not to appear ignorant or foolish in front of the whole yard.

"Good morning," he said. He shot a faintly amused glance at the bystanders. Every horse he'd ever broken had attracted an audience; not that Annie-May came into that category, but long reining is not a skill widely practised by everyday riders and their interest was natural enough. Just the same, his chief concern this morning, after the horse, was Sophy's education; she needed to learn how to do this, for future reference if for nothing else, and an experienced ex-racehorse would be the ideal guinea pig. He turned back to her.

"Have you brushed her?" he asked, and she nodded without speaking. He approached the stable and hung the tackle over the door. He beckoned her over to him before he went in.

"Don't speak," he said, quietly and for her ears only. "Just watch me. Even when I bring her out, don't speak. If I need you to do something, I'll tell you. Follow me wherever I go. Keep beside me if you can, but not too close and don't speak. Watch all the time. Watch the horse and watch my hands. Then we'll talk about it. And then *you'll* do it. OK?"

He met her eyes and smiled again, and some of his confidence rubbed off on her. It was perfectly clear to everybody watching, including Miss Brown who had suddenly appeared from somewhere, that he had done this many times before and was equally indifferent to an audience of one, or a hundred.

Nearly an hour later he was sitting on the school fence smoking his pipe, watching Sophy struggling with the novel concept of lunging with two reins and trying not to get them into yet another tangle, while Annie-May drifted on to a wider and wider circle.

A voice he remembered said close behind him, "Good morning to you, Peter Holt."

Mrs. Kenley nodded to him, but she transferred her attention immediately back to her horse. Annie-May was now again under some semblance of control and showing occasional moments of accepting the invitation of the players on the bit to lower her head and come into a rounder shape, but even so, the overriding impression was of chaos and incompetence with the horse clearly much more in charge than she should have been.

"I can see you've dropped May and Sophy right in it together," her owner said, with doubt in her tone if not outright disapproval. "Was that wise?"

The look she cast towards the other spectators, now no longer including the taciturn estate manager, also suggested she did not entirely approve of their presence either.

"Perhaps you've caught me out after all," Holt said coldly. "but it's not only the horse who has to learn, and the only thing Annie-May doesn't know about this work is the shape we want from her." He raised his voice to speak to Sophy.

"Stop her," he commanded. "Let me take her again."

He slipped off the fence, tapped out his pipe and took a pair of black leather gloves out of his jacket pocket before taking it off and hanging it on the fence.

Flushed and frustrated, Sophy thrust the long lines into his hands, the pair of them hopelessly jumbled together. He immediately dropped the tangled mass into the sand, only retaining one line to keep the horse waiting while he patiently and precisely separated them and gathered them in figures-of-eight loops over each hand. Detaining Sophy beside him with a quiet glance, he spoke again so that only she could hear him.

"You're doing OK," he said gently. "It takes time and practice, and we all get in a muddle when the horse is green or does something unexpected. Don't worry for now. We're a bit unlucky because Mrs. Kenley's turned up." He smiled at her encouragingly. "Go and be sociable while I finish off the work for today. And then we'll boost your morale with a lesson on Gypsy. We might look at shoulder-in today, if he goes well enough."

He turned his attention then to Annie-May, and what happened next became the stuff of legend on that quiet DIY livery yard at the foot of Fairgate Down. Put on his mettle by the owner's evident disapproval of his methods, and having seen the signs when he'd worked the horse earlier, he determined to show both her and anyone else who cared to watch just what he could do with a talented horse without actually riding it.

Annie-May, sensitive to the moment as all Arabs are, flicked her dainty ears back as he gathered the contact, and in a moment she was trotting on a wide circle, in perfect control, her elegant, elevated steps seeming barely to touch the sand as he softly invited her to answer the reins and fold sweetly into his hands. And then the miracle came as she understood at last the meaning of the gentle, insistent request of the unfamiliar bit and the softly seeking reins.

The magic, tentative strides of a horse feeling its way into a rounded and balanced carriage for the very first time are as precious to the trainer as the crown jewels are to the Keepers of the Tower. And Annie-May was not a mare to do anything by halves. As she shaped herself to the pattern the man and the tackle were making for her, she seemed to grow nearly a hand taller, and the wonder of her presence and her pride in who she was grew by the same measure.

Holt never once took his eyes from her, but nor did he speak, He jogged a few steps on the spot as the horse flew round him, her outline established now as though she was on old hand at the dressage game, and then he invited her to leave the lunging circle and spread her strides as he followed her offset around the school, across the diagonals, into turns and loops and changes of hand, changing his own pace to keep hers' constant; and always he held those long, impossible-to-manage twin reins softly stretched, controlling and comforting the horse both together, and reminding Sophy irresistibly of the contact she knew he offered Gypsy when he rode him and which she could never quite achieve herself.

He crossed behind her to change the rein for maybe the twentieth time, and this time, as he turned her again on to the lunging circle and the bend changed, as the side of her face became visible he caught a glimpse of her eye and knew the moment had come. A vertical loop flowed softly along the outside rein to drop across her hocks, and with the confidence of a horse at peace with the man in charge of her, Annie-May stepped into canter, accompanied by an involuntary murmur of applause from her adoring public.

Whether the man heard it or not was impossible to determine, for he had his hands full now. The quality of the canter, seen for the first time even by her owner in an outline, and performing an exercise where speed was not the sole consideration, was breathtaking. Annie-May, above any Arab he had ever seen, was possessed of the lift and balletic cadence for which the breed is famed in that waltzing pace, to a quite astonishing degree.

Inspired by the beauty dancing around him, and forgetful now of Mrs. Kenley or any other human presence, he was tempted to emulate a feat he had seen only once in his life, performed on a world famous stage by a specialist master of the art of working horses from the ground. He took the reins in one hand, and drove the cantering horse away from the circle to surge down the long side in an extended half a dozen strides. It was a spectacular demonstration of balance and control on both their parts which tested the man's abilities to the limit as he strove to allow the horse room with the reins and yet still retain command to return to the circle a moment later.

He did not hear the gasps of incredulity from beyond the fence as he took her through a simple change across the school to repeat the exercise on the other rein, still with the long reins in only one hand and this time with Annie-May flying down the fence less than a yard in front of the spectators.

He was breathing hard with the unaccustomed effort when he brought her at last to a halt, and they both stood for a moment motionless, with the mare eyeing her master standing behind her shoulder with one ear turned towards him. A huge, wide smile spread over Peter Holt's face, but when he spoke only the horse was near enough to hear him.

He dropped the outside rein and approached the horse's head; with indescribable tenderness he reached up to caress the side of her face, letting his hand wander softly over her eye; then he stroked her behind her ear and his lips moved in a whisper for her and for her alone. Annie-May lowered her head to his shoulder and rubbed her warm nostril against his cheek, and the two of them were alone together in a private, world apart.

The watchers beside the fence were silent, awed by the majesty of the horse and the skill of the trainer, and now by a strange feeling that they were intruding on an intimate moment where only the two principals had any right to be.

Sophy blinked back tears as she watched her instructor unclip the side reins, re-attach them to the roller, and gather up the long lines to lead the mare towards the gate. It suddenly dawned on her that she'd been so rapt with the man and the horse that she hadn't yet even spoken to Mrs. Kenley, standing beside her. When she turned to her now, an apology forming on her lips, she saw with a slight shock that Mrs. Kenley, businesswoman *extraordinaire,* was as moved as she was.

"That man," she heard her say under her breath, and then he appeared in front of them with beads of sweat on his brow beneath his cap.

Whatever he might have been feeling a moment before, he was brisk and to the point as he handed the reins to Sophy.

"Put her away," he said. "A pat and a quick rub down, she's not that hot. Unlike me," he added ruefully, picking up his jacket and dabbing his cheeks with a non-too-clean handkerchief. "Then bring Gypsy."

He was turning towards Mrs. Kenley when they were both distracted by Kitty tugging at his elbow.

"Can I do that with Blackie?" she said eagerly. "Will you show me?"

He sighed a little wearily. "Not now Kitty," he said looking down at her. "You know you and Jennifer have a lesson at twelve. We'll talk about it then."

Her father appeared to remove her with an apologetic grin which did nothing to conceal his admiration for the demonstration whose conclusion he'd just witnessed. It seemed for a moment as if he would say something himself, but in the end he just nodded, presumably thinking that he too would have his chance later. Holt stared after them, momentarily lost in thought and shrugging into his jacket.

"It seems I owe you another apology," Jennie Kenley said quietly. "So you had already worked her before I came. I don't know how you can run like that in those boots."

He removed his cap to mop his forehead again. "You don't think about it," he said absently. "When you're committed the horse just takes you." His fingers, one hand still gripping the handkerchief, moved slightly, apparently of their own volition. He came back to himself with a jerk.

"Sorry," he said. "Miles away. I haven't done that for a very long time. I suppose I should be glad I still can. Yes, of course I gave her a few minutes before Sophy took her. I had to show the girl anyway. Talent can't make up for lack of experience in something like that, but I wanted her to start from scratch with the mare as far as possible. It'll help their relationship later on. The horse knew all about it right off. I thought she would. Racing people know their stuff. I worked on a racing yard outside Wetherby once, just briefly when they were short handed. I didn't expect to see you today," he added, "but since you're here we can talk about tack. How much do you want to spend on a saddle? We'll need it in a day or two, and Gypsy's is far too wide even for a stop gap."

"I'd like to see Sophy when she rides her for the first time," Mrs. Kenley said. "Or will you do that first too?"

He frowned. "When you've got one of your board meetings," he said, "do you always know what you're going to say before you go in? Well, I don't make hard plans when I'm teaching either, but it's my job to teach, not to get on every five minutes. When you're the instructor, the point is not what the horse will do for you, but what it will do for the pupil." He grunted. She had the impression this was a conversation he'd had many times before, although probably not lately.

"There's too many instructors who ride all the time, and that's not much help to the client, is it? I only ride in a lesson when I feel I need to, to demonstrate or get a horse to do something for the first time. Mostly, I try not to." He realised then he was giving her a lecture about his professional beliefs, and stopped in some confusion.

Their eyes met, he raised a doubtful eyebrow and suddenly they both laughed.

"I'll take that as a 'maybe' then," Jenny Kenley said, still chuckling. "Why don't you have lunch with me in that famous pub of yours? I probably really won't be back again for a week now, although I dare say Agatha will keep me informed."

"I bet she will," Peter Holt said with a wry grin, looking up over the stables and towards the attic windows in the roof of the big house, and she laughed again.

Impulsively, she put her hand on his arm. "You're a very remarkable man," she said to him. "And I don't just mean with the horses. You're not afraid of me, are you?"

He was astonished. "Why would I be afraid of you? I don't see what you mean."

"Most people are," she said quietly. "You really don't know who I am or what I'm worth, do you?"

There was a pause. Gypsy's hooves sounded on the concrete path leading to the school, a reminder that their impromptu tête à tête was coming to an end.

"I'm afraid I can't come to lunch," he said quietly, "I have to teach Sophy now, and at twelve I have those two girls and their ponies, but I do hope you'll ask me again. And no, I don't know who you are, except you say you're Mrs. Jenny Kenley, and I certainly don't know what you're worth. Does it matter? I do know we seem to be on a similar wavelength every now and then." A frown crossed his face. "Bit disconcerting, actually. You must have noticed."

"Oh, I've noticed," Mrs. Kenley's frown was far less concerned than his. She chuckled not quite privately at his apparent discomfiture, and added inscrutably, "of course, I have the advantage of a woman's intuition to help me understand it. I'll call you in a few days time about the saddle."

She held out her hand, and he took it automatically, and as Sophy and Gypsy came to the gate she left him without looking back.

Chapter Twenty Five

The luckless Terry Godwin had scant chance to say much more than "Hello" in the "Shepherd and Flock" that evening before Sophy commandeered the conversation to enthusiastically proclaim herself in charge of the most wonderful horse and to be actually being paid for it.

In amongst her excitement her admiration of Peter Holt's ground work skills was not lost on the younger man, and as the evening wore on he became progressively more gloomy. In the end Sophy realised she was getting carried away and starting to show off, and finally checked herself and asked him self-consciously, and with an obvious lack of interest, how his cars were getting on.

Even to an enthusiast like Terry, the notion that his cars might be "getting on" or not, as though they had feelings of their own, was bizarre in the extreme. It seemed to point up the differences between them, and coming on top of an extravagant panegyric of someone who, in spite of his age, he was half convinced was a potential rival, plunged him even further into a mood of depressed annoyance.

"Cars don't 'get on,'" he said irritably. "Don't talk rot. They just break down and get fixed." He stared at her reproachfully across the table. "Like I fixed yours'," he added, unable to stop himself reminding her that of the two of them he was the one bringing something practical to their relationship.

It was the first time he'd been cross with her, and the jolt bitterly brought back the realisation that nowadays she had less than complete control of her life. She stared back at him, frowning, confused but annoyed in her turn. Perversely, although he couldn't possibly have known that yesterday was her birthday, and she hadn't even mentioned it today, a small, totally illogical part of her was also disappointed that he hadn't found out somehow and bought her something. What was she doing here with this stupid man anyway? He knew nothing about horses, he wasn't her sort and he couldn't even ride.

It was one of those moments when the right word would have defused the tension and restored the status quo, and between older heads such a word would probably have been found, but that Sunday evening in the "Shepherd and Flock," between two young people drawn together more by age, need, curiosity and accident than common ground, it remained unspoken.

Sophy peevishly fiddled with her orange juice, turning the glass round and round on its beer mat. Terry was cross and disappointed that she had made so little attempt to pretend an interest in his own activities, especially since she knew how he felt about her and he knew too he had been seriously helpful to her in recent days. Unbeknown to her, he also had to contend with Bert constantly referring to the pair of them as 'beauty and the beast,' a connotation which he sometimes felt was only too true when his lack of sophistication was exposed at odd moments during their conversations.

The silence lasted perhaps half a minute. Terry roused himself. He looked at her with his brow contracted into a deep frown. His pride wanted him to say, "It's not working, is it?" but he couldn't bring himself to do it. Instead, he asked her if she wanted another drink or some crisps from the bar.

Sophy looked down at the table, glanced around the room, and back at the table. She didn't *not* like him, she didn't really know what she felt just then. She thought vaguely that mother was right, she hadn't, well, done this sort of thing before. Perhaps if she had she'd know what to do. She looked up at him.

"Actually," she said slowly, "I think I'm going home. I'm awfully tired."

"I'll walk you," Terry said. It was a relief to both of them to have something to do at that moment, even if it was only getting up and going outside.

On previous occasions he'd taken her arm for the brief stroll back to the flat, but tonight he walked silently and rather nervously beside her, as though any attempt at physical contact would provoke the break he wasn't sure he wanted; he couldn't know that Sophy was feeling equally ambivalent about the relationship.

There was an awkward pause outside her front door as she let herself in.

"Well, goodnight then," Terry said rather carefully, and Sophy gave him a weak, uncertain smile. Unexpectedly, their eyes met. For a terrible moment Sophy thought he was going to try to kiss her, but he didn't. Suddenly, he held out his hand, shook hers vigorously, and walked briskly away down the street. She watched him go, frowning uncertainly, before she closed the door and turned to climb the stairs.

"You're back early," Edith said as her daughter pushed open the upstairs door. She glanced over her shoulder and saw the expression of total bewilderment on Sophy's face. "Whatever's the matter?" she asked her.

"Men are awfully complicated," Sophy said. She collapsed into a chair. Her mother burst out laughing. "Oh my dear," she said at last. She looked at Sophy, frowning back at her. "I bet he's saying exactly the same thing about you right this minute," she said.

Whatever she thought about Terry or his automotive ambitions faded quickly into the background over the following days. She had never in her life been so busy, or felt so tired at the end of every day.

As well as twice the stable chores with two horses to look after, Gypsy had to be ridden every morning, Annie-May worked from the ground under the school lights in the evening under the watchful gaze of Peter Holt, and usually also in the presence of several less critical young spectators who were still intrigued by the process of re-schooling a racehorse; and in between she was on her feet in the shop for the bulk of the day; with Christmas less than a month away now and the footfall inevitably increasing, the seasonal fare flew off the shelves, leading to frequent trips across the yard to the store room for replenishments.

It occurred to her one weary Friday night ten days before the holiday that maybe she could stop working in the shop now that Mrs. Kenley's first cheque had arrived. It would make a huge difference to the pressure she was under, and there would be so much more time to spend with the horses.

She made the suggestion to her mother over breakfast the following morning. It was a work Saturday, and seemed the ideal opportunity to give Mrs. Mullins notice. Her mother, however, was still a little sceptical about Mrs. Kenley and Annie-May as a long term, paying prospect, and was less than enthusiastic about the idea of her giving up a reliable source of income, however paltry it might be.

"I think you should wait," she said. "Why don't you ask Mr. Holt? I know it's hard, but you are managing and….." she paused. She wanted to say 'every little helps' and 'Christmas is coming,' but the thought brought last Christmas to mind and might remind Sophy of it too, just when her preoccupation with her new life was beginning to banish the old into a fading memory.

Peter Holt's opinion when she asked him at the end of Gypsy's lesson was brusque and to the point. "I can't decide for you," he said, "but I'll be disappointed if you leave that old lady on her own just when she's at her busiest. It would hardly be fair, would it? Wait till after Christmas at least. And suppose Annie-May or Gypsy goes lame?"

He gave her a meaningful look.

"We both have good reason to know how unpredictable life can be," he added. "I never felt comfortable without at last three regular paying clients, people I could depend on. Bills have to be paid whether you're working or not. And next month you'll start competing again. Entry fees cost, even at the lowest level."

It was exciting for her to be reminded that she'd be riding in public again soon, although it was only at an inconsequential little show at a venue nobody had ever heard of, but what he said next sent a shiver down her spine.

"Annie-May can have the day off today," he said. "Turn her out for half an hour when you come back this afternoon. Don't let her get cold. We'll ride her tomorrow morning and try out that new saddle. It's time. Oh, and Mrs. Kenley is coming, so it's best behaviour time too."

She stared at him. She was becoming relatively capable at long reining, and Annie-May was looking more and more like a riding horse and less like a race horse, but she'd had the impression there was much more to do yet.

"Your face is a picture," he said, laughing at her. "If I could bottle that expression and sell it I'd make a fortune. Now go on or you'll be late for work. I'm going up the hill with Teddy and then I've an errand in Chichester. And don't go gallivanting with Terry tonight, we'll need to be on our toes tomorrow just in case."

Somehow, the rest of the day happened. The only thing she remembered about it was Terry coming into the shop to order some flowers for his mother to be delivered on Christmas Eve, but he dealt with Mrs. Mullins and only glanced at her on his way out. After he'd gone she thought she ought to have said something, even if it was only 'hello,' but really it was enough of a struggle to attend to the customers with what she had on her mind.

Annie-May trotted briefly round the small turn out paddock in the last of the daylight, head and tail aloft in the time honoured silhouette of all her kind suffering excitement, but she settled quickly to nibble at the stunted grass. With her chores complete, and only Annie–May to feed when she brought her in, Sophy leaned on the gate in the chilly, still winter twilight watching her charge with excitement of her own churning inside her. It was a shock to turn and see Miss Brown standing quietly beside her.

"Big day tomorrow," she said, with what might have been a smile. "I thought I'd wish you luck. Going well, isn't she? I do keep an eye. And square off the midden before you go. Your friend Kitty has just tipped a barrow out and left it. You know the rules."

She paused. Sophy couldn't tell whether the estate manager was remembering a previous, similar admonition all those weeks ago, but she was astonished to find her own reaction was anything but similar.

"Okeydokey," she responded with cheerful indifference, and as Miss Brown turned to go she couldn't be sure she didn't hear her mutter something half audible which sounded suspiciously like, "that's my girl."

Chapter Twenty Six

Sometime after midnight tiredness overcame trepidation and she actually overslept by half an hour. Her mother, still in her dressing gown, watched her tear through a bowl of cornflakes with a mixture of amusement and anxiety, with anxiety in the ascendant as her darling daughter fled down the stairs seeking to make up for lost time.

The fierce, frosty morning air of the street snatched away the last of the cobwebs as she opened the front door and blinked in the bright winter sunshine, but her car started as usual with the first turn of the key in spite of the coldest night of the season so far. She was briefly reminded of the boy who'd put it together for her, but she bundled him out of her head with an unconscious grimace; there were far more important things to think about this morning.

She drove into the yard at nine twenty instead of the nine o'clock she'd promised, but in spite of the various vehicles already parked there only horses' heads greeted her as she climbed out of the car. The old Landrover was there, and Joe Fittleworth's car, and Jennifer's mothers', and a couple of others she recognised as well as Miss Brown's in its usual place. She had just enough composure to realise with relief that there was no sign yet of the famous Bentley, but there was no sign of Annie-May either, who was usually taking a keen interest in her neighbours at this time of day.

Momentarily uncertain, she grabbed her riding hat off the car seat and hurried through the arch and down the short path to the school. A cluster of keenly interested spectators was watching Peter Holt lungeing Annie-May, with only one orthodox lunge line this morning attached to the bit and wearing her new dressage saddle with the stirrups pulled own and flapping against her sides. He saw his protégé arrive and beckoned her into the arena. Nervous and awkward, she climbed though the fence.

"Good morning," he said quietly as he checked the horse and went up to her, coiling the line over his hand as he went. He patted the mare's neck and she rubbed her nose on his shoulder as he caressed her.

Sophy was afraid for a moment he was going to chide her for being late, but instead he gave her an encouraging smile.

"Are you ready? Put your hat on. I will ride her first if you like, but it would be better if you did, for you and for her."

The butterflies in her stomach became a storm. Dumbly, she put her hat on and fastened the strap. Automatically, she checked the girth and moved to put her foot in the stirrup to mount.

"Not like that," the quiet voice said, and she turned to him in surprise. He explained quickly. "Racehorses are usually mounted with a vault or a leg up. It's quite possible she's never been mounted with the stirrup in all her life. Let's not frighten her. Give me your leg. Be sure to land as soft as you can. And jump properly – I'm not Tarzan to lift your weight with only one hand." He grinned suddenly and gave her a broad wink. "This is what a horseman's life's about," he said then. "I'm quite envious it's your turn to be first."

He stood beside her, his left hand holding the bridle. Sophy had been legged up before, of course, although not for a long time, but this wasn't the moment to say so. She tentatively bent her knee, she heard him say "Now!" in her ear and in a moment was sitting in the saddle looking down at him. Annie-May flicked her ears back and forth in the manner of a horse who has not been ridden for a while, but her back beneath the saddle was relaxed and Peter Holt still held the bridle. She stood calmly enough while Sophy's feet found the stirrups and she took up the reins and made herself comfortable.

Then he released her. "Follow me." he said, and led the way to the end of the school with Annie-May walking steadily behind. He stopped at the fence and looked up at her. The butterflies had flown away.

"You're on your own now," he said, and his smile seemed to stretch from ear to ear. "Go and get acquainted. Nice and easy. Don't canter unless she offers it." He walked away to join the little group watching over the gate without looking back.

"She's so *brave,*" Kitty said in a hushed voice to no one in particular, and her father looked enquiringly at the instructor over her head. Along with everyone else, he'd been expecting the master to ride first rather than the pupil.

Peter Holt, feeling his professional decision was being challenged, was faintly irritated, and without taking his eyes off the horse was moved to justify his action although there was no need. With Sophy and Annie-May the centre of everybody's attention no one noticed Mrs. Kenley approaching behind them, extravagantly swathed in fashionable faux furs and a smart woollen coat.

"She's going to be Sophy's ride," he said, "so I want the horse to think of her first, even if she doesn't go very well to start with. As for brave, it's a judgement call. I think Sophy's good enough, and I think the horse is calm enough. If I'm wrong….," he inclined his head towards the horse and rider, trotting a brisk circle now in the middle of the school. A small smile escaped him. "I'm not wrong," he said then, and the smile widened.

He turned in response to a tap on his shoulder and Mrs. Kenley was saying good morning.

"It seems I'm just in time," she remarked, and she too transferred her attention to her mare and her young rider in the school.

Left to her own devices, Sophy felt a tiny moment of doubt and then pulled herself together. She walked Annie-May along the fence, and already the freedom and the length in the stride contrasted sharply with Gypsy's more measured steps. She turned to cross the school, and as she approached the track again gingerly asked her to trot.

The effect was immediate. With the tiniest touch of her leg, Annie–May responded with alacrity and set sail along the fence as though she'd been waiting for a rider to ask her that ever since the day she'd arrived. Sophy was taken by surprise, and briefly left behind, but her former, automatic instinct to snatch the reins at such a moment was instantly overcome as the habit of greater awareness, so carefully being cultivated by her watching mentor, smothered the old reaction and she offered the rein instead.

Annie-May took instant advantage of her freedom to raise her head, but although the outline was lost Sophy comfortably managed the stride, started to rise to the trot, and with the instinct of a dressage rider rode on to a circle to steady the balance and give herself a chance to re-establish the shape she wanted.

It didn't work. For the next ten minutes Annie-May was quite happy to trot wherever she took her with her head half up and her back half down, but politely declined to lower into the bridle in flat defiance of the hours of education she'd undergone in exactly that shape without a rider on her back. And from Sophy's point of view it didn't help that the trot was too fast and hugely dissimilar to Gypsy's, with a lift and a cadence unlike anything she had ever felt before and which took some getting used to.

She couldn't know that it wasn't as bad as it might have been, and Peter Holt was actually not displeased with either of them. Sophy was riding with sympathy and intelligence, and she could not yet be expected to have the experienced hands required to convince an ex-racehorse to oblige her with a completely different way of going at the first attempt. As for Annie-May, although she was going forward with excessive enthusiasm, she was behaving calmly and in spite of her hollow top line still showing a supple, athletic step and clearly relishing not only being ridden again but also being the centre of attention.

"She always used to show off like that in the paddock at the races," Mrs. Kenley said. and there was no denying the mare still looked more like a racehorse than a dressage horse, and there was more than a trace of disappointment in her owner's voice. She took Peter Holt to one side.

"I've been checking up on this dressage business," she said to him. "I know it'll take time, and I heard what you were saying as I arrived, but I'm a bit surprised you're not riding her yourself this first time." She looked over towards Sophy. "The girl looks well on her," she said. "And I can see why you like her. She has a bit of presence herself. But it doesn't look like dressage, does it?"

"It will," the instructor said. He looked at her, not apologetic but not quite as sure of himself as he usually was. Still, he didn't want to ride the horse this morning; his instinct told him it wasn't necessary.

"Do it for my sake," Jenny Kenley said quietly, and he frowned as he realised she had once again guessed the thought behind his expression.

"I wish you'd stop doing that," he said, knowing she would understand him and trying to look put out, but their eyes met and he failed dismally.

She put her hand on his arm with a private smile. "I shall be about all day today," she said. "I'm thinking about buying a house in Stepford for, well family reasons and to give myself a change from the town whenever I want it. I'm viewing it at two this afternoon. I'll take you to lunch and then you can come with me and give me your opinion. I need objective feedback from someone who isn't on the payroll or desperate to please me. Preferably a man. Now ride my horse and show me what I came to see."

Her habit of assuming she could always get what she wanted should have irked him, but it didn't. On the other hand, he wouldn't allow himself to be commandeered without having some say in the matter.

"I'll ride the horse," he said. He lifted her hand gently off his arm. "And then we'll see. I'm already booked all morning." He glanced towards Kitty and Jennifer as he spoke.

Sophy was walking the mare now, having realised she was getting nowhere with such a hollow trot and uncertain what to do about it. It was something of a relief when she saw Peter Holt coming towards her.

He looked up with a smile.

"Excellent," he said. "We couldn't have expected more, from you or her. On another day, I'd be happy with that and we'd stop now, but Mrs. Kenley's here and wants me to ride her. If I thought it would do harm I'd refuse, but in a month's time I don't think it will matter much, and it's her horse and she's the one paying. It's what happens when you ride for other people. Sometimes you have to compromise."

He surprised her with what he said next.

"Do you mind?" he asked her as she dismounted to stand beside him, and it was clear from his expression that her answer mattered to him. It wasn't until much later, in the cool reflection of a hot bath, that the significance of the question came home to her. It had to be a sign he was beginning to have professional respect for her.

She frowned under her riding hat and responded with relief.

"I wish you would," she said, sounding a little tearful. "I'm making an awful mess. She just won't come down for me."

He checked himself in the act of preparing to vault into the saddle and turned to face her. "You did well," he said earnestly, "and that's the truth. There's a lot about riding, and feeling things, which only experience can teach you. You learned some today, and you'll learn more next time. I don't know any more than you what this mare will do for me, the joy is in finding out, and so I'll be learning too. Whatever she does, you watch my hands as well as how she goes and try and feel what I'm feeling."

He vaulted into the saddle and his feet found the stirrups in the same instant. Annie-May twitched under him, and threw her head in the notorious, circular motion Arab horses all over the world are famous for; he looked down at Sophy with a wry grin.

"Well," he said to her, "at least that's one thing she didn't to you. Maybe she won't like me after all. Go and be nice to Mrs. Kenley. We'll have a proper de-brief later, and we have to change the work pattern for next week now we're riding her."

He turned the horse away from her then, and she made her way a little nervously towards the gate, her hat dangling from her hand, where Kitty was beaming at her in undisguised admiration and Mrs. Kenley's neutral expression could mean anything from approbation to disappointment.

Chapter Twenty Seven

It had been a long while since the man on the horse had found himself with a point to prove to a demanding owner, and with a watching gallery whose expectations, while probably less knowledgeable than hers', were likely to be even higher.

As always, there was no guarantee that either he or the horse would live up to their expectations. Such moments as this had been the spice of his professional life for nearly forty years, offering a challenge far removed from competitive performance on a prepared mount he already knew well, for truly great horsemanship rarely takes place in a public arena; often it occurs in front of a mere handful of spectators, or even in private isolation, when a rider and a strange horse achieve a joyful rapport known only to themselves.

He savoured the moment, walking on a circle on a long rein as far away from the gate as possible. There was no doubting the quality of the horse, or the fact that he and Sophy between them had laid the right foundations, but even putting aside the inevitable unpredictability of the entire canon of horse flesh, Annie-May was not only a mare, she was a pure bred Arab, a breed whose potential for temper and temperament had been a legend among horse folk for centuries.

The challenge today was charged with a further, private consideration which had no connection at all with how successfully he might be able produce the horse, and which would mean nothing to anyone else.

In these situations in the past it had been important to achieve the maximum effect to convince the owner to engage his services, but on this cold and sunny December morning, far from his beloved Yorkshire and many months since his last such ride, there was also Sophy to consider.

She was progressing better than he could have hoped, not just technically but becoming more sensitive and identifying more and more with the horse she was working; and in the paternal attitude he always unconsciously felt towards his students, he was quietly proud of the way she was now becoming accepted into the stable community, and more and more prepared to meet her changed circumstances with equanimity. Nevertheless, he was also acutely aware of the fragility of her softened approach to life, and years of teaching teenaged girls had left him with a deeply cautious approach to denting their self esteem. Assuming the horse responded, it would not do for Sophy to suffer another shock to her ego today comparable with the one he had given her the first time he rode Gypsy.

At the same time, he had to show Mrs. Kenley something more than she had seen already. He gently shortened the rein, and it was almost a relief when Annie-May objected and hollowed her back. Sophy would be sure to have noticed it even if no one else had. Not that he could allow it to continue.

He asked for a trot, and unlike Sophy the response did not surprise him. He carried his mare into the rhythm he wanted in half a dozen strides, active and forward but undemanding and above all not hurried, not the hasty, always-on-the-edge-of-running steps which Sophy had been suffering. Not that the outline was much improved, and as he passed the gate the sense of disappointment among the watchers was almost palpable.

He smiled then, although Sophy was again probably the only one who noticed; for in those few yards, a mere half circuit of the school, he had found the measure of the mare, body and spirit and soul together; and he knew that in a moment she would love him, as he loved her and all her kind, and together they would sing their private, silent song and dance their private dance which others would see but only a very, very few would understand.

He rode on to a large circle at A, close to the gate, mindful that he had asked Sophy to watch his hands, and his fingers closed on both the reins.

Annie-May instantly objected to the interference, as he knew she would, but as she sought to take hold and hollow further the pressure fell away to a sudden softening, a yielding, compelling invitation to lower her head and feel the joyful, come-to-me-I-love-you contact he was offering her.

Annie-May was taken by surprise, and for a few lifted and elegant steps she rounded and carried herself on the circle as though she had never worked in any discipline other than dressage in all her life; but in spite of a week's work from the ground it was a new bewilderment to make such a shape with a weight on her back, and harder work too, and she quickly sought to escape and return to her usual carriage.

But there was no escape. His rising trot was as soft as a feather, but the tempo was unbreakable and carried her seamlessly on; and the contact was never strong but ever-present, ever-so soft but constantly containing.

A circle came and went, and then another. He took her on to the other rein, and still there was no way out. He was asking her to shape round his leg a little now, helping the balance through the turns, and then, when he stroked her neck with one hand, even without the slight support of the inside rein it was becoming easier to keep this strange, new way of going this implacable, gentle man was making for her.

He felt her relax beneath the saddle and come at last completely into his hand, finally persuaded, and the reins became alive with conversation and willing understanding. Again he stroked her neck, this time with the other hand, to be rewarded with a appreciative fold of her ear as she paid attention and made an effort to answer the shaping pressure of his inside leg.

The trot was swinging now, an easy, forward step, nicely engaged for a working pace, and the outline was accepted and secure. The potential for progress to higher things was self evident, and Annie-May, confident now and clearly enjoying herself, was half eyeing the spectators as she passed the gate and beginning to show off as all Arabs do at every opportunity.

Her rider was tempted to show off himself - a canter, shoulder-in, even a leg yield, were there for the taking as Annie-May's carriage became more established, but the last thing he wanted to do today was underline the difference between a lifetime's experience and the best efforts of a talented but novice student. He contented himself with a few strides of medium trot, and he could almost feel the mare's disappointment when he forbore to ask for more; his restraint notwithstanding, those few steps brought gasps from his audience, and a beaming smile from Mrs. Kenley.

He rode to the gate and dismounted. The horse was nuzzling his ear and automatically he put up his hand to stroke the side of her face. It was plain Mrs. Kenley was about to speak to him but Sophy was looking at him with exactly that expression of self-doubt, envy and admiration he had tried so hard to avoid, and he spoke to her first.

"It's not about how well you sit or what you know," he said to her. "It's about this," he touched his forehead, "connecting with this," and he put his hand between Annie-May's ears. He made Sophy look at him and their eyes met. "You know what I mean," he said, and she nodded slowly.

"I .....," she started to say but he interrupted firmly. "It's coming," he said. "You know it is. If it wasn't, she'd have dumped you on your backside or you'd both be in Northumberland by now. Don't underrate yourself."

He opened the gate and gave her the reins. "Put her away and make much of her," he told her then. "Take Gypsy for a hack this afternoon." For the first time he glanced at Mrs. Kenley. "I'll be busy."

Kitty was tugging at his sleeve and he looked down at her. "Is it time for us now?" she demanded, and he laughed then.

"Alright," he said to her. "You and Jennifer go with your Dad and get your ponies ready. I have to talk to Mrs. Kenley." He took his pipe out of his pocket. "Go on then."

"Nice of you to find the time." Mrs. Kenley, for all her admiration of the man and his skills, was not accustomed to being the last in line, and especially not when she was bankrolling the performance.

She seemed for a moment about to say as much, but Holt was completely unmoved by her sarcastic tone and was lighting his pipe, regarding her thoughtfully. She realised then, as had happened before, that he was reading her mind as she so often read his. What was it about this man, with his equine intuition and seemingly limitless ability to take control of every situation, that she found so magnetic and so disturbing? It was a startling question for a woman of her experience, and she looked away from him, more in self-defence than a pretence of avoiding his pipe smoke.

"I beg your pardon," he said, taking the pipe out of his mouth, and she made an impatient, deprecatory gesture.

"It's coming together," he said to her. "Annie-May will be ready for some Prelims. for experience in four or five weeks time, and up to Elementary by the summer if all goes well. And it might not look like it today, but Sophy's at least as good as I thought she was, and with that bit of presence she has that you noticed yourself, and the horse looking a million dollars, heads will be turning I promise you."

"I still wonder you don't want to ride her yourself," Mrs. Kenley said perversely, knowing she was treading on thin ice but unable to keep from voicing the thought. "The way you and that horse talk to one another, you must want to."

He was cross with her then, as she knew he would be. Even so, his answer was measured and professional.

"I'm too tall," he said, "and I'm not elegant. I'm a nagsman, and while it's OK not looking too smart for showjumping or even eventing, it won't do for dressage once you get off the bottom rung. Sophy's made huge strides with her own horse and she's learning fast. Most of all she's learning that horses need to feel wanted themselves or they don't want to please you."

He frowned irritably. "Anyway, you know damn well why I won't ride in public. Not now, maybe never. Don't take advantage."

There was a short, uncomfortable silence. Mrs. Kenley was not accustomed to being spoken to in such abrupt terms and at the same time felt slightly ashamed of herself for putting the suggestion again when she knew she shouldn't have. Such discomfiture was an emotion she hadn't experienced in a very long time. It was also slightly shocking to feel a bond with this man who was so far removed from her and her world, who had absolutely no need of her or her money, and who treated her exactly as he treated every one else, without fear or favour.

The sound of ponies' hooves on the path interrupted them, and Kitty and Jennifer came into view.

"This house," Peter Holt said suddenly. "Do you *really* want my opinion?"

She was obliged to look at him. It was impossible to tell him the truth, that she wanted to spend time with him, that it was refreshing to spend time on almost any excuse with an intelligent man who owed her nothing and had no interest in her wealth or standing. It was a thought which had intruded on her at infrequent intervals throughout the past week. Unfortunately, or perhaps fortunately, she realised with wry resignation from his slightly raised eyebrow that he probably already knew it.

He smiled then, with unexpected warmth.

"There's quite a nice pub in Stepford," he said. "Meet me there about one. And I'll take *you* to lunch."

Chapter Twenty Eight

The conurbation of Stepford, about six miles east of Fairgate, was barely larger than a hamlet, being a random collection of mostly old houses with an eighteenth century church, a shop and a pub clustered round a minor cross roads on the Steeplehurst road. The surrounding farms were largely arable nowadays, with asparagus much in evidence, although the towering Downs less than a mile to the south, basking in the bright winter sun, suggested that sheep husbandry had once been the principal local agricultural activity here, as it remained in much of the county.

The Bentley loomed large in the small car park behind the "Crooked Crook" as he drove in; he couldn't know she'd already been waiting for ten minutes, and *nobody* had kept her waiting since she couldn't remember. Eddy instantly emerged from the driving seat to open the rear door for his employer to alight.

"You're late," she said irritably to Holt as he descended from the Land Rover, immediately turning to attach a lead to the whippet who promptly jumped out to join them.

It was three minutes past one.

"I was explaining intermediate rein effects to young Kitty," he said. He raised a tentative eyebrow. "Joe took an interest too. Would you like......"

"Oh, for goodness *sake*," Mrs. Kenley exclaimed peremptorily and with more than a trace of pomposity. "Intermediate *what?*"

Eddy was closing the Bentley door behind her, and the instructor caught his eye as he glanced over her shoulder. The chauffeur was too obviously trying to hide a smile. He grinned back, an expression intercepted by Mrs. Kenley, who was irritated further that these two men, as different as chalk and cheese, had somehow found common cause and were laughing at her.

A vague sense that Holt and her driver had between them and in their own different ways taken her measure was disconcerting as well as aggravating. It was probably Holt's fault – on his own Eddy would never have had the nerve. And the man Holt had still given no indication that he knew who, and how important, she really was in the wider world. It was just possible, of course, even after more than a week's acquaintance, that he still didn't know; perhaps more disconcerting was the notion that he knew exactly who she was and simply didn't care.

He straightened his face and offered her his arm.

"Shall we go in?" he said.

She tried to look at him severely but the impression she gave was more of confusion than ill temper. Since Gerald had died, nobody had ever laughed at her, or taken anything she said less than *very* seriously. She noticed that Eddy was carefully not looking in her direction, and realised with a flash of insight that the man was afraid that his brief, silent exchange with her new friend might cost him his job, or a dressing down at the very least.

She glanced up at her escort. He refused to meet her eye and looked down at the dog. On this occasion, it wasn't hard to guess what he was thinking.

"Dammit," she said with exasperation. "I'm really not an ogre. It's just that....."

"Shouldn't that be 'ogress'?" Peter Holt interrupted. "Or are you all male now, like actresses are actors?" Now he did look down at her, and his eyes were chuckling and his eyebrow was rising again.

The man was quite shameless. It was impossible to keep a stern face as he held the door open for her. In another moment all four of them entered the bar together, although the smile on Eddy's face was tinged with relief.

Business executives of any rank, high powered or mere minions, were only infrequent visitors to the "Crooked Crook," a hostelry significantly less sophisticated than its Fairgate equivalent and whose principal claim to fame was home baked bread, delivered to the patrons via a locally celebrated ploughman's lunch which was invariably served in a basket.

Although perfectly palatable, it wasn't the Sunday lunch Mrs. Kenley had been expecting. Nor had she anticipated sharing a table, in what was in effect a public bar, with her chauffeur as well as her host; not to mention a grey whippet, who lay on the floor with his nose resting on her foot.

Peter Holt, something of a regular customer here, realised she was not entirely comfortable but in the same moment determined not to give way to his first impulse and ask Eddy to take himself and his beloved dog off to another table. Damn the woman. He was fully aware of the potential consequences, as he knew she must be, of the lively connection they felt for one another, but he refused to allow himself to be intimidated by her wealth and her apparent assumption that she was in sole charge of their relationship. For the first time it occurred to him that perhaps he ought to have taken steps to find out more about her; he thought ruefully that his lack of a computer, or any interest in the internet or IT generally, needn't have prevented him asking Sophy to look for him – or indeed for both of them if it came to it.

Unusually, the conversation between them was stilted and awkward, although Eddy was discreetly silent. Eventually, she asked for another glass of wine, and when he returned from the bar Eddy and the whippet were on their way to the door.

"I thought they could wait outside," she said, defending their dismissal as he sat down with frown. "After all, we won't be long and Eddy'd finished his lunch and he can't have another drink because he's driving."

He did not reply, but his disapproval was almost tangible.

"I know what you're thinking, " she said suddenly, "but it's not true. I'm really not snobbish, but I haven't eaten in a place like this for years and Gerald and me never ate with the help. It, well, it just wasn't done, somehow."

"Don't I qualify as help?" he interposed then, and she was confused and looked down at the bare oak table.

"That's different," she finally responded, and this time he raised both eyebrows. "I don't know why, but it is."

"Well, it shouldn't be," he said. "And it's Sunday. Doesn't that driver ever have time off? The least we could do is give him lunch and not leave him out in the cold. And Teddy will need a coat on if he's out there for any length of time. It can't be more than five or six degrees today."

He was regarding her steadily across the table, and it was her turn to frown.

"No one has ever talked to me like you," she said uncomfortably, feeling obliged to explain herself in spite of not wanting to and knowing she didn't have to, "at least, not since Gerald." She steeled herself to go on. After all, she could dismiss this man with the blink of an eye and never see him again if she so decided. But that was the one thing she didn't want.

"My family was, well, what's left of it still is of course, wealthy I suppose you'd have to say. Very wealthy, some would say. I grew up with a nanny and a cook and a housekeeper and two maids and a gardener and Daddy had a driver, and Gerald was already many times a millionaire when I married him and it's just carried on ever since. I'm a middle aged woman who was married for thirty years and I've never washed clothes or even dishes, or even fried an egg in my life. I just never had to."

"Well, you don't have to fry eggs for me," he said, laughing at her out loud. He checked himself. "I don't see that money has much to do with it. We're just friends, or associates if you prefer, with a common interest in horses. Why don't we just leave it at that? I don't really care much for anything except horses and dogs." He winked at her unexpectedly. "Of course, I could be persuadable about people as well, if the right person came along."

She stared at him. His impertinence was breathtaking, but his blue eyes were dancing and she knew she was blushing like a schoolgirl. It was absurd that this man could so affect her. She was fifty four years old, a mother and a widow, widely respected in the business communities of three continents and hugely experienced in the ways of the world, who could buy this pub and the whole village if the fancy took her and spend the change on a stately home in every state in Europe. And none of it mattered to him. She was just a woman he liked and felt a connection with, and was not afraid to acknowledge it.

The quick wit she was famous for in difficult board meetings came to her rescue.

"Do you always flirt with your patrons?" she asked him. With a sense of mocking the pair of them as though they were teenagers, she put her head on one side and smirked at him with exaggerated coyness.

The effect was more engaging than she knew, or intended. His smile widened, but his reply was interrupted by her mobile phone sounding with a text message, and he waited as she checked the screen.

"The agent is waiting for us at the house," she said.

"I knew you were going to say that." Peter Holt was secretly as relieved as she was to call a halt to a conversation which was accidentally beginning to stray into territory which he himself was not yet ready to explore, and which he could foresee embarrassing the pair of them in another minute or two. He went to the bar to pay the bill, and she was already outside and waiting in the Bentley when he turned round expecting to escort her out.

Eddy handed him Teddy's lead. "The house is just around the corner, sir," he said to him. The 'sir' didn't sound quite right to either of them, but each supposed that in the circumstances it inevitably had be said. "Mrs. Kenley suggests you follow her – us, I should say. I understand there is parking at the property for several vehicles."

'Just around the corner' was true enough; the Land Rover was still in second gear as he followed the Bentley into a wide, ungated driveway beside a handsome, if not especially large, Jacobean house set back about a chain from the minor road behind white painted, pointed iron railings. Anticipating they might be here some time, he paused to put the whippet's coat on before leaving him, looking bereft as only a whippet can when he knows his beloved master is likely to be gone for quite a while.

The agent was a grey suited, white shirted and dark tied, smart young man who was deferential to the point of fawning when he spoke to Mrs. Kenley.

"Such a privilege, Mrs. Kenley," he smiled. "Please ask me anything you like. Shall we go in?"

He glanced at her companion with surprise tinged with alarm. A middle aged man in riding clothes, none of them new, with a pipe in his top pocket and muddy boots, was an unexpected complication when he was already on edge at dealing with a client he'd never met but knew by reputation was a seriously wealthy, internationally known businesswoman. As a dedicated follower of his profession, and unlike the riding master, he had done his internet homework. Apart from numerous appearances in the business pages, both before and since her husband's death, Mrs. Kenley was sufficiently well known to have also featured infrequently in the society columns.

His concerns regarding her companion proved unfounded. Peter Holt followed the pair of them a pace behind as they toured the house, and while Mrs. Kenley's frequent glances over her shoulder satisfied her he was taking a keen interest, he asked no questions and made no contribution to their conversation.

The house was immaculate throughout, and featured what were obviously newly installed bathrooms and a re-equipped kitchen, but was totally devoid of furniture or furnishings. The décor even in the two attic rooms perfectly complemented the pale cream rendering of the façade, symmetrically divided by the front door and two stories of pastel blue, sash windows.

While Holt had little knowledge and even less interest in property values, it was evident even to him that a five bedroom house in such condition and in such a location was unlikely to be worth less than a seven figure sum. Backing on to open farmland, the property also boasted a well kept garden of at least half an acre, divided by paths edged with low box hedges in contrast to the taller, well established evergreen trees behind the railings bordering the road.

They were standing beside the Bentley in the bright, pale sunshine of the short December afternoon, watching the agent's little bubble of a car back down the drive, before she finally asked him what he thought.

He'd had plenty of time to devise a considered reply.

"That depends on who, or what, you want it for," he said, and she frowned at him.

"I knew you'd say that," she said. "Just generally, though, do you like it?"

He would not be drawn. "Liking it is not the point," he said, and repeated his first response. "I don't see why you wanted another opinion unless you tell me more of what it's all about. All you've let on so far is you don't want to live in it yourself except maybe at weekends sometimes. I dare say it would be perfect for that. Bit of a waste, though, don't you think?"

She regarded him thoughtfully. He could not know, but for her it was a watershed moment. Since the death of her husband, while there had been no limit to the number of his associates offering her business opinions she did not need, disinterested personal advice, especially involving family matters, had been hard to come by.

If the truth was told, having initially felt drawn to him at their first meeting, and knowing instinctively that he had felt the same, the lack of someone to simply talk to and be herself with had struck her lately with increasing force. It was ridiculous for someone in her position to feel lonely, and she thrust away the notion as pathetic and not worthy of her, and yet deep inside herself she knew that it was so.

Again he made the connection before she expressed it.

"You need someone to talk to," he said to her. He smiled then, as though she was a neighbour and they were chatting over the fence. "Come and have a cup of tea with me. Do you have the time? It's only a few minutes back to Fairgate, and it must be on your way if you're going back to Chichester."

Chapter Twenty Nine

Whatever Eddy's opinion of his boss's eccentric friendship with a semi-retired professional horseman, his expression was carefully neutral as he followed the Land Rover down Rosemary Lane and turned behind it into the small driveway in front of Peter Holt's cottage. Unusually, Mrs. Kenley had opted to travel in the front of the Bentley for these few miles, and had spoken to him quite conversationally once or twice. Nevertheless, he lost no time in alighting and hurrying to open the door for her.

The sun was low now as the short afternoon was drawing to a close, and there was a keen chill in the clear air as Holt greeted her, his pipe in one hand and the dog's lead in the other.

Eddy was hovering awkwardly behind her, clearly at a loss as to whether to wait in the car or expect to be invited in. The host, with no inkling of what his guest might wish to talk about, realised that whatever it was she would possibly not want the driver to be a party to it. On the other hand, it went distinctly against the grain to leave such a long suffering and presumably loyal retainer quite literally out in the cold.

He had an outrageous idea, inclined his head towards her and spoke quietly.

"Why don't you give Eddy the rest of the day off and let *me* take you home?" He glanced at his Land Rover, and then at the majestic Bentley and a small smile appeared on his face, rapidly expanding into a genuine chuckle. "I'll brush off the seat and Teddy can go in the back. There's luxury for you."

Jennie Kenley was nonplussed by the strangeness of the suggestion and piqued by the fact that this time he really was laughing at her, although the good humour in his eyes robbed the remark of any offence. But he had guessed one thing right. There was no reason for Eddy, discreet though he always was, to know in advance about a private family matter which would probably make the gossip columns eventually whatever the outcome.

She recovered herself and looked at him sternly. "I'm not made of porcelain," she stated tartly. "We'll do it. And," she added with some determination, "I actually quite like dogs, although not on my lap when I'm wearing a designer dress." She spoke briefly to Eddy, who touched his cap and departed, reversing his large, expensive charge carefully into the narrow lane.

Unlike his previous female guests, Mrs. Kenley took only a cursory interest in Peter Holt's domestic arrangements when he escorted her into his kitchen through the back door. There was a wood burning stove against the wall opposite the door, lit and closed down since he'd left home this morning, which had been unlit on that earlier occasion, and which he prodded briskly into life before placing a chair in front of it for her. The whippet had swiftly preceded both of them into the house, and was already curled up comfortably on small square piece of carpet, strategically placed to maximise any available warmth.

She unbuttoned her coat and positioned her feet carefully so as not to disturb the animal, but he promptly laid his chin across the nearest ankle and looked up at her as if daring her to dislodge it. She could hear Holt moving about behind her, and the chinking of crockery, and then a small grunt as he removed his boots, but she was accustomed to being waited on wherever she went and didn't turn round.

Her eye was caught by the flames licking about a small, misshapen log in the now open grate. As the warmth reached out to her, creating a comforting, vivid contrast to the chilly world outside, the hypnotic effect of the flames began to persuade her that this was normal, to be here in this quiet, strong man's house, waiting for him to bring her a cup of tea when she would tell him something that only a handful of people knew, and most of them were on the other side of the Atlantic.

She was roused from what was becoming a warmth-induced, drowsy reverie by a small table being placed beside her, another chair appearing on its other side, and a moment later a huge, white mug of tea being handed to her. He put his own tea on the table as he sat down, and spread his hands wide to soak up the heat in front of the fire.

"Well, now," he said hospitably. "How's the tea?"

"I don't remember ever having such a large receptacle," she said demurely, poking fun at him in her turn, and he laughed out loud.

"Touché," he said. "It saves going back to the teapot so often. At least that's my theory. You didn't really suppose I'd have a fine china tea set, did you?"

She shook her head and looked back into the fire. It was time to explain to herself, as well as to him, what she was doing here so far from the world of wealth, privilege and surface sincerity she habitually inhabited, where any expressed opinion was either designed to impress her or else was coloured by at least a particle of potential self interest.

"I know it sounds selfish, stupid even, but it's not always easy to be what most people call 'filthy rich,'" she said quietly, and the flames licked and climbed all over and around the misshapen log and they were both watching it now. "Everybody wants something from you, and while I expect that in business and some say I'm even tougher than Gerald in giving as good as I get in meetings and negotiations and so forth, it's hard to know who to trust with personal things." She turned abruptly to face him.

"Gerald always said that horses knew who to trust because they always ran better for someone they liked. He always tried to use the same jockeys, and we had the same trainer for twenty years."

"Makes sense to me," the horseman said. "You're in big trouble if they don't trust you, believe me."

"It's not just that," she was less sure of herself now. "Ever since we two met there seems to have been some odd common instinct between us. Agatha keeps going on about it."

He stopped her then. "I do know," he said softly. "I am the other half. It's a bit unnerving sometimes. I just thought we'd let things take their course. Let's face it, except for Annie-May we don't have much in common."

"That's just it," she replied. The log shifted slightly deeper into the fire and threw up a small shower of sparks. "In a way it almost helps. You're sort of detached from my problems and yet....well, anyway, I have to talk to someone. And I've seen you with Annie-May, and that girl as well. They'd both die for you in a minute."

He took his eyes from the fire and glanced towards her. She was staring at the flames, and seemed suddenly younger, and pensive and vulnerable. Very deliberately he turned to take a pull at his tea, and the movement altered the mood as he'd hoped it would. Quietly businesslike, he said, "You'd better tell me then."

He reached down and stroked the dog's warm stomach, and he stretched luxuriously to cover every inch of his piece of carpet. Jennie Kenley was distracted from the fire and looked down at the whippet, deeply content with his lot and in a world all his own.

"It's about my son," she said. "Tony. The house is for him, if he wants it."

Holt reached for his pipe, considered for a moment, and changed his mind. He did not smoke in other people's houses, and although he was at home in his own kitchen it had to be possible she might not like it and yet feel embarrassed about mentioning it. Still staring into the fire, the slight movement escaped her.

"He's in America," she went on. "It's not a long story, but it's not a happy one. Gerald sent him to New York six years ago to get a handle on the American side of the business, as they say over there, with a view to him taking it over eventually. It didn't work out.

"You know how important money is to some people, and they say it specially matters in America." She turned to him with a small, sad, smile. "I don't think the famous American dream is all it's cracked up to be, sometimes. Anyway, I know I'm his mother but after a few months it was clear he wasn't working at all, he was just spending his time and the company's money enjoying himself, and his bosses weren't checking him because of who he was. I tried to make allowances, after all he was only twenty three when he went, but really he was out of control and although I can't be sure I think he was taking drugs of some sort."

She absently sipped her tea, the big white mug an incongruous contrast to her expensive suit and the pearl necklace revealed by her open coat. Their eyes met briefly over the rim, and she looked again into the fire.

"I suppose we could have done more, tried harder with him, but he was over twenty one and when you have a global business lots of people depend on you and often your life's not your own. Gerald was distracted by manufacturing problems in China and he spent nearly a year in Hong Kong dealing with politicians and I don't know what else. I was left to cope with the UK end, time went by and then suddenly we hear out of the blue Tony's married some up and coming Hollywood actress. That was three years ago. Now they're getting divorced, and they're both claiming adultery and mental cruelty and damages and God knows what else, and she's quite well known now, so the American media are having a field day with it. He wants to come back to England to escape some of the fuss. He says he can't walk down the street without photographers all over him, and because his wife is who she is he's being flooded with hate mail, real mail he says, not just on social media.

"He came over for his father's funeral in the summer, but then he had to go back for some legal business and I haven't seen him since."

There was distress in her voice now, and he put a comforting hand on hers. A tiny sound formed in the silence as the burning log moved lower and the flames moved higher, spreading wider to begin their assault on two of its companions.

"I'm expecting him mid-January," she said, and her hand moved under his, "and if he lives at home with me I know we'll fall out in five minutes. I want him close so I can keep an eye on him but not under my feet. He's still my son whatever he does. Would you believe I've never met the woman he married? Thank God there are no children." She paused. "I really don't know why I'm putting all this on you," she said finally. "I was going to tell Agatha, but she used to bully us all those years ago, not physically but she always had to be the one in charge, if you know what I mean. She sort of talks *at* you not to you all the time. I'd explode if she started telling me what to do now, and you can bet she would."

"I'll certainly agree with that," Holt said with a smile. He took a sip of his own tea, cooling a little now in spite of the warmth from the fire. "I should think that house would do very well for a bachelor pad. He'll rattle around a bit, though."

Mrs. Kenley's mind had moved on. "I'll get my PA on to it first thing tomorrow," she mused, more to herself than to him. "I won't haggle. We'll get it bought and furnished, shouldn't take more than a couple of weeks altogether if I tell my people to skip the searches and just get on with it. I'll get an agency cook housekeeper moved in right after Christmas. I expect he'll want to drive himself. With a bit of luck I should be back in England myself about the same time as him, mid January or thereabouts."

"Back?" he said in surprise. "Are you going away?"

She turned to look at him and shook her head with a frown.

"I have to. On Tuesday. There's a trade fair in Vienna next week and we're launching a new product for the space industry, something to do with gyroscopes and measuring degrees of cosmic latitude, or something like that, I really haven't got a clue what it is or what it does but I have to be there. It was one of Gerald's last projects. And then I have to go to Budapest to sign papers about a factory extension, and a government person wants a meeting about a contract for tractor parts."

He was astonished, and it showed.

"One of these days I'll explain to you what Kenley Industries actually is," she said. "What I – we – actually do."

"I'm not sure I want to know," he said, eyebrows raised in alarm. It was her turn to touch his hand.

"It's no big deal really," she rejoined, "It's just work. I'd usually be back by next weekend, but in a moment of weakness I agreed to spend Christmas with some of Gerald's friends at their ski lodge in France. I think they felt sorry for me, and I can't back out now. I won't be home again for at least three weeks, p'raps four."

Holt dragged his mind back to the practicalities of the world he was familiar with.

"It's all very well, this globe trotting and high finance and stuff," he said in a matter-of-fact tone, "but what about Sophy and Annie-May while you're gone?"

"You mean who's going to pay her while I'm away?" The business woman in her saw through him instantly. "And you too, I suppose."

His face puckered with annoyance and his fingers paused in their caress over the dog's neck. Knowing she shouldn't have said that and couldn't unsay it, she braced herself for his answer.

"My interests are not in question." The icy calm in his voice cut her to the bone, a bitter contrast to his sympathy of only a moment ago. "I have all I need, with or without your contribution, but Sophy does not and Christmas is very close. I must look out for my pupil's interests."

She stared again into the fire. Apart from her husband, in half a century of moneyed comfort, she had never met a man who cared so little for what she had or what her influence might do for him, and who spoke to her with no hint of malice or of currying favour. However close she felt to him, it was sometimes hard to deal with.

"I will make arrangements," she said weakly, and was rewarded with a broad smile.

"Forgive me," he turned again to face her. "Jenny. I'm a bit....touchy sometimes. I never thought you wouldn't."

It was her turn to put her hand on his, and for just a second it seemed he might lean across the little table and kiss her cheek, but the moment passed and he didn't. Later, on odd occasions when she was alone, she remembered the moment and wondered how she would have answered, without ever coming to any conclusion.

He stirred himself then. "Come on," he said briskly. "We must get you home or Eddy will think I've kidnapped you and send out a search party."

"That's not funny," she said, and he stopped dead in his tracks. For a moment they stared at each other. It was another indication of the huge gulf between their respective circumstances. It flashed across Holt's mind that kidnap must be an ever present concern to someone in her position, a concern which presumably extended to her son also, however much of a waster he might be.

"I'm sorry," he said quickly. He helped her on with her coat, damped down the stove and all three of them stepped into the cold, dark December evening.

True to his word, he did brush the passenger seat, but the effect was rather spoilt by Teddy jumping in first with muddy feet before he was pushed into the empty load space behind the cab.

For most of the half hour journey the conversation was sparse, as each was contemplating a relationship with no apparent end or objective: it occurred to Jenny Kenley that had she been a dizzy seventeen year old, and he her riding master, she'd be looking at him rather like that girl Sophy did, as though the world began and ended with his presence.

As for Peter Holt, independent to a fault and slowly coming to terms with the rest of his life after the unspeakable tragedy that still coloured his thoughts a dozen times a day, the idea of a serious friendship, or perhaps more, with any woman seemed faintly incongruous. And when that woman was Jenny Kenley, an apparently famous millionaire, the complications appeared endless and were probably insurmountable.

Into the minds of both of them crept the idea that it might be better all round to nip the whole thing in the bud, and stop now, just keep a quiet distance and concentrate on what they did have in common, the horse.

When they reached the city ring road she had to direct him, and he was not surprised to be confronted by tall wrought iron gates set in a red brick wall bordering the road, which swung open invitingly as the Land Rover approached.

Nor was he disappointed by the Kenley residence, a handsome, four storey Georgian house floodlit from the extensive gravelled forecourt with lodges to each side of the main building. The bonnet of the Bentley was visible, gleaming in the half dark aperture of a car port a few yards away from them.

He switched off the engine. There was a pregnant pause as they looked at each other. Peter Holt grinned.

"Do you suppose I should open the door for you, or shall we start as we meant to go on?" He checked himself suddenly, and added quietly, "Or shall we not go on? I'm not very good at this sort of thing."

A middle aged woman in an apron was hurrying towards them from the house. She came to the passenger's door and unhesitatingly opened it wide.

"Oh, Mrs. Kenley," she said excitedly. "You're safe then." She stepped back suddenly as the whippet's nose appeared over her mistress's shoulder.

"Of course I'm safe," Jenny Kenley was annoyed at her concern. She released her seat belt and turned to her driver. "Ever since Gerald died they're all terrified I'm going to be got at or run away with. Will you come in for dinner?"

He should have been expecting the question, but still he hesitated. Their eyes met in the half light.

"I think," he responded, carefully formal for the benefit of the listening housekeeper, "that today has been enough for me. I look forward to renewing our acquaintance when you return after Christmas, and if all goes well we should also by then be planning a competition campaign for Annie-May."

Her first instinct was to smile at his caution, but she could not prevent a small sense of relief that the evening should end now. On an impulse, she squeezed his hand where it was resting on the steering wheel. As she did so, the thought came to her that a younger woman would probably have kissed him, but really it wasn't the time for that.

"Have a good trip," he said, and he might have winked at her but it was too dark to see.

"I knew you'd say that," she said, moving to step down on to the gravel.

"And I knew you knew I'd say that," he rejoined, and when she glanced primly over her shoulder she had to join in his gentle, quiet laugh.

His confidence waned rapidly in her absence. As he drove home, with Teddy curled up and re-established on the front seat beside him, the appeal of normality, contrasted with the unknowable consequences of a complicated relationship with a woman, however attractive, who might as well come from another planet, grew ever stronger.

Chapter Thirty

Outdoor activities in a Sussex December are necessarily hostage to the weather, and so it proved over the following days for Sophy and everyone else whose horses lodged at Fairgate Stables.

The ten days leading to Christmas proper were characterised by wet, wet and yet more rain, leading eventually to a waterlogged manège and no possibility of lessons for anyone, or even sensible schooling; with standing water much in evidence even when it wasn't actually raining, mindful of the possibility of permanent damage to the surface and to the membrane beneath, Miss Brown finally declared the riding arena out of bounds until further notice.

For Sophy, the frustration of a sudden halt in her professional career when it had barely begun was tempered by her mother's pride in the arrival of a cheque from Kenley Industries, and the promise of many more to come. Life at home was also easier than it had been, and Edith made no bones about telling her it was her contribution that was making the difference.

The grey skies shortened even further the brief hours of daylight, and it was all but dark when she left work at the shop at four o'clock to drive to the yard. Hacking was out of the question on unlit roads by then, and although it was just possible to ride out on Gypsy for half an hour in the mornings before she had to get to work, Annie-May had not been worked since she'd been ridden that first time. While Gypsy seemed to accept his regular soakings with resignation if not equanimity, it was clear that Annie-May was becoming increasingly irritable at her lack of activity and the discomfort of a soaking wet rug during her brief sojourns in the paddock.

As the days passed even Kitty and Jennifer, on holiday from school, were losing their pert enthusiasm after returning drenched from ride after ride and having to spend so much time drying their ponies and cleaning tack.

Peter Holt put in an appearance from to time to time, and made encouraging noises to all his pupils, but in truth there was not very much any one could do. Even Teddy the whippet, in spite of being comfortably clad in a bright blue, fur lined waterproof coat, seemed out of sorts with the seemingly unremitting gloom of midwinter.

Finally, and at last, on Christmas Eve the skies relented and a bright morning dawned, frosty but clear.

Sophy was saddling Gypsy tied up outside his box at a quarter to eight when Miss Brown appeared. At almost the same moment the old Land Rover arrived, and Peter Holt stepped out in jacket and riding boots with an ancient, peakless crash hat in his hand.

"I hope you're not thinking of schooling," Miss Brown said, approaching Sophy but looking over her shoulder at the instructor with a mixture of surprise and disapproval. She said loudly, in a voice clearly intended for both of them, "The school is not to be used for at least another two days even if it doesn't rain again."

"I was just going out for a short hack," Sophy said, "I thought I'd feed and muck out when I come back." She too was regarding Peter Holt with some surprise. Whatever was he doing here so early?

"That's two of us going out for a hack," he said cheerfully. "That mare must be going mad with nothing to do all this time. I'm coming with you." He grinned suddenly. "I shouldn't wonder if we both didn't learn something this morning."

"You're going to ride out on Annie-May?" Unusually, it was an incredulous Agatha Brown interposing in a conversation about a horse rather than merely imposing yard discipline. Holt's grin widened, but he frowned at the same time.

"It could be a bit chancy," he admitted, "Ideally, she'd have worked in the school a few times first, but she must do something. And the longer we wait the more chancy it gets. In the end, I have to trust her, I have to trust myself, and she has to trust me too."

He turned to Sophy. "This is a job for me," he said quietly. "Make sure you watch, whatever happens. That's what I mean about learning. You'll have to do it yourself one day. Taking a measured risk is what most professional riders get paid for. At least, it is for those of us who live in the real world. We can't all win the Hickstead Derby or go to the Olympics on horses worth a million dollars."

He disappeared into the tackroom and came out carrying Annie-May's brand new saddle and bridle, a body brush and a hoof pick. "I'll be five minutes," he said. He raised his eyes to the Down beyond the lane, its wooded slopes shining with melting frost in the brilliant morning sun. "I'm looking forward to this. It's been a long time since I rode out on a fine morning."

The casual, automatic remark crashed into his memory with sickening force. His expression changed and he turned quickly away from them and went into the stable. A moment later he placed the saddle on the door, but without showing his face.

The two women looked at one another without speaking. Sophy put her hat on and fastened the strap. She took Gypsy over to the mounting block and put her foot in the stirrup. Miss Brown was moved to break the small, awkward silence.

"I had a Christmas card from Jenny this morning," she said. "She put a note in asking how you were all getting on."

"Well, we haven't been getting on," Sophy retorted rather rudely and without thinking, looking down at her, "with no school."

"I can't help the weather," Miss Brown responded with equal acerbity.

"No, you can't," Holt emerged from the stable and led the grey mare into the middle of the yard.

"Quiet please," he said authoritatively. He glanced at Sophy, who was adjusting her stirrups, and then said to Miss Brown, "better stand well back, just in case."

He waited while she retreated, checked the girth and vaulted into the saddle, light as a man could be in long boots and a hacking jacket, and his feet found the stirrups as though they were magnets. Sophy, who still had to look down and fiddle to put her feet in, was about to comment when he caught her eye and she paused. It was evident he had other things to think about.

Annie-May's feet were planted four square, but she was trembling all over, her back arched, a bomb on the brink of exploding. He sat quite still, the reins loose in his hands, and it seemed to Sophy it was the longest minute since the world began. Gradually, the trembling eased, and he moved his left hand forward with infinitesimal care to stroke her neck, but still her back was raised and the bomb was not yet defused.

"My little grey lady thinks she might be going racing," he said softly, perhaps to her or perhaps to his rapt audience. Another minute passed, and still the mare would not relax beneath him. In spite of his decades of experience and absolute concentration, the outcome of the next few seconds could not be foretold, and to wait longer might even compound the problem.

With a tiny, invisible movement of his weight and no other aid of any kind, he suggested she walk around the yard. She took a stiff half pace forward and instantly stopped, arching her back higher. Again he sat still and waited, and then picked a moment to ask again, this time achieving half a dozen strides before she halted, visibly more relaxed this second time. The relief on the man's face was unmistakable. He looked across at Sophy, who was watching spellbound with a mixture of awe and terror.

"Walk on out the gate," he said to her. "Give me a lead down the lane. In five minutes she'll be fine. It's not like she's a half-broken three year old."

Sophy pulled herself together. Gypsy, short of work himself, stepped forward almost eagerly and Annie-May followed obediently and without hesitation, joining a string as she had done countless times before.

Miss Brown watched them go with mixed feelings. She hadn't ridden herself for thirty years, and however brilliant and inspiring that man might be, and however much her friend Jenny might admire him, it was moments like that which reminded her why she never intended to start again.

She turned back to the house to finish her breakfast. It was only seeing Sophy tacking up earlier than usual that had brought on to the yard at that time of day – it had crossed her mind that in spite of her express prohibition the girl might try to use the school if she thought there was no one about,

As she passed the Land Rover she could see the whippet curled up on the front seat in his familiar blue coat. He half opened a sleepy eye to meet her glance through the window and then closed it again. The estate manager mentally reproved herself. It's Christmas, she announced almost out loud. Don't keep thinking the worst of people.

A hundred yards down the lane the two horses were walking steadily side by side in the sunshine. Annie-May's ears were sharply pricked and she was intermittently high-blowing with excitement, and clearly wanted to jog at the first excuse, but she had recovered now from her hysterical overreaction at being mounted again with a vault on a stone yard with another rider close by, and for all she knew the exciting, imminent prospect of spreading her legs in the racing gallop she was usually asked for at that time of day.

"Can I talk now?" Sophy said. "Why did she do that?"

Holt answered without looking at her, well aware that while his horse might have got its head together after that initial episode it was still waiting for an opportunity to dispose of a huge amount of physical and nervous energy, built up over more than a week of confinement and relative inactivity.

"Only she knows for sure," he said. "Lack of work, expecting to go to the gallops, a strange place, feeling cold, not liking the way I got on – there could be lots of reasons. And she is an Arab, and the female of the species." He glanced at her and grinned. "Even no reason at all. It's what I said about learning. Whenever you do something with a horse for the first time, even if you know the horse has done it many times before with someone else, be prepared. Don't take anything for granted."

"It was frightening," Sophy said with a slight shudder. "I never saw a horse do that before. Will I *ever* really ride her, properly, in the ring, I mean?"

They had come to the corner where the forestry track which ran through the woods and eventually to the top of the Down joined the lane on their left. Less than a hundred yards ahead, the rush hour traffic could be seen pursuing its ceaseless dance of passing and repassing across the T junction on to the main road.

"Take me to the top of the hill," Holt said. "A good brisk trot for a mile up that track will sort 'em both out a treat. Maybe we'll canter the last bit."

After days of hardly riding at all, it was an offer she couldn't refuse. She shoved the guilty thought that she might be late for work in the shop, and that on a day when it was sure to be busy, quickly into the background as the horses set off at an eager, competitive pace between the dripping pine trees bordering the hoggin path.

He rode comfortably beside her, and she noticed at once that although Annie-May was calmer now he was making no attempt to persuade her into the shape they were trying so hard to establish. Gypsy, in contrast, despite taking a keen interest in where they were going and plainly enjoying the company, was relatively round and swinging smoothly into the contact.

"Gypsy's looking good," he said to her as the track swung left handed in a wide arc, opening up a view down the valley over a field and still climbing steadily towards the ridge which overlooked the village. It was just a casual, conversational observation, but still she was inordinately pleased with herself. He never offered her praise unless they both knew it was due, and she was emboldened to ask about Annie-May.

"She's fine," he said. "I know what you're thinking, but you can't force the issue. We have to let her enjoy life or she'll never do anything for us. She's spent eight years when all she had to do was run fast, and now she's been mostly shut in a box for over week. It'll be a while before I want you to ask her dressage questions when she's out hacking. We'll all know when it's the right time, you and me and her." He looked ahead, where the track was straightening for the last three furlongs before the open meadow which spread across the summit of the Down.

"It's time for that canter," he said. "I'll race you to the top."

Their eyes met, bright with comradeship and mischief across the yard of space between them, and the horses leapt forward together.

He did not allow Annie–May to engage the flying gallop she undoubtedly possessed, and they came to a halt still more or less together on the hilltop overlooking the village, the house roofs alternately sparkling or in deep shadow in the low winter sunlight, and the church tower with its bare flagpole casting a long shadow across the graves in the churchyard.

"Not such a stick-in-the-mud as you once thought," he said to her, looking at Gypsy.

"I never thought hacking could be so much fun," Sophy said, almost as out of breath as her sweating horse. In contrast, neither Annie-May nor her jockey seemed remotely put out by their exertions.

"People need to ride out as well horses," he responded calmly. "It's sharing experiences which builds confidence between the species. If I asked you what Gypsy was thinking right now, I bet you could tell me."

She stared at him. It was true. Her mind flashed back to only a few weeks ago, when so far as she was concerned Gypsy's sole intention had been to frustrate her at every opportunity, assuming he had any mind at all. She patted his neck rather guiltily. Holt grinned at her, and then looked away over the shining village.

A large tractor was parked outside the shop, and a tiny figure descended from the cab and disappeared inside.

"I have a feeling a certain young man is planning a surprise for you over the holiday," he remarked. "I had the Land Rover serviced the other day. How are you getting on with Terry these days?"

Sophy blushed under her riding hat.

"I haven't seen him for ages," she said, and remembered the vaguely unsatisfactory feelings they seemed to have provoked in each other the last time they'd been together.

She followed his gaze down hill, and they both watched as the tiny figure emerged from the shop and remounted into the tractor cab.

"Mrs. Mullins hates it when he parks outside the shop like that. He got a ticket once," she said half to herself. A thought struck her and she looked at her watch.

"Oh, no," she said, "I'm going to be late for work. I haven't even mucked out yet." She turned her horse to hurry back to the yard.

Holt was unperturbed, and unrepentant for bringing her farther than she had intended.

"There's plenty of time," he told her. "We can't trot down that hill anyway, they'll be falling over their own feet and jarring their knees. Besides, we are at work. Don't you worry. You shoot off when we get back and I'll do the horses this morning. It's high time I swung a fork in anger again. Mind you," he looked at her with a wry grin, "I shan't be making a habit of it."

He turned Annie-May to walk beside her, and the horses matched companionable strides homeward bound on a long rein over the wet field.

Chapter Thirty One

There was just room to park in a corner of the little yard behind the shop and when she pushed open the door at five to ten, she had never seen so many customers all at once.

Mrs. Mullins looked flustered and seemed to be trying to serve two people at the same time. There was hardly room between the aisles to turn round.

"Sophy, thank goodness," she said to her. "Don't bother changing, put a pinny on and start the other till." The shop door bell rang, and then rang again, underlining the urgency.

Sophy threw her bag under the counter and hurriedly tied her usual apron on.

"I thought we'd be busy," she said, taking a box of mince pies from the first customer in her queue, "but not like this."

The woman she was serving, always up for gossip whenever she came in, was quick to explain.

"There's been a accident on the Chichester road," she told her. "Someone skidded in the wet, don't know who, patch of ice first thing or something. The road's closed all morning at least, so my postman says. And my kids must have their mince pies. And my old man's out of fags. He'll be unbearable if he can't smoke over the holiday. I was going to town, but I ain't got time today to go all round the houses there and back. I got family comin' tomorrow."

Sophy was about to suggest it might have been better not to leave it all to the last minute, but it was clear the woman was not alone in having her arrangements disrupted, and with a shop full of hard pressed customers there was simply no time to do or say anything except serve, explain how much was owed and take the money.

It was a hectic morning, but as time wore on the pressure eased and by lunch time the flood of customers had slowed to a trickle and finally dried up altogether, at least temporarily. Mrs. Mullins collapsed into a chair behind the counter, and Sophy, still in her riding boots, was despatched to put the kettle on. They were both sitting down, cups in hand, when Harry the policeman came in hat in hand and bought a bottle of lemonade and a biro.

"I'm sure you heard about it," he remarked conversationally. "One casualty, not too bad but bad enough right before Christmas, poor devil. You can tell folk the road's open again now. All back to normal." He looked quizzically at Sophy. "That young man of yours did pretty well," he added. "Bit of luck, him being on the spot like that, and that tractor of his came in handy."

He left without saying any more, and the two women exchanged glances and watched through the shop window as he returned to the police car and spoke a word to his companion through the open door before he got in they drove away.

"I saw Terry come in here this morning," Sophy said. "I was riding up on the hill. He must have been on the way back to the farm. I wonder what he did."

"I know he parked outside again," Mrs. Mullins grumbled. "And he didn't buy anything. He just left this for you. It's the first chance I've had to give it you. I wonder why they'd want that huge tractor for a car crash, but whenever there's an accident they always seem to need big machines to do something."

She gave her a small packet wrapped in Christmas paper from under the counter and what was evidently an accompanying card. With a sharp pang of guilt, Sophy realised she had made no attempt whatsoever to reciprocate. Subsumed in her own affairs and worrying about Annie-May, she had in truth hardly given Terry a thought since their last, vaguely unsatisfactory meeting. And there certainly wasn't time to start thinking about him now.

The flow of customers increased again after about half an hour, and by four o'clock there wasn't a box of chocolates, a mince pie or a cake left on the premises. Mrs. Mullins, closing early on account of the holiday and not reopening until the New Year, slid the bolt on the door and turned the sign to 'Closed' with a huge sigh of relief.

"I suppose you'll be wanting to rush off," she said to Sophy, "but being as it's your last day I do want to say how pleased I am with how it worked out for us. I'm going to give you an extra twenty pounds, and you mustn't worry about leaving me without any help. After you gave notice I had a word with my sister, and she's going to come and help. She's younger than me so she'll be able to do some of the lifting you did. The Council made her retire early, I know I told you about it, she was so cross when they did it."

She opened the till and gave Sophy a twenty pound note as well her wage packet, already made up. "Oh, don't forget your present," she added, and picked up Terry's little parcel from where Sophy had put it back under the counter for safe keeping.

"I haven't got him anything," she said unhappily to her now ex–employer, shrugging her way into her anorak. "I didn't think we were, well, like that, somehow. Did he say anything when he left it?"

Mrs. Mullins shook her head. "He was in and out pretty quick," she said, and grinned a little smugly. "I think he was afraid Harry was on the prowl." Unexpectedly, she gave her a quick hug. "Happy Christmas," she said. "Now get off to your horses and make us all proud of you next year. I shall hear all about it, you know what it's like in here."

It was embarrassing as well as gratifying to be made such a fuss of for just doing her job, and it was a big relief to be leaving; but still it was slightly daunting to think that from today she was a full time, independent horsewoman, and however much Peter Holt might help, she was solely and totally responsible for making her own decisions and making her own living.

The bright day ensured that it was not quite fully dark when she drove into the yard a few minutes later, although the contrast with the heavily shaded lane was sharply pointed by every possible light appearing to be switched on. She stepped out on to the cobbles a little wearily, and headed for the muck forks leaning against the wall by the tack room; the idle thought came to her that if Peter Holt hadn't mucked out properly this morning, it was going to be hard work tonight. Not that there was any reason to suppose he hadn't been as good as his word.

Kitty appeared in front of her beaming excitedly and offering her a Christmas card, and what looked like a box of chocolates wrapped in sparkly paper, quickly followed by Jennifer and the two other girls bearing similar gifts. She stopped in confusion and her mouth fell open.

Joe Fittleworth, hovering in the background and wearing a broad, festive smile, was sufficiently astute to notice the expression on her face and came to the rescue.

"Now then," he said. "Sophy'll have her work to do before she can keep you lot happy." He led her away from the chattering girls, and followed her to Gypsy's stable. She looked at him tearfully.

"I feel awful," she said miserably. "What will they think of me? I just never thought."

There was no need to tell Joe Fittleworth anything, but she wanted to, to somehow explain that she wasn't really so mean, or so poor any more; she'd just never bought Christmas presents before, except for Mum and Dad. And she'd never had any from anyone else, either. Not really, not from anyone who mattered, at least, and certainly not from little girls, two of whom she barely knew.

"I only used to buy presents for Mum and Dad. Dad's secretary did all the cards and stuff for everyone else. I don't know who got what, I just never thought about it." She could have added with perfect truth that in those days she didn't care about it much, either.

She patted Gypsy's broad neck, and there was comfort in that firm, warm, familiar strength. Joe watched her over the half door, sympathetic but frowning too. Inevitably, like everyone at the stables, he had some knowledge of her past and had observed with approval the change in her since that man Holt had come on the scene. And his daughter worshipped the ground she walked on, and her best friend Jennifer wasn't far behind.

He had an idea.

"There is a solution," he said to her, and she recovered herself and returned his gaze. "Give 'em all a riding lesson for Christmas. They can all ride together. They'll love that, and we can pretend it was your plan all along. Soon as the school's in use again."

She stared at him, eyebrows raised. Could she really teach four children all at once? It must be hugely difficult just knowing where they were, never mind what they were all doing.

"I....," she started to demur but he forestalled her.

"Have a word with your friend Mr. Holt," he said to her. "I bet he can tell you how to do it. Teaching must figure somewhere in your new career, and you surely know a lot more than they do." He smiled then, a wide, genuine, confidence boosting smile from a man much older than her, and a parent to boot.

"You don't realise how those kids look up to you," he told her. He chuckled then. "I'll spread the glad tidings. All very seasonal. Is it agreed?"

With her hands full of cards and five packages, including Terry's, she dropped one outside the flat door as she put the key in the lock, and Edith heard the commotion and came to investigate.

"You've done pretty well, my girl," she said to her daughter with a smile as she let her in. "All I got was a card from Geoff, oh, and a half share in one from your Mr. Holt. It came this morning addressed to both of us."

Sophy dropped her parcels on the kitchen table and started to pull her boots off.

"It was horrible," she said. "They all gave me something, even Terry left something at the shop, and I didn't have anything to give to anybody. I never felt so rotten and useless ever." Alone with her mother, the shame overcame her and she started to cry.

"Now then," her mother said, "I don't suppose anyone said anything. You can make it up to them later." She frowned, and felt a little guilty herself. It had not occurred to her any more than it had to that her daughter that half the world exchanged cards and gifts at Christmas on the slightest excuse or acquaintance, and would naturally assume the practice was mutual.

In her own previous existence, Christmas had been the occasion for very superior, very expensive parties, with each hostess vying to present a more impressive event than the last one. Exchanging folded pieces of paper with bland greetings and robins on had had very little to do with anything, and religion had nothing to do with it at all.

Truth to tell, Christmas was a tradition the Taylor family had never embraced with much enthusiasm, or needed to, although Derek had been accustomed to spread flamboyant largesse amongst his business associates every year. She couldn't remember exactly, but Sophy had probably not given or received a card or a seasonal gift involving a non-family member since primary school. Now, living in a different world, where friendship was not dictated by mutual interest, social standing or wealth, Christmas cards had a whole new meaning. She realised with another little jolt of guilt that until very recently very few of her daughter's horsey acquaintance would have wanted to give her a Christmas present, and Sophy wouldn't herself have cared much either way if they had.

She sat down beside her and hugged her hard.

"What's that for?" Sophy said, wiping her tears with her sleeve.

"It's because I'm so proud of you," her mother said. She kissed her cheek. "Now I want to talk to you about Mr. Holt. Do you think he'll be on his own tomorrow?"

Chapter Thirty Two

He certainly wasn't on his own first thing. All three of his charges rode out with him on another brilliant, crisp morning, waved off cheerfully by Joe and Mrs. Fittleworth and Jennifer's mother, paying a relatively rare visit in honour of the day to her daughter's favourite out-of-school destination.

Sophy's professional doubts about sharing her instructor's time and wisdom with Kitty and Jennifer, even on an informal hack, were quickly dispelled when it became clear that while he was very definitely in charge, on Christmas morning he was not about to offer serious advice to any of them, and was chiefly intent on enjoying his own ride and encouraging Annie-May to do the same.

By the time they had left the lane and were trotting in pairs up the hill, with the ponies behind, Kitty and Jennifer were alternately giggling and pretending to be serious, while Holt himself, discreetly keeping a close eye on the ponies as well as their riders' behaviour, was content to allow Annie-May a long, swinging stride as he listened to Sophy's hesitant invitation to Christmas dinner that evening.

"Your mother's very kind," he said to her, again glancing behind at the following ponies. Kitty caught sight of his frown and took her reins back into both hands. Instead of replying at once to her invitation, he returned to more immediate matters and spoke loudly enough for the girls behind to hear him too.

"You know Kitty and that Blackie pony better than I do out hacking," he said to Sophy with a broad, conspiratorial wink. "Can they be trusted if we have a canter?"

Sophy looked over her shoulder at the two girls' eager faces, flushed and grinning from ear to ear beneath their helmets.

"Well, I don't know," she said teasingly. She tried to wink back at him, but she wasn't very good at winking and his own grin widened.

"Well, it's Christmas," he said. "We'll chance it." He swung round in the saddle and faced his two young charges squarely. "No overtaking," he said severely.

"Annie-May is quieter today," Sophy said, looking at his mare moving easily over the ground and shortening Gypsy's reins in preparation. The mare was still not down in his hand but was plainly content within herself.

"She's good," he agreed. "We'll give them both a day off tomorrow, and then we'll swap the next day if the school is still out of action. I specially want you to do as much as possible with her. The closer the relationship you can make with her, especially when she's still not sure what we really want from her, the better for your training and more she'll offer you later. We can talk about it tonight, if you like."

"You'll come then?" Sophy said.

"Why wouldn't I?" he responded. "I love Teddy to bits but he can't cook." A thought struck him. "He'll have to come too," he said.

"Mother won't mind that," Sophy rejoined. "We always used to have dogs in the house. Labradors, usually, for when dad went shooting."

Two young voices in unison shouted behind them, "So when are we going to canter then?"

There wasn't much chance of the ponies doing any overtaking. The leaders set off at good strong pace, and once Peter Holt was satisfied his two younger riders were safe in the saddle he allowed himself the luxury of adopting a forward position with his weight out of the saddle. Annie-May joyfully spread her legs into an extended stride and flew away from all three of them up the hill, to be pulled up at the summit and wait a few seconds for the others to join her.

Sophy was very aware that Gypsy fell on his forehand as he trotted into a ragged halt beside his Arab friend, but it wasn't the occasion for pedantic insistence on balanced correctness. In any case Holt wasn't looking; he was staring out over the valley and the village, rooftops shining in the sun from the overnight rain, and as she followed his gaze the church bells began to ring, calling the faithful to celebrate the day.

From high on the Down the congregation could be seen straggling through the churchyard and Sophy wondered idly if her mother was among them. They'd never been churchgoers, either of them, but Edith had suggested over the breakfast table that she might attend this morning.

"If your friend Mr. Holt does comes to dinner," she'd said with something of a wry grin, "me and the turkey could both be in need of divine assistance."

Sophy, hurrying to get out the door, and with no time even to open her unexpected parcels, had not paid much attention, but as Kitty and Jennifer arrived on puffing ponies to join them it occurred to her that the combined culinary skills of her and her mother six months ago had barely amounted to boiling an egg. But that was six months ago, half way back to what had been life in another universe, and it seemed in that crystal clear moment, on a happy horse on a glorious morning, and with friends on both sides of her, that she'd never been properly alive until this minute.

Chapter Thirty Three

He was punctual that evening, and arrived with whippet attached and carrying a bottle of wine and a box of chocolates, with a small dog's bed folded under his arm.

Sophy opened the door and he said, "Happy Christmas, again," with a broad smile. His eye was caught by a new brooch she was wearing on her jumper, a silver stock pin with a horseshoe motif.

"That's nice," he said, and was surprised when she blushed slightly in response. "Not from your mother then," he smiled again.

"No," Sophy said defensively and in some confusion. She hesitated, but apart from her mother he was the only person she had to talk to properly. "It's from Terry. I wasn't going to, but I just thought I'd wear it, for a change. After all, he's not my boyfriend. It's engraved 'To Sophy and Gypsy' on the back."

He recognised her doubts, but experience warned him against expressing too firm an opinion about a teenager's personal emotions.

"Well," he told her, "at least he's gone to some trouble over it. I'd be flattered if it was me." He looked at her quizzically. It occurred to him then that there must be times when her lack of worldly experience, however engaging it might be to others, could make things very difficult for her.

"Life's not all black and white," he said. "You can have boy friends who aren't your *boyfriend*, if you know what I mean."

She was still contemplating the wisdom of this remark when Edith appeared from the kitchen looking anxious.

"Do come in," she said. "I hope you'll be forgiving. I'm not too sure about the cooking. I..., well. we've never done Christmas like this before."

"Neither have I," he said gallantly as he handed her his contributions to the occasion. "I'm usually on my own, 'cept for the dog. Thank you for inviting me. Even in the far off days when I had girlfriends, as a penniless riding instructor with no prospects I was mostly kept well out of sight of a family Christmas dinner." He grinned. "But all that was a long while ago. I don't usually cook much when I'm at home, I just follow the instructions on the packet, but I'm happy to help, so long as I have direction. Where would you like me to put Teddy? He'll stay put, so long as I tell him to. Well, mostly at least," he added, knowing from experience that whippets as a breed were not generally top of the class for obedience.

"Can I take him?" Sophy said, and she led him into the corner of the main room beside the television and dropped the bed on the carpet. His master looked at him from the door and raised an admonitory finger, and the dog obediently sat on it.

"That's impressive," Edith said.

"It won't last," Holt said. "As soon as he thinks I'm not looking he'll be checking out the premises."

There was slightly awkward pause. Sophy said, "Shall I open the wine?" and in the same moment her mother spoke.

"Mr. Holt," she began, and he frowned then and she understood him at once. "Peter. I just wanted to say straight off how grateful I am for what you're doing for Sophy. I just can't tell you what it means for us." His frown deepened, and she hesitated.

He spoke more seriously than Sophy could remember since that day at his cottage.

"We're all helping each other," he said quietly. "Isn't that what friends are for? Let's just leave it all there and look forward."

The sound of a pan boiling over interrupted them. "Oh, hell," Edith said and vanished into the kitchen.

"I'd better go too," Sophy said. "Mother's never cooked a turkey before."

"Well, I don't think there's much I can do," he said, laughing. "I'm OK with spuds and sprouts, but that's about all. Turkeys don't have enough legs for a horseperson."

It would be an extension of the truth to say that the meal was as good as any of them had ever tasted, but the food was acceptable, the wine was excellent, and the goodwill far outweighed any other shortcomings. With the remnants of the turkey still on the table, and cups of coffee before them, the guest looked at his hostess and asked, "Do you mind?" before breaking of a piece of the bird and throwing it to his dog, watching them wistfully from his bed in the corner.

Both Sophy and her mother were scandalised when he offered to assist with the washing up. Edith caught herself again comparing this life with how they had once lived, where such a suggestion from a guest would have been a calculated insult, as if the host could not afford her own domestic staff. She thought ruefully that Derek would probably have thrown him out on the spot.

She tried to look offended, but he was not deceived.

"I know it's been a lot of work," he said. "Mostly I don't care about living alone, but Christmas is different even for me and I appreciate being asked."

"Actually," Sophy said, a trifle too artlessly. "You can help me with something."

He chuckled then and took a sip of his coffee.

"I might have known," he said. "As a matter of fact, I think I do know. You need a little advice about giving a lesson to Kitty and her friends. I had a quick Christmas drink with Joe Fittleworth in the pub last night."

"If you two are going to talk about horses," Edith said, "I'm definitely *de trop*. I've promised Sophy I'll come and watch her compete whenever I can," she paused momentarily, "just like before. But really, well, I just don't do horses. If I'm absolutely honest, I'm a bit nervous with them. It was always Derek who handled all the horse stuff. Why don't you two sit down on the sofa while I clear away?"

"How do you do it?" Sophy said, pushing her chair back with alacrity. Holt and her mother exchanged an amused glance at her transparent enthusiasm to avoid the dirty dishes. "With four of them, I mean. And I've promised, so I must do them all together. I never taught even one at a time before."

Holt regarded her dispassionately. He stood up more slowly and followed her to the sofa, carrying his coffee cup. "I know you've helped Kitty already," he said, sitting down and placing his coffee on the small table beside him. "I'll just give you one or two pointers and you'll be fine. We were going to have to talk about this anyway. Most professional riders teach as well, it goes with the territory. I mean, if you're good at something, no matter what it is, other people who are trying to do the same thing are bound to ask how you do it and want advice. And it all helps to pay the bills. I got injured in a fall once, and teaching was all I could do for over a month. I'd have been in big trouble money wise without it. If I'm still helping you in a year's time, and things go the way I hope they will, we must think about you getting some proper qualifications, perhaps taking a course somewhere."

"Now that sounds good to me," Edith checked herself in the act of stacking their three plates together and shot her daughter a meaningful glance. "You'll have something to fall back on."

Sophy digested this new aspect of her professional career with a thoughtful frown. "But I don't really want to teach all that much," she said doubtfully, and Holt laughed then.

"Nobody said it was compulsory," he remarked. "And if you don't make a name for yourself you won't have any customers anyway. Let's not get ahead of ourselves. But your mother is right. It can be tough, and if things don't work out and you need to work in a riding school," he raised his hand defensively as the protest formed on her lips, "you'll need to have letters after your name. It can't hurt. And teaching other people is a great way to learn yourself. You also get the chance to ride different horses and you see things you otherwise might not."

He frowned himself then as it became clear that Sophy was not convinced. "If I could ride like you.....," she started to say, and stopped when it was obvious he wasn't listening.

"I'll give you some basic ideas," he said, "and then I want *you* to do something for *me*," and he indicated her laptop, folded closed on the sideboard. He gave a glance of thanks to his hostess as she replenished his coffee before disappearing into the kitchen. "You might want to write down some of this to remind you later. I often took notes when I was your age. Mind you, I always had to share my instructors with a whole class."

Sophy made a face at the idea. It wasn't much like Christmas, more like being back at school. He shrugged then. "Well, no matter," he said. "I shall be there when you do it anyway. Just in case. There's things like insurance and liability which you and Joe probably never thought about. Does your insurance cover teaching?"

She was nonplussed by the question. "I.....," She stopped, abruptly guilty, and he realised instantly she had not taken his advice and had still not insured herself.

Now, and suddenly, and Christmas notwithstanding, he was quite seriously annoyed with her.

"I've told you already," he said, and the sharp change in his tone brought Edith to the kitchen doorway with a tea towel in her hand. "There's more to riding other people's horses than just riding them, The day after tomorrow you're going to hack Annie-May, or rather you were. I can't possibly allow that now. She's a valuable animal, maybe worth thousands as a racehorse, a riding horse and not least as a brood mare with her racing record. If you make a mistake and she puts her foot in a hole, or springs a tendon while you're riding her, can you pay what she's worth? Or suppose a horse you're riding, even your own horse, kicks a car or a pedigree dog, or even a person? If Kitty falls off in your lesson and breaks her leg, suppose Joe sues you for asking her to do something that's beyond her? Being Joe he probably wouldn't, and if he did he might not win, but you must be insured just in case. You wouldn't drive your car without insurance, would you? It's a professional requirement. As soon as the holiday is over, you have got to do this."

"Oh, she'll do it," Edith said determinedly from the doorway. She turned to Sophy. "You never mentioned this insurance business to me," she said accusingly.

"I just didn't think it was important," Sophy said miserably. "You know Daddy did all that stuff. Or I suppose he did. Anyway, I never had an accident like that."

Silence crashed into the room as the enormity of the one accident they all knew about filled each mind.

Holt recovered first and spoke more calmly.

"There's no harm done," he said. "We'll just mark time for a day or two. Mrs. Kenley won't be back for a fortnight anyway. Get yourself public liability cover to ride or work anything with four legs, and to teach for a few hours a week. Some owners are covered anyway, but you can't depend on it. You have to be prepared – I know myself you can never tell what opportunity may come along, and you could be asked at a show say by a complete stranger to help out when you least expect it. A freelance has to be ready for anything."

He paused before he went on with a small smile. "You don't have to insure yourself, of course. No one will care if you break your own leg, and when I was starting it was far too expensive for me. But that's up to you."

"What do you want me to do for you?" Sophy said, trying to deflect attention from her own, all too evident shortcomings.

"In a minute," he said. "First, this lesson of yours. If I'm there, and I will be, I'll be technically responsible, supervising if you like, like a driving instructor in the passenger seat, so it will be my insurance covering everybody and the kids won't have to wait till the New Year for their Christmas present. Of course, I won't say anything unless I feel I must, and the girls won't know you're not the one in charge.

"So here's the drill. Line 'em up, single file, work 'em round the school, circles and rein changes, you'll soon get confident just telling 'em where to go. Correct their positions and explain the aids – talk about weight and stuff which I know you know about and I bet they don't. You don't have to use canter, but if you do, make 'em canter one at a time so they don't race each other. Keep changing the leading file so they all have a chance to go in front. Make sure you can see 'em all all of the time in case one has a problem, so keep to a corner or one end of the school and not the middle. If you think things are getting out of hand, or a pony is playing up, stop everybody instantly. Safety is always number one.

"And two most important things – speak to each one in turn, so none of them feels unfairly left out, and whenever you teach people on their own horses or ponies, if you want to ride one to demonstrate, *ask first*. In this case it could only be Rufus, I guess, since he's the only one big enough, but who knows what your next class will be?"

He paused. Sophy was beginning to wish she'd taken a few notes after all. It was a lot to take in all at once.

"You've given that speech before," Edith said from the doorway and he looked up with a smile.

"That's true," he agreed. "But not for a while." He turned back to Sophy.

"Because it's a Christmas present," he went on, "we should try to make this lesson a bit special. What do you know about formation riding, you know, simple drill with more than one rider? It's terrific fun for kids – novice adults too come to that although they don't get the chance very often - you know, riding in pairs and turning together and passing on opposite reins and stuff like that. They'll certainly remember it. Did you ever ride it yourself? I often did it with my students, having to keep up and be in the right place helps make people more effective."

Sophy was silent. Her mother spoke for her.

"Sophy always had private lessons," she told him. She did not add that in those days Sophy was not inclined to share anything, and certainly nothing to do with her riding or her horses.

He thought for a moment, his frown expressing both disappointment and disapproval at such an isolated equestrian education, and then offered a further suggestion.

"You teach them for half an hour or so," he said, "and then I'll join you and we'll drill 'em together. That way you'll get some control experience as well as them. It'll sort things out nicely all round. Do me good as well, I shouldn't wonder. I probably need the practice. Why don't you came and watch?" he added, turning again to the mistress of the house.

"I will," she said, with a non-rider's polite interest in what sounded as though it might be more of a spectacle than people riding in eternal circles to no apparent purpose.

"Teaching sounds much more complicated than riding," Sophy said, frowning again in her turn, and he laughed at her then.

"Not really," he rejoined. "Just different. What really makes a good instructor is experience. You get to recognise and correct things the riders' can't see themselves. And it's very rewarding when things start coming together." He looked straight at her, his meaning was plain, and she blushed hard and her mother went over to her and squeezed her shoulder. Then she bent down and kissed her daughter on the top of her head.

"So what's this favour I can do for you?" she asked him again, shaking her head to discourage her mother from any further public demonstrations of affection, and his answer took both of them by surprise.

"You both have one big advantage over me," he told them. "I'm not a machine person, and like you don't do horses," he glanced at Edith, "I don't do computers. I did have one once, but I hardly ever used it, and now they seem to have got so sophisticated and every day there seems to be some new criminal scam going on and I'm rather wary of getting involved."

He looked again across the room at Sophy's laptop.

"I'd like you to look up Kenley Industries for me on the internet. I'm interested to know a bit about our new benefactor. Or have you done it already and not told me?"

"I never thought," Sophy said. "Do you think she'd mind? Didn't she say it was her business now her husband had died?"

"It can't be private if it's on the internet," Holt said reasonably. He did not add that he had his own, very personal reasons for wanting to know a little more about their absent mutual friend.

"I'm interested too," Edith said, and in spite of her guest's careful tone her female antenna twitched and she shot a quick, surreptitious glance at him. He was good company, informed and polite, but apart from Sophy they had nothing in common and he wasn't her type at all. Not having met Mrs. Kenley herself, it was faintly intriguing to imagine that perhaps he was hers.

Kenley Industries website was as impressive as the business itself, but offered no personal insight whatever into its principal shareholder and new Chairperson. The company, still in private hands, was a global manufacturer of specialist parts for the aerospace and automotive industries, with its headquarters in London, factories on three continents, a reputation for innovative technology and several thousand employees worldwide. Sophy lost count of the noughts attached to its turnover figures.

All three of them gazed at the computer screen as Sophy scrolled through the editorial describing the company's *raison d'être* and achievements.

Peter Holt raised his eyebrows at last.

"Well, now we know," he said. "The lady is force to be reckoned with. No wonder she didn't tell us exactly who she was – who would have believed her?" He turned to Sophy.

"It makes no difference to us or how we work Annie-May," he said. "And from what I know of her, she would not expect it to. If you think about it, we are privileged to have her horse. She could have been sent to an international rider with an indoor school and every possible facility. You must have impressed Miss Brown without knowing it or she wouldn't have recommended you."

He was smiling at her now, thinking that for a Christmas guest in her home he might been a little hard on her earlier.

"From where I'm standing it looks like a team effort," Edith said.

Sophy was pensive and silent. A year ago, in that other life, no one had ever asked her to ride a horse for them, and certainly never suggested paying her to do it. She'd competed against professional riders of course, and even beaten them sometimes, but there had been numerous, rather annoying occasions when some person in a less than smart jacket and worn boots, riding a tidy but very ordinary cob, had beaten her smart warmbloods out of sight.

Now, after three months of working with a man like Holt, and the difference he had made to her and Gypsy, she was beginning to understand why. Proper riders, professional or not, made the best of whatever horse they were riding by showing how much they cared about it.

"I'm so grateful to you," she said to him suddenly. It might have been the wine, but she felt like bursting into tears.

He made a deprecatory gesture. "There's a long way to go yet. As a matter of fact, with learning about horses, the road never ends."

He stood up. "Talking of roads, I should be taking the road home and leaving you both in peace. It's been an evening to remember. May I?" he said to Edith, and he kissed her on the cheek.

A moment later he was gone with his whippet into the night.

"I wonder if he's driving," Edith said. "We had nearly two bottles of wine between us."

Sophy pulled back a corner of the curtain and looked down into the street. The man was plainly visible a few yards away, standing beneath one of the three street lamps illuminating the road junction in the centre of the village. She saw him light his pipe, glance down and speak to the dog, and walk away taking a torch from of his pocket, leaving as ever a wreath of tobacco smoke drifting behind him in the still, cold night air.

Chapter Thirty Four

The weather continued cold but fair, with frosty mornings, and two days after Christmas Miss Brown lifted the embargo on using the school.

Sophy's eagerness to take another step forward with Annie-May, or even to work Gypsy properly, was tempered slightly by misgivings about the impending lesson she would have to give, and sure enough the prospective participants instantly engaged her for the following afternoon as soon as the notice indicating the school was now available appeared on the tack room notice board.

Their carefree enthusiasm contrasted sharply with her own growing feeling of apprehension when the next day dawned fine and the hours passed. At Peter's suggestion she worked Annie-May in long reins again rather than ride her first thing, under his watchful eye, and then he gave her a brief lesson on Gypsy, which did not go as well as she expected.

It was not much comfort when he told her that a week's hacking with no schooling in between would inevitably lead to horses whose outline was not firmly established regressing to some degree; perhaps the best that could be said of the morning's work was that it took her mind off the coming afternoon.

Her mother was surprised at how little appetite she had when she returned home for lunch and to collect her, and how quiet she was during the short drive to the stables.

Sophy's nerves were not improved when it became clear that the world and his wife had come to observe her teaching début. As she went into the school to join her class there was Peter Holt, of course, leaning on the fence and smoking his pipe as usual; and Joe and Mrs. Fittleworth, and the parents of Kitty and Jennifer's young friends, as well as her own mother. In fact the only obvious absentee was Jennifer's mother, who according to her daughter had gone to the sales in Chichester. Miss Brown had come too, and was looking at the school surface and frowning. For a brief, ecstatic moment it seemed she might cancel the afternoon's activities, but instead she gave her a small nod and engaged Peter Holt in conversation.

Then Terry Godwin appeared from nowhere. He nodded politely to Peter Holt, as a regular customer, and offered her a broad, happy smile of greeting. He clearly had every intention of waiting until the end and then persuading her to go out with him somewhere. She realised with a start that as well as Dad's medallion round her neck, she was wearing his brooch on her jacket, and a feeling of confusion muddled her head still further.

. Out of the corner of her eye she saw Holt was watching her more closely than anyone. He slightly inclined his head as their eyes met, and the moment could be delayed no longer.

Her four pupils were wandering about the school on their ponies chatting to each other and giggling; a warning voice inside her head said, 'that Kitty child will start showing off if you're not careful,' and in that moment the nerves subsided and she knew what she had to do. She raised her head and spoke loudly and for the first time in her life with a real feeling of authority.

"Form a ride behind Kitty at B walking on the left rein," she ordered, and the giggling stopped on the instant and the line formed at the marker, exactly as it had on those infrequent occasions when she'd watched class lessons being taken by proper instructors in the past.

The four ponies walked steadily round the school, awaiting the next instruction. Sounding more confident than she felt, she commanded the ride into trot and Kitty obediently led the way, going large and conveniently rising on the wrong diagonal. Already, she had something to say, and then she asked for a circle and suddenly it was easy; careful to watch every moment, she asked for changes of rein and circles and a serpentine and began to make basic corrections up and down the ride as the class trotted around her.

Rufus was happily following Blackie wherever he went, with the other two, smaller ponies behind when Sophy, mindful of what she'd been told, asked Jennifer to take over as the leading file. As Kitty turned Blackie away to take her place at the rear, Rufus promptly stopped, so abruptly that his rider was propelled half way up his neck and the following ponies were obliged turn in to avoid a collision.

Jennifer recovered her seat and smacked him, and his ears flattened, his back feet lifted six inches off the ground but he still refused to go in front. All four ponies were now stationary awaiting direction.

Jennifer, feeling she was the centre of attention, fearful of the result if she smacked him again and so helpless to make her pony behave, was becoming tearful.

"Please will you ride him?" she said to Sophy, and her lower lip quivered as Sophy dithered, uncertain what to do. It was a massive relief when Peter Holt stooped through the fence and came towards her, carrying her hat. He put the hat in her hand, and went to hold Rufus as Jennifer dismounted. He spoke quietly to Sophy, and obediently she put on her hat asked the others to come to the centre of the school.

He gave her Jennifer's whip and held the pony as she mounted and adjusted the stirrups. Her legs were far too long for a pony this size, and Jennifer's stirrups were barely long enough for her on the last hole, but somehow she managed. He was still standing by the pony's shoulder as she took up the reins.

"Lean slightly back, soft leg and open your hand," he said quietly, looking up at her. "Just walk away. If it doesn't work, pull his head round to your foot, so he has to move sideways to keep his balance, and then walk away, any where you like. Don't smack him. If you smack him he'll buck."

She stared down at him. The pony felt tiny, insubstantial beneath her, giving her an unnerving sense of insecurity.

His smile was reassuring. "It's OK," he said. "He's not evil, just naughty." He stepped away from her.

She let her weight drop back and gave away the rein. Rufus hesitated, apparently assessing the situation and the capabilities of his new rider, and then moved forward a few paces. Still sitting slightly behind the balance, she was able to keep him going.

Holt was walking beside her half a dozen yards away. She became aware that every eye inside and outside the school was watching her intently, but it was impossible to concentrate on anything except the pony. What would he do, would he stop, would he buck, and then suddenly she thought, how can I make him like me, so he wants to do what I want? Instinctively, she leaned forward and stroked his neck, and for the first time his ears flicked forward.

Through the mist of concentration, she heard Holt's voice say, "You pick the time, take a light contact, lie a little back, make an easy sitting trot and keep going." He stepped away from her.

She walked on to the end of the school. As she came to the corner and tentatively asked for a slight bend, the step softened and she knew that this was the moment. Rufus trotted quietly forward, a relaxed, gentle lift in the step with his neck stretched out and a minimal contact. Compared with Gypsy, he was easy to sit, and as the long side of the school drew them on towards the spectators by the gate, they both began to enjoy themselves.

Watching from the centre of the school, Holt was experiencing his own satisfaction. Three months ago, even four weeks ago, she probably wouldn't have been able to do this. Technical expertise came from the head, but the sensitivity needed for this sort of riding job had to come from the heart. He could see the pony smiling from the other side of the school, and knew there was more to come. After all, Rufus was fifteen years old. Somebody must have taught him something at some stage of his career. He beckoned her over to him. Her eyes were shining with the joy of unexpected achievement and the sheer pleasure of feeling this unknown pony offering himself to the rhythm she was making.

Holt caressed the pony's neck as he spoke to her.

"Do it again," he said. "Then when you're ready make the trot a little bit stronger and ask for an outline, nicely mind you, and if it comes, and I think it might, rise to the trot straight away. If he resists, I mean if you feel the contact go tight against you, open your fingers without lengthening the rein." He paused. "Don't force anything. Don't worry if it doesn't work. Whatever happens ride on both reins, make a circle on both reins, always nice easy steps, and after five minutes come back to me. I don't need to tell you to *carry every step* and *concentrate* for every step, do I?"

She took up the reins, beaming down at him. "He's rather lovely," she said, a remark overheard by Jennifer, who was standing beside Kitty sitting on Blackie a few yards away. She smirked proudly up at her friend, and Kitty made a face at her.

Peter Holt chuckled and took his pipe out of his pocket. "They're all lovely when they're good," he said. "Go off now and make a name for yourself."

It was easy to reproduce the trot she'd had before. Rufus readily adopted the same swinging stride and seemed content to continue in such a long, loose shape indefinitely. Half way down the next long side, she asked a little more and closed her hand. She felt him tighten through the back beneath her and object to the constricting rein, and the step shortened sharply. It took a moment to quell her first instinct, to harden the aids and insist on the answer she wanted, and then Peter Holt's words came back to her. What was happening was exactly what he'd said might happen.

There seemed no logic to opening her hand just then, but she did it anyway, still trying to keep the same length of rein.

The pony shook his head slightly from side to side, as though a long forgotten memory was stirring from deep in the long ago, and he dropped his head to the softer, gentler touch of the bit, lifting his back to complement the now graceful curve of his neck. It was a transformation. Sophy was astounded, and gasped out loud. It was a glorious, magic, enchanting moment, an intimate expression of confidence and affection from a horse she had never ridden before.

And she forgot to rise to the trot, and she forgot to ride forward, and the pace slowed and the shape changed and finally Rufus walked and then stopped.

She was still on the track, sitting motionless in the saddle with her head bowed and trying not to cry, partly at that breathtaking feeling of connection with the pony and partly at her own stupidity for not keeping him going.

Holt came over to her.

"I know," he said, looking up at her with a private, empathetic smile. "Now get a grip. Ride the pony and make me proud." He glanced over his shoulder. "And we mustn't keep the others waiting much longer. It's not very warm, standing about."

She pulled herself together. It occurred to her then that Peter was probably the only person she'd ever met who would know what she was feeling, or why she'd stopped when she did. She gave Rufus a pat, redolent with the gratitude she was sure he understood, and over the next few minutes he did not disappoint her, or her watching public.

She rode those five minutes in a kind of wonderment, with the pony travelling sweetly beneath her around and across the school as though he had never worked in any other shape in all his life. The step was lighter and smaller than Gypsy's, and she knew she was impossibly tall for a pony of barely fourteen hands, and yet sometimes the feel was similar, especially when the contact tightened a little as Rufus found a corner difficult, or when her too long legs tried to wrap under his belly.

Left to herself, absorbed in the strange, joyful new awareness she was feeling, she might have worked the pony beyond his endurance in a shape he had long since abandoned for a less taxing way of going, but Peter Holt called her to him when he was satisfied she could achieve no more.

"Put Jennifer back up," he said to her. "We can discuss your work later if you like." He smiled at her and drew on his pipe with evident satisfaction. "Well done for now." He turned then to face the others.

"I'm going to work you lazy lot in a formation exercise" he told them. "So you'll have to concentrate. Then Sophy will take over."

"Like they do on the telly?" Kitty said, exchanging a slightly worried glance with Jennifer, now remounted and with Sophy standing beside her readjusting her stirrups. Jennifer did not respond. She was staring down at Sophy shoving her foot in the stirrup with a mixture of awe and admiration.

"OK?" Sophy said, looking up at her. She met Jennifer's gaze, and feeling slightly embarrassed at being the recipient of such undisguised hero worship, withdrew hurriedly to stand beside her own instructor. It was even more embarrassing to realise she had very likely looked at him in much the same way more than once in the last few weeks.

"I'm afraid it may not be quite like they do it on the telly," Holt said to Kitty with a smile and a glance at the spectators. "But that's the idea."

He lined them up side by side, numbered them one to four, worked them in single file around the school and then used the centre line to develop opposing pairs and finally a quartet abreast coming down the centre line to resume a single file. Fortunately, Rufus was on his best behaviour after his recent experience with a rider who was more able, not to mention more sympathetic, than his usual pilot, and did not disrupt the pattern when it was his turn to lead his partner. In fact, it seemed to the spectators that the ponies had enjoyed the performance as much as their riders had.

The four of them were trotting round the school with Jennifer proudly leading the way and Kitty bringing up the rear when Holt turned to Sophy, and told her, "Now it's your turn. Concentrate on the drill, but still make corrections if you have time. Start at A. Make 'em do it twice with different partners, and no stopping!"

It was daunting, but there was no time to think; already, Jennifer was approaching the H quarter marker. She snatched her thoughts together, was dimly aware that Holt had left her alone in the arena, and commanded the first turn down the centre line.

Edith and Miss Brown were standing together, coated, gloved and scarved against the cold and a little apart from the others, when Holt joined them through the fence.

Edith said to him doubtfully, "Can she really do this? Won't there be an awful muddle?"

He swung round to watch. The ride was dividing at C; as Kitty turned, the last in the line, Blackie fell in on to his shoulder and Sophy rasped out an order to correct the bend.

"I think she'll be fine," he said. He grinned. "Those kids don't know what they're in for."

Miss Brown said enigmatically, "I've seen enough girls on this yard over the years, but never one like her."

Neither Holt nor her mother was quite sure how to take this observation, but she did not elaborate, and all three of them unconsciously assumed a similar stance, with their hands resting on the top fence rail, as they watched the exercise progress.

Sophy was actually enjoying herself. Increasingly confident, her voice rang out clearly and both the four and two legged participants seemed to draw extra enthusiasm from her undoubted concentration and commitment. When the second pattern was finally completed, and she ordered the ride into walk, the sense of anti-climax was palpable.

Terry Godwin said to no one in particular, "Wow, that was a workout," a sentiment cheerfully echoed by Joe Fittleworth. "I knew she could do it," he said. He looked at Terry, someone he did not know, but still he guessed the reason for his presence. "I'll bet she keeps you under control too," he said to him, and Terry grinned a little ruefully. "I wish," he said.

Sophy remembered how Peter Holt always insisted on letting her horse relax after a lesson, and then asked for any questions. As the first lesson she had ever given drew to a close, and the ponies were stretching into a long rein, she asked the same question.

Four eager faces turned towards her, and Kitty, as was only to be expected, spoke for all of them.

"That was the best lesson *ever,*" she said. "Can we have another one?"

Sophy brought them off the track to dismount, suddenly conscious in her own turn of how exhausted she was. Now that the mental pressure of the last few days was lifted, it was easy to forget that she had also mucked out, groomed and worked two horses herself this morning, as well as riding Rufus under her own instructor this afternoon.

"Maybe next Christmas," she said happily, feeling weary, relieved, and hugely pleased with herself all at the same time.

Chapter Thirty Five

The stable yard was more bustling than she could ever remember it as the girls put their ponies away, talking excitedly amongst themselves and with their parents joining in.

Her mother was saying to Peter Holt, "I never thought of Sophy as a teacher before," Holt was listening politely while evidently thinking it was high time he took the dog for a walk before it became too dark, and Miss

Brown was, typically, standing a little to one side overseeing the proceedings with her usual air of impassive disinterest.

Terry Godwin suddenly appeared beside her.

"Happy Christmas," he said, adding a little diffidently, "you were terrific."

Sophy blushed, and then remembered she was wearing his brooch.

"This is lovely," she said. "Thanks ever so much," and he was embarrassed in his turn.

"Well," his voice was uncertain. "I know we're not, well, you know what I mean, but I just thought…." His voice stumbled into silence.

The unexpected arrival of Miss Brown spared both their blushes. She spoke to Terry with what was, for her, a surprising degree of approval.

"That was a fine thing you did on Christmas Eve," she said to him, and he turned towards her with an awkward, disparaging gesture.

"I just happened to be there," he muttered. "Just coincidence, really."

"I've heard about this," Holt said. "If I hadn't been so busy with other people," he shot a glance at Sophy, "I'd have done this before," and he shook the boy's hand with real enthusiasm.

"You're talking about that accident," Sophy said. She looked at Terry. "What did you do? Tell me about it."

"Nothing much," he said. He was evidently about to change the subject, but Peter Holt would have none of it.

"That's not what I heard," he interrupted. "I heard the driver had gone off the road and the car was stuck between two trees, the doors were jammed, and you smashed the back window to get in and gave the driver the kiss of life. Then when the police and ambulance people came you pulled the car free with that huge tractor of yours so they could get him out. Doesn't sound like nothing much to me."

"Nor me," Sophy said with feeling. "Is the driver alright?" She realised the inanity of the question as she spoke, and added "I mean.. .."

"He'll be OK," Terry said awkwardly. "Broken ribs and stuff. That copper Harry came round to tell me. Makes a change from getting torn a strip off."

"You ought not to park outside the shop," Sophy said, and he made a face at her.

He took a deep breath.

"I probably wouldn't if you weren't inside," he announced, laying his cards on the table in front of everybody. The other three exchanged glances. Even Miss Brown managed what might have been a smile.

"I think we should leave these romantics to sort themselves out," Holt said, and these was no doubting the conviction of his smile. "Let me take you home, Edith. Sophy has to feed and put her horses to bed. If she can escape from her fan club."

He nodded at Kitty and Jennifer, huddled together by the tack room door and obviously up to something. Fortunately Kitty's parents came past and ordered them to get on with their evening stables so that they too could go home.

Briefly, Terry and Sophy were left standing alone in the middle of the yard and only Gypsy, leaning over the stable door and waiting for his supper, was watching with any kind of attention. Terry hesitated; he'd been rehearsing what he wanted to say since this morning, and now, kicking himself, with all that talk of the accident, he'd forgotten it.

Sophy fingered the brooch on her coat. He was rather sweet, really, for all his heroics and his huge tractor and mechanical abilities. Buoyed by the confidence of her successful afternoon, she commandeered the conversation.

"You want to take me out," she said.

"I do," Terry said, hugely relieved that the responsibility for saying those words had been snatched from him. He was emboldened to say what he had intended from the start. "Actually, I was going to ask if you'd like to go to the theatre in Chichester with me. Tonight. What do you think?"

Sophy was taken aback. Terry Godwin and live theatre were not an equation she would naturally have put together. Expecting he was just going to ask her to the pub like before, she hesitated in her turn.

"What's on?" she asked, temporising.

"Puss in Boots," he said, and grinned shamefacedly.

Sophy stared at him. He went on hurriedly. "Bert was going with Alice, you know the barmaid he's going out with, she likes all that "he's behind you stuff," she's already dragged him to some amateur Aladdin thing in Petersfield, but she's got the flu and so he gave his tickets to me. I haven't been to panto since I was ten. Will you come? I can't go on my own, I'd never live it down. There's some TV actor starring in it, I forget who."

"I suppose it might be fun," Sophy said slowly. She could vaguely remember seeing 'Aladdin' herself, once upon \a time.

"Oh, great," he snatched eagerly at her cautious acceptance and added quickly, before she could change her mind. "I'll pick you up at seven. It starts at quartet to eight." Having secured his object, he vanished into the darkening late afternoon with a brief wave, and a moment later his van followed Peter Holt's Land Rover out through the gate.

There was no way of telling whether she would enjoy the show, but her mother was delighted for her and between them they agonised over what she should wear. She still had one or two dresses which fitted her from last year, and Terry had only ever seen her in jodhpurs or jeans. Without quite knowing why, it was seriously important to impress him, to make him realise she was not to be taken for granted in even the smallest way. Finally, having tried on everything which was even remotely possible, and looking at herself critically in front of the mirror, with her mother cooing appreciatively in the background, she made another decision.

"We'll go in my car," she announced when Terry presented himself. "I'm not going to the theatre in a van, not for anybody."

Terry, tidier than she had ever seen him and wearing a shirt with a crooked tie, had spent half an hour cleaning his van in her honour, but faced with her determination and, in his eyes at least, her sensational appearance, did not argue.

"You can drive," she said, handing him the keys.

As she said in response to her mother's enquiry the following morning, 'Puss in Boots' was highly entertaining, if you like that sort of thing and can suspend your grown up sensibilities for an hour or two, but she had more to tell her about what happened afterwards, as they were leaving the theatre.

"There was a woman from the Chichester paper taking photographs of the children and asking them what they thought," she said excitedly, pushing her cornflakes round the bowl. "She had a badge on her coat that said 'Press,' just like a proper reporter, and she recognised Terry from that accident. She'd been sent to photograph it, and apparently she got there just as he was pulling the car out with the tractor. She made us pose for her. She said Terry and his tractor will be in the paper when it comes out tomorrow, and now we'll both be in it next week. She made notes about who we were and stuff. I said I was a dressage rider and she thought that was great, you know, different. And Terry kissed me when he brought me back, properly, you know." She paused. "I was going to wake you, but, well, it was half past twelve and I didn't in the end."

Her mother took a moment to digest this information, delivered at a breakneck pace very unlike Sophy's usual, more deliberate, just-got-out-of-bed manner first thing in the morning.

"It seems a good time was had by everybody," she said eventually, smiling across at her. She added in a slightly different tone, "I'm sure Terry Godwin is a perfectly respectable young man, and we all know now how resourceful he is, but do be careful, darling. You be sure he's what you want before....." She let her voice tail into silence.

"Oh, it's not like that at all," Sophy said dismissively, and her mother frowned slightly. She wanted to tell her that while she might think it wasn't like that at all, it was unlikely that the young man shared her opinion, but she was wise enough to keep her own counsel. Sophy would certainly fly off the handle if she suggested it, and that would help nobody. Not for the first time, she was reminded that in most families any teenage daughter of the house would have been in this position three or four years ago.

It was food for reflection, but not for now. Geoff was already ringing the doorbell to take her to work; normally, the gallery would have been closed until the New Year, but he was planning an exhibition for local artists in mid-January, and there was, as ever, much to be done.

"Have a good day at the stables, dear," she said as she slipped into her coat. "And do wash up, if you have time."

Chapter Thirty Six

It was a bright, sunny morning, and perhaps as a result of being out so late last night the day seemed fresher and more promising than usual. By the time she'd finished mucking out she was looking forward to riding with an eagerness she hadn't experienced for ages.

Even so, she felt a slight uncertainty about whether to hack or school Gypsy, and Annie-May was clearly on edge and full of herself having only worked in hand yesterday. The dilemma was resolved by Peter Holt arriving just as Kitty began to pester her to go out with her on Blackie.

Holt knew exactly what he wanted her to do this morning. He tapped out his pipe on the Land Rover wheel and strode over to her. He was wearing breeches and boots himself, but it seemed he did not intend to ride that day.

"It's time you rode Annie-May properly in the school," he said. He looked at the mare across the yard, with her ears pricked and an expectant gleam in her eye. He chuckled then. "I hope you're on your toes," he said. "It looks as though she is. Tack her up and come down to the school. We'll see how she goes for you."

"Can I bring Blackie?" Kitty wanted to know. Sophy checked on her way to the tackroom and spun round, horrified that a naughty little pony might upset her first serious session riding Annie-May. But Kitty was talking to Peter and not to her.

"You're just as entitled to use the school as anyone else," he said mildly. "But the rules are strict. You must keep out of the way if there's a lesson going on."

He caught sight of Sophy's expression, and the furrow in his brow and the slight inclination of his head reminded her that not so many weeks ago she had herself not behaved very well in a similar situation. She blushed in spite of herself at the recollection. It seemed like a hundred years ago, but the boot was on the other foot today and no mistake.

Holt knew her well enough to know what she was thinking.

"Touché," he said to her, and grinned. Kitty didn't understand that, looked blankly from one to the other, shrugged and went to brush her pony before tacking up.

Nevertheless, it was absolutely infuriating to have to share the school with Kitty and Blackie while in any properly arranged world she would have the school to herself. After all, she was a professional rider now, being paid to ride a high quality horse with unlimited potential, albeit under supervision. Surely she ought have the school, and her instructor, to herself if she wanted. Especially this morning.

It took a moment to realise it was typical of Peter Holt to adamantly apply the same impartial, professional criteria to a child on a scruffy pony as he would to her, or even, she supposed, to somebody famous.

"You'll have enough to do without worrying about Kitty," he told her then. "And it won't help if you're in a bad temper before you start. Annie-May will certainly know if your mind's not on the job." He suddenly looked at her earnestly, and with a trace of anxiety.

"This is a judgement call for me," he said quietly. "I am taking a chance that you are ready for each other. I think you are, and I have faith in you, but you cannot ride a horse like Annie-May without a clear head, especially if she's fresh. And there will be more days in your career when you have to share a school than when you don't, and sometimes the horse you're riding will be very much more difficult than Annie-May. So you have to get used to it. And there may be days when you don't have a school at all, just a not very flat field. I know that happened to me more than once. Now let's get on. I want to talk to you about Gypsy later."

Kitty and Blackie were already wandering about the school when he legged her up on Annie-May, keeping a precautionary hold on the bridle. She looked down at him nervously. Annie-May felt like a rocket with the touch paper lit.

"Get settled," he said to her. "Long rein, just walk off quietly. Let her stretch long on a big circle. Ease into trot whenever you both feel ready." He released the rein. Out of the corner of her eye she saw Miss Brown appear by the gate.

Annie-May strode vigorously forward with huge walk steps, barely keeping her balance, and Sophy realised she would have to trot at once whether she wanted to or not. Gingerly, fearful of the response if she even whispered with her leg, she allowed her weight to ease a fraction forward and the mare leapt down the long side in a bare handful of canter strides, threw her head wildly at the corner in that characteristic Arab gesture, fell into trot and ran round the short side.

She had just enough presence of mind of mind to ride on to a circle, and Annie-May swerved sharply away from Blackie, ambling about in the centre of the school. She recovered her balance, and was dimly aware of Holt's voice as the mare swept on, smoothly and fast, but head up and completely hollow, back on to the track.

"Stay on the circle," he ordered. "Keep going and she'll settle. Kitty, you come to this end out of the way."

The next few minutes were a gradually diminishing nightmare for a rider accustomed to the more solid feel of an educated, balanced warmblood beneath her rather than a narrow framed, under worked Arabian racehorse, who had only the barest idea of working in a riding arena. Peter Holt, watching with increasing confidence as his student came to terms with a first experience he knew she must find unnerving, but which he had himself encountered many times in a journeyman's riding career, saw the horse slowly accept the discipline of the circle and progressively ease into a steadier tempo.

He was momentarily distracted by Kitty riding up beside him in wide eyed awe at Annie-May's speed in the trot and Sophy's rapid but careful rising to stay with her.

"She's so *fast*," she said.

Satisfied that Sophy was managing somehow, Holt allowed himself a quick glance at the pony and nodded too to Miss Brown, watching stony faced by the gate.

"She's doing fine," he said, half to himself, but with real relief in his voice. He told Sophy to change the rein and keep trotting, and as the edge slowly faded from Annie-May's wild enthusiasm, she was able finally to start actually riding her instead if just following the step and the pattern the horse was making.

If the instructor was relieved that his judgement had been vindicated and Sophy had been able to cope, if only just, his pupil was thankful at last to be breathing freely again, with nerves subsiding and a growing sense that surely the worst must be over by now. She wanted to stop, walk, give herself a chance to think, but the implacable man standing in the centre of the school with that silly little pony beside him would not allow it.

"Keep trotting," he said firmly as she passed by. "Keep rising. She'll come to your hand if you're clever enough and soft enough. Use the school."

For a long while, nothing happened. Annie-May was amenable enough now to be ridden wherever she wanted her to go, but still she had her head in the air and every attempt to ask her down was met with a sharp resistance.

Holt was beginning to think he would have to ride her again himself when at last he saw a tiny hint of yielding from the horse's end of the rein. In that minute fragment of a second, if she offered the rein the mare would come to her, a friend for life. But would she feel it, would she know? There was never time to tell a rider this was the instant; they must feel it themselves, or the moment is lost.

Sophy was tiring. Her concentration was intense but the nervous energy which had sustained her was giving way to not physical but nervous exhaustion. She turned her mare for the umpteenth time across the school, just ahead of the still stationary Blackie and that accursed man who would not let her rest, and as she changed the rein the lightning flashed.

In the very act of turning to the track, as she opened her hand Annie-May lowered her head sweetly to the contact and in half a stride it was a trot to dream of and never wake. She was too tired not to ride it, and she did.

Dimly, through a golden, ecstatic haze she heard that wonderful man say, "*Now* you can walk whenever you're ready," but she didn't want to walk, she wanted to ride that trot forever and forever in circles around the school, with that floating stride soaring below her and that secret knowledge of love and infinite trust soft and secure in both her hands.

Miss Brown, standing gloved. coated and shivering slightly beside the gate, was better placed than anyone to witness the transformation. A tiny, involuntary gasp of approval escaped her and carried to Holt a dozen yards away. He turned at the sound, and for a brief moment exchanged a smile with her. In spite of his continuing concentration on his pupil, it crossed his mind that the woman was human after all. And then he was distracted further by remembering that she was Jenny's friend, and so must have something to recommend her whatever outward appearances might suggest.

Annie-May began show off. Still fresh in the cold air, and feeling confident now in Sophy's soft, containing contact, this strange new way of going encouraged her hocks to come powerfully beneath her, and she began to experiment, lengthening her stride more and more and becoming progressively less balanced. It occurred to Sophy then that she might canter, and a hint of panic entered her head. If she cantered from this sort of trot there'd be no controlling her.

Peter Holt was at least as conscious of the danger as she was, and found himself torn between wanting, urgently, to tell Sophy to stop, and hoping she had the feel and experience to make the decision for herself. Annie-May in a proper shape under saddle was as breathtaking as he'd known she would be, but there were mental processes to go through as well as just responding to the aids.

It was a sign of Sophy's developing horseman's instinct that she rode into walk from rising trot just in time, realising with a flash of insight at the last second that to sit for the transition would invite a leap into canter. Holt was beaming as she came up to him, reins in a loop, the mare snorting with satisfaction and excitement, and Sophy herself elated and exhausted in equal measure.

Kitty was staring at her wide eyed from beneath her blue helmet.

"*Wow*," she said. Holt grinned.

"I wish you'd stop saying that," Sophy said. She turned towards her instructor. He was lighting his pipe and winked up at her through a small cloud of blue smoke. If she hadn't been so tired she would have started to cry.

Chapter Thirty Seven

"She's the most gorgeous horse I've ever ridden," she said with a catch in her voice. "That trot's just amazing. It's just...."

"Better than Rufus?" Holt interrupted her with a smile, and she was nonplussed at the suggestion. Confusion took hold of her. How could he say that? And yet her mind flew back to the pony, with his paces a world away from Annie-May's extravagant, brilliant stride, but still an honest soul who had tried to please her. Unconsciously, she flexed her fingers, remembering.

Holt saw her frowning. "I never like to say one horse is better than another," he said, "although people often ask. After all, they may have secret talents we don't know about, or had bad experiences. They're all different, of course. We take what we learn from each of them and bring it to how we ride each of them. It was Rufus yesterday who taught you how to ride Annie-May today. Be grateful. Think about it while you're cooling off."

He wrapped his hands round the warm bowl of his pipe and glanced at the gate, where Miss Brown had already decided the entertainment no longer justified the bitter cold and was retreating towards the house.

"I'm freezing," he said as Annie-May walked away, stretching luxuriously and with her rider's mind racing. He looked at Kitty. "You must be too. And you can't ride out here on your own, you know your Dad won't like it. We'll put the kettle on in the tackroom and have a cup of tea. Perhaps Sophy will take Gypsy out with you later." He called over to her, "in the tackroom whenever you're ready."

With Annie-May safely rugged up, having been awarded a heartfelt but discreetly applied cuddle, on her way to join them she passed Blackie standing in the stable with his own rug thrown over his saddle. Kitty was evidently determined to be ready should the chance come to go for a ride.

Pensive and quiet, she stood in the doorway. Peter Holt was warming his hands on his mug of tea and Kitty was nibbling a bar of chocolate. A car could be heard arriving behind her, presumably Jennifer or one of the other girls coming to attend to their pony.

"I'm learning so much," she said in a low voice, and they both looked up at her.

The man replied in the same, measured tone, stating the complaint of every tutor of every practical skill the world over.

"It's doing it as does it," he said. "Only the horses can offer you experience. All I can do is try to open your mind to it." He smiled at her then. "I don't mind telling you that talent helps, because the moment you get conceited Annie-May or one of her friends will dump you on the seat of your pants, or worse. But the road never ends. After forty years, the more I know, the more I know I don't know. The day I, or you, forget that, our careers are finished. When it comes to riding, every horse in the world knows more than any horseman ever will."

He was silent, thinking perhaps of his own early days in a different time, when in comparison with today almost the only constant in the equestrian world was the horse itself.

Sophy was thinking that a few short months ago the idea that a horse, or even most horse people, could ever know more than she did would have been so far off the radar as not to exist.

He broke his reverie and spoke briskly.

"Now then. Gypsy's your horse, not mine or Mrs. Kenley's, so you have to make the decisions about him. Downside's next show is on the fourteenth, two weeks from Sunday. I called in and collected a schedule."

He took it from his pocket and gave it to her.

"The woman said you could enter online, but you know I'm not into all that so I brought you an entry form anyway. I see they have an Intro, two Prelims and a Novice class. So what do you want to do? If you do the Intro I'll never speak to you again." It was clear he was more than half serious. "And remember, you'll have to hack there and back, all roadwork, so his shoes must be up together."

Annie-May fell out of her mind and for a long moment panic set in. It was nearly a year since she'd been in the arena, and it had only mattered so much then because she'd wanted it to. With real life beginning in real, deadly earnest, it really mattered now, and what was more her standards were different. It wasn't just about her being queen of the party any more, it was about making the absolute best of herself and her horse whatever might happen.

"Are we ready?" she said doubtfully, and he smiled. That little word 'we,' not 'I,' introduced without thinking, spoke volumes to him about her altered approach to her once 'useless' horse.

"I think so," he said seriously. "For me, the question is whether to enter both Prelims or only one, or one Prelim and then the Novice. I know what I would do, but it's up to you. Equally important, it gives the work a proper focus, something to work towards. We might get Annie-May to Downside before the end of the season, but we can't count on it. She'll take as long as she takes. And I've got an idea about her first show, starting with a bit of a splash, but I must run it past Mrs. Kenley first."

She looked down at the schedule. Entries closed a week before the show, and there was a list of the season's dates reaching to the end of March, when there was a championship show for the winners of the most points throughout the winter.

Her heart was thumping unexpectedly, and she told herself severely to get a grip. It was an unaffiliated Prelim, not the Regional Finals where she'd won a minor rosette in two classes last summer. Or rather, the summer before, she realised with a jolt.

"So what would you do?" she asked him, and he grinned and wagged his finger at her.

"No cheating," he told her. "You decide. There'll be owners asking *you* these questions one day, if you're lucky."

She thought for a moment. "I'll do the second Prelim," she said. "That way there'll be plenty of time to get there, and Gypsy will have time to get used to things. I....," she frowned and paused. "I don't think he's ever been to a show before."

"Sensible choice," Holt said, nodding approval.

"Blackie's been to lots of shows," Kitty said, eagerly interrupting. "Can I come too?"

They both looked at her.

"There's no leaving you out of anything, is there?" Holt said with a wry grin. He sensed rather than saw the horror on Sophy's face at the idea of playing nursemaid to Kitty when she would be desperate to concentrate on her own performance, but it was an open show and Kitty was quite capable of riding the movements of a Prelim test. There was no reason why she couldn't go. Then he had an idea.

"Why don't you ask Sophy?" he said to her, deliberately and somewhat mischievously putting his star pupil on the spot.

There was a brief silence as Sophy wrestled with her reply. Every fibre of her soul rebelled at the thought of Kitty tagging along like a sort of interfering appendage, but after only a second she realised that Kitty could easily go anyway if she wanted, perhaps with Jennifer or someone else, or her dad might even hire a trailer, as she knew he sometimes did for Pony Club events.

Six months ago the idea of going to a show with a child in tow would never have formed a part of any plan she would even consider; helplessly, she cast about for an answer, knowing all the while that only one was possible. Holt was looking at her and his brow was furrowing as he waited. Heroically, she stamped on her own wishes, and then realised there was no point in being half hearted about it.

"I don't see why not," she said. "We'll ride over there together, just like a hack. It'll be fun." She forced a not too unnatural smile, and was rewarded with a beaming ear to ear response from her young devotee, the effect enhanced rather than diminished by the smear of chocolate on her upper lip.

"Excellent," Holt said, and the look of approbation he bestowed on Sophy very nearly made her blush. He stood up then and rinsed out his tea mug.

"You two have horses to ride out," he said, "and I've got Teddy to walk. We'll start thinking about that show in a day or two." He looked at Kitty then. "I doubt that Rufus will be ready," he said to her, "so don't be giving Jennifer any ideas."

Chapter Thirty Eight

Terry knew all about Downside Equestrian Centre when she announced rather diffidently in the pub that evening she was about to begin her new competitive career in two weeks time.

"Dad sells them hay," he said. "I usually deliver it. It's an awkward gateway off the road with a big trailer. They take out one of the posts on show days to get the lorries in, but nobody bothers just for me."

Sophy fiddled with her orange juice and delicately extracted a crisp from the packet on the table in front of her.

"Is there anywhere you haven't been with that tractor of yours?" she asked him, crunching the crisp and wiping a fragment off her lip.

"Oh, we get about," he said airily, and he started as a hand dropped on his shoulder.

"You certainly do," the man said, and they both recognised Harry the policeman, out of uniform now he was off duty.

"There's a drink for you both behind the bar," he said. He grinned at Terry. "In recognition, and to show there's no hard feelings. So long as you don't do it again, of course." He winked at Sophy, and she realised he was referring to both the accident and to Terry's predilection for illegal parking.

"He won't be stopping there again on my account," Sophy said.

"I had heard," Harry said. "You young people, no staying power. A new job every five minutes. Just don't fall off that horse of yours." He squeezed Terry's shoulder again, almost paternally. "Bloody good show," he said. "And it's in the paper. Happy New Year to you both."

As he returned to his friends at the bar, the landlord proffered Terry an empty glass, confirming his offer.

"Well, that's a turn up," Terry said. "Who'd have thought a copper would ever buy me a drink?"

"And me," Sophy pointed out.

"It's no surprise any bloke wanting to buy *you* a drink," Terry said gallantly, but Sophy wasn't listening.

"So what's this about the paper?" she asked him. "That reporter woman said you'd be in it. Are you on the front page?"

Terry's brief hour of fame, for he was indeed pictured on the front page, complete with tractor in the very act of dragging the crashed car out of the trees, faded rapidly into merely a memory over the following days.

With a fixed goal to aim for, intermittent bad weather occasionally disrupting the best laid plans, and two horses to ride each day, Sophy was beginning to find the pattern of life very full compared with the irritable, empty indolence of just a few months ago.

The pending exhibition at the gallery also involved her mother sometimes working later than usual, and for the first time in her life she found herself taking responsibility for a few basic household chores; twice she even managed to prepare supper with reasonable success, although that was largely due to Mrs. Mullins' advice about what was easiest to cook when she saw her standing in the shop weighing pre-packed TV dinners in each hand.

There were days when it was a positive relief to meet Terry for a couple of hours in the pub of an evening, and relax with a feeling that she had achieved all that could reasonably have been expected of her that day. As for the young man himself, although he had not attempted to kiss her again, without realising it she was beginning to take for granted his steady, uncritical admiration, not to mention his availability whenever she wanted to escape from mother or the washing up.

Gypsy was progressing well. At least, Peter Holt seemed to think so, in spite of his occasional lapses into a flat shape and a tendency to lean on her hand and fall on his inside shoulder, especially when cantering left. It was maddening, and when he rode the horse himself it didn't happen, as he was able to demonstrate by offering the old devil a loose rein. Those were the days when he had to remind her that 'if it was easy everybody would do it,' and that he'd been practising for forty years rather than four months.

Annie-May, of course was quite different. Actually remaining in control was much less of an issue now, but as the paces became less volatile some of the brilliance was also fading. She was able to produce her round and swinging without difficulty, and she had cantered her once or twice without losing the shape, but it was almost as though now the mare had understood what was being asked of her, she was becoming bored with the whole enterprise.

Half way through the first week of the new year, satisfied she had finally insured herself, in the mid-morning after her lesson on Gypsy Holt surprised her by telling her to take the mare out for a hack.

"She needs variety," he said. "Arabs have a notoriously short attention span, and some say they're smarter than other breeds too so endless schooling makes them sour quicker than say, warmbloods. That may be why there's relatively few Arabs at the top in dressage. Considering their natural advantages you'd think there'd be more." He winked at her. "If we want to make Annie-May the exception, we'll start by keeping her mind fresh."

Sophy remembered her own carefully bred and prepared dressage horses of yesteryear.

They'd been quite content to work round the school indefinitely, in any pace or exercise asked of them, in measured, adequately forward, balanced steps which would always score at least a seven; perhaps they too would have benefited from a brisk canter over the common, or a hack down the road and through the village for a change of scene; looking back, compared with Annie-May, or even Gypsy on a better day, it seemed to her now that they were just following orders without much enthusiasm or interest in what they were doing. Bit like me when I started at the shop, she thought.

She did not have time to pursue the parallel. Kitty and Jennifer, as usual close enough to overhear the conversation, and due back at school the next day, instantly demanded to go too.

Sophy, with Gypsy's tack still over her arm, and already a little doubtful about how Annie-May might behave for her out on the huge expanse of the open Down, demurred. Peter Holt frowned.

"In that case I think I'd better come as well," he said. He spoke to Kitty. "I bet you know every ride round here for miles. Isn't there a bridle path off the Steeplehurst road? Can you get back from there?"

He turned to Sophy.

"It won't hurt to keep off the hill for your first ride out. She could be a handful up there with the wind under her tail. And she's only been out once since she's been here. I think you'd have been OK on your own, she'd feel dependent on you, but if one of those ponies gets excited….." He left the sentence unfinished, relieved her of Gypsy's saddle and waved the two girls away. "Go and get ready then," he said, opening Gypsy's stable door to tack him up again.

Sophy was still hesitating. Annie-May was so, well, Annie-May, and on the road with traffic, and motor bikes, and tractors, even dogs, anything might make her spook, or buck, or just run away. She was confident with her in the school now, and of course that was why Peter wanted her to go out with her, but she was so unlike all the horses she'd ridden before, she was narrow and quick and so *off the ground* all the time.

It didn't help that until lately, on solid old Gypsy, almost her whole riding career had taken place in the safe confines of an arena or a collecting ring.

Miss Brown watched the little convoy leave the yard from the office window, with Kitty riding proudly at its head, with unaccustomed, slightly proprietorial feelings. From being more or less totally detached from her livery customers, regarding them as a time consuming distraction from the more commercial aspects of running the estate, since recommending her yard to her friend Jenny she'd found herself taking a more personal interest in both her human and equine clientele. And since opening this morning's post she also knew something they didn't, which might matter a great deal to everybody in the not too distant future.

While it had suited all the concerned parties at the time to circulate the rumour that the Fairgate Estate was owned by an absentee Arab sheikh, in fact it had been bought as an investment vehicle by a Russian oligarch with long term retirement pretensions to enjoy the life style of an English country gentleman. Having since fallen out of favour, and now coming under increasing political pressure at home, all of his UK holdings as a consequence were about to be put on the market.

Although the estate's farmers, with binding, long term tenancies, were unlikely to be materially affected, the livery customers were all on monthly notice agreements. It was entirely possible she herself could be out of a job before very long.

Also in the morning mail was a brief note on Kenley Industries memo pad notepaper, in her friend's remembered, spidery handwriting, announcing her return in a few days time, and expressing the cryptic hope that her horse was 'behaving as well as her instructor.'

In spite of her other, more disturbing news, Miss Brown allowed herself a small, wry smile. It seemed that Peter Holt was still on someone's mind even after a fortnight's absence and at a distance of many hundreds of miles.

The principal object occupying Sophy's mind for most of that morning's ride was remaining in control of an irritable, wound up, volatile ex-racehorse who seemed perversely intent on reminding both herself and her rider just how difficult a highly strung Arab mare can be once the torch has been lit.

To be fair, it wasn't Annie-May who started it. Passing through the village they were trotting comfortably past the shop when Rufus, in spite of being second in the file, took sudden exception to a pram on the pavement. A violent spook almost dropped Jennifer into the road, and Rufus himself backed abruptly into Annie-May's chest trotting behind him.

She threw her head wildly in that familiar circular motion, ripping the reins from Sophy's hands, and jinked a huge leap right into what was fortunately a clear carriageway. Holt, bringing up the rear of the ride, was powerless to directly assist either Sophy or Jennifer, and they were necessarily obliged to help themselves.

Still in front, Kitty stopped and turned round. Rufus, having now decided the pram and its occupant and driver were harmless, allowed his jockey to recover herself and quickly resumed normal service.

Annie-May, well accustomed as she was to working in a professional, well mannered string, was seriously annoyed and demonstrated her displeasure by snatching at the rein as Sophy tried to retake it and setting off down the road in a sharp hand canter.

It was frightening, or it would have been if she'd had time to be frightened. Her mind racing, feeling the mare unsure of her footing in canter on the tarmac, Sophy just had the sense to sit as still as she could and overcome her first instinct to pull her up and break the stride, hugely increasing the chance of a fall. Two cars coming towards her pulled over quickly and stopped. Gingerly, she steered her round the corner: there was a grass verge opposite the pub, and it was possible to guide the mare on to it. Roughly and without ceremony or any attempt at sensitivity, she hauled on the reins and stopped her on the grass, largely by main force. Annie-May planted her feet deep in the turf with her ears flat back and snorted angrily. Keeping the reins stretched, Sophy rested her hands on the pommel of the saddle and took a deep breath of relief as the rest of the ride appeared around the corner.

Peter Holt was ashen faced beneath his ancient riding hat, but still watching his charges and riding with his usual automatic competence.

"Thank *God*," he said as he rode Gypsy up to her, and the fervour in his voice astonished her. Then she remembered the last time he'd seen a rider leave his ride along the road, and what had happened next. She gasped herself then, at the horrific thought that it could have happened to *her* this morning. Watching his face, she saw him striving to take charge of his emotions and the situation. He took a deep breath and caught her eye. His deliberate manner steadied her own nerves, and she looked back at him with a weak but determined smile.

"Alright then," he said. "I'll go in front, Sophy at the back. Kitty, you can tell us where to go."

Kitty's local knowledge brought them back to the stables along a circuitous farm track of dubious legality as a public bridleway, but feeling as he did Holt was not about to suggest a lengthy detour.

As for Sophy, Annie-May was obstinately refusing to settle into any sort of relaxed stride, constantly tossing her head and fidgeting with the bridle even when they were only walking.

Matters were not improved when it started to rain with increasing intensity, a cold, hard, early January rain driven on a rising wind which froze hands and quickly penetrated even Sophy's expensive riding anorak. All four of them were heartily glad to finally return to the stables after a ride which it seemed to Sophy had set back her progress, and Annie-May's, by a huge measure.

The man had the advantage over his three companions of vast experience and extra strength, and in a bare ten minutes Gypsy was rubbed down, rugged and furnished with a hay net.

Sophy, struggling with a still fractious mare who simply would not stand still, saw him pass her stable door without a glance on his way to assist with the ponies.

It was another ten minutes before he came at last to join her and took hold of Annie-May's head collar. Finally, the horse allowed herself to be massaged dry and have a rug thrown over her. She was standing on her saturated, rumpled quarter sheet, and he lifted her front feet to release it.

"You'd better take this home and wash it," he said, hanging it over the door beside the saddle.

Sophy, with Annie-May at last behaving herself and taking an interest in her hay net, turned towards him with tears in her eyes as inactivity finally drained the last vestiges of adrenalin from her.

"I was so frightened," she whispered, looking down at the straw. Without realising she was doing it, she patted the horse beside her and began to toy with the rug surcingle. Annie-May half turned her head, as though she was listening.

"So was I," Holt said in a firm voice. He did not need add that he had every excuse to anticipate the worst; instead, he resorted to the commonsense practicalities of everyday riding.

"It was just a simple, silly spook," he told her. "It was worse for you because you don't know the horse very well and you were nervous already. It was nobody's fault, and it happens somewhere to somebody a hundred times a day, with generally no harm done. You did well, you kept your head and you kept her on her feet, and I've certainly known a few with more experience than you who wouldn't have." He paused. His tone became more matter of fact as he went on.

"There's more to being a professional rider than schooling and winning prizes," he told her. "Dreaming about applause and red rosettes is only a small part of it. You've got to be able to deal with situations that other people can't or don't want to. Think of today as a good start." He smiled at her then, and she rubbed her eyes with her soaking coat sleeve and smiled weakly back.

"Attagirl," he said. "Now we've got to do something with these wet children. They can't stand in front of the tackroom heater all day, and Joe's at work until five, Kitty says. Can you take them home with you for a few hours, until you come back for the evening feed? Thirty years ago I'd have taken them home myself without a thought, but not the way things are today. Do you mind? We could have asked Miss Brown, but her car's not here and the office is locked."

Sophy picked at the sleeve of her saturated coat. Those kids must be a least as wet as her. "OK," she said doubtfully. There wasn't really much alternative.

Chapter Thirty Nine

Anthony Kenley was bored.

Those who knew him well enough to call him Tony would have said he was dangerously bored. As the son of a man whose all-consuming twin passions were business and engineering, with family a distant third, the restraining influence of a responsible father had never figured in his upbringing; and six years of more or less pleasing himself in America, paying less than lip service to what he was supposed to be doing for the company, had encouraged him to believe implicitly that the family fortune automatically entitled him to whatever he set his mind to. Whenever Anthony Kenley was bored, the consequences usually boded ill for someone.

A dark haired, well favoured man of not quite thirty who barely looked twenty five, he was confident and successful with the opposite sex and even after his misguided nuptials had continued the relentless pursuit of any woman that took his fancy. The fact that the young actress he'd married, initially dazzled by his family's wealth and what it might do for her career, had behaved with equal abandon on several film sets was making the financial aspects of their divorce especially complicated.

Since landing at Heathrow two days ago, a week earlier than his mother was expecting him, he'd had little to do except loaf about the Chichester house getting in the way of the staff and pretending he was out when his American lawyers telephoned.

His mother's resident PA, Hilda Gordon, a smart young woman in her mid-thirties, was already struggling to cope with his non too subtle advances, and in an attempt to distract him, or better still persuade him to move out, told him about the house his mother had bought for him in Stepford.

A spark of interest shone in his eyes. The notion of having to stay in the same house as his mother for any length of time was less than appealing, and she would be certain to cramp his style and expect him to work for a living doing something tedious, unnecessary and irrelevant. His father, belatedly aware of his son's sexual proclivities and talent for evading responsibility, had left him very little money of his own, merely tied shares in the company, and unless or until he could persuade her otherwise his finances were largely dependent on the whim of his mother.

He leaned forward slightly over the desk, quite unashamedly inspecting the woman's cleavage while he spoke to her.

"Sounds interesting," he said. "Ready, is it?"

She pushed her chair back from the desk, away from him.

"The furnishers finished last week and the housekeeper moved in yesterday," she said. "Your mother left it to me to manage before she left."

He moved round the desk. She was quite attractive, with her horn rimmed spectacles, pleasantly full figure and businesslike, efficient manner. An hour or two in her company this afternoon would break the pattern nicely. Or he could go and look at this house.

"How will I get there?" he asked her.

"Eddy can take you in the Bentley or I'll hire a car for you," she said, reaching for the telephone, fortunately on her other side.

"The hell you will," he responded. "You think I'll be seen dead in a cheap runabout? And as for that misery of a chauffeur and that great mausoleum of a Bentley......Give me that paper."

She was momentarily confused. On her desk was an open copy of the 'Financial Times,' and the just delivered local paper, still folded. He reached over and picked it up, turned to the motoring section and scanned the advertisements.

"That one," he said, stabbing the page with his finger. "Have it brought round. Pronto. Tell 'em it's on approval, or buy it if you have to. I dare say the firm can afford it. It'll be on the firm's insurance then too, won't it."

"I'm sure it can," Hilda said frostily. She was plainly less than enthused by the prospect of spending a significant sum of her employer's money on no other say so than the sudden fancy of her notoriously extravagant son.

He looked down at her with a frown, and this time he wasn't inspecting her chest. The threat behind his eyes was unmistakeable. Hilda Gordon was intimidated, as he'd known she would be, in just the same way as his managers in America had been. He was the boss's son, and so far as they knew could make or break their careers on any whim he wanted.

"I'll see to it," she said lamely, and the frown was replaced by an engaging grin. In spite of herself, she grinned back, a grin replaced by a frown of her own as soon as he'd left the room. There was no doubting his attraction, but his reputation had preceded him and she felt like kicking herself for responding. She reached again for the phone, and noticed he'd taken the paper with him.

His head reappeared round the door. "I'll have a sandwich before I go out. Tell the cook. ASAP. Salmon or ham." The door closed again.

*

With all four of the girls back at school there was a feeling of the 'Marie Celeste' about the stables as Sophy turned in the gate and parked beside the house. Unusually for that time of day, Miss Brown's car was also absent. Still, the rain had stopped and although the cloud persisted it was briefly warmer than yesterday; according to the radio, a sunny afternoon would be followed by a fine, frosty night, clouding over later with a suggestion of snow before morning.

She paused for a moment before she opened the car door, reflecting as much on yesterday as on what she might do today. Playing Scrabble with Kitty and Jennifer in the flat yesterday afternoon, with all three of them wearing her old jumpers while their clothes dried, had been more fun than she would have imagined; on the other hand, she'd allowed herself to be persuaded into giving just the two of them another lesson this evening after school, which might not be quite so much fun with raised expectations to fill.

A tap on the car window surprised her, and Peter Holt was standing there in his usual flat cap, an open anorak and walking boots, his pipe in one hand and Teddy in the other, and no riding gear in sight. She opened the door.

"'Morning," he said cheerfully. "Just passing with some ideas about a programme for today. After what happened yesterday, I think it's specially important that you school Annie-May first, and that I'm not there. You both need to get some confidence back into your relationship, and it's best if you can do it by yourselves. I think you're good enough now, and generous enough, not to need me for that." His gaze seemed to penetrate deep inside her head at that moment, and she knew exactly the value of the compliment contained in that word 'generous' as soon as he said it. It was a far cry from......She felt herself redden slightly in the chilly morning air.

"Take lots of time and be nice to her," he ended with a smile.

"But I thought I'd ride Gypsy first," Sophy said uncertainly. "I sort of wanted to feel I was prepared a bit, if you know what I mean, in case…"

He understood her apprehension, but he had ridden and worked Annie-May himself enough to feel he knew her, and there were other reasons to insist on her doing as he asked. She got out of the car, and as she bent down to fuss the dog he explained.

"Annie-May's not a horse to compromise," he said. "Think of it like this. You had a row with her yesterday, and if she sees you ride Gypsy first today she'll think you'd rather ride him than make up with her." She stared at him, and he had the good grace to laugh at himself.

"I know," he said. "Stupid, isn't it? But I always think of horses as people, especially when there's problems. I used to get ragged for it dreadfully when I was a student, and the racing lads took the mickey no end, although I do know some of them did it too, on the quiet. You find these things out after a few beers sometimes."

He stopped himself and turned away.

"No good going down memory lane," he muttered. "Certainly not after yesterday's shenanigans." He physically shook himself before he looked back towards her.

"Anyway, it'll be better for you too. You won't be worrying about Annie-May while you're working Gypsy. Now about Gypsy. It's still far enough away from the competition to ride through the whole test without him learning to anticipate, so warm him up, ride it twice, and then go out hacking for half an hour to keep him sweet. And I'll see all three of you tomorrow."

"But I haven't learnt the test yet," she objected., and he wagged his pipe at her.

"Well, learn it when you go home for lunch," he said, and with a word to the dog he turned on his heel and was gone.

*

After a moment's pause she opened the library door without knocking. Damn the man and his conceit. It was a public room, why should she knock?

Tony Kenley was sprawled across an armchair hiding behind the paper. She put the car keys beside the empty plate on the adjacent table.

"I spoke with your mother," she said to him as he lowered the paper. "She'll be back on Sunday. She says to buy you the car and you can move to Stepford whenever you want."

"Thought she would," he said indifferently. Mother was tougher than dad had been, but he'd always been able to handle her in the end. Not that he wasn't fond of her, of course, well, to some extent at least. At a distance. He realised the prim and attractive Miss Gordon was looking at him with something very like disapproval. He grinned to himself.

"You could move in too if you wanted," he said to her, and it seemed he was more than half serious. The secretary was scandalised, but he disarmed her with another grin and indicated a photograph on an inside page of the Chichester paper.

"Mother said in a letter she'd retired Annie-May to do dressage and was sponsoring a local rider," he said. "Is this her?"

Hilda Gordon had never met Sophy, and the full colour photo of a young man in a white shirt and a crooked tie escorting a strikingly pretty girl outside the theatre meant nothing to her. She read the caption underneath.

'Terry Godwin, the hero of last week's accident, takes his dressage rider girl friend Sophy Taylor to the pantomime.'

Like most local people, Miss Gordon had heard of the Christmas Eve accident.

"That boy saved a life," she said.

"Never mind him," Tony said impatiently. "Is that the girl?"

She might not know the face, but she knew the name. It was the one on the cheque she sent to Fairgate every month.

"Must be," she said, a trifle reluctantly. The man's intentions were transparent even to someone who had only known him a few days. Whoever the girl was, surely she didn't deserve Tony Kenley's dubious attentions. Not that she could do anything about it.

"Hmm," Tony mused. "I think I might stop by and see Annie-May. Where are they keeping her now?"

Chapter Forty

It took her nearly an hour after Peter had departed to feed, muck out, fill hay nets and tidy up the yard and her two horses' rugs, and to put Blackie and Rufus out in the paddock with some hay. The other two ponies lived out all the time, and someone had already put hay in their field and gone. One of them had obviously rolled since, and his rug was crooked and in danger of sliding off completely.

It was none of her responsibility, but still she caught him and sorted it out, although not without slipping in the mud a couple of times as the pony was wary of a stranger. It was a voluntary gesture not lost on Miss Brown, who drove in just at that moment from a meeting on one of the farms. Her business suit contrasted sharply with Sophy's grubby jodhpurs as she came over to her.

"That was a Christian gesture," she said to her, with evident approval, knowing exactly who was responsible for what throughout her small empire. She also looked approvingly at the just swept yard, but made no further comment.

"Mrs. Kenley will be back on Sunday," she informed her. "Perhaps you'd like to pass that on to Mr. Holt."

It crossed her mind to also tell her that the future of the yard could be in doubt, but it was perhaps a little too soon for that. A few minutes later, glancing through the window as she settled at her desk, she saw Sophy emerge from the tackroom with a saddle and bridle over her arm and open the door to Annie-May's stable.

Annie-May allowed herself to be saddled and bridled, intermittently interrupting the process by pulling at her hay net, and finally it was time to bite the bullet and take her down to the school. It wasn't until she led her up to the mounting block in the corner of the arena and had checked the girth and slid the stirrups down, that the full significance of what she was doing struck her.

For the first time in her life, and with no support from Peter Holt close at hand, she was about to ride someone else's horse, and be paid for it; and a year ago, even six months ago, it was the sort of horse, with the sort background, that Sophy Taylor would not have ridden for any amount of money.

She stood for a long moment before she stepped on to the block, pondering where she had been and who she had been all that time ago, and where she was today, and Annie-May turned her elegant head towards her as if asking what she was waiting for. She could have sworn the horse was frowning. Even that was not a thought she would have had a year ago, before that man had explained that horses had thoughts of their own and were not merely vehicles to obey their riders' instructions.

She settled herself into the saddle, and preoccupied as she was did not at first notice that the mare, unusually for her, did not fidget or attempt to walk away as her feet found the stirrups and she checked they were not twisted.

Ready at last, she asked for walk and Annie-May gave an audible, soft sigh and did not move. A firmer pressure with both legs also had no effect, and she felt the mare's back rise under her.

Uncertainty gave way to apprehension. What was happening? She was always a keen handful for the first five minutes. The awful thought came to her that perhaps she was lame after yesterday, but she'd walked to the school perfectly sound and there wasn't a mark on her. Even more awful was the abruptly conceived idea that perhaps she was about to buck her off, in revenge for that terrible yank in the mouth she'd given her on the verge outside the pub which had upset her for the rest of the morning.

She sat motionless, her mind a blank but knowing there must be a solution. It might be dangerous even to get off. What would *he* do now?

Gently, she took up a contact, and felt the tension in the mare increase. Again she waited, and again Annie-May waited with her. In desperation, she looked about her; there was no one there, and the only sound was the quiet rustle of the winter breeze through the scrubby beech trees beside the footpath.

With trepidation in her heart, she tried to remember everything she had learnt in these last months, from the laws of balance in that half forgotten book she still hadn't returned to how Rufus had unexpectedly shown his true colours in that now famous lesson. At last, with a soft and trembling hand, she asked Annie-May to turn to the left.

The contact tightened against her hand, and automatically she strengthened the aid. Annie-May turned her head, stiff and angry, but the tension through her back caused her to lose her balance and her forehand shifted half a pace to the left. The contact slackened on the instant as the turn deepened, and the horse fell forward in a tight, stuffy walk along the fence, with the reins loose and Sophy gasping with relief.

They walked all the way round the school, and the tension eased away by slow degrees, until the walk was swinging and forward but still with a bare minimum of contact. Half way round on the second circuit, with her nerve steadying as the horse relaxed more and more, and still on a long rein, Sophy thought she might dare to trot for a few steps towards the corner.

For the very first time in all her years of riding, through ponies and warmbloods to despair alone with Gypsy and inspiring tuition with Peter Holt, the *thought was aid enough*. It was *magical*.

Annie-May understood the idea without needing the physical application, and at once stepped calmly into a loose-limbed, easy trot that barely needed the rein for balance. It wasn't engaged, or round, or dressagy in any way, but somehow at that moment she *knew* with certainty that she and her lovely mare were closer than she had ever been to any horse or any person.

She rode in sitting trot, her seat as soft as the stride below her, and she could have cried with the realisation that Annie-May had forgiven her for her rudeness and roughness yesterday, and that now they were friends forever.

She changed the rein, and even rode circles in each direction, and the tempo and the stride never varied and not once did she feel any need to take the reins to actually steer. When at last it was time to walk and to stop, Annie-May seemed to read her mind as she had before and came smoothly to a halt in the centre of the school, as precisely as if the aid had been given by Peter Holt himself.

Alone in the school, she fell on her horse's neck and embraced her with both arms, rubbing her cheek on her mane, heedless with trust now that she would not be bucked off or run away with whatever she did. Annie-May stood patiently and endured this passionate demonstration as though she expected nothing less and it was only her due, and after a moment Sophy sat up and gathered her thoughts together.

If it had been possible, she would have asked Annie-May out loud if she would like to be schooled a little now; after all, they really should do some proper work; and then she knew, with the insight which comes to those few horsemen who don't just ride, but who truly identify with the person carrying them, it *was* possible to ask, though not in words.

She straightened her back, lifted her stomach and opened her chest, and eased her legs longer. As her seat deepened, she took up the reins, and Annie-May came willingly into her hand and waited to be asked the next question.

It would be an overstatement to say the work was flawless; Annie-May undoubtedly did her best, and managed to maintain her shape for most of the trot exercises, but when she needed a little help Sophy's lack of experience every now and then let down them both; and the canters, although brief, were far from balanced or elegant; nevertheless, when Peter Holt, returning from his walk, came by with Teddy and waved cheerfully over the fence from the footpath, the approval in his smile was unmistakeable.

Neither horse nor rider knew he had been observing them intermittently from high on the hill for much of the morning, half afraid he had jumped the gun with his own judgement and with yesterday's terrible reminder of the dangers fresh in his mind; yet knowing that it was time, and Sophy had to be trusted to find her own way along the stony path she had chosen.

Annie-May was rewarded with a few extra nuts in her lunch, and even Gypsy, dozing over his door, received a pat he hadn't yet earned before she drove the few minutes home for her own lunch. Mother was at work of course, so there was no one to tell of the morning's joyful miracle, and she hugged what she knew close to her soul, how she knew now how that man Holt made horses do things that most riders, including her before today, could only dream about.

There was a light blinking on the answering machine with a message from mother at the gallery. Geoff was hosting a function that evening for the exhibitors at the forthcoming exhibition, and so she would be late home.

The incongruous image of her mother handing round cocktails on a tray for presumably bearded and eccentric local artists was briefly upsetting. It was yet another, if belated, reminder of their altered status in life, but she realised then that her mother had learned to cope with …well…. poverty, much sooner and much more graciously than she had.

High with the remembered elation of those aids she hadn't needed to give, it was easy to resolve that from now on things would be different, she would never complain again, and mother would truly be proud of her and not have to only pretend any more.

There was plenty of time to ride Gypsy before she was due to teach the girls, and after looking at the test she was going to practice she spent half an hour dusting and tidying the flat before she left again. It was an unusual feeling to know that mother would be genuinely surprised and pleased with her when she got home, and then she caught a glimpse of herself in the driving mirror and could not resist a wry smile. Whatever she might feel now, she knew herself too well to expect this new, selfless person to last long. "Must try harder," she said to herself, unconsciously echoing forgotten school reports of long ago.

Miss Brown indulged in a sandwich and a pot of tea later than usual that day, in consequence of a lengthy telephone conversation with a prominent London estate agent recently commissioned to undertake a first valuation of the estate prior to putting it on the market.

Returning to her desk, she allowed herself a small sigh. It was already clear, whatever happened, that a great deal of extra work was about to come her way which had little to do with the actual running of the business, and there was no guarantee she would have a job, or a home, at the end of it.

She glanced out of the window over the sunlit yard. That coloured horse's stable was empty, and the girl's car was back in its usual place. She thought idly of the transformation in that young lady since the man Holt had come on the scene with his home truths and no nonsense; it was odd how he and her friend Jenny seemed to be a pair every time they were together; you could hardly say they had much in common.

And then she started with a sharp double take of surprise. The girl's nearly new sports car turned in the gate and parked exactly where *she* always used to park it, too damned close to the house as though she owned the place.

A young man got out, faintly familiar to her, and then as he straightened up and looked about the yard she recognised him. She'd last seen Tony Kenley just after he'd left college, before he went to America where he had apparently not been as successful as his parents had hoped. Jenny had let slip one or two details about his private life too, which were rather less than complimentary coming from his mother.

Gypsy had a lot to live up to that afternoon, and it was too much to hope that he would suddenly find a miraculous balance and cadence that had never been in evidence before.

Even so, she was pleased with him. Without realising it, the empathy she had found with Annie-May spilled over into her expectations of his very different paces and manners, and the honest gelding responded with what she first noticed as greater sensitivity to the aids, and then with a canter circle on his difficult left rein which seemed much more controlled and together than usual.

It was warm work in the sunshine in spite of the chill in the air, and she rode over to the gate and took off her jacket just as Miss Brown and a man she didn't know were coming down the short path from the yard.

Not especially interested, and keen to get on with her work, still it seemed only polite to wait; surely Miss Brown hadn't found something else to complain about.

The woman looked up at her with a neutral expression.

"This is Tony Kenley," she said. "He is home from America and come to see Annie-May."

"Hallo, Sophy," the man said, and flashed a smile at her. "I saw your picture in the paper. Doesn't do you justice, I must say."

Miss Brown, in spite of not being as familiar with his reputation as Hilda Gordon, shot him a sideways glance. When introduced to his mother's horse, he had paid her only the most cursory attention and had immediately asked about her rider. The real focus of his interest was now abundantly clear.

Sophy blushed beneath her hat.

"Pleased to meet you," she said. She was increasingly aware that she was making a favourable impression on this well dressed and very attractive young man. He was exactly the sort of person mother used to invite on social occasions and then place next to her for dinner. In those days she didn't care tuppence about any of them, but now she hadn't met someone like that for ages and he did look interesting.

Tony, astute as ever, could see he was making progress without even having to try.

"Why don't you have dinner with me tonight?" he said, cocking his head engagingly to one side as though he was pleading with her. "You can tell me all about Annie-May and what your plans are."

Terry and Bert were playing in a darts match at some pub in Chichester that evening. In fact, she wasn't going out with Terry again till Sunday. She hesitated, but Tony didn't.

"I'll pick you up here about seven," he said. "How's that?"

Swept away by his confidence, and the fact that he was Mrs. Kenley's son, she was on the point of agreeing when she remembered Kitty and Jennifer.

"I have to give a lesson," she said. "I won't be finished by then."

A feeling of relief swept over Miss Brown. She had no responsibility whatsoever for Sophy Taylor, but she was starting to like her, had sensed her naivety and she had no illusions now about Tony Kenley. He would literally eat her for breakfast, or dinner anyway, with even half a chance. Perhaps she should have a discreet word with her mother, or even Peter Holt.

Her relief was short lived.

"No problem," he rejoined. "We'll make it eight." He flashed his famous smile again. "I'll see you then." He glanced appreciatively at her stretch jodhpurs which left little to the imagination. "Look forward to it."

Before she could respond he turned back to Miss Brown.

"So how do I get to Stepford? I'd better go and look at this house. Have you seen it?" He touched her arm and led her back towards the stables.

The older woman knew they were both being manipulated, and Sophy could well pay the price, but it was hard to see what she could do about it just at that moment. It might be none of her business, but still she made a resolution to speak to Miss Taylor later in the day if the opportunity arose.

It might be in both their interests. It was hard to imagine that Kenley boy had more than one thing on his mind, dating Miss Taylor, and she knew his mother would be furious if he got the girl into trouble of any kind, and she herself had not intervened when she might have done.

Chapter Forty One

The lesson went well, in spite of being interrupted after about ten minutes by the other two girls arriving and demanding to be included.

Jennifer insisted she ride Rufus again, although he wasn't actually misbehaving, and with Joe Fittleworth leaning on the gate chatting to the other two mothers under the lights as she rode by, and hearing their flattering comments, it proved an agreeable end to what had turned out to be a long and demanding day.

If the truth was told, chatting in the tackroom afterwards and caught up in the aftermath of her lesson, she had all but forgotten about Tony Kenley until Joe, glancing out the window, suddenly exclaimed, "Good lord, here's your old car come back. I don't believe it."

Tony Kenley had made the most of his time since he'd issued his invitation. Arriving unannounced at the house in Stepford, the housekeeper had opened the door to him with a doubtful expression, only resolved after a phone call to Chichester to confirm he was who he said he was.

However, with his identity established, he rapidly took charge. The housekeeper, a highly experienced agency professional in her fifties well accustomed to the autocratic peccadilloes of wealthy, spoilt young men, showed him over the house with its elegant, almost all new furnishings and asked him when he would be moving in.

"Oh, whenever," he said vaguely. "But I will be dining here tonight, and probably staying over. Get a bed ready. Cook for me and one guest. For about nine. I don't suppose there's any wine in the house. Get a couple of decent bottles from the pub on the corner. And after you've served the meal, make yourself scarce."

He didn't actually wink at her, but he might as well have done.

The housekeeper, very well paid to do as she was bid and mind her own business, accepted the instructions with the indifference of someone who is not personally involved on any level with any forthcoming events, whatever they might be.

She did ask what he would like for dinner, but it seemed the food was not his primary concern and he just waved a negligent arm and said, "Oh, I don't know, not too fancy, do what goes with the wine."

Sophy followed Joe's gaze and saw with a slight shock that it really was her old car under the yard lights, and the man getting out was Tony Kenley.

It took a moment to adjust her thoughts.

"I'll have to go," she said awkwardly. "It's Tony Kenley, he's come to take me out."

The murmur of surprise was checked by the man himself appearing in the doorway. He made no pretence at sociability and addressed himself only to Sophy.

"Well, Miss Taylor, are we ready?" He held his arm out to her.

Sophy was embarrassed in front of the others, and she could sense Joe Fittleworth's irritation at being totally ignored and also at the rudeness of the man not even glancing at the other two women present.

"Well, hardly," she demurred. "I'll have to go home and change." If he was taking her out to dinner, it would scarcely be appropriate to arrive at a smart restaurant in riding clothes, and redolent of horses.

"Oh, you'll do fine just as you are," he said. "Why don't you leave your car here? I'll drive you and bring you back for it later."

It wasn't quite what she'd expected, and momentarily she was taken aback, but just like this afternoon it was hard to resist his breezy, confident, just-trust-me-and-I'll-deal-with-it attitude. He seemed to take it for granted it that people would agree with him, which made it very difficult to suggest something else. Anyway, she reasoned, not taking two cars made some sort of sense. She grabbed her coat and handbag from the back of her own car and got into his as he held the door open for her.

A flood of confused emotions gripped her as she settled into the passenger seat; there was the well remembered scent and feel of luxurious, expensive leather invading her senses; the familiar dashboard with its speedometer reaching to improbable speeds she had never attempted, or wanted to; the radio, by chance still tuned to the last station she had listened to driving into Chichester that last time. He couldn't know it had once been her car, how could he? Presumably he just wanted something fast and flashy and this was it.

Thoughts were hurtling around her head like sparks spinning from a Catherine wheel. She fingered her father's St. Christopher medal round her neck with a lump in her throat and real confusion now over how she would talk to him, and how somehow she had got herself into this position without ever really agreeing to anything. It had all just happened, as though he'd wanted it to and so it had to be.

He got in beside her and slammed the door. A moment later the engine started with that remembered, low, rumble of power, and he revved it with obvious satisfaction, attracting disapproving attention from the small group watching from the tackroom door.

"I do hope this isn't going to end in tears," Joe Fittleworth said grimly to no one in particular, and one of the young girls' parents exchanged a knowing, faintly concerned glance with him.

"What do you mean, Daddy?" Kitty said, tugging at his sleeve. "Isn't he a very nice man?"

The woman frowned, and mouthed, 'out of the mouths of babes' at him and he made a wry face.

"Never you mind," he said to his daughter. "Say goodnight to Blackie and tell Jennifer it's time to go home."

Tony Kenley drove skilfully and fast along the dark country road, exploiting the car's performance in ways that she never had.

"Useful sort of motor, this," he said to her without taking his eyes off the road. "Lucky to find it in a one horse town like Chichester. Only one lady owner, apparently."

She did not reply. In fact, it was hard to think of anything to say.

"Do you ride yourself?" she asked him at last, and he shot a glance at her over his shoulder.

"Did once," he said. "Dad thought I might like polo. Didn't take to it." He didn't add that having realised it would require effort and application to achieve any sort of competence, he simply couldn't be bothered.

He stopped the car unexpectedly outside a pub fronting directly on to the road.

"Nearly there," he said. "I'll just be a minute," and he got out and left her.

Unsure where she was, and relieved to have a moment to herself, she peered out of the window. The pub was a few yards from a cross roads and the sign, a stylised image of sheep and a twisted pole, hung out over the pavement, but there was no name on it.

He returned with a hessian bag. The contents, clearly bottles, clinked together as he put it in her lap. He turned left at the cross roads, and then almost immediately left again into a communal drive which led to the rear of a handsome old house which shared its parking amenities with its neighbour.

He opened the car door, and when he smiled at her he seemed even more attractive in the dim, interior roof light.

"Home," he said. "Are you hungry? Let's see what's for dinner."

He led her round the corner of the building and clattered the heavy knocker on the front door.

It was a relief to find there was someone else in the house. For all her inexperience, Sophy was finally beginning to realise that although he was Mrs. Kenley's son, and so handsome his smile and his eyes turned her inside out, for all that he still could be, from her point of view, well, anybody, really.

As if sensing her doubts, once in the house he became charm personified. He helped her off with her coat and hung it in the hall along with her bag. He waited while she took off her half chaps, and at his suggestion she removed her jodhpur boots.

"It's all carpets," he said, "isn't that so, Mrs......?" He mumbled the housekeeper's name as she hovered in attendance. In fact, as a matter of no importance to him, he hadn't so much forgotten it as never asked what it was.

The woman was unperturbed. "That's so," she agreed. "Dinner is ready, sir, whenever you would like it."

"Oh, we'll get stuck in," he rejoined. He handed her his hessian bag. "Pour me a double v." He looked at Sophy. "Do you want to powder your nose or whatever it is you women do every five minutes?" The smile robbed the words of any hint of criticism, but still she hadn't even washed her hands since leaving the yard.

"I think I will," she said, and the housekeeper escorted her upstairs and left her on the landing with an indicative gesture.

Her stockinged feet felt odd on the thick piled carpet, and next to the bathroom a bedroom door was open, with a neatly turned down double bed in evidence. Much later, in retrospect, she had the idea that the presently nameless housekeeper might have left that door open on purpose, as some hint of what she might expect later in the evening.

Anthony Kenley was no fool. For all his wayward habits, he was sharp and perceptive in his own interests.

It quickly became clear to him that while Sophy's manner and hesitant conversation seemed altogether too innocent for a girl who must be at least twenty, in other ways she was socially sophisticated; the housekeeper, no doubt seeking to impress her new master, had raided the local shop with a vengeance after he'd left that afternoon, and had produced a five course meal with all the cutlery and condiments to match.

Sophy negotiated this repast as though she was accustomed to such fare everyday, which indeed she had been until a few months ago, but unusually for one of his prospective conquests she resolutely refused to drink anything but orange juice. Moreover, his attempts to flirt with her met with a disappointing lack of response.

In fact, as the evening wore on, he became increasingly persuaded that she could be pursuing an agenda of her own, and whatever slight conscience he might have had about his intentions slipped easily into abeyance.

She couldn't possibly know he was technically still married, or actually anything much about him at all. On the other hand, riding for his mother, she could hardly be unaware that married or not he was possibly the most eligible prospective partner in the south of England.

There was only so much interest he could pretend in Annie-May and the trivial happenings at Fairgate Stables, and when she politely asked him about his work in America, although patently she could know nothing about it, it was surprisingly difficult to convince even himself that his transatlantic sojourn had been a huge success.

Under the influence of his opening double vodka and most of a bottle of wine, by the time the housekeeper brought their coffee to the table and announced she was retiring for the night he was beginning to feel irritated, with her and with himself. The evening was not progressing quite as he'd hoped. Sophy, still in her white riding shirt, had undone the top button in the warmth of the dining room exposing a delicious, tantalising glimpse of white skin behind a silver chain; and what with one thing and another, he hadn't been with a woman for several weeks. Probably a record, he thought to himself, grimly. He put down his coffee cup and with a sudden movement shifted his chair next to hers.

"Now have a glass of wine," he said, "and let's not be so silly." He filled her glass and put it in her hand.

She felt his breath on her ear. It was alarming, but the glass was in her hand and he was smiling that smile only a foot away and she drank it.

In seconds her head clouded and the room swayed, and all the reasons why she didn't drink and didn't like alcohol leapt forcefully back at her. She put down the glass, gripping the table with her other hand to steady herself.

"That's my girl," he said, and he put his hand quite shamelessly on the inside of her thigh. It was firm, strong and warm, and breathlessly exciting beneath the tight, stretchy material of her breeches. The surge of too long contained, eager desire ran through him. This girl wasn't just beautiful, hell, they were all beautiful; she was athletic, lissom and active. He *wanted* her, wanted her to expend her strength and physique for his pleasure, while he pleasured her in ways which he flattered himself had never yet failed him.

Sophy was struggling to stop her head swimming; for a moment she was unaware, and then tried to pull away from him.

"Don't," she said, but still the alarm in her voice was muted. "I don't want it." It was hard to sound angry when the room was shifting around her. She tried again to move away from him but he had his arm around her and unexpectedly he kissed her neck below her ear and a sudden strange tingle made her shiver and he felt her resistance pause.

Encouraged, he went too far, too fast.

He pushed his hand hard up her thigh and deep into her crotch, parting her legs and softly churning his probing fingers against the shielding, yielding fabric.

She gasped with the shock, and the shock cleared her head. She crashed her hand across his face with all her strength and his chair tilted backwards and then fell behind hers, with the man in a heap on his back with his legs akimbo in the air. She leapt up and ran to the door, not hearing the foul imprecation which followed her.

The light was still on in the hall, and she snatched her bag from the hook and picked up her jodhpur boots. There were sounds from the room behind her through the open door and it was urgent to get away. His coat was hung on top of hers, and there wasn't time to unhook it; she slid the bolt on the front door, turned the latch and fled from him into the dark night.

Chapter Forty Two

The gravel of the front path pressed painfully into her stockinged feet, but the road was a mere ten metres from the house. She opened the gate in the iron railings protecting the front garden and ran down the empty lane towards the junction, her handbag flailing wildly in her hand, and then she dropped a boot on the tarmac with a dull clatter.

Commonsense grabbed at her racing emotions. She *had* to put her boots on. She sat down panting on a low wall fronting the last house before the main road, and the pause gave her a moment to look about her and take stock. He probably wouldn't follow her, why would he? There'd be no sense to it, but still he might and she had no illusions that she'd hurt him badly enough to stop him. She shuddered slightly. She might have made him so angry he would come anyway.

She got to her feet. The cross roads was lit by a single tall lamppost, and the hospitable lights and sounds of an ordinary pub evening were filtering out through the misted windows of the adjacent 'Crooked Crook' into the cold night air.

Did she dare go in and ask for help? They might know him and not believe her, and the prospect of explaining what had happened, of talking to strangers just then, was appalling beyond words. She simply could not do it, no matter what.

The sign beneath the lamppost pointed left to Steeplehurst and right to Fairgate. A car went by towards Fairgate, headlights boring into the pitch black night beyond the halo cast by the street lamp. It didn't take us long to get here, she thought. It can't be that far, and her watch told her it was still only a quarter past ten.

There was no sign of life from the way she had come, and she slung her bag over her shoulder and set off firmly down the Fairgate road, the fear of pursuit and sense of outrage fuelling a rising anger that somehow she was herself at least partly responsible for finding herself in this position.

How could I be so stupid? She repeated to herself, over and over again. How could I be so *stupid?*

The starless dark folded over her like a dense black duvet as she left the village behind. It was just possible to see the white line in the middle of the road, and she followed it as the road swung left and then right, the lodestar leading her home. Without pausing in her stride, she fumbled in her bag for her mobile phone.

The first thought, to phone mother, was quickly banished. She wasn't at home, and anyway she didn't have a car. She strode on, and Peter Holt and Terry came into her mind. The phone lit up, she found Terry's number, and the screen announced there was no reception. Doggedly, she strode on.

Two cars passed her, one in each direction, loud in the quiet night and giving her plenty of time to step to the side of the road. It was a relief that neither driver paused in his steady career, although she must have been plainly visible in her bright white shirt. Had one of them stopped......panic struck her. Should she go with them, or run? Desperately, she forced herself to think calmly.

It started to rain, rain mixed with tiny shards of ice as the night and the cold deepened, and the sweat of her rapid walk was chilling against her skin whenever she paused. The sleet intensified and a slight but icy wind blew through her thin, wet shirt and made her shiver.

The lights of the last car to overtake her had lit up a bus shelter a hundred yards ahead. In the sleet and the dark she almost walked past it, despite frequent glances to the side of the road. It was a haven, of sorts, at least from the wind and the sleet if not from the cold. She sank on to the bench and wrapped her arms around her chest to rub herself warm. And the phone had a signal!

It was shirt-sleeve order for Terry and Bert too as they took their turns on the oche in the crowded bar. They were winning the match, just. And then Terry's phone rang, with Sophy's name in evidence.

"Hi, Soph," he said cheerfully. "What's up?"

For a long moment she couldn't speak. The sounds of a warm, busy, congenial pub carried easily past his voice, and it seemed as though she was connected to another planet as a wrinkle of wind found its way inside her shirt and briefly made her shiver uncontrollably.

"Help," she said then, automatically speaking the first word that came to her. The shake in her voice abruptly alerted him that this was no ordinary phone call. Glass of shandy in one hand and phone in the other, he stepped away from his friends into a corner.

"Tell me," he said, and Bert, glancing towards him as his turn to throw came nearer, saw his face change as she answered.

"That's the 'Crooked Crook,'" he said as she described the pub sign, the only reference she knew to tell him where she was. "I know it. I know that bus shelter too, but there's no buses on that road after eight. But what're you doing out there? I'm coming, but it'll be half an hour at least." Unaware of the extremity of her situation, he made an attempt at levity. "Jump up and down to keep warm. I'll be as quick as I can."

He put the phone back in his pocket. Bert thrust his darts into his hand.

"Double twelve," he said.

"I have to go," Terry said. He faced the board. His second dart scraped into the double. "I'm sorry, guys, I do have to go. It's an emergency."

Bert and one of the opposing team tried to protest but he forestalled them. He said to Bert, "Sophy's got stranded somehow on the Stepford road." He looked across to the bar, where a mutual acquaintance was chatting to the barmaid. "Get Simon to stand in for me."

He stepped outside into the car park. In spite of being accustomed to working outside in all weathers, the cold struck him forcibly after the heated bar as he pulled on his jacket, and a few flakes of wet snow were dancing in the air. It definitely wasn't the kind of night to be stuck in a bus shelter half way to nowhere. He got into his van and drove out of the City slightly faster than the speed limits allowed.

The housekeeper's expression was a study of careful neutrality.

"I came down when I heard a bump," she said to the master of the house as he was closing the front door. "Is everything alright?" She noticed Sophy's boots were missing. "Has the young lady gone?"

He turned towards her. The right side of his face was a livid red and the eye was closing.

"We suffered a disagreement," he said evenly, as though it was a simple, everyday occurrence. He frowned pointedly. "I'm sure I can rely on your discretion, Mrs....."

"Branksome," she supplied for him. "Of course, sir." She paused. "Since I'm downstairs, I might as well clear away now instead of in the morning."

"You do that," he said, irritably indifferent. "And get me another drink, and a packet of frozen peas."

She turned away quickly, or he would have seen the smile and heard the subdued chuckle she couldn't quite suppress.

It didn't quite take Terry half an hour, but the twenty five minutes it did take felt like half a year.

By the time his tatty white van made its appearance, and he pulled in to the bus stop lay-by with its hazard lights flashing, Sophy was chilled through to the bone and beginning to think she would never be warm again. She was so cold and shivering so hard he had to help her into the van, and he quickly threw his own coat over her, turned up the heating and revved the engine in an attempt to force more heat from the fan.

"What the hell are you doing out here?" he asked her as he pulled out into the road, and she'd had time to decide what to tell him.

"I came with a friend and we had a row," she said. "And I'm not saying any more so don't ask me."

She was so cold her voice was unsteady, but there was no doubting the conviction in the last sentence.

He was briefly silent. In these last few weeks Sophy had become the darling of his every waking hour, but he did not delude himself that she shared his devotion, at least not to the same degree, and it was quite possible her 'friend' was male. He did not even like admitting the strength of his feelings to himself, and he certainly hadn't shared them with Bert, his usual confidant in matters of the heart.

"So where's your car?" he inquired at last, thinking that might give him a clue to what was going on. "Is that where you want to go?"

She didn't answer. Her ears and fingers were tingling painfully as the circulation returned, and she was beginning to feel just cold instead of absolutely freezing. If she could only get out of these wet things and feel normal she could start thinking straight and get life sorted out again. She glanced sideways at him across the dark cab and remembered he was supposed to be playing darts.

"Thanks for coming," she said. "Please just take me home."

"Any time," he responded. Greatly daring, he reached over and gently squeezed her leg. "God, you're cold," he said.

It was impossible not to recall the last time a man had touched her leg, but far from wanting to slap him down she wanted to hug him for a gesture of protective affection, when she had never needed one more.

Chapter Forty Three

The sleet turned to snow in earnest as the temperature dropped in the small hours, and walking to work in the morning a little later than usual the village and the Downs were picture postcard pretty in the sun, coated in a pristine, white blanket a couple of inches thick. It was a beautiful morning in spite of the cold, and already the traffic was clearing the roads, although most of the cars which passed her were travelling slower than usual.

The old coat she'd pressed back into service from the far reaches of the wardrobe was thick and heavy, but it was warm and serviceable. It seemed unlikely she'd be able to ride this morning, with the snow and the frozen ground, but in reality she was still thinking about last night rather than what had to be done today.

As she passed the shop she exchanged a wave through the window with Mrs. Mullins, who was sticking a notice on the glass about reduced Christmas puddings. After the hectic recent events it was bizarre to remember early December, when they'd both expressed doubts about the wholesaler's optimistic sales forecasts.

She'd been soaking luxuriously in the hottest bath she could bear when mother came home last night, at nearer midnight than eleven. She'd knocked on the door and said in surprise, "Are you still up, dear? I thought you were going to have an early night. Did Terry call after all?"

It was the ordinariness of the question that finally tipped her over into having to talk about it. Terry had behaved with perfect courtesy, in his own bumbling way, and escorted her carefully to the door before rescuing his coat and leaving her with anxiety both in his voice and his expression, but there was no way she was going to cry or tell *him* what had happened.

It was a bit of a shock to her mother to be invited in; she'd become accustomed to her teenage daughter jealously guarding her personal privacy, and she pushed the door open with exaggerated care. One glance at Sophy's face was enough to tell her that something untoward had happened, and she sat down on the edge of the bath with concern in her eyes.

Sophy looked up at her tearfully.

"It was Mrs. Kenley's son," she said. "He.....attacked me."

Edith was astounded, and looked it. As Sophy explained, with chapter and verse from beginning to end, her mother was left once again with a faint feeling of guilt that her daughter was so unprepared for the random buffets of life which inevitably collide with every young person as they take responsibility for their choices. Not that that was any excuse for the man's appalling behaviour.

She listened soberly, but with growing relief that no real harm had been done.

"It's partly my fault," she said at last. "We lived in a small, safe world until....., well, you know when. When I was your age, I didn't have the protection round me that you grew up with, so I was better prepared for...., well, how things are now for us. And for men. Most men aren't always gentlemen but they wouldn't do that in a month of Sundays. Just the same, we all have to remember there's always a few who want what's not theirs to have, and try to get it one way or another. You did right. You know you did. And you'll know better next time. Thank goodness for Terry, eh?"

Sophy met her mother's comforting smile with a weak one of her own.

"I suppose," she said. She pushed herself wearily into a sitting position. "And I'm so tired. I rode three horses today, and gave a lesson."

Her mother had been on her feet herself for the last six hours, which had included fending off one or two amorous advances of her own from half inebriated artists, but it wasn't the moment to mention it.

Instead, she let her smile widen.

"The perils of being a professional horsewoman," she said, as she stood up stiffly and left her precious daughter to ready herself for bed.

The lane to the stables was virgin snow, glistening in the sun, and there was a childlike satisfaction in looking back at her own footprints. Under the influence of that bright sun, and the prospect of horses to ride tomorrow if not today, and of imminently meeting people she knew were beginning to respect her as well as like her, it was impossible to dwell too much on yesterday. As she pushed open the yard gate, Annie-May saw her coming and whinnied a welcome.

While there was no denying the snow was picturesque, it was a serious hindrance to trying to work efficiently. The morning tasks all took longer than usual, although that was partly due to a phone call from Peter Holt.

First he wanted to know how she had fared with Annie-May yesterday and it was gratifying to be able to tell him they were friends again. He grunted at that, and she could imagine his wry raised eyebrow before he went on.

"I'm not coming in till Sunday," he told her then. "Somebody's asked me to be a godfather, and me and Teddy are going to Yorkshire for a couple of days to check out some Ripon rabbits. They say this freeze is going to last till the weekend, so it won't make much difference to you and me anyway. You'll just have to cut their feed and put them out for an hour or two."

She heard him chuckle. "That Annie-May'll be a bit fresh by Sunday," he said. "Don't forget your hat that morning, will you?"

She told him Mrs. Kenley was coming back that day too, although she couldn't tell him if she would also be visiting her horse. He made no comment about that, and after a warning to be careful of ice about the yard he said, "See you Sunday," and hung up.

By mid-morning her four charges were brushed off and out in their separate paddocks and there was only Gypsy's box left to do. With not being able to ride, there was plenty of time and she was sitting in the tackroom listening to the radio, her fingers folded comfortably round a hot cup of coffee, when she heard a car drive in.

The man Kenley was suddenly standing in the doorway with something over his arm. She leapt to her feet, heedless of the knocked over coffee, and fled to the back of the room.

She hadn't even seen Miss Brown this morning. The yard was deserted.

He raised both hands in a placatory gesture and deposited her coat and half chaps on the table, carefully avoiding the spilt coffee.

"I thought you might need these," he said lamely. In spite of his judicious application of frozen vegetables, there was a lurid blue and red bruise spread over his right cheek and the eye was half closed.

Her panic at seeing him was hardly flattering, and for all his experience and sophistication it also unnerved him. It was broad daylight. Suppose she screamed?

"It's alright," he said hurriedly. "I won't touch you. I just wanted to, well, call it quits between us. I hope you got home OK last night."

She didn't answer.

"I should say sorry," he muttered. "I guess I'm not used to girls like you."

"You never bloody will be if I can help it," Sophy said bravely, emboldened by his unexpected contrition when she'd been more than half expecting angry recriminations, or worse.

There was a short silence between them. With sublime incongruity, the radio DJ announced a classic love song.

He tried to rescue some self esteem from a situation which he knew now should never have arisen.

"At least you gave better than you got," he remarked with a rueful gesture towards his face.

As one of his smart arse American friends had told him once, 'If you don't know when to keep it in your pants, sooner or later it'll get you in trouble.' It occurred to him then that her robust defensive action had probably saved him from himself. A clumsy, indiscreet fumble could be explained as a misunderstanding, albeit with difficulty. It had happened before. Going further was something else entirely....and even now, it was impossible to look at her and not be aware how attractive she was.

In two days, his mother would return. She obviously had some regard for this girl, and he could not afford any more disapproval from her when his financial future depended on her goodwill.

"I think I should go," he said then. Still she was watching him warily without speaking. "I, well, no hard feelings, eh?"

He saw the flash of anger come into her eyes as she recalled that agony of cold flight last evening, and still she said nothing, and he was obliged to leave without the understanding of closure between them he had hoped for. And yet even as he drove out the gate, there was something about her that lingered in his mind; he fingered the bruise on his face; she wasn't going to be easy to forget.

She wiped the table and made herself another cup of coffee and gradually the turmoil in her head stilled. She was actually thinking about Terry, and last night's rescue, when the phone lit up with a call from him.

"I wondered how you were this morning," he said. His tone was cautious, as though he was half expecting a firm instruction to mind his own business. After all, she hadn't been very communicative last night.

"I'm good," she told him, and the conviction in her voice helped to convince her too. She had the idea then that it might be nice to give him a little present for helping her yesterday. She looked down at the table and fingered his brooch on the coat that man had just brought back. She hadn't even given him a Christmas present.

"So we're still on for Sunday night, then?" he asked, and she gladly said 'yes' while wondering what on earth you bought for a man who'd practically saved your life and wanted to be your boyfriend but wasn't quite, because you were dithering.

There would be time to get to Chichester and look round before she had to come back for evening stables if she got a move on. She ended the call with a muck fork in her other hand on the way to Gypsy's stable.

She'd put her proper coat back on, checked the horses in the field and was brushing the last of the snow off her car when Joe Fittleworth drove in unexpectedly. He parked beside her and got out quickly.

"I'm glad I caught you," he said. "I didn't think you'd be riding today so I pinched an hour off. Are you off home for lunch? Have you got a minute?"

"I'm only going shopping," she said.

Joe smiled. "Ah, good," he said. "I wanted to give you this and just have a quick chat while the girls aren't around."

He put an envelope in her hand.

She was confused, and looked it. Joe laughed at her.

"Don't panic, it won't go off," he said. "Now listen. Me and the other parents, we've been talking and we'd like you to teach our kids every now and then, you know, once a fortnight or something like that. Peter is a super guy and he knows so much, but he is a bit high powered for them sometimes. He said so himself the other day. And you're light enough to ride Rufus, and Jennifer says he's so different afterwards. We thought we'd pay you what's in the envelope for your time, even if sometimes there's not all four of them. It's not as much as we pay Peter, but we think it's fair. Now what do you say?"

She opened the envelope. There were four five pound notes inside. It was exactly what she paid Peter herself. She could not know it was also exactly half what Joe paid him. She hesitated. It seemed a lot of money for doing what she actually quite enjoyed, especially when she could see a difference in how one of them was riding.

"I can't do jumping and gymkhanas and stuff like that," she said doubtfully.

"Oh, Peter can do all that if they want it," he said. "Thing is, they've got this dressage bug watching you, and you're so much nearer their age."

She nodded then. "So long as Peter doesn't mind," she said.

"I have spoken to him," Joe said. "In the pub the other day. He said he thought it would be good for you, but if I was doing him out of a job I should buy Teddy a packet of crisps."

He grinned at her.

"As matter of fact I have a feeling he's had another offer himself from that yard down the road, Downside is it? I suppose a man like that's bound to get noticed when he comes out of hiding. I don't know why he retired in the first place when you see him ride, and he obviously loves it."

Sophy of course knew exactly why he'd 'retired,' but she wasn't about to say so. Feeling quite proud of herself, she said eagerly, "It's a deal," in the most businesslike voice she could muster, and they shook hands on it with both parties feeling highly satisfied.

Chapter Forty Four

Almost as if by mutual arrangement, the old Land Rover and the Bentley followed one another into the yard on that grey, damp Sunday morning. In fact, with most of the livery clients' vehicles already in evidence, there was barely room for them in the area Miss Brown insisted was kept clear for parking.

She came out of the house to greet her friend just as Peter Holt was closing the Land Rover door, and he nodded to her before they both descended on Mrs. Kenley, adjusting her coat and looking about her after driving herself this morning.

Holt reached her first.

"Welcome home," he said. "May I?"

He leaned forward and kissed her on the cheek.

"I knew you'd do that," she said to him, and they both laughed. Again Miss Brown was struck by how close they always seemed; she felt a twinge of envy; even in the days when she'd had boyfriends of her own, she'd never really identified with any of them.

Mrs. Kenley turned towards her, and the two women embraced briefly.

"You and I need to talk," Mrs. Kenley said to her "But first I want to know about Annie-May." She looked over to where Annie-May's box was empty and transferred her attention back to Peter Holt. "You had some snow, I believe, How have you managed?"

"I've been away myself," he told her. "Sophy's been in charge. She must be in the school with her now. Shall we?" He offered her his arm with exaggerated gallantry, as though he was about to lead her on to the dance floor at the Ritz, and Jenny Kenley, international businesswoman and multi-millionairess, giggled like a school girl and pushed it away.

"I've missed you," she said to him. "Everybody I meet is so damn serious all the time, or else they want something." A momentary cloud passed over her face. "I do miss Gerald sometimes," she added, mostly to herself. Then she changed her mind, and took his arm anyway.

He glanced down at her.

"Don't say it," she said, and he grinned and mouthed "I knew....."

All three of them joined the little group of spectators watching Sophy struggling to contain the enthusiasm of an exuberant Annie-May, who after two days off had remembered she was a racehorse and in the nicest possible way was letting everybody, including her rider, know all about it.

Sophy saw them arriving and rode over to the gate. Annie-May snorted and tossed her head, snatching the reins from her rider's hands.

"Thank goodness," Sophy said to Peter Holt, hurriedly re-gathering her reins, "Will you ride her? I can't do a thing with her this morning."

He released Jenny Kenley's arm, went into the arena and led her away from the gate. Satisfied they could not be overheard, he looked up at her.

"I'd love to ride her," he said. "Don't tempt me. But I mustn't. Mostly because she won't respect you if you get off now, but also because the boss is here." He glanced over to Mrs. Kenley chatting to Miss Brown by the gate. "We have to show her we're making progress, and only you can do that."

She was perplexed and disappointed. Annie-May was fidgeting and stepping eagerly from foot to foot as they talked. It was evident to Holt, if not to Sophy, that she was bubbling over with energy and would buck or worse if she had to wait much longer.

"Here's what you do," he said to Sophy. "Ride on to a twenty metre circle, loose-ish rein, let her trot as fast as she likes for a minute or two, canter if she wants, but stay on the circle. Change the rein when you can. Just go with the flow. Give her ten minutes and the edge'll come off and you'll be able to ride her properly. Go now or she'll explode."

He stepped back and Annie-May surged forward. He watched Sophy guide her gingerly on to the line of the circle at the far end of the school, with the horse in a charging trot but just enough contained by the constant turn for Sophy to stay more or less in control.

Satisfied his pupil had the skill and awareness to stay safe, he rejoined the spectators by the gate.

"She's come over all unnecessary with not being ridden for a couple of days," he said to Mrs. Kenley.

"That girl is coping pretty well," Miss Brown said. She very nearly smiled at her old school friend. "We had the same problem at the beginning of every holiday, remember. Of course, our ponies weren't racehorses."

"She'll be fine in a minute or two," Holt said, and it wasn't clear whether he meant the rider or the horse. He felt a faintly familiar tug at his elbow.

"Will Blackie do that when I ride him next?" Kitty asked anxiously. "He hasn't been ridden since Wednesday."

"He might," Holt said, looking down at her with a serious expression. "You just watch Sophy and do what she does, and you'll be fine."

Sophy was rising to the trot like a demented puppet as Annie-May seemed determined to trot as fast as was equinely possible, but gradually the steadying effect of the circle took hold, and after the third or fourth it was possible to introduce a little lateral bend and instantly the balance, and the breakneck pace, became more civilised. She essayed a few strides of sitting trot, changed to the left rein, where Annie-May was always less confident, and soon was riding on a consistent contact with the mare paying much more attention.

She was tempted to approach the gate and ask what she should do now, but the instructor was chatting to the 'boss' as he called her and not even looking in her direction. She was piqued at his apparent lack of interest, not realising that he wanted her to show Mrs. Kenley how far she had come and what she could do without his assistance.

Jennifer, Kitty and Joe Fittleworth and the other girls and their fathers, it being Sunday, were still watching though, and suddenly it became important to put on a show for them. If she was going to teach those girls as part of her profession, she had to prove she was better than they were.

There was enough spark and energy left in Annie-May for her not to worry about forward momentum, and she began to ride a series of serpentines, the exercise which had worked the last time she rode her, and again the mare responded readily, coming into her hand and softening over her back just like she had before when there was nobody to see.

She wasn't the only one aware of her audience. Annie-May, having run herself out of nonsense, was quite sensitive enough to know she was the centre of attention, and proceeded to upstage her rider by producing a quality of work which even Peter Holt would have been proud of.

Sophy was delighted and astonished together; Annie-May was answering her aids almost before she gave them, the contact was magically soft and it seemed as the horse kept saying, 'yes. yes. come on, what shall we do now then?' She tried a medium trot, and flew across the school barely touching the ground. Greatly daring, she tried a ten metre simple change, which always before had resulted in Annie-May throwing her head and losing her balance, but today it worked perfectly. She cantered half way round the school, came forward to walk and gave her lovely mare a heartfelt hug. She'd forgotten the spectators minutes ago in the ride she was enjoying, and when some of them clapped, albeit a little hesitantly, she sat up with a start of embarrassment.

It was a far, far cry from the days when she'd scorned to show any affection for any horse. Even her famously expensive warmbloods of last year were lucky to get a pat in public, even when they'd won a class.

She walked over to the gate.

"You'll do," Holt said to her with a broad smile of approval, and it was high praise indeed, and she blushed alarmingly. He turned to Mrs. Kenley. "That mare does love an audience," he remarked. "That could be worth a mark a movement one day. She's got to be correct, but a bit of pizzazz can't hurt, even at the lower levels. I've got an idea for her début I'd like run past you." He looked up at Sophy. "Well, both of you."

"Come to dinner one day next week," Mrs. Kenley said. She smiled herself as she echoed his words. "Both of you. My son is home from America." Then she remembered something her PA had said. "But perhaps you knew that."

Sophy nearly fell off the horse. She grabbed the mane, steadied herself and dismounted. She gripped the gate for a moment and forced herself to be calm.

"I'd love to come," she said. "I have to ride Gypsy now. Will you all excuse me?" She led Annie-May back towards the stables, pursued by Kitty and Jennifer both asking her questions at once.

As the others turned to follow, Miss Brown and Joe Fittleworth accidentally met each others' gaze. If either of them had noticed Sophy's reaction to the mention of Tony Kenley, neither of them owned to it.

Chapter Forty Five

She hadn't seen Terry since before the snow, that terrible night when he'd rescued her from practically freezing to death in a bus shelter.

It was only a few days ago, and yet it seemed like a year. As she walked to the 'Shepherd and Flock' that evening, fingering the package in her anorak pocket, she was looking forward to seeing him again more than she would have admitted to anyone, and certainly not to him.

And Gypsy had gone well too this morning, after Annie-May's owner had disappeared into the house with Miss Brown.

Gypsy's idea of extra enthusiasm after two days off was to lean on the bridle, but she was wise to that game by now, and soon brought him into line with his usual standard of work. Peter Holt, enjoying a leisurely smoke of his pipe as he watched her cope successfully with a very different problem, while at the same time avoiding Blackie who was running about the school only half under control, congratulated himself on the vindication of his first impression of her potential, and suggested as she dismounted that they might introduce Gypsy to some lateral work in her next lesson.

It had been such a good day she refused to let the shadow of possibly having to meet Tony Kenley again spoil it, or interfere with her anticipation of spending the evening with a young man who didn't just fancy her, unlike some, he would treat her with proper respect.

Without intending to, she started to make comparisons. You couldn't pretend Terry was as good looking as that other man, or had anything like his, well, you'd have to say it, sort of magnetism, but when you came right down to it there was a solid, decent quality about him which was definitely not part of Tony Kenley's character.

Terry's van was in the pub car park. It was a bizarre thought, but his honest, useful van and her old car, all red paint and image and flash performance, seemed to sum up their two characters. It was a bit of a jolt to realise that she'd been very enamoured of that car herself not too long ago.

As she pushed open the pub door, it was a sobering thought. Had she been like that too, only concerned with appearances and money and what *she* wanted, regardless of anything else? No wonder that man thought he could do what he liked with her, when he had so much and she had nothing. Not any more, she said to herself with fierce determination.

"Hi," Terry said as she joined him at their usual table. He looked up with a grin. "You look warmer than you did the last time I saw you."

On an impulse, she stroked his hair and kissed the top of his head before she sat down. Sensing his surprise, and slightly embarrassed at herself, she spoke quickly.

"I see you've got me a drink already," she said, and took a sip of the orange juice in front of her. Inevitably, the memory of that glass of wine she'd drunk without wanting to came back to her and her face clouded.

Terry was not completely without perception.

"You're not going to tell me about that night, are you?" he said to her.

She put the glass down and looked over at him.

"No, I'm not," she said. "Don't ask me about it. But I bought you this to say thank you."

She put her package on the table.

It was a Swiss army pocket knife with his initials engraved on both sides.

He was astonished and delighted.

"You needn't have done that," he said. She realised it was a sign of how much he thought of her that he was almost tearful.

It was necessary to change the subject.

"Are you coming to the show next Sunday?" she asked him.

"Wouldn't miss it," he said roguishly grinning at her. "Are you allowed to cheer at dressage shows? I've got a rattle Dad used to take to the football."

"You'd better not," Sophy was horrified at the idea, and he grinned even wider and they both laughed. It was amazing how easy she felt with him.

His affection was transparent, but he wasn't afraid to tease her, and she knew now that he would put her first whenever she asked him. Thinking back, except for Mum and Dad, nobody had ever done that for her before. In the same moment, she remembered what she'd been thinking about her old car. It wouldn't be right, or fair, to ask him too often.

She was very much less comfortable driving to Chichester on Wednesday night for dinner with Mrs. Kenley. Even without the probable presence of her son, sharing a social occasion with someone who was paying her as an employee was a new and rather off-putting experience. She liked Mrs. Kenley well enough as a person, but Peter calling her the boss the other day had rather underlined how much she depended on her to keep going, financially.

The man himself was disembarking from his Land Rover as she drove through the gates into the floodlit courtyard in front of that impressive house. He gave her a brief wave, and then turned his attention back into the cab.

She parked alongside, seeking moral support and grateful that they could go in together. He finished fitting a warm coat on Teddy, who would have to remain in the truck for the duration, and turned to her with a smile.

"I did a double take when I saw that," he said, indicating her old car parked a few yards away next to the Bentley.

Sophy said awkwardly, "I think the son bought it." She hesitated. The man was obviously here, and there would be no hiding the fact that they knew each other. "I met him last week," she admitted, trying to sound non-committal.

He did not comment. Smartly dressed himself in a jacket and tie, as they moved towards the front door he complimented her on her dress, and then as they waited to be admitted he glanced around the courtyard and smiled, broadly.

"Very democratic, this car park," he said. "From a Bentley to a banger, and we're all going to dine together." He deliberately looked straight at her then, sensing her unease at the prospect.

"Just be who you are," he said to her quietly. "We're all proud of you, you know. I don't want to be patronising, but I thought you ought to know."

Of course, he couldn't know that the major element in her apprehension was the imminent, inevitable meeting with a man who had attacked her, but still they were the right words at the right time.

The wide double doors opened in front of them and they stepped side by side into the lofty, brightly lit entrance hall. A polite young woman took her coat, and Mrs. Kenley appeared beside the foot of the stairs.

"Welcome to you both," she said. "Did you come together? Do come in."

They were five at dinner that evening, with the fifth participant introduced to the guests as "Hilda, she's my right hand person and lives here too."

It quickly became clear that Jenny Kenley was an experienced and able hostess, and had it not been for Tony Kenley, unfortunately sitting directly opposite her, Sophy would soon have felt able to relax herself. Indeed, the occasion was not dissimilar to many other dinners she had attended when her father was alive; a handful of guests invited for mainly business reasons, a serviced meal superbly presented, and measured conversation.

Peter Holt, as she would have expected, was immediately casually at ease with Mrs. Kenley and her aide, and even managed to inveigle a smile from the waiter, who was attending to the table as formally as though it was a papal banquet.

"You're incorrigible," Jenny Kenley told him as she saw the waiter smothering a giggle, and when he caught her eye and said, "I knew you were...." he got no further before they both burst out laughing.

Tony Kenley, who knew Peter Holt only by name and had never seen him with his mother, was distracted from surreptitiously watching Sophy trying to avoid looking at him, and said irritably, "For God's sake, mother, it wasn't that funny."

Holt frowned, although carefully not at him.

He understood now why even the boy's mother had doubts had about him. There was something about this young man, with every possible advantage life could offer him, which his instincts told him was not quite right. Had Tony Kenley been a horse, however outstanding his pedigree and performance, he would probably not have bought him. It was a test he sometimes applied to people when he met them for the first time, and over the years it had rarely failed him. It was disappointing, when he was the son of a woman he valued so highly even after such a short acquaintance, but he could not resist the impression.

His horseman's sensitivity also told him there was a tension between Tony Kenley and his pupil which there ought not to have been, but he could only guess at the reason for that.

Mid way through the meal the waiter leaned forward and spoke softly into Mrs. Kenley's ear, and she frowned in her turn.

"I'm so sorry," she said to the table at large,. "I asked them not to call until tomorrow. It's the time difference, I suppose. I must take this call. Hilda, why don't you tell them my news while I'm gone. Tony, you haven't heard it yet either. Please excuse me."

As she left the room the waiter resumed his station by the sideboard, and even Tony's attention focused on the secretary sitting discreetly quiet at the foot of the table.

Hilda Gordon was unperturbed at assuming the limelight, and smiled slightly in acknowledgement. She too had noticed the frisson of dis-ease between Tony and Sophy, but unlike Peter Holt she had her suspicions about the cause; she had also noticed that the man Holt, who like his protégé had previously been merely a name on a cheque she despatched once a month, appeared to have an unusual rapport with her boss.

Astute as all good PAs must be, it occurred to her as she marshalled her thoughts that just maybe that might have some bearing on the decision she was about to unveil. Then she saw that Tony had finally torn his eyes from the face of the girl opposite him and was watching her, waiting to hear what she had to say. He was probably the only man in Chichester who could make her blush without saying anything; it was hugely distracting.

With the advantage over Sophy of far greater experience of men in general as well as men like Tony Kenley, her smile faded as their eyes met.

It had been perfectly clear for days that Tony Kenley would bed her without a thought if she gave him half a chance, simply to pass the time. It would mean nothing to him, and quite possibly little to her either after a period, but the deceit would be disrespectful to her employer, a woman she liked and got on with, and might eventually compromise her work, even her job. And she knew all about the man's current situation; most of the paperwork about his divorce, even the personal stuff, crossed her desk en route to the English lawyers advising his mother.

Still, she couldn't stop herself sighing inwardly. Whatever her head said, his physical attraction was undeniable. His imminent transfer to Stepford couldn't come soon enough.

She ripped her eyes away from his with more than a trace of regret, as well as a renewed determination not to succumb to his persuasive charisma.

As an excuse for the accidental pause her emotions had promoted, she took a sip of wine and then said, "Contact has been established between Kenley Industries and a Russian oligarch who wishes to remain anonymous."

A mystified expression appeared on each of the faces of the three very different people she was talking to. There was a moment's silence. Sophy automatically looked to Peter for some explanation, but his reaction of polite confusion mirrored her own.

Tony Kenley had no such compunction.

"Don't play silly buggers, Hilda," he said irritably. "What *are* you talking about?"

"It's not generally known, but the Fairgate estate is for sale," she told them then. "Mrs. Kenley has it in mind to sell this house and move to Fairgate. She's already had a look round the house, and our property people have been asked to assess the farms and the land to agree a valuation. Fairgate House is much larger than here, and has potential to become something of a hub for the company. For instance, there are the facilities within the house itself to host business meetings. And there are potential tax advantages as well, but that's a bit complicated." She paused.

Sophy and Peter Holt looked interested; Tony Kenley was scowling. Mrs. Kenley was returning to the table and paused behind her secretary's chair.

"There's a memo on your desk, Hilda," she said. "Their MD is coming over next week. Set up a meeting, would you, oh, and you'd better be there too."

She beckoned the waiter to refill her glass as she sat down and looked round at them all. "Well, have you told them? What do you think? I'll be able to keep a proper eye on you pair. We might even get another horse or two, if all goes well." She raised her glass as though she was toasting her horsemaster, and her smile embraced Sophy as well, sitting on the other side of the table. Not included was her son, whose scowl intensified.

"I don't get this dressage business," he said. "Where's the profit in it?"

"Life's not just about business," his mother said evenly. "You know we've always had horses. Dad liked racing, I like dressage."

"It seems to me," her son said then, pointedly glancing sideways at the man sitting on his right between him and his mother, "it's not only the horses you like."

There was short, uncomfortable silence. His mother was upset and glared at him. Even Tony Kenley had the grace to look slightly abashed. He really ought not to have said that to her, not in front of other people.

"It won't affect you if I move," she said at last. "You've already said you like the Stepford house. And we have to find you a job, either in the company or somewhere."

He didn't relish that idea, and certainly would not discuss it in front of strangers, and was silent in his turn. Nor did knowing that the hugely desirable young woman sitting opposite him was currently unattainable, and probably never would be, and Miss Gordon was also steadfastly resisting his charms, improve his sociability. The fact that he had indulged in a couple of large vodkas before dinner also played a part.

His mother was reminded of a sulky teenager who had found solace in his father's laxity whenever she disciplined him. The faint hope that he might have become less selfish in recent years was evidently not to be realised. Even so, it was good to have him close again, and there was undoubtedly something of Gerald in the cast of his features.

It was far too early to tell what her relationship with Peter Holt might turn into, but it was hardly fair to expose that worthy man to baseless suggestions of ulterior motives when of all the men she had ever met, he was the least likely to entertain them.

Holt himself rescued the situation with a natural question about the stables.

"Will you keep on the other liveries?" he asked her. Most of his wealthy clients in the past with yards of their own had preferred to keep them private.

She turned to him with relief.

"I think so," she said. "I don't see so many children these days. Those kids at the stables, I've missed that innocence. You forget what it's like to be young when the only people you ever meet are deadly serious grown ups. Mostly grey men. In dark suits. And mostly with only money on their minds." She made a wry face.

He chuckled. "Well, at least you can't accuse me of dark suits, " he said. "Now, about Annie-May...."

He was interrupted.

Tony Kenley emptied his glass and stood up.

"I'm going out," he said in a loud, petulant tone. "I really don't think I can stand any more talk about dressage." He looked at Hilda. and for a moment she thought he was going to ask her to go with him and her careful heart suffered a sharp twitch, but he didn't.

"Miss Gordon," he said to her. "There must be a nightclub somewhere in this town. Where is it?"

"There's one in the High Street," she said.

His mother frowned.

"I'm not sure you should drive, darling," she said to him, and he waved his hand dismissively.

"I'll get a cab," he said. Only Sophy and the waiter noticed he checked in the doorway and gave her a long, lingering look before he finally vanished.

Sophy felt a massive relief with his departure. He hadn't spoken two words to her all evening, and yet his continuing fascination with her was obvious, to her at least. Presumably no one else had noticed, although she did have the impression that Peter didn't like him.

It was impossible for his mother not to notice the lightening of the atmosphere once her son had gone. She wondered a little sadly whether that boy would ever learn that the universe did not revolve around him and what he wanted. Perhaps it was already too late.

Hilda was asking Sophy about riding, and the two of them were chatting now with a freedom which neither of them had shown five minutes ago. Even the waiter serving the coffee seemed more at ease with himself and what he was doing.

Peter Holt stirred his coffee slowly, happy that Sophy had finally found her tongue and something to say, and at least as aware as his hostess of the altered ambience, and the reason for it. When he finally looked up at her, and her preoccupation was broken, the close relationship between them seemed stronger than ever.

"Now about Annie-May," he said again, deliberately leaving unsaid what they were both thinking. Only his eyes told her of his empathy with her feelings.

"Oh, yes," Sophy said, apologetically turning round and abruptly breaking off her conversation with Hilda as she heard the mare's name spoken.

"I'm all ears," Jenny Kenley said, forcing a small smile for him.

"Well now," he said. "I don't think you'll enjoy watching your mare competing in endless Preliminary and Novice classes, and I don't think she needs to start there, so here's my plan. I propose we bring her out at Elementary level at a decent show when she's ready, in about three or four months' time I should judge. It's not like she's a novice horse like most novices, if you see what I mean. She's used to travelling, and performing in different places, and crowds and all that. Young horses aren't, so all that's part of the learning curve, and she's already done it. On the other hand, we don't want her to make a fool of herself either, so we'll do a couple of quiet tests at Downside at the end of their season just to be sure.

"And we've got another piece of luck on our side. The jockey's well experienced at Elementary, I think you rode at Medium too once or twice, didn't you?" He turned to Sophy as he finished.

She nodded as her mind turned over what he'd said. It was all true. Annie-May, whatever her schooling quirks might be, certainly didn't ride or behave like a young horse. She'd overheard a well known trainer say once that Elementary was where proper dressage started, and it was hard to imagine a woman like Mrs. Kenley enthusing over anything less.

Even so, it was a huge challenge, to produce a feisty ex-racehorse with a huge personality and paces to match to perform a respectable Elementary test in only three months.

"I've been checking out dressage on the web," Mrs. Kenley said. "You really think you can leapfrog two levels just like that?" She was looking at the pair of them now.

"Annie-May's a horse," Holt said with a rueful grin. "Nothing's ever guaranteed with a horse. You must know that from racing. And Annie-May's a mare, and an Arab, which you can bet won't help. But it's being who she is that makes her special. You get her registered and we'll give it a go."

"Well, Sophy Taylor," the boss was looking at her now. "You'll be the one in the hot seat. What do you think?"

Sophy looked down at the table, suddenly aware that everyone's eyes were on her. Her first thought was to thank God that the son wasn't still there. Then she thought of Annie-May, and how she had come to love her, and the feel she gave her, and how forgiving she could be if she knew you were doing your best. A fierce emotion gripped her. If any horse in this world could do it, Annie-May could.

She caught Peter's eye across the coffee cups, and he winked at her, a broad, conspiratorial wink expressing not just confidence and encouragement but respect between two professionals. She realised with a start her opinion mattered. There was a lump in her throat and she swallowed hard.

"No problem," she said proudly.

Mrs. Kenley's good humour had returned.

"That's decided then," she said, beaming at them. She realised her aide had been excluded from the conversation longer than was quite polite, and deliberately spoke to her.

"Maybe we'll get you riding a horse instead of a computer if we move to Fairgate, Hilda. What do you say? I might even start again myself."

Hilda looked distinctly doubtful. Peter Holt grimaced.

"Not more women on horses," he said. "Everywhere I go I'm surrounded."

His current companions exchanged amused glances. Mrs. Kenley chuckled. "We will be gentle," she told him, "so long as you're gentle with us."

Chapter Forty Six

Going to a show this time last year, all she'd had to do was turn up, get in the lorry, ride the tests and then dismount to be taken home.

Not today, she thought ruefully as she arrived at the yard at first light on Sunday morning.

Gypsy's first ever test was scheduled for seven minutes past eleven, and Blackie's was two tests later. Taking Peter's advice, she had to allow at least an hour to ride the three miles to the venue and give the horse time to look about him and have a canter in the practice arena before the bell went. And there was Kitty to consider. It would not be fair to trot Blackie's legs off all the way there just because she wanted to hurry.

Running over the test in her head as she mucked out Annie-May, she thought wryly that being unselfish, however worthy it might be, did sometimes have drawbacks. Then Kitty and Jennifer arrived, bubbling with excitement, and Kitty's first words changed her mind.

"Oh, you've got him in," she said, happily grateful. She almost ran over to the pony, tied up outside his stable, caked in mud and pulling contentedly at a hay net.

Joe Fittleworth looked in over the door and said good morning. He watched her, expert now with many weeks of practice, forking over the mare's bedding.

"That was kind," he said quietly. "You must be stressed enough this morning."

She looked up at him, flushed and untidy, and Annie-May chose that moment to give her an affectionate rub on the shoulder. She staggered slightly.

"You could say that," she responded. He grinned at her.

"Not all beer and skittles, this horse business," he said with a chuckle. "At least it's a fine morning. I'd better go and help those girls get some of that mud off. It's a good job Rufus isn't going too."

Yesterday's arrangements were working out, or so it seemed. Jogging down the road in the sunshine, with Blackie and his chatty little rider beside her, and Gypsy taking a keen interest in this new route they were taking, Sophy's spirits rose. It might be only a Prelim. in the back of nowhere, but she hadn't been to a show for months. Peter was taking her mother and her show jacket, and Joe was bringing Jennifer and whatever Kitty might want, and the redoubtable Terry was expecting to appear in the nick of time. He'd been insistent on knowing exactly when she was going to perform.

"I have to check the sheep," he'd said to her. "Bert doesn't work Sundays."

They were half way there when the old Land Rover passed them, with Joe's car following and Jennifer waving enthusiastically through the passenger window.

As they arrived she remembered what Terry had said about the gate, and sure enough one of the posts had been taken out and was lying beside the driveway.

Downside Equestrian Centre was about half way between Fairgate and Stepford, and once upon a time had been a substantial dairy farm. Nowadays it was a combined livery business and riding school boasting a manège and an indoor school, once a barn, which on show days served as the warm up area and the arena respectively.

It was evident from the relaxed conversations and greetings between the competitors and their followers that many of them were regular attenders at Downside's informal dressage shows. Sophy and Kitty, as newcomers, were met with interested smiles, friendly faces and even enquires about their mounts, a far cry from the splendid isolation Sophy was used to at more senior events, where everyone was deadly serious and dedicated almost exclusively to maximising their own performance.

Peter and Edith, Joe and Jennifer, found a space on the manège fence and watched the new arrivals mingling with the other riders.

Blackie was behaving with his usual pert confidence, being well used to collecting rings from Pony Club shows, but after a three mile hack along the road Kitty had him under reasonable control; Gypsy, on the other hand, had only ever shared a school with a single pony; he had never been in this situation before, and Sophy was struggling.

There were perhaps half a dozen other horses preparing for their tests, and at any moment three or four of them were trotting or cantering on either rein, avoiding each other in the disciplined way that riders do in such circumstances, but for the inexperienced Gypsy the sight of another horse coming rapidly straight at him, only to divert at the last minute, was novel and disconcerting to say the least.

In the first five minutes he must have shied twenty times, and Sophy was bewildered and not a little unnerved as she struggled to keep her seat. What on earth was the matter with him?

Watching from the fence, Holt recognised the problem but knew there was nothing he could do to help her. In some ways it was for him too a reminder that in spite of riding since childhood, her equestrian experiences had always been sheltered and artificially controlled; the rough and tumble of naughty ponies or Pony Club games, which gave Kitty and Jennifer their cheerful confidence, had never featured in her expensive dressage career.

Sophy rode over to him, frustrated and tearful and unsure what to do. It was impossible to warm up properly, or do anything sensible at all. When she looked over her shoulder, it was infuriating to see Blackie trotting about like a veteran. Actually, he was going rather well.

Holt looked up at her with quiet concern.

"He'd afraid of the other horses," he told her. "Give him time. He's warmed up anyway, just with getting here. Just walk about gently and let him get used to things. I know we talked about practising a few canter transitions, but you've got twenty minutes yet. And if we can't, well, we can't. And remember, the more frightened he is, the more confident you have to be."

"May I have the track?" a voice demanded from fifteen yards away, and she was obliged to move to the inside. A sharp, sixteen hand bay thoroughbred passed between her and the fence in a brisk trot, and Gypsy shifted abruptly another yard away. Sophy realised the anxiety on her mother's face was probably mirrored on her own.

She pulled herself together. Peter was right, of course. A space appeared at the other end of the arena. She headed for it, and after another minute she tried a short trot, and then another. Gradually, Gypsy woke up to the fact that he wasn't under attack from every horse that came near him. Even so, she never did manage a canter transition; not that she would have wanted one anyway with how Gypsy was going, tense and hollow with his head in the air.

The steward called from the gate, "Sophy Taylor," and there was no help for it. Ready or not, time was up. The girl with the clip board preceded her to the indoor school and Gypsy followed her readily enough, through the big double doors into the familiar territory of a marked out 20 x 40 metre arena.

The girl turned to go out, wished her good luck, and closed the doors behind her. Without the comforting presence of a human close to his head, Gypsy's feet froze, immoveable, glued to the spot in trepidation. She could feel him trembling under the saddle.

The fact that the horse might never have been in an indoor school before had escaped the attention of both the rider and the trainer.

Terry arrived, breathless and just in time, to join the group watching through the gap above the kicking boards beside the doors.

"How's it going?" he said cheerfully.

"It's not," Holt retorted grimly. He urgently wanted to go to Sophy's aid, but he dare not. The judge might take exception to his intervention, although she had not yet rung the bell, and in any case there was not much anyone could do in the few seconds remaining. Whatever was going to happen next, it was down to Sophy and the horse and no one else.

Sophy guessed what was the matter. She was carrying a whip, and once upon a time that would have been her first resort, but she knew now that that was not the way. She stroked his neck, and remembering Annie-May she tried to turn him off balance. Gypsy half turned, half reared which he had never done before, and then walked with stiff steps into the centre of the school.

The bell rang.

She gathered the reins and was able to walk the length of the arena. It was unfortunate that although the actual building was over 50 metres long, enabling a space at each end and allowing the horses to enter at A from outside the arena proper, it was only 20 metres wide, which meant the long sides had to be ridden along the wall.

She persuaded him into trot and he progressed down the centre line more of less straight in a lumpy, reluctant stride with his head held high and quite clearly bemused at being asked to work in what he evidently thought was an outsized stable.

Turning right at C, he backed off the white boards, saw the wall approaching and would have stopped altogether without a sharp prod from Sophy's heels. As they went down that first long side she was able to hold his forehand on the track, but the quarters were on another track altogether, well inside the wall. It might have been adjudged a passable travers with a better quality trot, but it was definitely not on any Prelim test agenda.

As they came towards F Sophy's mind was in a whirl. Nothing in all her competition experience had prepared her for anything like this. Surely she mustn't retire. Gypsy could do this, she knew he could. There had to be a key.

They passed the F marker, still crooked. The next movement was a 20 metre circle at A. He was looking at the boards and about to stop. On an impulse, she *told* him to stop, and inspiration struck.

Trust was the key.

Stationary at A, she knew she had twenty seconds before the bell would end the test for her. It wasn't a rule which had ever mattered before, but it mattered today. Heedless of the spectacle she was making of herself, and counting the seconds, she leaned right forward whispering and caressing his ears and his neck just behind the poll, something she knew he loved in the stable after work. His ears flicked gratefully back towards her, and she persevered for as long as she dared. Finally, she resumed her seat and asked him to commence trotting on the circle.

He moved off in the same reluctant step as before, but approaching the centre line the miracle came. As she asked for the turn to continue, his head came down and the rein softened, and she felt the tension seeping away from his back as he started to bend. He was wary of the wall as it came closer, but he stayed down and he stayed straight. In another few moments they were trotting straight as an arrow down the long side to H.

Watching from the far end of the arena, Peter Holt turned to her mother and spoke with pride and a catch in his voice, "That's horsemanship. You don't see that often. I couldn't have told her to do that. Only the rider could know that was the answer. This is a tiny little show in the backwoods of Sussex, and nobody's doing anything fancy or even trying to, but you won't see a better rapport with a horse in the Olympic games." He grunted. "I wonder of the judge is smart enough to see it. That's the thing about horsemen. It takes one to know one."

Terry was confused. "She's not supposed to stop there," he said. "I helped her learn it."

Holt, still watching the horse, clapped him on the shoulder. "I dare say she'll explain," he told him. "There'll be other things for *you* to learn as well, I shouldn't wonder."

Standing on tiptoe to see over the kicking boards, waiting for the test to conclude and to call the next competitor, the young steward knew more about it than Terry.

"That's a super trot now," she said.

And it was. As the test proceeded, Gypsy seemed to come to terms with his surroundings. For the final trot movement before the first canter, on the diagonal, Sophy knew he was working as well as he'd ever done at home, but her elation was short-lived. When she asked him to canter he fell hard on to his inside shoulder, clearly still not quite prepared to trust himself working so close to the wall in the faster pace, and indeed the entire canter tour was sketchy, unbalanced and inconsistent as he broke and backed off the wall whenever it came close.

She came down the centre line at last to halt and salute, and the relief on her face as well as on the faces of her mother and trainer was almost palpable. Unexpectedly the judge, sitting high above the arena, opened her cabin window and beckoned to her. She was a hard faced, bespectacled woman of a certain age well known among the local horse fraternity for her severity and precise application of the rules.

Sophy looked up at her nervously. What had she done? Surely she wasn't going to be eliminated after Gypsy had tried so hard. Her mind raced back over previous competitions. She'd never been called by a judge before.

The woman, leaning out with one hand on the window catch, was unable to speak to her without being overheard by the others.

"I never saw a test ridden quite like that," she said. Her habitual frown was wrestling with a smile. Eventually, the smile forced its way through.

"I thought you were done for before you even started, but you made it somehow. Well done. I have a feeling we'll be seeing more of you."

She closed the window.

The young girl opened the doors and she passed the next competitor entering the school as she went out. In a moment she was surrounded by eager, upturned faces congratulating her. Gypsy threw his head nervously at being the centre of so much attention, and Peter Holt motioned the others to step back. Sophy dismounted, gave her horse an appreciative pat and turned to her instructor.

He didn't say much, but his smile spoke volumes.

"You proved yourself today," he said to her. "And if you don't know what I mean now, you will when you think about it later. And as for him," he leaned forward and stroked Gypsy's nose, "he'll score twenty per cent more next time, count on it."

Joe Fittleworth came up to them from the practice arena, where he'd been keeping an eye on his daughter and Jennifer was hanging over the fence enviously watching her friend.

"How was it?" he asked of no one in particular.

Sophy wrinkled her nose. "Not good," she said. "He was frightened. I suppose it could have been worse. We did get through it."

Holt said, "Is Kitty ready?" and her father grinned. He glanced behind him to where Kitty was waiting for her turn by the practice ring gate.

"She's always ready for anything horsey," he said. "Jennifer's going to call it for her. I was going to, but Jennifer's desperate to do something, you know how it is with kids. I think Kitty knows it anyway."

Holt chuckled. "She'd better, if Jennifer's calling it," he said. He said to Sophy, "We must try and get that Rufus pony sorted out. It's not good when someone feels left out."

Sophy thrust Gypsy's reins into Terry's hands. "Hold him for me," she commanded. "I want to watch Kitty."

If Kitty was nervous, it didn't show. She sat up straight with her Pony Club badge and tie very much in evidence, and Blackie rounded to her hand just like he had been doing at home lately. It was a cheerful, engaging picture and the pony went forward merrily with his ears pricked and clearly enjoying the limelight. Jennifer called the movements well enough, but as Joe had said she probably didn't need to.

"If there was a mark for personality that pony would score ten," Peter Holt said, smiling broadly as Kitty saluted at the end with the widest, proudest smile of the day.

There were twenty eight horses in the class, and with more than a dozen still to compete it would be another hour and a half before the result would be known.

Anti-climax set in. Terry gave Gypsy back to Sophy, and she thought about re-mounting, and didn't. Kitty was beaming and kept saying, "He's so good," and hugging the patient Blackie over and over again. Edith dithered. She knew just enough about dressage to know that Sophy's test, by her usual standards, had been a disaster, and she didn't quite know why the man Holt thought she'd done something wonderful. Joe was beaming along with his daughter, Jennifer was feeling sulky and not quite part of things, and Terry in his innocence was waiting to see what would happen next.

Peter Holt had plans of his own, and advice for everybody else, especially his pupils.

"We can't keep the horses hanging about here all day," he said "Ride 'em off home and sort 'em out and come back later in Sophy's car. That OK with you, Joe? I've got an appointment with the owner here in ten minutes, he's asked me if I'll come in once a week and teach his students, they've got exams coming up and it's exactly what I used to do before I moved down here."

He turned to Sophy's mother. "It won't take many minutes, and then we can go to lunch somewhere and have some peace and quiet."

"What about me?" Jennifer said. "I want to go back with the horses."

"Don't fret," Joe said. "I'll drop you there on my way home for my lunch. Then you can come back with Sophy too."

Sophy gathered her reins and said to Terry, "Leg me up," and he looked at her in blank confusion.

"I said you had things to learn," Holt said with a chuckle. "Watch."

They made their way through the busy lorry park, following Joe's car, and out on to the road home. Gypsy was stepping out firmly, but Blackie was tired now and they walked most the way back to Fairgate, offering Sophy plenty of time to reflect on her first, public professional performance.

It wasn't one to write home about, but it was hard to see how she could have done better. Peter's words came back to her, about proving herself. She'd been disappointed at the time that he hadn't said more, but walking down the road in the quiet aftermath, she realised with a flush of pleasure that actually it was the highest praise.

When Gypsy had been confused, frightened almost, and wanted simply to stop, she'd kept her head, thought about what to do, identified with the horse and somehow completed the test. Walking home in the sun, keeping half an eye on Kitty and the occasional traffic, she knew that even six months ago she would not have been able to do any of those things. It was all very well Peter giving her the credit, but she knew where it really lay.

"You're ever so quiet," Kitty said, looking up at her from beneath the peak of her riding hat. "Didn't he go very well? I didn't see."

"He was frightened," Sophy said. "It was his first time. It was not very good, but he did his best."

"Blackie always does his best," Kitty said proudly, and her sublime confidence made her smile.

"I'm sure he does," Sophy agreed. She rubbed Gypsy's neck where Kitty wouldn't see she was stroking him as they turned at last in through the yard gate.

Jennifer was sitting on the bench outside the tack room idly swinging her legs back and forth as she waited for them. Rufus was tacked up and tied up outside his stable. She stood up the moment she saw them.

Sophy dismounted a little wearily. As she lifted the reins over Gypsy's head he stretched his neck and sighed, as though he was weary himself after so many new experiences, and glad to be back on familiar territory. He nuzzled against her midriff, and suddenly it didn't matter that the kids were watching, she cuddled his head briefly before leading him into his stable.

Jennifer followed her.

"It's not fair," she said. "If I can't go to the show I want a lesson for half an hour."

Sophy came out of the stable with her arms full of tack. She regarded the unhappy child with a frown. There was a strange sense of déjà vu about the moment; not that many years ago it was exactly the sort of thing she might have said herself. On the other hand, however unavoidably, Jennifer had been left out of the action today, while her friend was covering herself with glory.

"Alright," she said. "But it'll have to be a quick half an hour. And it's only for today."

Chapter Forty Seven

In spite of Jennifer's quick half hour, it was still only mid afternoon when she drove gingerly back into Downside's lorry park, picking her way slowly and carefully among the vehicles, people, horses and ponies randomly thronging the area adjacent to the two schools.

With more time to look about her now she was horseless, the variety of the clientele was quite remarkable. Unaffiliated open dressage shows were an alien environment for someone who had always prided herself on being better than that. Every type of horse and age of rider seemed to be represented, all pitting themselves against each other on a completely level playing field. Oddly, in spite of all her past successes, she didn't feel superior at all; in fact, with friends to greet, she felt quite proud and glad to be part of it.

She found a space and the two girls promptly decamped and left her to lock the car and make her own way between the trucks and trailers towards the indoor school, where the Novice class was in full swing. She saw Peter and her mother first, down by the practice arena where Peter was talking to a rider over the fence much as he'd talked to her this morning. She felt a twinge of jealousy, and then remembered he was forming an association with this other yard. The feeling of discontent increased. Did that mean he would have less time for her?

Piqued at the idea that he wasn't just waiting for her, she resisted the impulse to go and join them and went instead into the indoor school gallery, where the secretary was ensconced adding up the scores and fielding riders declarations and enquiries.

The results and scores of the previous classes were pinned on a board on the wall, and the unclaimed score sheets were in tidy piles on a table below, with the placed horses' sheets laid out separately with the appropriate rosettes.

Kitty and Jennifer were standing in front of the table giggling and peering at the results on the wall. Kitty was tightly grasping her sheet along with a bright, multicoloured rosette with '4th.' in a large numeral in the centre and the name of the establishment printed round it.

She turned to Sophy in triumph. "Beat you," she said, and smirked at Jennifer.

Sophy turned her attention to the scores. The riders were listed in their order of competing, not the finishing order, with their scores in the adjacent column, and it took a moment to find Gypsy's name.

51.1% was by far the lowest score she had ever had. It was *devastating*. She stood there in shock for a long, long moment, with Kitty and Jennifer giggling behind her and other, later competitors passing on their way to and from the secretary.

Someone she didn't know appeared beside her to look for their own score, and she was in the way and automatically stepped aside.

"Aren't you going to collect your sheet?" Kitty said, still smirking. "I scored 67%."

She shuffled through the pile and found it. The woman she didn't know waited for her, and then found her own sheet.

"You were on that coloured horse," she said to her in a friendly tone, and Sophy nodded without speaking. "I saw you in the collecting ring. He didn't look easy."

"He's very green," Sophy managed to say, feeling obliged to respond. The woman looked down at her score sheet.

"I can't read that board without my glasses," she said. "61.4. Better than last time. See you again, maybe." She went out into the sunshine, and all three of them followed her.

Peter and her mother were coming towards them, and she could see Joe parking his car beside hers' in the distance. Kitty had fitted her rosette into the lapel of her jacket, and had she looked any more pleased with herself would probably have exploded.

Peter Holt met her smile with one of his own and glanced quickly through the score sheet she gave him.

"I always said that pony had more cheek than was good for him," he said, giving it back to her. "Caught it off you, I shouldn't wonder. Well done. Now go and tell your Dad all about it. I need to talk to Sophy."

Sophy's expression said it all. She could feel her lower lip quivering and fought to conceal it, but her mother was not deceived.

"Oh, dear," she said. "I knew it wasn't very good, but was it so bad?"

Holt took the proffered score sheet from her but did not immediately look at it.

"No, it wasn't," he said in a definite, there's no argument about it tone. "You found the best performance your horse could offer, today, in today's circumstances, and you did it with empathy and determination. That's exactly what a professional rider should do. It's up to you to make the best you can out of whatever horse you're riding whatever the situation, and you do it with kindness and proper regard for the horse's future. If you'd got cross with him today, next time he very likely would be even more frightened. And you certainly wouldn't have got through the test.

"There's only one mark on this sheet that matters today and it's the last one. I haven't looked at it, and I bet you haven't either."

He gave the sheet back to her.

"What is it?"

Her eyes ran down the numbers. Last of all was the rider mark.

"Seven and a half," she said in disbelief. There wasn't another mark on the sheet above six, and most of them were much lower. It was highly unusual to see such a discrepancy.

"No fool, that judge," Holt said then. "And she took the trouble to speak to you. It's been a good day. We've all learned a lot. And it's not over yet. Mrs. Kenley's coming to see your lesson on Annie-May in half an hour. We'd both better get moving. I'll take Edith home and you'd better go and get tacked up. And I bet you've had no lunch. Better grab a sandwich to eat on the way." He gestured towards the refreshment van.

She stared at him. It had been so much Gypsy's day, Annie-May had faded from her mind.

"I bet you forgot something else too," he said with a grin. "What happened to Terry?"

"Oh, Lord," she said. "I did forget him. Where is he?"

Edith said, "After you left, he said he might as well go back to work. I think he was a bit fed up you didn't even say goodbye."

Sophy frowned.

"I'll have to make it up to him," she said thoughtfully. She looked suddenly determined. "I'll be more organised next time. We both will."

Her mother thought she was talking about Kitty, but Holt knew better.

Chapter Forty Eight

Joe's two young charges were putting their ponies to bed in the field, and their cheerful voices as they explained the day's events to the other two girls engaged on the same errand carried easily on the slight breeze as far as the school gate.

It was a moment of calm in what had already been the fullest day. It was twilight now, and getting colder, and Annie-May was wearing her racing quarter sheet as a precaution against the chill. She switched on the lights before she led the mare towards the mounting block. Even now, she never threw that switch without remembering the days when she couldn't ride in the dark for fear of not being able to pay to see what she was doing.

As if sensing her fatigue, and used to the procedure by now, Annie-May stood statuesque as she mounted and settled her seat in the saddle and her feet in the stirrups. As they moved off in walk, her flowing, eager stride contrasting with Gypsy's steadier step seemed to drain the tiredness out of her. Annie-May deserved her full attention and abilities, and she would have them; in any case, as Sophy knew well by now, she was not a horse who would tolerate being taken for granted.

Annie-May had been stood in all day, and with that and the chilly evening air she was quite fresh enough to keep her rider fully occupied for the first few minutes just remaining in control of a wildly exuberant trot. It was something of a surprise when she looked up from a circle at the opposite end of the school to see what appeared to be a small crowd gathering beside the gate.

Mrs. Kenley had brought Hilda Gordon with her; the four girls from the yard had finished their chores and come to watch, coercing the long suffering Joe as well as two other parents to come too; Peter Holt was just arriving, having changed into riding breeches, and then Terry emerged from the shadows behind him.

She rode over to the gate. Annie-May was fidgeting from foot to foot and high blowing. Twice she threw her head in the typical Arab motion that Sophy had learned now to anticipate when she was excited. Automatically she slipped the reins and took them back.

Hilda Gordon nervously stepped back a pace and bumped into Joe.

"God, that looks dangerous," she said.

Holt was unmoved. He nodded agreeably to Jenny Kenley and said to Sophy, "Bit fresh, is she? No sweat. Let's get you sorted out. How long've you been up? Five minutes?"

He knocked out his pipe on the gate post and walked beside her to the centre of the school.

"Are you going to ride her?" she asked him, assuming that was why he'd changed.

"Not necessarily," he said. "I always change to teach if I can. It's a matter of respect to the horses. And it's as well to be prepared. You should take note, I suppose, now you're a teacher too."

It was a surprise to think of herself as a teacher, but there wasn't time to dwell on the idea just then.

"You were riding on a circle when I came," he said to her. "Go back on to it, rising trot. Rise slowly, stay soft but make yourself heavy and dwell in the saddle when you sit down so she really has to push you to make the rise. Concentrate on the bend as much as steadying the tempo."

It was a new development of a concept they'd talked about before, of how the horse follows the rider and not the other way round.

The circle began at the same breakneck pace, but as her understanding grew of what he was asking for the effort of lifting her forward with every pace started to tell, and within a minute or two Annie-May was working far more sensibly. It seemed to Sophy, sitting on top, that the horse was as relieved as she was to stop rushing about unbalanced and half out of control.

Holt observed the change without comment. You couldn't do what Sophy had just done without an established seat and a certain sensitivity, but he was not a man to spread compliments like confetti. He worked the trot on both reins, finally allowing her to go large and still maintain the balance and tempo. Experience told him the horse would revert to running if they essayed a canter without some further work, and so he took another tack to conclude the session.

He spoke to her while she worked round him on a circle in the centre of the school, deliberately dividing her attention between what he was saying and the horse working beneath her, knowing that this kind of multi-tasking was an integral part of every professional horseman and riding instructor's education. It was the first time in their relationship that he hadn't stopped her to explain what he wanted, and Sophy's initial reaction was to stop anyway and listen, but he would not allow it.

"Keep going," he said. "If you stop now you'll break the flow, and you have to learn to ride and still feel the horse while you're thinking about something else. Go into sitting trot, go large, position left, and keep it. Ten metre circle in the next corner. We're going to try a shoulder-in."

The trot was still big enough to make sitting difficult, but the position and the volte steadied it to a still robust but more measured working step. Sophy realised with a start of understanding that Annie-May, sharp as a tack, knew something different was about to happen before she did.

Holt sent her across the short side into another ten metre circle, and then demanded a shoulder-in out of it.

It wasn't quite a complete disaster.

Annie-May had spent her entire career to date being asked to travel at over thirty miles an hour in a straight line, and the concept, or purpose, of proceeding in what to her was merely a crooked trot was totally bewildering. She stayed beside the fence for a couple of steps, more or less on three tracks and still in a round outline but hanging on the outside rein, then turned into the school hanging on the inside rein. She threw her head in irritation. Whatever *nonsense* did they want her to do now?

This time, Holt did stop her.

"You're asking too much," he told her. "And you're asking for too much shape with the hand and not enough from the leg. And you must carry the stride *through* in the direction you want to go."

Sophy looked down at him in some distress. Annie-May stretched out her neck and shook herself from end to end, expressing her own opinion and, perhaps deliberately, giving her rider an uncomfortable wobble into the bargain.

She had ridden shoulder-in before, of course, and the aids were familiar enough. But those horses knew how to do it; the thought also came to her then that they didn't have Annie-May's temper or temperament; on the other hand, someone must have taught them, and that was going to be her job now.

"Please show me," she asked him then.

Holt paused. There was of course no guarantee that a racing mare with minimal school experience would do it for him either, but faced with such an appeal he knew he had to try. His original idea had been to use the position in the exercise to keep the horse steady in possible preparation for a final canter, but as sometimes happens the lesson had developed differently.

"Alright," he said. "It might not work, but you watch my seat and legs especially. The hands are the easy bit."

She dismounted and gave him the reins. As she watched him vault into the saddle, tiredness overwhelmed her. For the first time in her life, she really didn't want to be asked to get on again. Not until tomorrow.

He slipped his feet into the stirrups and rode away from her, adjusting them as he went.

Already, he knew that Annie-May would do this for him.

He took up the reins. Sophy had good hands, softening almost daily now, but this man was the master. He placed his mare into trot, and to the watchers by the gate the step seemed instantly taller, more elastic, prouder, and it was clear even to Hilda Gordon that something special was about to happen.

He rode in decreasing circles, twenty, fifteen, then ten metres wide, and the man and the horse were indistinguishable. When he asked for a shoulder-in along the fence opposite the gate, Annie-May answered the axis of his inside leg and the satin softness of the inside rein as though she had been a dressage horse for all of her life. She danced gaily along the fence, elegant, eye-grabbing and relaxed, understanding the question and plainly intent on letting the world know exactly how smart she really was.

"I simply don't *believe* that man," Jenny Kenley said under her breath. "That horse would *cartwheel* for him."

No one else said anything. He carefully repeated the exercise on the other rein and returned to Sophy in the centre of the school. He stepped off the horse and caressed her neck. Annie-May half closed her eyes and leaned her head on his shoulder.

"I wish I knew how you just *do* that," Sophy said.

"It's not magic," he told her. "Just experience." It was evident, tired as she was, that she needed some encouragement. "I'll tell you something else, Sophy Taylor. You'll do it yourself one day, sooner than you think and rather better than me. Why do think you got this job in the first place? I've got round shoulders, but you've got style. And you can't beat that for dressage."

Looking into her eyes, he realised she was more than tired, she was worn out.

"It's enough," he said. "Go and make your peace with Terry. I'll take her back to the yard."

The pony fraternity melted away home, and he was followed into the yard by Jenny and her assistant, who watched him over the stable door as he untacked and gave the mare a quick rub down before putting on her overnight rug. Terry and Sophy were chatting quietly beside his van on the other side of the yard. Whatever they decided, Terry drove out almost immediately, and Sophy came over to join them.

Hilda said to her, "I was never this close to a horse before. I'm impressed."

"It's not me you should be impressed with," Sophy said. Peter Holt came out of the stable and she turned to him. "There's a feed made up in the tackroom for her. I'll get it."

She had her back to the gate when a familiar sound spun her round in her tracks. Her old car swept into the yard slightly faster than was quite safe and halted beside the Bentley. She was a yard from the tack room door and jumped inside.

Tony breezed across to Annie-May's stable.

"Hi, guys," he said cheerfully. "Taking some stuff to Stepford, thought I'd stop off and see how it's going."

"You're too late," his mother said. "We're all going home."

Sophy gritted her teeth. She couldn't hide in the tackroom all night, and there were three other people here. She emerged with the feed bucket.

It was natural for them to look at her as she approached, and the man Tony, perhaps deliberately, was standing exactly where the stable door would have to open.

"Excuse me," she said nervously, and as he stepped aside his arm brushed over her breasts. Awkwardly, she emptied the bucket into the manger and Annie-May buried her nose in it. As she came out, he'd resumed his position and the same thing happened again. The others were talking amongst themselves, and he was actually joining in, and no one else noticed. It was necessary to get away as quickly as possible, and yet not upset Mrs. Kenley.

"I have to go home and change," she said. "I'm meeting Terry for dinner at the 'Shepherd and Flock.'"

"That sounds like a good plan," Tony said instantly. "Why don't we all join you?"

"Not me," Peter Holt said, rather too quickly. "I have a small grey friend who wants his tea." Jenny Kenley looked at him with a frown. With their mutual perception he could not hide from her that he did not like her son, and knowing that they had only met once she had to wonder why.

"Me and Hilda have to go home too," she said. "It may be Sunday night but you know perfectly well we have to prepare for a meeting in London tomorrow." She turned to Peter Holt.

"Every time I come here," she said to him, "you and Sophy surprise me, you especially. Is there a college in Yorkshire somewhere that teaches you to speak horse, and then you teach it to your students?"

He was grateful she had included Sophy in her compliment. "I suppose Teddy could wait for his tea if you didn't have to go," he told her.

She wrinkled her nose in disappointment.

"But we do," she said. She put her hand on his arm and their eyes met. "Next time," she said to him softly. Her tone was unmistakeably affectionate, and Tony glowered angrily, an expression rapidly transformed into a smile as his mother turned back to him.

Miss Brown, nursing a heavy cold picked up on a visit to one of the farms two days ago, watched from an upstairs window as the diverse trio of vehicles departed in convoy, with Sophy's little car leading the way, and finally the twilit peace of a cold, clear winter evening descended on Fairgate House Stables.

A little over an hour later, peace was definitely not on the menu in the 'Shepherd and Flock' dining room, although the evening had started well enough.

Terry was as smart as Terry was ever likely to be. Scrubbed almost to the point of shining, in a white shirt and red tie, he was congratulating himself on sharing a table with the prettiest girl in Sussex as she studied the menu, idly twirling a fork at the same time.

Sophy too had made a little effort for him, and just for a change was wearing a relatively low cut dress instead of her usual jumper and slacks. Her shower had refreshed her, and she felt less tired than before. She felt his eyes on her, but she was comfortable with him, confident that his diffident ways would not push their relationship into areas she was not yet ready to explore.

"Since I'm going to pay," she said, peeping at him demurely over the top of the menu, "shall we have some wine?"

"I think you should, definitely," said a voice she knew, and she turned with horror to see Tony Kenley standing beside the table staring down at them, or rather at her breasts.

Terry looked up, surprised at first more than annoyed. He didn't know this man from Adam, and waited to be enlightened. Tony did not oblige him, and Sophy was momentarily too taken aback by this unwanted apparition.

"Why don't I join you?" Tony said. He took a vacant chair from an adjacent table and sat down between them.

Terry was disconcerted by his presumption, and still waiting to be introduced.

Sophy saw his brow darkening, and said hurriedly, "Terry, this is Tony Kenley, Mrs. Kenley's son, you know, Annie-May's owner, you saw her this evening."

"How do you do?" Terry said without much enthusiasm. Tony acknowledged him with a minimal grunt and turned his attention back to Sophy. "You look terrific," he said. His eyes dropped again to her chest. "That's a handsome….necklace," he added with a knowing grin.

Sophy was appalled and increasingly nervous. Tony, fortified by a stiff vodka supplied by Mrs. Branksome, and remembering the feel of her firm thigh and frustrated by his lack of action these last few weeks, was determined to make a last throw of the dice for her. If the truth was told, he had been unable to get her out of his mind since that first evening had ended in disaster. He supposed it must be because she was so, well, fit, not to mention beautiful, but he was not much given to introspection and seeing her again today had relit the fuse. And, anyway, what the hell, there was nothing to lose.

"Tell you what," he said to her. "After we've eaten, there's a half decent club in Chichester. We'll go on there. What do you say?"

Terry was barely included in the invitation.

It was hard to cope with the sheer nerve of the man. The situation was momentarily relieved by the waiter, who recognised her and Terry as regular bar patrons and knew their names. Although he was standing opposite Tony, he spoke first to Terry and then Sophy.

"Are you ready to order, Mr. Godwin? Miss Taylor?"

Tony took the menu from her. A quick glance showed him the most expensive item was rump steak, offered with a wide range of trimmings.

"We'll have three of those," he said, pointing. "And a bottle of champagne. And get a move on if you want a decent tip."

Terry found his voice.

"Just a minute," he said, and Tony instantly turned to him. "Don't like steak?" he said aggressively. "Well, have something else." He swung his attention back to Sophy.

The brief distraction had given her a chance to get her thoughts together.

"I'm not going to any club," she said. "I'm tired. Anyway, I don't do clubs."

"Bit of champagne'll soon perk you up," Tony insisted. "You won't know yourself."

Then he smiled at her, and her heart twitched just as he knew it would. The resolution in her face started to fade. The man was impossible, and he'd frightened her, and she hated him, and there was poor Terry stranded on the other side of the table, but still....and then he administered the *coup de grace* and winked at her. She tore her eyes away from his. She was unhappy, trapped, tempted, bewildered, and none of these emotions was lost on Terry watching from only a yard away.

The waiter appeared with a bottle of champagne and showed it to him.

It was the last straw. Terry smashed his fist down on the table. The crash drew every eye in the restaurant. He was so angry the last wisp of timidity left him.

He stood up and he seemed to swell with anger. The waiter stepped back in alarm.

"You," he said to Tony. "Outside. Now."

He was briefly astonished at the farm boy's temerity, and then he leaned back in his chair and started to smile. Sophy thought Terry was going to kill him, but Tony Kenley was unmoved.

"This isn't the wild west," he said with sublime confidence. "Don't you know who I am? Behave yourself."

Terry recovered a modicum of poise, but his anger was no less for being controlled. He knew he loved Sophy, and he had a growing feeling that this smug bastard might have had something to do with her distress the other night. He took hold of Tony's jacket, hauled him to his feet and manhandled him across the room past two tables of startled diners and out into the car park.

He threw him ten feet down the tarmac, and Tony stumbled awkwardly as he regained his balance. The two men faced each other in the cold semi-darkness. Sophy appeared in the doorway on trembling legs and holding the door post for support.

Terry was terse and to the point. He said to her. "Do you like this man? What's he to you?"

"I…..know him," she said feebly.

"Do you want to go with him?" Terry asked her and she shook her head.

Tony spread his arms wide in a huge, melodramatic gesture of appeal to her; now the man had released him, and the imminent physical danger had passed, the whole situation was ridiculous, even faintly amusing.

Finally, Sophy found the courage to say it.

"I hate him. I *hate* him."

Terry looked back at his rival.

"You go *now*," he said to him, "or I'll make you." He flexed his powerful hands. Tony had taken a few judo classes, and knew something about self defence thanks to his father's fears of kidnapping when he'd first gone to the States, but he'd be no match for the strength of a man who worked the land for a living, and he knew it.

It went heavily against the grain to be bested by a yokel, but what the hell. Mentally, he shrugged. He'd given it a good go, but he'd have to get over the girl. There were other fish in the sea. Even if he could beat that man, this one wasn't going to bite.

Sophy leaned heavily on the door post. The whole episode, and now Tony Kenley's abrupt departure, so alien to her whole life's experience, made her head spin.

Terry, confused himself when he saw the man leave in his girl friend's old car, did not immediately notice her distress. When he turned towards her she was slipping slowly to the ground, and he hurried to support her.

"It's OK," she murmured as his arms folded round her. "Really." He raised her unsteadily on to her feet and she held on to his arm. Her coat was still in the restaurant cloakroom. "I'm cold," she said. "Take me back in."

He opened the door. No one in the room was unaware of the manner of their exit a few minutes earlier, and all eyes turned towards them. A middle aged man dining with his wife at a nearby table looked at Terry half carrying her and said, "Is she alright?" and he nodded rather grimly and found the way back to their own table.

He helped her back into her old seat. Everything was just as it had been before the arrival of Tony Kenley; the champagne, even the extra chair, had vanished. Satisfied she was recovering, he resumed his own seat. Gradually, attention drifted away from them and the quiet, mingled sounds and conversations of the other Sunday evening diners filtered over them. It was as though the entire incident with Tony Kenley had never happened.

The impression was reinforced by the same waiter reappearing with the same smile and the same polite enquiry.

"Are you ready to order, Mr. Godwin? Miss Taylor?"

They looked at each other across the table. Unaccountably, Sophy wanted to giggle. Terry nibbled his thumb nail.

"Shall we?" he said to her. She took hold of herself. There was a jug of water on the table and as she reached for it the waiter forestalled her and poured some into her glass. It was astonishingly revitalising.

"OK," she said stoutly.

Very slowly, Terry smiled at her. The pride and the steady commitment in his eyes was embarrassing and she blushed and looked down at the tablecloth. He picked up the menu. Neither of them ordered steak, or champagne.

Usually, when they met at the 'Shepherd and Flock' he walked her home and then went the few yards back to collect his van, but tonight he drove her round the corner and parked outside the door. It was still only ten o'clock, but Sophy by now was exhausted beyond words.

The deliberate small talk, about the show and horses, and even the companionable silences during dinner, had skirted round the issue of Tony Kenley, but there was one question which Terry knew he had to ask, whether she would answer it or not.

He waited until he was helping her out of the van, and then finally he said, "That bus shelter business. Was that him?"

Safe at her own front door, she nodded and frowned at the same time. She reached back into the van for her handbag, and as she straightened he took her in his arms and drew her into the shadow under the lintel. She melted into his arms as held her against his chest and gently kissed her lips, his strong, masculine hands caressing her face and softly finding their way to her neck beneath her hair. For a long, luxurious moment she gave herself to that soft, enveloping feeling of security with his lips on hers and his arms around her; even so, she was so tired she could hardly stand.

"I'm sorry," she whispered. "I have to go. I'm so tired. You were wonderful."

He held her hand to the last minute as he released her.

"I'll phone tomorrow," he said, and the last thing he remembered as he turned to go was her smile as she vanished inside.

Her mother was watching television when she collapsed on to the sofa beside her.

"You're home early," she said. "Is everything alright?"

It was hard to know how to answer. "That man was there," she said at last. Edith switched off the TV and turned to face her.

"Tony Kenley?" she said, and Sophy nodded. Her mother frowned.

"And what happened? I can't imagine Terry was very pleased."

"He wasn't," Sophy said. "He…..chased him off."

Had she been less tired, she might have said more, but it really didn't seem worth the effort. There'd be time tomorrow for details and explanations.

Her mother took a moment to weigh up this information, and then was struck by a thought which clearly had not yet occurred to her daughter. It had to be possible the son had influence with his mother and would prejudice her against Sophy continuing to ride her horse. Her frown deepened. Surely poor Sophy wasn't about to be hit by another catastrophe which was not her fault, not now, just when things were looking up for her.

Sophy was already falling asleep, her long legs angled untidily across the sofa like a tipsy spider. Edith knew how tired she'd been before she went out, but she'd insisted on going and now there had been even more stress and shenanigans which couldn't have been foreseen. She prodded her awake and sent her to bed. Any fears she might have about Annie-May could wait until the morning.

"I'll bring you some cocoa in a minute," she said instead, and Sophy turned sleepily in the doorway.

"If I'm awake to drink it," she said.

Chapter Forty Nine

It was round about then, as the days steadily lengthened and it was possible to anticipate the prospect of spring, that life began to assume a pattern shaped around a fortnightly excursion to Downside's little dressage shows.

She rode her two horses every day, a couple of times a week under Peter Holt's ever more demanding supervision, and with Mrs. Kenley occasionally arriving to watch Annie-May; she gave a lesson to Kitty and Jennifer and their friends every now and then; and she spent one or two evenings a week with Terry, happily chatting about what she'd been doing and letting him kiss her goodnight afterwards.

By the time of his third visit to Downside, Gypsy had become accustomed to the indoor school and was rapidly climbing the order of merit, producing work comparable to the quality Sophy was used to at home. Kitty was faintly disconsolate when eventually he began to beat Blackie, although the pony continued to score pretty well with every judge who saw him.

It was a red letter day for Jennifer when for the first show in March, on a damp, misty morning, all three of them set off down the road together; it was also a big day for Gypsy; Peter Holt had decided it was time for him to show his mettle in the Novice class, and Sophy had a few extra nerves of her own. She'd managed to come third in the Prelim class last time, Gypsy's first ever rosette to hang on the tack room wall alongside Kitty's collection, but would he be confident in medium trot with the school wall approaching? She had a horrible feeling he would stop and back off like he had before, that first time.

Her ears were full of the two girls' excited chatter but her head was preoccupied with what she would do if that happened, and she was only half listening. Then her old car went by and her heart jumped. It pulled up a few yards ahead and they were all obliged to stop.

Kenley got out and came towards her. She hadn't seen him since.....

Agitated as she was, she still noticed there was a woman in the passenger seat. He stepped up to the horse's head.

"Good morning," he said. "That's not my mother's horse. Where are you going?" His manner was harsh and unpleasant. Nevertheless, looking down on him gave her the confidence to answer with relative indifference.

"It's my own horse," she said to him. "And we're going to a show." She very nearly added , "What's it to you?," but she didn't.

"We mustn't stop, we'll be late," Kitty said.

"Quite right," Sophy agreed with her. "Good bye, Mr. Kenley. You can tell your mother I'll be riding Annie-May later." She nudged Gypsy forward and he was more or less pushed out of the way. All three of them trotted past his car and kept going.

It was another minute before he re-passed them, perhaps deliberately faster and closer than he should have done, especially with children present, but the road was narrow just there and it could have been unintentional. Still, Rufus shied slightly and Jennifer gave a small squeak as she got hold of him again.

"Bloody man," Sophy thought to herself. She could only suppose he was going to his house in Stepford; it was a miracle their paths hadn't crossed sooner, with him living so close. And of course he could come to the yard with his mother whenever he wanted, although these days she usually brought Hilda Gordon and they spent as much time in the office with Miss Brown as they did watching her ride.

Kitty and Jennifer were entered in the morning Prelim class and the Novice was not until the afternoon, so first Sophy and then other two would have to wait for each other, as nobody wanted the ponies, especially Rufus, out on the main road for six miles unsupervised.

Thanks to Peter Holt's connection with the show centre, she was able to borrow a stable for Gypsy while the kids warmed up and performed, but even so it was a serious nuisance having to waste all day waiting to spend six minutes in the ring. She thought with a rueful smile it was just one more circumstance which would have been unthinkable this time last year.

Faced with the prospect of hanging around most of the day until Sophy's test in the afternoon, her mother had declined Joe Fittleworth's offer of a lift and would be absent today. Terry wouldn't be there either; he had an engine in pieces, he said, the parts had been late arriving and it was promised to his customer for tomorrow.

Peter had brought Gypsy's rug over, and she untacked him and left him looking out at his new neighbours and surroundings with wary curiosity while she wandered down to the collecting ring to see how the other two were getting on.

Blackie was his usual pert person, and Kitty was showing off with a string of entirely unnecessary canter transitions which must have been trying the pony's patience severely. Joe was leaning on the fence looking pensive, next to Jennifer's mother, putting in a rare appearance for her daughter's first show, and looking decidedly anxious.

Peter Holt, against his better judgement and proper protocol, had felt obliged to go to Jennifer's assistance, and being on foot amongst eight randomly working horses in that relatively confined space he was himself in danger and a potential hazard to everyone else. Rufus, in spite of all his own show experience, and as if to make up for his good behaviour on the way, was taking advantage of Jennifer's nerves and lack of experience and making life very difficult for her. His latest trick was to repeatedly snatch the reins from her and then throw his head up, regardless of any other rider in the vicinity.

Holt finally got hold of the pony's bridle and led him over to the fence. Jennifer was tearful and in no fit state to stay in the saddle. He put his arm round her waist and lifted her off to embrace her mother.

He saw Sophy with a relieved smile.

"There you are," he said. "Get on this pony and ride the nonsense out of him. He's taking the mickey like he used to do at home. He's not due in the ring for half an hour, and if you can do a job on him we just might get Jennifer back up by then."

Kitty rode up, smug and smiling. "I'm in next," she announced loudly. "Who's going to watch me?"

Peter Holt and Joe exchanged an amused glance.

"You're always in next," Holt said. "Don't crow. It could be you in trouble next time."

He kept hold of Rufus while Sophy adjusted the stirrups. She thought he was going to stay with her, or at least stay by the fence, but he stepped through the rails and walked off to the indoor school with Joe, leaving her without a backward glance.

Unsurprisingly, Rufus, now with a much heavier and highly competent jockey on his back, decided to behave himself. Even so, for Sophy it was a new experience to be working a pony surrounded by much bigger horses, all intent on their own purposes and inclined to look down on a pony rider in more ways than one.

It took a few moments to accustom herself to Rufus' smaller stride, but she still rode him occasionally when she was teaching and he came into her hand readily enough. After a couple of trot circles he began to work like the schoolmaster pony he'd been bought for, and when a space opened up between the other horses she asked him to canter and he responded calmly. It was much the same pattern as when he was playing up in a lesson; Jennifer was gradually mastering his cheek, but in a show situation when she herself was a nervous debutante the pony was bound to sense it and take advantage of her uncertainty.

Peter Holt was nowhere to be seen, but after fifteen minutes Rufus was behaving impeccably and she rode over to Jennifer and invited her to get back on him. Her mother looked doubtful, but Jennifer was irked by Kitty's insufferable superiority and was made of sterner stuff. Having seen her pony working properly, she set off into the mêlée of riders warming up with far greater determination than previously, and Rufus, without assuming quite the shape he had shown for Sophy, seemed to have learnt his lesson.

She was watching by the fence with Jennifer's mother when a female voice behind her said, "You did a good job there," and she turned to see Peter Holt and a bespectacled woman she didn't recognise also taking an interest in Jennifer's progress.

The woman introduced herself.

"Hello, I'm Felicity Harris," she said. "I'm a livery here and I've got a little brown cob, he's 15.1 and Peter's been giving me lessons and he's told me all about you. I wanted someone to do a few Prelims on him and hack him out sometimes for me before I start again myself. I know it's pathetic, but I lost my confidence after a fall last year. It's taken me this long to be riding again, but Toby needs to do more or he'll get too strong for me. He's only six. Would you be interested? I know you're busy, but I would pay you of course."

She didn't know what to say, and Peter was no help. He just stood there looking neutral. Felicity Harris was a small, earnest looking person with greying hair who could have been any age between forty and fifty five; she pushed her spectacles back up her nose as she waited for Sophy's answer.

"Where is Toby now?" she asked finally, fighting back her first impulse to politely decline out of hand. Holt smiled. It was the right answer. No freelance professional should dismiss a potential client without some investigation. Sophy was learning, and not just about riding.

Toby was in the stable next to Gypsy. Gypsy saw her coming and pushed his nose out with a faint grunt of greeting, and she stood there stroking his ear while Felicity paraded Toby on the cobbles for her. Clipped and hogged, with one white foot, he looked round and placid; he wasn't her type, of course, but he seemed a nice enough little horse, although there didn't seem to be anything special about him.

She thought for a minute. There wasn't any reason why she shouldn't ride him. She could probably fit it in. After all, Downside was only ten minutes in the car.

"Once or twice a week?" she said tentatively.

"Agreed, on one condition," Felicity said instantly. "He's in the Prelim in twenty minutes, last to go. It'll give me a chance to see you on him, and you'll get the feel of him." She turned to Peter Holt, still standing beside her, clearly seeking his approval of this arrangement.

"Sounds good to me," he said. "Now if only I was four inches shorter and a stone lighter my pupils wouldn't be doing me out of business….."

He looked at Sophy and grinned.

"You'd better get moving if you're in the ring in twenty minutes. In the meantime, I'm going to check on Jennifer. At least one of us ought to see her test."

Sophy had forgotten all about Jennifer. "Oh, lord," she said. "I hope she's alright." Another thought struck her. "How did Blackie go?"

Holt grinned again. "The usual," he said. "I think that pony'd score 65% with his eyes shut. We must try and get him up a level over the summer."

"You do seem to be connected with an awful lot of horses," Felicity said.

Sophy had turned her attention to Toby. "I suppose I am," she said absently. "It's all down to Peter really."

"I think he's rather wonderful," Felicity said, gazing admiringly at his back as he disappeared towards the indoor arena.

Sophy frowned. After being his only pupil for so long, she still hadn't quite got used to sharing his professional attentions, especially with people she didn't know.

"I suppose he is, a bit," she muttered in agreement. "Hadn't we better get Toby tacked up?"

Toby was quite at home in the collecting ring. As a Downside resident, nothing was happening that he hadn't seen before. Unfortunately, as his owner had hinted, his confidence translated into a fixed, leaning jaw and a rushing, unbalanced trot pace constantly verging on the edge of what would undoubtedly have been an equally unbalanced canter. The placid image he presented when not being ridden was a complete contrast to his eagerness to disregard any attempt to restrain him once he had a rider on board.

He was also short striding, even for a cob, and the rapid tempo took a moment to get used to. Sophy was briefly reminded of a sewing machine as she quickly decided to sit rather than rise; the movement was just too fast for words, and seemed to encourage him to go even faster.

He was nothing like Annie-May, but she started to deploy what she'd learned about steadying a running trot on her, trying at the same time to invite a lighter contact. It didn't exactly work miracles, but to Felicity and her watching Fairgate friends it was clear the horse was paying her at least some attention, and very gradually the pace became less fraught. The stride even lengthened slightly, but ten minutes was not enough time to establish anything. He was still working above the bridle, and there had been no opportunity to canter, when the steward called her to the gate.

The girl knew her by sight by now, but she knew Toby better.

"Have fun," she said with a quiet, knowing grin as she let her into the school. Waiting for the bell, Sophy would have had second thoughts about this whole enterprise if it hadn't already been too late.

The bell rang. She realised with a shock of embarrassment that she didn't know the test; how could she? She was booked to ride the Novice today. She looked helplessly towards the door, and a weight lifted as she saw Peter coming in with the sheet in his hand. Of course; out of all of them, he would be one to realise that she wouldn't know it.

"Enter at A in working trot and proceed down the centre line without halting," he read. "Track left at C."

So far, so good. Toby still had his head in the air, but being indoors steadied him further and it was relatively easy to at least perform the movements with some degree of accuracy and maintain a consistent tempo. She even had time to debate whether to canter or not. It would be a string of noughts if she didn't, but was it safe? If only she could ask her trainer, but this was a competitive test and she couldn't. Familiar with other Prelim tests, she guessed the last trot movement before he called it and tried to catch his eye across the arena. He looked up from the sheet, keen to see as much of the test as he could while commanding, and saw the question on her face. He could just see her brow furrow beneath the peak of her riding hat, and in a moment of inspiration realised her dilemma.

His thought crystallised in a moment. She was indoors on a short striding cob, she had a sound seat and a head on her shoulders. Had it been allowed, he would have said, 'Go for it,' but it wasn't. Instead, he very slightly inclined his head, and twitched one corner of his mouth into a grin of encouragement.

For Sophy, it was enough. He called, "Canter right between A and K," and as she passed the end marker she gave the aid.

Toby leapt forward as though he'd been shot in the rump, but the stride was only eleven feet for all his enthusiasm, and she was easily able to turn him on to the required circle in the centre of the arena, which necessarily slowed him further. As she returned to the track at E, in spite of the heavy contact she was even beginning to enjoy herself. There was no malice in the horse, he reminded her a little of Blackie trying his luck a bit as he did sometimes. And Toby, for all his energy and wanting his own way, short of deliberately throwing her off simply didn't have the physique to disrupt her seat.

If you'd suggested a year ago she'd get on a common cob she'd never seen before and immediately ride a test on it, for money, well, it would have been so far beneath her it would never have happened; and yet she came down the centre line to salute feeling quite pleased with herself. Toby was never going to set the dressage world on fire, but still he had his own way about him. Next time, she thought, I'll have you down in my hand a bit better.

As she moved off from G towards the doors, where Peter was waiting to let her out with a broad smile on his face, it also occurred to her that a year ago she probably wouldn't have been able to do it anyway.

Chapter Fifty

There was absolutely no reason for Tony Kenley to drag a nightclub hostess who had expressed no interest in horses whatsoever to a minor local dressage event, but midway through the afternoon his expensive sports car parked in the Downside liveries' car park, blithely ignoring the notice directing all show traffic into the field.

"I thought you were taking me home," the young woman said. "What are we doing here?" Sitting in that low slung car, the horses looked enormous. "I'm a bit frightened of horses," she added.

Tony could not himself have explained why he had turned in through Downside's gate, but after seeing the show sign, and remembering this morning's encounter on the road, the impulse had been overwhelming.

"Well, stay here then," he said indifferently. "I just want to see somebody."

He made himself smile at her. There was nothing wrong with the woman, but she was just another casual fling. He might see her again at the club, or he might not. His divorce had finally been resolved last week, and he was only human; some sort of celebration had been called for.

He got out of the car and vanished.

There were more people about than he would have expected, and to his untutored eye it seemed that every type of horse he'd ever heard of was represented.

Then he saw her, sitting on that coloured horse in the middle of the car park, surrounded by people and children and ponies and to all appearances the centre of attention. The man Holt was there too, looking up and speaking to her. The whole group seemed pleased and excited, as though she'd just done something extraordinary.

And she had. Gypsy, perhaps piqued because he'd seen her ride Toby first, or perhaps because he'd finally got to grips with the indoor school, had produced a medium trot and canter fit to complement the undoubted quality of his other work, and even drawn a discreet round of applause as he left the arena.

Sophy's eager smile said it all. He had no interest in dressage, even had it been his mother's horse, and it was nothing whatever to do with him, but still he experienced an unpleasant feeling of exclusion. She was fifty yards away, and he had no illusions left about what she thought of him, but she was an exceptional girl and still he felt drawn to her. What else was he doing here? Damn the woman. Why couldn't he just forget her? The evil thought came to him then that he might queer her pitch with his mother, and then reintroduce her. Horse mad like she was, that might bring her round.

A young female voice behind him said tentatively, "Excuse me, is that your car in the yard car park? Could you move it please?" He turned round. A teenage girl was looking at him anxiously. There was a home made paper badge pinned on her jersey with 'Car Park Steward' printed on it.

"I'm leaving," he said abruptly.

There was nothing to do here, and if she saw him there would probably be some unpleasantness with her instructor. That man Holt seemed to have some sort of hold over his mother, although he couldn't imagine what, and there might be repercussions. Just to irritate him further, his mother was now talking about placing him in the London office – "Now that American business is finally over," she'd said to him, "perhaps it's time for a new start."

There are moments in life, of no special significance in themselves, which somehow stick in the mind long after the event. The ride home to Fairgate became such a time for three tired riders and their respective horse and ponies; Kitty had again been placed in the top six and Blackie was sporting yet another proud rosette in his brow band, Jennifer was pleased that she had recovered her nerve and actually completed her first test with a not too terrible score, and Sophy and Gypsy had been leading the novice class when they left Downside, although there were another eight competitors still to ride. Eager to know if she had won, she was debating with herself whether to ride Annie-May first, or drive straight back to find out. Professionally speaking, the icing on the cake was Toby; he'd beaten Rufus, although not by much, but Felicity's expectations had not been high and she was pleased just to see him finish the test without a major disaster. She'd been even more pleased with his score sheet, and that contract was now well and truly confirmed.

In the end she rode Annie-May first in the last of the daylight, unusually with no spectators at all. With no one to show off to, the mare seemed a little flat, and Sophy confined herself to a few circles and loops without asking too much of her. As she was winding down, walking on a long rein and looking forward to dashing back to Downside before going home to tell mother all about it, Miss Brown appeared at the gate looking agitated.

She waved to her urgently.

"That Rufus pony," she said. "They decided to keep him in tonight. He's cast in his box. Can you help? They've all gone home. I know what to do, my own old pony sometimes used to do it, but I'm not strong enough by myself."

She dismounted in a hurry.

Annie-May was turned into her box without ceremony, and the two of them went into Rufus' stable.

Somehow, the pony had managed to roll on to his left side across the back corner of the box with all four legs folded against the wall. He raised his head when he saw them, and then it flopped back into the straw. He'd obviously been struggling to get up, and was now exhausted. The paint was chipped off the planking where his hooves had struck it.

"He could have been stuck for a while," Miss Brown said. "I came down to the office to get some papers and I heard a clatter."

There was a lunge line looped around his front pastern. "I couldn't get him over," Miss Brown explained. "It'll take the two of us. Pity that instructor of yours is not here. There's never a man around when you want one." She made a wry face, picked up the line, handed it to her, and took a good grip herself. "Are you ready?"

It was the nearest Miss Brown had ever come to a wry or humorous remark, at least in Sophy's hearing. A cast pony was also a new experience; of course, she'd heard about it happening, but it had never happened to one of her horses.

They took the strain, and heaved together. Rufus was astonishingly heavy, or so it seemed to Sophy, and it seemed an age before he rolled slowly on to his back, legs flailing dangerously close to them, and then fell on to his other side away from the wall. Instantly he got up and shook himself hard. He regarded his rescuers rather balefully, as though it was all their fault. Clearly unscathed, he shook himself again.

"It's been a big day for Rufus," Sophy said, amused by the pony's antics.

"It's not that funny," Miss Brown responded. "They can hurt themselves quite badly. Still, no harm done this time."

Sophy removed the lunge line from his leg. Rufus ignored her and attacked his hay net.

"I must finish off Annie-May and get back to Downside," she said as Miss Brown slid the stable bolt.

"You're a busy girl these days," the manager said. She very nearly smiled. "Onwards and upwards, is it?"

Sophy was faintly embarrassed. "Well, maybe," she said.

Suddenly, Miss Brown put her hand on her arm. "You take care," she said. "You're a handsome girl and there's one or two who'd like to get their hands on you. And I don't mean Terry Godwin."

She walked away quickly. Sophy's initial confusion crystallised in an instant. She could only mean Tony Kenley. But surely she, or rather Terry, had dealt with him. Did Miss Brown know something, or was she just guessing? Surely he wouldn't persist, not now.

It was a disturbing thought, and rather took the shine off Gypsy coming third in his first Novice class.

When his own interest was in question, Tony Kenley was not someone who let the grass grow under his feet. Apart from his lingering designs on Sophy, he had persuaded himself that Peter Holt was a malign influence on his mother where he was concerned, and if possible should be removed from his position of apparent friendship with her.

To be fair, in his own selfish way he was fond of his mother, and while she was adamant Holt was not exploiting her, his father had not been dead a year; perhaps she was seeking solace in the first half presentable, available man who came along. He'd seen something like it once before with an heiress of a similar age in America, and the resulting dénouement had been messy and expensive.

Despite living now in Stepford under the efficient domestic management of Mrs. Branksome, he invited himself to dinner at the Chichester house on Tuesday evening. He would have gone on Monday, but he had tickets to a show in London, and there was a girl he wanted to meet he'd known before he went to America…..

His mother was dining alone and was pleased to see him, and said so. At the same time, she had questions of her own. Mindful of the generous allowance the company, or rather she, paid him every month, she wanted to know what he intended to do now he was back in England and finally a free agent.

"I haven't decided," he told her. "I'm considering some ideas. I'm not sure about the London job. I mean, do I have the qualifications?"

Jenny Kenley smiled sympathetically, but inside she sighed. The boy was being evasive as usual. He'd been home for weeks now, and so far had used his incomplete divorce as an excuse not to take any firm action about his future. With that prevarication now concluded, it seemed he was seeking an alternative impediment.

"Actually," he said., "I really wanted to talk to you about something else. It's this business with the horse. And buying this estate in Fairgate."

His mother frowned.

"So what about the horse?" she said. "I didn't think you were interested."

"I'm not," he said. "Not as such. But I wonder of you're being conned by the two of them, the girl and that man Holt."

He saw his mother's brow crease deeper.

"You'd better explain," she said coldly.

It was a warning sign, but he chose to ignore it and ploughed on.

"I saw them on Sunday afternoon," he said. "The girl took her own horse to a show. Holt was there, and some kids on ponies from the Fairgate yard. I know for a fact the girl had been there all day because I passed her on the road in the morning. And I met your friend Agatha in the Fairgate shop yesterday. She was quite chatty. It seems your Mr. Holt has taken a job teaching at Downside, and the girl is now riding a horse for someone else over there too. It seems to me they're both taking your money and not doing much to earn it. I mean, she's using what you pay her to school and compete your horse, to school and compete her own. There was no sign of Annie-May on that showground."

He picked up his glass, drained it, and reached for the decanter.

His mother observed mildly, "You weren't here when Peter outlined his plans for Annie-May. If Sophy takes her own horse to shows in the meantime, I don't think that's any of our business."

She paused. In spite of his earlier hints, the idea that Peter Holt, or Sophy for that matter, would take advantage of her had never seriously exercised her thoughts for a moment. And it wasn't as if she was paying them much. On top of which, although she couldn't answer for Sophy's financial circumstances, she knew that Peter was indifferent to the money. With his quiet lifestyle, he didn't need much, but he was a fiercely proud man beneath that easy going exterior. If she even suggested such a thing, he would walk away in an instant and that was unthinkable.

"I'm not sure about buying the estate either," Tony said. "I mean, do we really need it? You don't think your friend Agatha and this man Holt aren't somehow getting something out of it?"

A maid came in to clear the table. She asked if they would like some coffee, and Mrs. Kenley nodded. Tony motioned to her to leave the decanter. As the door closed behind her trolley, his mother resumed the conversation from where Tony had left it.

"As for that question, no, I don't," his mother said flatly. "There were confidential political circumstances surrounding the vendor's decision to sell which very few people knew about. I only knew it was going to be sold myself from a chance remark from a friend in Switzerland over Christmas. I dare say Agatha might have got some advance warning from the vendor, but Peter couldn't possibly have a clue about any of it, then or now. I don't suppose for a minute he'd be interested anyway."

It seemed the time had come for a few honest words between mother and son. She reached out and put her hand on his wrist.

"I think we should clear the air between us. I loved your father, and I do miss him, but he wouldn't have wanted either of us not to get on with our lives. The business doesn't run itself, and although we have good managers doing the day to day stuff someone has to make the decisions Gerald used to make and so now as the owner it's down to me. I suppose it's lucky we worked side by side for so long.

"I know working in the business is not for you," she raised a hand as he seemed about to protest, "so I've made decisions about the future for both of us. I intend to go on working as I am for another ten years or so, unless things change, say I stop enjoying it or fall ill or something else happens, after all you never know. At that time I'm thinking of selling perhaps a half share in the firm so when I do pop off you won't lose out even if you're not involved. I want to buy the Fairgate house and estate and make it home, not just for now but as a place to retire to, where I can have some horses to enjoy with people I like around me. I'm hoping that over time we can develop the stables and have a real string of Kenley competition horses, jumpers as well as dressage horses. For now, it's nice to see Annie-May, the last of your father's horses, enjoying life and still doing something worthwhile. Later on, perhaps we'll breed from her. It may not mean much to you, but it matters to me. I think he'd approve."

Tony digested this information in silence. It seemed his mother had every detail worked out except where he figured in the scheme of things. He sipped his wine with a preoccupied frown, considering, while his mother stirred her coffee.

"Peter Holt is a good man," she said suddenly. Her voice was quiet but earnest. "You may not like him, but he and I have a sort of common feeling which is hard to explain. We may never be more than friends, but I very much want him to be part of my plans for Fairgate. At the moment he and Sophy are working Annie-May for me – it's hardly a full time job and they're both technically freelance and self-employed, so it's not exactly surprising they've taken on other work."

"Well, I still think you're being short changed," Tony insisted. "You didn't see that girl lapping up the attention she was getting and you didn't even know she was going to a show that day. And who's looking out for Annie-May if she's not even on the premises half the time?"

His mother looked at him reflectively. Ever since he was tiny, whenever he wanted something and was unsure he would get it, her son had displayed a consummate mastery of persuasive petulance; whatever did he want now?

"There's no urgency about you finding an occupation," she said then, seeking to mollify him. "You'll always be provided for, you must know that. But you really can't go through life doing nothing." She frowned. The only thing she knew he did with any consistency or enthusiasm was chase women; he'd done it since he was nineteen, and the hope that his marriage might have had a mitigating effect had quickly been dashed. And then, suddenly, the daylight dawned.

"It's Sophy," she exclaimed. "You've tried her out and she wouldn't have it. I remember now, I thought it was odd at the time. She wouldn't even look at you when she came to dinner that day. Was that black eye you wouldn't talk about something to do with her?"

He was her son, and she loved him dearly for all his faults, but the temptation to laugh at him was overwhelming. She twisted her lip and fought it for a moment, but it overcame her.

"Oh, Tony," she said eventually. "You really can't have every woman in the world just because you want them. Sophy's lovely, and innocent, and naïve, and wouldn't have a clue about a casual affair unless the other party had four legs. Oh, Tony," and she shook her head at him, still smiling broadly.

He was mortified and looked down at the table. It occurred to him then, as he should have realised before, that ever since he was ten his mother had seen through his wiles better that his father ever could.

Chapter Fifty One

Spring was interrupted by a cold week in late March which brought bright days, a bitter wind and bone in the ground, which lingered beneath a white frost until after ten in the morning. The faint shimmer of budding green on the twigs of the trees was checked in its progress, and the first stirrings of grass growth stilled in spite of the sunshine.

Sophy's busy days followed a pattern of riding, lessons, yard work and twice weekly trips to Downside to ride Toby and chat with Felicity, with occasional interruptions to what was now a familiar routine when the farrier called, or Mrs. Kenley came, sometimes unannounced, to see how they were getting on with Annie-May.

Downside had only one more show before the season ended with the championship show, scheduled for the third weekend in April, and both Blackie and Gypsy had already qualified for the Prelim. class final, with Gypsy close to achieving an entry in the Novice. Even Jennifer and Rufus had managed a score of 60%, although only once, and he still had a distance to progress to catch up with Blackie.

Sunday that week was a non-show day, and when Peter Holt arrived in his truck in the middle of the morning, jacketless in the sun, his suggestion that all his charges and their horses should have an easy day was met with general approval.

"We'll all go for a ride," he said. "Back for lunch, and then the afternoon off."

"Now that sounds good to me," Joe Fittleworth said. "The missus would very much like to see Kitty for more than five minutes at a time now and then. Do you suppose you can be a pony widow if you're actually the mother?"

Peter Holt grinned. "That's too technical for me," he said. "I dare say it amounts to the same thing."

He turned to Sophy. "I'll ride Gypsy," he said. "OK? I think it's time Annie-May went to Downside, so you need as much time as you can with her this week. We'll put her in the Novice and see how she goes. We'll have an extra session on Thursday. I know you'll have Gypsy in the same class too, so I might have to ride one of them over there for you. We'll have to see how the times work out. It's not worth the expense of hiring a trailer just for three miles. I dare say Joe or maybe that young man of yours will bring the rugs and jackets and stuff.

"And since you're the jockey, you can tell Mrs. Kenley. I'll bet a pound she'll want to come." He winked at her. "It's all happening. But we'll kick of the week with a nice relaxing hack over the hill. And my poor neglected little whippet can have a good long walk this afternoon." He glanced behind him, where Teddy's nose could be seen poking out of the driver's window.

Peter Holt's idea of a relaxing hack, as all the participants well knew by now, was anything but relaxing by most amateur rider standards. He tended to trot or canter wherever it was safe, which generally resulted in tired but exhilarated riders, especially the kids on their ponies, and the horses having their school cobwebs well and truly blown away.

"It's not just about fitness and knowing how to do the work," he told Sophy the first time she asked why he seemed always to go so fast when they went out together, and why he wasn't too concerned about niceties of outline when they were cruising along a bridle track at twenty miles an hour. "It's the psychology as well. God didn't intend horses to go round and round in circles on plastic floors all day. Specially not indoors. It's keeping 'em fresh that makes 'em want to do it. You must have seen lots of high quality horses in the ring working as though they couldn't be bothered. Your dressage work can be as correct as you like, but it's keeping the spark that wins the high marks. You can always tell when a horse is happy and keen and not just going through the motions."

He grinned at her. "You can't tell me you don't know when Gypsy's in a good mood, or if Annie-May's having a strop when you're riding her."

It was true, of course. Once upon a time all she'd wanted her horses to do was what they were told, a bit like robots. But Gypsy and Annie-May, in fact all the horses and ponies she knew these days, well, they naturally weren't exactly *people* but they weren't *just* horses either. And they were all different.

She was pondering this tricky question as she let herself in to the flat at lunchtime. Nowadays her mother's cooking was more adventurous, and today being Sunday and Sophy being expected home at a sensible hour, she had essayed a lamb roast.

The warmth and the smell of cooking greeted her as she took off her boots and hung up her coat. Edith called cheerfully from the kitchen, "Is that you dear? Come and stir the gravy."

Unusually, with it being midday, they ate at the kitchen table facing each other instead having plates on their knees in front of the evening television.

Sophy went to the sink for a glass of water.

"It's very good," she said, sitting down again and referring to the lamb. Her mother looked over at her, put down her knife and fork and sobbed suddenly.

Sophy was startled and stared at her. "What...," she started to say but Edith waved her into silence.

"I never thought we'd make it," she said emotionally. "But we have. When....it happened, I thought we were finished. Life was over and done with. Derek was gone, and the house, and your horses, and pretty much everything else with them. But look at us now."

She smiled though a tear. "We've got a home, you've got horses to ride and new friends, between us we can pay the bills and keep warm and I was going to tell you, Geoff's giving me a small rise and he wants to get me a little car to go round the craft fairs looking for new exhibitors for the gallery."

She paused. "It's not like it was," she said. "I suppose it never could be. But you're happy again and that's what matters most to me." She caught her breath. "I can't tell you how proud I am to be your mother when I see you and Gypsy doing so well, and someone by the ring says 'Is that your daughter?' and I say 'yes' and you've done it all yourself."

It's especially embarrassing to be embarrassed by your mother, even when no one else is present, and Sophy blushed and looked down at the table. Her mother's emotion was infectious, and for a moment they were both tearful.

Sophy said slowly, "Its not been a year yet."

Unconsciously, she fingered her father's St. Christopher. She met her mother's earnest gaze and remembered how she herself had felt when it happened, how penniless they were when they moved here, how Gypsy had been driving her to distraction and despair, that silly, false humiliation she'd felt starting work in the shop, then the advent of Peter Holt and the difference in her life since that first, fantastic autumn day.

She drank a little water and picked up her knife and fork, aware that her mother was still watching her fondly.

"Please don't look at me like that, mother," she said. "It's only living, really, isn't it? And I have to get to Downside to ride Toby this afternoon."

A teasing thought came to her.

"You never know," she said, looking across the table with an arch grin and carefully pretending to sound as though she meant it, "Perhaps we'll be millionaires again this time next year."

The mischievous thought gave way to a sudden, serious realisation. Speaking for herself, it wouldn't much matter one way or the other; she wouldn't be any happier if they were.

Terry Godwin had never been a millionaire, although, as is the nature of farming, his family had experienced good and bad years from time to time. It was doubtful if he'd ever thought much about it, except as an abstract concept that would never happen. Nevertheless, feeling more independent now he was past twenty one, and with what he considered a 'steady' girl friend in Sophy, and with his motor business expanding in spite of its unusual location, he told his father he wanted to stop working on the farm altogether.

His announcement wasn't unexpected; the uncle of one of his school friends owned a vehicle hire company based in Petersfield, and had recently approached him with the offer of a maintenance and servicing contract for his van fleet, which at a stroke brought another twelve motors under his care. It also provided him with a reliable monthly cheque far in excess of what his father could pay him.

When Sophy pushed open the door of the 'Shepherd and Flock' that evening, later than usual after being kept at Downside chatting to Felicity and the yard owner when she still had late stables to do at Fairgate, he was sitting at the bar with Peter Holt and telling him all about it.

Both men turned at the sound of the door closing, and Sophy found herself greeted by two smiles when she'd expected only one.

Emboldened by his new found independence, and eager to tell her of his change in fortune, Terry slipped off his stool and kissed her 'hello' on the cheek. Peter, with Teddy safely hiding behind his legs, looked on indulgently.

In spite of their regular embraces at the end the evening, he'd never greeted her like that before, in front of what seemed like half the village. It wasn't that she minded, particularly; I mean, with Mrs. Mullins knowing everything and everybody, it was hardly a secret. But still……she flushed slightly.

"Terry's got some good news," Peter said. "I think I'll go home and not spoil the party." He finished his beer. As he passed them on his way to the door, he dropped his hand on her shoulder.

"No late nights this week," he said to her with a knowing wink. "Lots to do before next Sunday. And don't forget to phone the boss."

He held the door open for the dog, and the cold night air briefly swirled around them. Terry led her to their usual table in the corner by the window and went to fetch her orange juice.

A warm yellow glow in the car park caught her eye through the leaded glass; Peter Holt was lighting his pipe before he and Teddy walked home under the bright, indifferent stars.

Chapter Fifty Two

She'd never phoned Mrs. Kenley before. Both she and Peter had been given her private number with the strictest instructions not to call her unless it was a dire emergency, and never to divulge it to a third party under any circumstances.

It was around ten o'clock on Monday morning when she called her, with slight trepidation, over a cup of coffee from the tack room after morning stables.

Hilda Gordon responded with an urgent enquiry. "Sophy? Is everything alright?"

It seemed like an anticlimax to explain about the show next Sunday. "Peter said to tell you as soon as possible," she said lamely.

Ms Gordon said she would pass on the message. For a moment she seemed inclined to chat. "I've never been to a horse show," she said. "Perhaps I'll come too."

"I'll have to phone again on Friday with the time," Sophy said. Ms Gordon hesitated. "You don't know now?" she asked.

"That's not how it works," Sophy said. "It's not like jumping. They have to see how many there are and work out a running order."

"Mrs. Kenley's going to Paris midweek," the PA said thoughtfully. "We have a meeting with some legal people about a contract dispute. I'm sure we'll be back by then. You have a good day now. Give that lovely horse a pat for me." There was smile in her voice as she added, "Don't fall off."

Sophy put the phone back in her pocket. She hardly knew Miss Gordon, but there was a confident, competent way about her that always provoked a slight envy. She thought back to that dinner party. It was perfectly clear that she'd had the measure of Tony Kenley, probably even better than his mother. Certainly better than me, she thought. Even after all this time, she still felt slightly ashamed of herself for being so naïve as to expose herself to him like that.

A shadow fell across her from the doorway, and she looked up with surprise to see Terry standing there.

"What's this, skiving?" he said cheerfully. She made him some coffee and he sat down beside her.

"Dad said I should come and see Miss Brown," he explained. "He thinks we might need to tell the council about my business expanding. He won't let me do anything illegal planning wise, he says. I don't understand it myself, and I don't really think he does either, but he says she will."

"I'm sure she will," Sophy said.

They were interrupted by the arrival of Peter Holt for her morning session with Gypsy.

"Meet me in the pub for lunch," Sophy said to Terry, taking her saddle from the rack.

"Can't," he said, "Got an engine in bits, promised for five o'clock. Have to get back ASAP."

"It's all go with you young people," Peter Holt said, swinging his shooting stick as he led the way down to the school. He opened the gate for her. "Get warmed up and we'll see how that shoulder in is coming."

It seemed that just about the only straightforward aspect of Sunday's show was going to be the weather, which had been set fair since Friday and was promised to continue for several days. It was a problem of logistics, and the tack room chat on Saturday afternoon was intense, involving five horses with no transport entered in two classes over a period of nearly six hours.

Kitty and Jennifer's entries in the Prelim class required their presence at Downside by nine thirty in the morning, and Sophy was engaged to ride Toby in the same class an hour later. Having two horses to ride in the following Novice class, she had requested times well apart, with Annie-May to go last.

With it being Annie-May's first public outing since her racing days, nobody could be quite sure how she would react; it was only sensible to give her the maximum time to become accustomed to the random movements of a showground rather than the more disciplined regime of racing preparations before she did her test. Annie-May being Annie-May, of course, it had to be possible her natural inclination to show off would boil over into becoming unmanageable. She also might think she was going racing again, with completely unpredictable consequences.

It was the nightmare scenario which Peter warned her might happen.

"If it does," he said seriously, "don't struggle and don't have a row with her. One of you might get hurt. Get off and we'll take it from there. That way, however fraught she is, she'll know you've made the decision and not her."

In the end, she rode Gypsy over in the morning with Blackie and Rufus, and thanks to them being recognised now as regular clients and Peter Holt's association with the establishment, she was able to put up Gypsy in a spare stable until it was time for his test. There was an awkward moment when she asked for a hay net for him, and the girl on the yard demurred, but Felicity solved the problem by giving him Toby's.

She rode Toby down to the collecting ring. Peter was talking to one of his Downside clients, Kitty was dismounted and talking to Joe, having just ridden her test, and Jennifer was waiting to enter the arena. The showground was the usual cheerful mêlée of people and horses enjoying the brisk spring sunshine, and at least half a dozen faces turned towards her with a smile of greeting. In spite of the hectic day ahead, a comfortable feeling of belonging came over her. She smiled down at Felicity in her turn, walking beside her, and gave Toby an appreciative pat.

Toby excelled himself that morning, completing most of his test more or less in the right shape and apart from striking off on the wrong lead in the second canter transition, without any serious mistakes. Felicity was delighted, but the watching Peter Holt was less enthused by the rider's performance.

"That wrong lead was your fault," he said to her as they watched Felicity leading Toby back to the stables.

Sophy, feeling quite pleased with herself considering the test as a whole, bridled at that. It was a measure of her growing confidence that she dared to argue with him.

"I don't see how," she said, rehearsing the movement in her mind.. "I sat to the trot to prepare, I asked him to bend, I gave the aid on the marker, and he just went wrong."

"The lateral balance wasn't right," Holt said. "If I could see it, you should have felt it. Think back. When you asked for the bend, what happened?"

It was true. She could remember asking for the shape, but then the marker came and she gave the canter aid without waiting for the bend to establish.

He said quietly, "These Prelim horses are always a bit on the forehand, so the canter often doesn't start from behind. Of course you know that. But think what it means when you ask for canter if the horse isn't properly bent. He falls on to the outside shoulder, in fact your aid is pushing him on to it, and so he starts to canter with that leg and that lead. I know it's a test, but the judge won't mark you down half as much if you wait a couple of metres to get the balance right and the correct lead instead of going exactly on the marker with the wrong one."

They both became aware that at least two other riders were near enough to overhear and were listening intently. Sophy was embarrassed at being corrected in public, however mildly, but Holt sensed it and was annoyed.

"Do you mind?" he said to them. "This conversation is private."

He led her away to the collecting ring fence.

"One other thing," he said. "Just general, really, between us professionals. It's always worth remembering, especially when you ride one for the first time, that short striding cobs like Toby find it easy to canter on the outside lead even on a circle, so getting the bend right first is even more important."

His remark about professionals cheered her up again, as he knew it would.

"So how do you know what the judges think?" she asked him then, and he shrugged.

"I used to sit on the other side of the fence sometimes," he said. "Not for a while, though."

Joe Fittleworth was coming towards them, frowning, Holt grinned then. He said to Sophy, "Now for it. We were all so concerned about getting everybody here on time yesterday no one thought about getting back. We can't keep Rufus and Blackie tied up to the fence here all day, and I hate to think what Kitty and Jennifer will get up to in the mean time."

"But I can't ride Gypsy back again twice," Sophy said. "Anyway, there wouldn't be time."

"No," he agreed with her. "Joe will just have to follow them back in the car. At least it's not far. Don't you worry about it. Now listen. You have to concentrate on the Novice now. It's a big day for you, and me, with Mrs. Kenley coming for the first time. We know Gypsy will do a decent test whatever happens, so use his test as a bit of a practice for Annie-May's, you know, get the feel of the turns and where the transitions come. I'll run you back to fetch her the minute Gypsy comes out so you won't have to hurry on the road, and we'll ride back together afterwards."

He was looking over her shoulder towards the gate where a white van was arriving. and his grin returned. "By the time Mrs. Kenley gets here you'll have more fans than a rock star," he said with a chuckle. "Here's Terry coming in with your Mum now. I'll go and buy them a cup of tea. You get Gypsy going and don't let that Felicity distract you while you're tacking up."

Annie-May's impeccable behaviour on the road from Fairgate disintegrated instantly as she entered the showground and realised this was a special occasion. Head and tail high in the air, she paraded down to the collecting ring barely under management and proceeded to trot wildly along the fence with a huge, elaborately suspended stride while snorting loudly.

It was an impressive performance and grabbed the attention of just about everybody within sight or earshot, no doubt exactly as Annie-May intended, but it was not easy to ride. Fortunately the handful of other riders warming up had sufficient experience, or sense of self-preservation, to keep out of the way.

Peter Holt, Felicity, Joe, Kitty and Jennifer who had come back to watch, and Terry and her mother, were all lined up along the fence; Peter Holt was smiling at the horse's antics, confident in his pupil's ability to handle her, but her mother was looking decidedly nervous.

In spite of her relatively elevated position, Sophy had her hands full and neither she nor any of the others noticed a Bentley, followed almost immediately by a bright red sports car, nose its way between the horse boxes to park a careful safe distance from the principal centre of activity. Eddy was clearly prepared to sacrifice a small element of his boss's convenience to safeguard his precious charge's paintwork. He opened the rear door for her, and the first thing Jenny Kenley saw was her son's car.

"Hello, mother," he said cheerfully, appearing from behind her. "Wasn't busy, thought I'd take an interest."

He nodded indifferently to Hilda Gordon, who was looking about her with a trace of nervousness as a large, half bred horse was led past.

His mother made a non-committal gesture. "Well, it's nice to see you," she said. She turned to the driver. "I think you'd better stay and watch the car, Eddy. That is why you came, isn't it?"

"Yes, ma'am," Eddy responded. He did not add that he wouldn't trust her, or indeed anyone else, to drive his lovely car across a muddy field, even one which did have some gravel thrown over the area beside the gate.

Hilda said, "Isn't that Sophy riding over there?"

All three of them followed her gaze to where Sophy's head and shoulders could be seen above the line of collecting ring spectators, travelling at an alarming rate on what was now a twenty metre circle, as very gradually she was beginning to have some influence over Annie-May's exuberant demonstration of her own brilliance.

Peter Holt greeted her owner with a wide smile. Terry regarded Tony with a certain surprise, which quickly became hostility, and removed himself from the group to assume a position some yards further down the fence. Tony was faintly amused by his rival's retreat, but feeling somewhat out of his depth in this environment decided himself to keep a low profile and await developments. There was only the faintest of chances he would find an opportunity to speak to Sophy, or that she would speak to him, but he had nothing to do today and nothing to lose either, so it had to be a chance worth taking.

As the final competitor in the last class of the day, Annie-May progressively ran out of companions until at last she and Sophy were alone in the collecting ring with only their own supporters lining the fence. By now, following Peter's advice, the mare had been kept working without a pause for nearly forty minutes, and for the last ten had been very nearly sensible.

Sophy was exhausted. She rode over to the fence to say a belated 'hello' to Mrs. Kenley just as the young steward, tired herself after a long day's duty, came into the arena and said, "Here you go, then, Sophy, are you ready?"

The hoped for couple of minutes to get her breath back were not going to materialise.

She entered the indoor school on a long rein, passing the penultimate competitor in the wide doorway. Annie-May looked about her with interest but with no signs of the trepidation Gypsy had displayed on his indoor début. That was a relief at any rate.

She walked own the centre of the arena. Annie-May was dark with sweat, worked into foam in the creases of her neck and loins, making a mockery of the intensive grooming she'd received for the opening day of her new career.

The bell rang, and Sophy's tiredness fell from her like rain into the grey surface beneath the horse's feet.

In the whole of her life, she had never wanted anything so much as to ride a good test today, *now,* on this lovely, difficult, dangerous mare who was teaching her so much and who she loved so hard that at this very moment it was nearly *painful.*

She took up the reins, and Annie-May did that awful Araby thing with her head. Disappointment crashed over her, but she was a professional now. They hadn't yet begun the test so it wouldn't count. Then the bell rang, she retook the contact and turned determinedly down the centre line.

Annie-May came to her hand, not softly but somehow. Her back was tight and she would not bend, but still the trot was even and they managed the first three movements without a catastrophe. It was time for the first medium trot, just an undemanding few strides, and Annie-May always loved to show off how far she could stretch, but when she asked, nothing happened. The step simply did not change.

Peter Holt did not take his eyes off his protégé, but he said to Jenny beside him, "That mare is a proper little madam. She's sulking because Sophy's got her under control." His voice dropped and Jenny couldn't be sure he was talking to her, or to himself, or to anybody at all.

"Will she know what to do? Surely she'll know what to do. Don't let me down, please *please* let her know what to do."

At the far end of the arena Sophy's mind was racing. What was the matter with the horse? She should have been showing the world how special she was, not moping about like a jaded school hack. She was half tempted to smack her, but prudence prevailed.

"It's not very spectacular," Tony Kenley said in a bored tone to his mother, standing on her other side.

Sophy niggled the mare with her heel, and gave her a small poke. For a moment she wished she was wearing spurs.

Peter didn't like spurs, especially on novices. "They should answer the leg," he'd insisted when she asked about using them on Gypsy. "Time enough for all that fancy stuff when everybody knows more about what they're doing. I never saw a novice rider yet who had proper control of their lower leg when it came to spurs."

Sophy realised in that same moment that using spurs on Annie-May might provoke an explosion, but not much else.

Another ten metres went by along the short side, stiff and reluctant and crooked with another corner coming.

And then the penny dropped. The old baggage was sulking. She was in a mood because she hadn't got her own way in the collecting ring, and now she wasn't even going racing and they were doing that silly slow stuff again.

It was impossible not to laugh out loud, and just as impossible not to reach forward and stroke her neck and giggle in her ear. At that exact second she loved Annie-May better than she loved anybody or anything else in the world, and Annie-May knew it too.

Jenny felt Peter grasp her arm without knowing he was doing it.. "Attagirl," he said in the same quiet, intense tone, and he definitely wasn't talking to anybody in particular this time.

In half a dozen strides, Annie-May agreed that perhaps she could stoop to doing this after all. With a passing good grace she allowed her back to soften and gave herself to the contact to produce the swinging step and the supple bend Sophy had felt so often at home. The second attempt at medium trot was a revelation; Hilda and Terry gasped at the difference, and even Tony was briefly impressed.

As they stepped into canter, with Annie-May showing every sign now of enjoying herself and playing to the gallery as usual, Sophy realised that even the few medium canter strides the test called for would offer her a golden excuse to really show off. It was very unlikely, once extended, that she would condescend to come back, and if she did she would certainly buck.

Peter Holt had the same thought, accompanied by an image of Annie-May and her precious pilot hurtling around the school as though it was a wall of death.

There was nothing he could do. Only Sophy's feel and intuition could make the right decision now, and she made it.

They cantered sedately round the school in an unvarying, sweetly lifting pace, including a careful change of rein, came forward to trot and turned from the half marker down the centre line to salute. Annie-May fidgeted twice, and then agreed to stand still for just long enough.

Holt realised he still had hold of Jenny's arm, and guiltily released it. The relief on his face was plain to all of them.

She turned to him with a smile.

"I think you rode every step of that with her," she said.

"That mare is so damn difficult," he said.

Annie-May was walking now towards the door, and it seemed to even the least knowledgeable spectators, as her ears flicked back to speak to Sophy, that she was saying, "Is that all? That's not much. I can go faster than that."

The steward looked up and said, "Isn't she lovely?" as they passed her and emerged into the late afternoon sun.

Sophy grinned feebly down at her, swamped with relief and slightly emotional. Looking over the girl's head, she could see her entourage approaching.

Chapter Fifty Three

Peter reached her first. Her face was a confusion of elation and disappointment. He patted Annie-May's sweaty neck as he spoke to her.

"Slip off and loosen the girth. It's the best way to reward her and she'll know she's finished, for the time being anyway."

Annie-May, as usual, revelled in being the centre of attention, but Sophy, with her mind in a muddle of different emotions, felt she was surrounded and being bombarded with questions and remarks from what seemed like everybody at once.

She had her back to them all wrestling with the girth buckle when Peter appeared beside her and took the reins out of her hands.

"I'll do that. I bet you've not eaten all day," he said in a quiet voice close to her ear. "Go and grab a sandwich while the van's still here. I don't want you fainting on me while we're riding home. I'll take care of her for now." He glanced over his shoulder. "And this lot," he added with a grin.

She was walking away when Tony Kenley, who in spite of the older man's discretion had been near enough to overhear, seized his chance.

"I'm a bit peckish myself," he said. "I think I'll join her."

It was a harmless enough remark, but with most of his companions having at least some idea of the antagonistic relationship between him and Sophy, and one or two of them knowing the reason for it, an embarrassed silence fell over them as he followed her up the car park.

Mrs. Kenley was furious. Damn the boy. Why couldn't he take 'no' for an answer? It was apparent to her now, as it very likely was to everybody else, why he'd come when he'd made no secret of his lack of interest in dressage.

Terry made an instinctive move to follow him, but was checked by a glance from Holt and Joe Fittleworth, both sensing a row which would spoil the day for everyone, especially the youngsters ready now to go home. Joe deliberately asked him if he'd ever ridden himself. Terry was obliged to reply, but even so he kept his eyes on Sophy moving through the rapidly dwindling crowd of showgoers while he answered.

The caterer was folding up the chairs around his two little tables in front of his van's serving hatch as Sophy approached.

"Yes, madam," he said. "My last customer." He smiled. "What can I get you?"

Sophy asked for a cup of tea and a sandwich. He stepped back into his van and she sat down wearily on one of the two remaining chairs. Tony appeared and immediately sat down on the other, and she recoiled from him with a shock of surprise.

"Don't be like that," he said hurriedly. "I know we got off on the wrong foot. I want to make amends."

The caterer appeared with Sophy's order. "Only cheese left, I'm afraid," he said to Sophy, setting it on the table. "I hope that's alright."

"Thank you," she said, and reached into her pocket to pay him.

"I'll get that," Tony said, and Sophy was angered even more. This bloody man was everywhere.

"No, you won't," she retorted. She gave the van man his money and he retreated in a hurry.

Tony offered her his most winning smile. "I do think we should at least be friends," he opined. "For mother's sake, at least. What do you say?"

She looked down the field.

The showground was emptying fast; only a handful of horseboxes remained and the little knot of people grouped around Annie-May was also smaller now, as Joe had taken the children home. Mrs. Kenley was encouraging Hilda Gordon to get acquainted with the horse, and she could see Peter explaining something about the bridle. Her mother and Terry were both staring in her direction, but they were at least fifty yards away.

No one was going to help her. No one could, really. Out of nowhere, she remembered what Miss Brown had said about taking care. She had to be grown up about this, and do it herself. And she knew exactly what this man wanted. And he wasn't going to get it.

She drank some tea to compose herself and buy a little time. The tea was just about warm enough to be palatable. Suddenly, the sandwich looked good. She picked it up, and paused.

She couldn't know that just at that moment, tired, dishevelled, sandwich in hand and with her riding hat on the table in front of her, she was the picture of desirability for a man like Tony Kenley, accustomed to a very different kind of sophisticated young woman whose chief object in life was a match for his own, the pursuit of her own gratification.

"I like Mrs. Kenley," she said, very obviously picking her words carefully. "She's been very good to me."

"Well, there you are then," he interrupted her with a note of triumph in his voice.

There was silence between them for a moment. Sophy realised he would deliberately misinterpret whatever she said if there was the faintest chance of getting his own way. She frowned, and even that failed to make her less attractive in his eyes; but there was no mistaking her determination now.

"Mr. Kenley," she said, trying to sound formal and official and once and for all, "I don't like you. I don't want anything to do with you. You tried to take advantage of me, and you frightened me. We'll never be friends. I'll talk to you if I have to, so long as I ride for you mother. But that's all. Now please stop bothering me."

She left the lukewarm tea on the table, picked up her hat and set off back to Annie-May.

The caterer reappeared as Tony sat frowning and watching her go.

"Can I get you something before I close, sir,?" he asked him.

"No, damn you," Tony said, and got up himself. Instead of following Sophy down the hill, he went across towards his car.

The caterer smiled the private smile of a man accustomed to witnessing the vagaries of human interaction, and glanced knowingly after each of them in turn. Pretty girl, that. He'd seen her here before. That man, with that flash car, obviously no better than he should be. It was none of his business, of course, but in a funny, disinterested way he felt quite pleased she'd shot him down.

Tony's car was driving out as she rejoined them, wiping her fingers, greasy from the sandwich, on her handkerchief; Terry came a step or two to meet her and put a protective arm around her.

"Alright?", he said in a concerned tone.

"Alright," she answered, and he had to be content with that.

Nobody mentioned that Tony had not come back with her.

Mrs. Kenley wanted to know what she thought about Annie-May in the ring.

"Peter says you did really well," she said. "But it looked awfully patchy. Why didn't you extend the canter, like it says in the list? She'd be good at that."

Thankfully, Peter stepped in. "Annie-May's still very green at this," he said, "and this is her first show. She might not have come back. I think Sophy did right not to ask. Let's go and see what the judge had to say, shall we? And we mustn't hang about too long, Sophy and me have to ride back to Fairgate before the light goes."

He took Hilda and Jenny away towards the scoreboard, leaving Sophy feeling much more comfortable with only her mother and Terry to contend with.

Her mother said, "You must be exhausted, sweetheart. You went out at six o'clock this morning. When do you think you'll be home tonight?"

"Oh, I'm not too bad," Sophy said. She thought for a minute. "Seven or eight, I suppose. I'll have to put them to bed when we get back, and then I have to bring Peter back here for his truck. That won't take long."

"His poor little dog must be desperate if he's been shut in that cab all day." Edith said.

Sophy said absently. "The dog's not here. He leaves him at home with the run of the back garden when he's away all day. I wonder what the judge really thought. I mean, technically I did miss out three medium movements."

Peter was coming back, walking between the two women. He had two sheets in his hand. He gave one to her and the other to Mrs. Kenley.

In what seemed like another age, Gypsy had scored 69.1% and was placed second.

She realised Mrs. Kenley was smiling at her.

"She liked you, and she liked Annie-May," she said. "Look." She put the sheet in her hand.

It was awful score, 51.4%, but she had a decent riding mark and the judge had written, 'This combination looks good for a big future,' and Annie-May had been awarded an eight for her paces. As if to underline the impression she had made, the original mark of 7.5 had been crossed out.

"All good stuff," Peter said. "now I'm going to put my breeches and boots on in the truck, and we must get moving." He turned to Sophy. "You stick to Annie-May," he said. "She won't want a change of jockey at this time of day. Is Gypsy's tack by the stable door? I'll meet you by the gate in ten minutes."

He was hurrying away when he stopped suddenly and turned round.

"OK," he said to Jenny. "Be about nine o'clock." He hurried on.

"What was that about?" Hilda asked of no one in particular.

"I don't know how he does it," Jenny said in a bemused voice. "I was going to ask him to dinner tonight, but with everything else going on I forgot. He seems to read me every time I meet him."

"From what I've seen," Hilda said, "It's a bit mutual."

"Yes," her boss's brow furrowed, "I suppose it is. I can't quite fathom it."

"Perhaps you'd like to come to dinner with us tonight?" Edith asked Terry. "I'm sure Sophy would like it."

"So would I," Terry said. "I've hardly spoken to Sophy all day, with all these horses she keeps riding. I'll drop you off and come back later, shall I?"

Eddy regarded the now well worn lorry tracks across the field with a certain misgiving as he held open the Bentley door for Jenny Kenley and Hilda to enter the rear seat. Nevertheless, largely thanks to his expertise with clutch and accelerator, he managed to negotiate a path to the gate without incident.

Half way along Downside's driveway, he crept past Gypsy and Annie-May, homeward bound in the last of the afternoon sunshine.

Chapter Fifty Four

"If I were a bookmaker," Peter Holt said to Sophy in the middle of the week preceding Downside's championship and final show of the season, "I'd probably make Gypsy second favourite to win that Novice class. He still has his forehand moments, and that little bay thoroughbred has beaten him every time so far, but he keeps improving."

She knew who he meant. "That's Elspeth's horse," she said. "He's lovely. He won it last year, Elspeth says. She's had him since he was a foal."

They were sitting in the tackroom drinking coffee after a long and frustrating session with Annie-May, whose determination to just keep going faster whenever she was asked to lengthen her canter was daily justifying Sophy's decision not to ask for it in the arena.

"*He* extends nicely," she said ruefully, thinking of the struggles she'd been having with Annie-May only twenty minutes ago.

"It'll come," Holt said. He drew comfortably on his pipe, with one eye on the open doorway. Miss Brown didn't actually forbid smoking in the tackroom; in fact, before his arrival, nobody ever had anyway; but he knew perfectly well she did not approve.

He took a sip of coffee. "We'll try a little psychology. Just go hacking until the weekend, then give her the day off when you take Gypsy to the show. If she's the lady I think she is, she'll be so miffed she'll be angelic on Monday." He chuckled. "Pesky females," he said. "You know where you are with a gelding like Gypsy. I bet you never thought six months ago you'd have him in a championship Novice class, even a little one like Downside, with a chance of winning."

"Thanks to you," she said, and he stopped her then.

"No," he said. "That's not how it works, as you'll find out soon enough when you've got pupils. The person who wins and takes the credit is always the rider, because he or she is the one who actually does it. Trainers just take the blame when things go wrong. And that's not just about horse riding. Everybody in the world has heard of Einstein or Shakespeare, but nobody knows who taught them, or made them interested enough in their subjects to do what they did. I certainly don't. Do you?"

"But that's not fair," Sophy protested.

"Yes and no," he said. "I've taught riding for a very long time. There's a perfectly sound argument, and believe me it's a disappointed parent's favourite, that if a pupil or a rider fails an exam or does poorly in competition, the trainer didn't do his job properly. I'm not much into football, but every time I open my paper it seems another top class manager's got the sack, but nobody ever sacks the team on the pitch when it loses a few games."

He stood up and stretched. "I have to get over to Downside for the student ride," he said. "We'll have a session with Gypsy on Friday morning, then you can give him a gentle jolly out on Saturday and that should set him up nicely. As for Kitty and Blackie," he grinned. "That damn pony could actually *win* the Prelim championship. I've seen the start list. He's never actually won a class, but he's beaten them all at some time over the season. Kitty will be insufferable."

"Kitty would be insufferable if she fell off and came last," Sophy said, and they both laughed at that.

He paused in the doorway. "By the way, get Gypsy registered and make sure your BD membership is up to date. It's time we started thinking forward for him now he's got some form."

She finished her coffee after he'd gone, reflecting on what he'd said about trainers. It rang true, but it still didn't seem fair. On the other hand, putting the world to rights was not her province. It was time for Gypsy to do half an hour's work in the school on transitions, with a few medium exercises in between, and then have a run up the hill before she went home to lunch.

There'd be time this afternoon for a surprise visit to Terry to inspect his newly extended workshop. And mother was due to come home this evening in her new company car for the first time.

She lifted Gypsy's saddle and bridle off the rack and stepped out into the bright sunlight, humming softly under her breath.

There were differing emotions on parade in the Fairgate House stable yard that Sunday morning.

Gypsy was tied up outside his box while Sophy washed bed stains off his flanks and neck and wondered if it was worth trying to plait his mane. After all, it was the Championship. In the good old days, when someone else was always available to do what she couldn't, her horses were always plaited for the arena, but she'd never done it herself. If the truth was told, it wasn't that she didn't know how, she just wasn't at all sure she'd do it as well as Kitty, who in less that twenty minutes had transformed Blackie almost into a show pony.

The radio was playing quietly in the background, Joe Fittleworth was cleaning Kitty's saddle for her sitting on a chair outside the tackroom while she plaited Blackie's tail, and only Jennifer was moping about with nothing to do, the other two girls having gone down to the school to ride.

They were due to set off for Downside in about half an hour, and Kitty was determined to make the most of the fact that Blackie had qualified for the finals while Rufus, for all he was bigger and faster, hadn't. It was no wonder Jennifer was feeling a bit left out this morning. She wandered over to watch Sophy picking out Gypsy's feet.

"I wish I was coming," she said unhappily.

Sophy straightened up and looked at her.

"Rufus is coming along," she said consolingly. "He's just not quite ready yet. Anyway, didn't you tell me he jumps better than Blackie?"

"I suppose," Jennifer said without much enthusiasm.

Sophy thought for a moment.

"Well," she said. "You could always come just for a ride. Can you be ready in time?"

Jennifer stared at her, spun on her heel and a moment later disappeared towards the paddock with a head collar in her hand.

Joe Fittleworth appeared behind her and gave Gypsy a pat.

"That was kind," he said. "Kitty has been rubbing it in a bit this morning." He glanced around the yard. "Is Peter not coming today?"

"He's meeting us over there," Sophy said. "I was going to ask you if you'd take my jacket and stuff for me. My Mum will bring it back, but she had to go to a craft fair in Petersfield first thing and Terry's working." She looked at him with a certain degree of satisfaction. "He's painting his new workshop," she said. "He's hoping to get over later."

"So you're not the only one going up in the world," Joe said with a smile.

Jennifer came hurrying by leading a rather muddy Rufus.

"You'd better be quick," Sophy said. "We're off in ten minutes."

The qualifying system for the Championship show always ensured three full classes, as the Downside management naturally needed to keep an eye on the bottom line as well as keeping the patrons happy. Part of the arrangement was not to allow any combination to compete in more than one championship class to give as many as possible of the regular patrons a chance to ride in the last show of the season. Although Gypsy had qualified at both Prelim and Novice level, thinking forward it had seemed natural to both his rider and trainer to choose to enter the Novice class.

A polite request to the secretary when they entered had given Blackie a start time near the end of his Prelim class, and Gypsy one close to the beginning of the Novice.

While there are worse things for horse folk to do on a sunny day than wander about a show ground, it's not so relaxing when you have your own horse in tow who must eventually put in a performance. While Kitty confidently expected there would always be a grown up on hand to take care of Blackie if she wanted to go off and play truant, Sophy had learnt by now that without a lorry to operate from it was better to take the horse home and then come back again to catch up with events. Today, Kitty would not have long to wait before they could ride home together as usual.

Having attended the last five or six shows, Sophy recognised nearly everybody as soon they rode through the gate, although some of her rivals for the Novice Championship had seemingly not yet arrived. Peter and her mother had also not yet come, and so Joe was left to hold Gypsy when Kitty, more nervous today because it was the top Prelim. test and this was the Championship, wanted someone to watch her warming up.

Blackie, cheeky as ever, sensed his rider was on edge and decided he would only canter on the right lead this morning. After fifteen attempts, and with her time approaching rapidly, Kitty was becoming tearful and frantic, and Sophy, watching from the fence, was at a loss to know what to tell her.

A hand dropped on her shoulder and she turned with relief to hear Peter Holt say, "Good morning, how's he going?"

Kitty rode up, breathless and anxious, and the words tumbled out as she explained what was the matter.

Holt calmly took his pipe out of his pocket and considered for a moment.

"Show me," he said, and Blackie duly declined to canter left, again. Kitty came back looking even more agitated.

"He's pulling your leg because he knows it's a special day and you're nervous," the instructor said. "Don't smack him, it won't work. Trot towards the fence, bend him the wrong way and canter at the last minute. He'll overbalance and go on the leg you want. After he's done it once, I bet he'll be OK after that. Try it."

Kitty rode away. A moment later, Blackie, heavily on his forehand, was nonetheless cantering on the left lead.

"That's not in the book you lent me," Sophy said.

Holt chuckled. "It's an emergency measure," he said. "You usually get the lead you want but it's an awful canter. Thing is, it gets 'em going on that leg and it's easier after that. They're more in the mood, if you see what I mean." He looked at her more seriously. "None of us can cope without the knowledge handed down in books," he remarked, "but in the end you can't beat experience and common sense. No one's going to write that down as a canter aid, are they?, but that doesn't mean you can't use it if you have to.

It's about compromising to get what you want without being unkind to the horse."

He beckoned to Kitty and told her not to canter again until she was riding her test.

"Psychology," he said to Sophy. "Just in case it does go wrong next time. Hopefully the pony will just pick up where he left off anyway, but more important Kitty will expect him to answer properly and when you assume a horse will answer 'yes' they generally do. If you give an aid wondering if the horse will say 'yes,' or expecting him to say 'no,' you can bet your life 'no' is what you'll get." He chuckled again. "I never read that in any books either, although I dare say it's written down somewhere."

Kitty's name was called and they followed her to the arena doors. Joe appeared leading Gypsy, anxious to see his daughter perform, and Sophy guiltily took her horse from him and left them to it. It was time she started warming up herself anyway.

It was about two thirty when the three of them left to ride home. Kitty, having come fourth after Blackie decided to behave himself, was as usual making sure that Jennifer knew all about it, but Jennifer did not rise to the bait. She waited until Kitty wasn't looking, caught Sophy's eye and mouthed up at her, "Wait till next week. It's jumping at the Pony Club."

Sophy, with the two of them under her care as they jogged down the road, was warily eyeing a huge tractor approaching with a hedge cutting flail attached to it. It was impossible not to remember Peter's experience. The tractor was not working, merely progressing sedately down the road, and it was evident the driver was fully aware of his responsibilities when passing equines as he had slowed his pace to a crawl, but even so she cast about for somewhere to get off the carriageway.

A field gateway appeared beside them in the hedgerow with the gate open into a grassy meadow, and she took her charges a couple of yards off the tarmac into the gap.

All three of them were watching the tractor creeping past when out of the blue a loose collie dog, barking its head off, attacked Blackie from behind. He shot forward just as the massive rear wheel of the tractor was turning slowly exactly in front of him.

Time stopped. Jennifer screamed. The driver braked. Sophy jammed her legs into Gypsy, reached down, snatched Blackie's bridle and pulled him crookedly off the wheel. Kitty fell in a slow, tumbling arc over the pony's right shoulder into the gutter beside the hard, black tyre.

The dog was still barking. The tractor man was climbing out of his cab, his face as white as Sophy's.

"God," he said. "Is she alright?"

The dog owner arrived, grabbed the dog without even looking at any of them, and vanished.

"I know 'im," the tractor man said grimly. "I'll 'ave 'im after. 'E's not allowed in that field."

He bent down over Kitty, but she was already sitting up and shaking herself. He helped her to her feet. Kitty adjusted her hat, and coolly took back her reins from Sophy. It was clear to Sophy, if not to the stranger, that she was not about to admit being frightened in front of Jennifer.

"I am perfectly alright," she said with all the aplomb which only a shaken child who is the centre of attention can muster.

"Are you sure?" Sophy said anxiously. "We're nearly back. Can you make it?"

"I am perfectly fine," Kitty said determinedly. As if to underline her determination, she put her foot in the stirrup and remounted. "It wasn't Blackie's fault."

"No, it wasn't," the tractor driver agreed. He looked up at Sophy, who was gradually recovering from the shock of what might have happened.

"Saw it in the mirror," he said to her. "Bloody marvellous, you were. I'll 'ave that bastard with the dog next time I see 'im don't you worry."

Sophy was anxious now to get home. Joe would be there by now and wondering where they were.

She led them back on to the road behind the tractor. shivering slightly as she passed that huge back wheel. The top of the tyre reached almost up to her waist. She thought of Peter with a greater understanding of the time it had taken him to get over that dreadful Yorkshire business. Perhaps it would be better not to tell him. She was about to say as much to Kitty when she realised that such a suggestion would instantly provoke her to do just that, and didn't.

There was no fooling Joe Fittleworth as they entered the stable yard. All three of them were unnaturally subdued, and he immediately guessed something had happened. Sophy disappeared into Gypsy's stable without pausing, but Kitty and Jennifer, especially Jennifer repeating the fact that Kitty had fallen off, were quick to tell him all about it. Finally satisfied his daughter wasn't hurt, he came to find Sophy.

She was giving Gypsy a brisk rub down, but he could see she wasn't quite herself.

"It seems you did a wonderful thing today," he said to her quietly over the stable door.

She turned to him and the sympathy in his face cracked the brittle shell of carrying on regardless.

"It was terrifying," she said, and sobbed suddenly, burying her face in Gypsy's neck.

He came into the stable and put his arm on her shoulder. "Come on," he said gently. "It's OK. There's no harm done, and Kitty and me will love you forever."

She turned to look at him. "Thanks," she said, sniffing hard.

"Don't let the kids see you crying," Joe said. "They'll just make more of it."

"No," she said. "You're right." She made an effort. "I have to get back to Downside. Mum and Peter are waiting for me. Kitty did so well this morning."

"Jennifer says you were leading the class when you left," Joe said then. "Good luck."

Driving back along the road below the Downs, as she passed the place where it had all happened, she couldn't help thinking that she, and Kitty too, had already had more luck that day than any two people properly deserved.

Chapter Fifty Five

The showground was already half empty as she drove in, and she pulled over by the gate to allow a couple of trailers and a lorry to pass her on their way out.

Peter and her mother were waiting beside the score board, and it wasn't clear from their expressions how well Gypsy had scored as she approached.

Peter said, "Did you all get back alright? I still have the odd misgiving about that Rufus pony."

"He was OK," she said. She turned to look at a departing trailer so as not to give away any hint of their adventure with the tractor. As she well knew, both her mother and her instructor were sufficiently sensitive to guess immediately if anything untoward had happened.

"So how did we do?" she asked, peering back at the results list on the board over the table, where most of the riders had already claimed their score sheets.

Incredibly, from an entry of twenty-eight horses, and over the seventeen movements in the test, the result was a three-way tie, with Gypsy sharing first place with last year's winner and another horse whose name was unfamiliar to her. Even the collective marks, the usual differential when scores were level, were the same for all three.

The secretary appeared beside them. "That's so rare," she said. "We had to go back to the cupboard for more 1st. rosettes." She recognised Sophy, still in her boots and breeches. "Well done. I never thought you'd be up there when you first came after Christmas. You've done wonders with that horse."

Sophy was embarrassed and grinned at her. The woman picked up her score sheet off the table, with its accompanying rosette, and gave it to her. She also gave her a small square envelope, smiled, and went back to her own table.

Holt clapped her on the shoulder. "Your first professional prize money," he said as she opened the envelope and found a ten pound note. He chuckled. "Don't forget to tell the taxman."

Her mother gave her a heartfelt hug. A tall dark woman of about thirty, immaculate in white shirt and stock and cream jodhpurs, came up and collected the last sheet, with the same 1st. rosette and envelope that the secretary had just awarded to Sophy. She saw the rosette Sophy was holding, and deduced who she was.

"Sophy Taylor?" she said in a soft, cultured voice. "I've heard about you." She held out a languid hand. "Thought I had this in the bag this year, except maybe for Elspeth of course. Then my new boy went lame before Christmas and he only came right last week so I haven't been able to school lately. Luckily we'd already done enough to qualify."

She turned to Peter. "You're Peter Holt, the trainer," she said. "We must talk. I'll call you one day."

She proffered a smile at all three of them and walked away towards a large, nearly new horse box with a magnificent, bright bay warmblood horse tethered to it who was being fitted with a travelling rug by a young woman in jeans and a baseball cap who appeared to be a paid groom.

Edith was irresistibly reminded of Sophy at much bigger shows in the past. The lorry, the help, even the horse, had a ring of familiarity which was at once nostalgic and upsetting.

"Who was that?" Peter asked of nobody in particular. He glanced around at the secretary, who was gathering her papers together at the end of the day. She heard him and looked up.

"That's Judy Sampson," she said. "She's a lawyer, works in London. It's her father's firm I think. She's been coming here for years."

"Sounds like a good client for you," Sophy's mother said to Peter, who did not immediately respond. Sophy was frowning. It wasn't so much that the woman seemed to have everything she used to have and didn't have any more; it was that Peter's professional attention looked like being diluted away from her even further.

She was at least partially reassured when he did answer.

"We'll see," he said. "I don't want to be run off my feet, after all I am supposed to be partly retired. It's no good taking people on if you can't give them the time they ought to have."

The secretary passed them with her arms full of spare judging sheets and the other accoutrements of her show day occupation. She spoke to Sophy.

"I suppose you'll be promoting yourself to affiliated now," she said. "We do have a summer series too, you know."

"Well, you know *I'll* be back," Peter said to her with a smile. "On Wednesday, actually. Didn't somebody say you were going to join my student ride? Let me help you with that." He nodded a farewell to Sophy and her mother and went off with the other woman towards the office in the stable yard.

As mother and daughter drove out, with Edith leading the way, his old Land Rover was the only vehicle left in the car park.

Within a few days, in spite of none of the equestrian participants speaking of it except among themselves, Kitty's brief drama on the way home that day was common knowledge at the 'Shepherd and Flock' and, as was naturally only to be expected, also among Mrs. Mullins' customers. Whatever Sophy's discreet intentions might have been, the tractor driver occasionally patronised the public bar, and had no compunction in describing the incident if only to draw attention to the verbal 'sorting out' he had delivered to the dog owner.

As luck would have it, the day Sophy's brisk, brave reaction came to Peter Holt's notice was the day before he, Sophy, Mrs. Kenley, Hilda Gordon and the estate manager all chanced to be on the yard at the same time.

Gypsy had been out for a hack that Thursday morning and was dozing comfortably in his box, but at three o'clock in the afternoon he was roused by the sound of vehicles and voices to peer lazily over the stable door and see what was occurring.

Mrs. Kenley and Hilda had come to see Sophy's lesson on Annie-May, and Miss Brown drove in from a farm visit just as Eddy was opening the Bentley door for his passengers to alight. Peter Holt's old Land Rover followed her through the gate.

Sophy was pulling on her riding boots in the tack room and hopped to the door on one foot to wave hello. Annie-May, tacked up and ready for work, banged her stable door, impatient for attention with all these people about and none of them talking to her.

Peter Holt acknowledged Jenny Kenley with a brief nod and made a beeline for Sophy.

"What's all this about a tractor and Kitty falling off last weekend?" he demanded accusingly. "Why don't I know about it?"

He seemed quite cross and Sophy dithered and did not answer. Mrs. Kenley and Hilda approached. Miss Brown was still fiddling with papers on the front seat of her car.

It was necessary to say something.

"It was nothing much," she said finally. "It was over in a second. Me and Joe thought it best not to talk about it."

A frown of confused concern came over his face. "I think I know why you didn't tell me," he said then. "I appreciate it. But it's OK. And bloody well done you."

"And this is about?" said Jenny Kenley, curiously.

Annie-May banged her door again. Miss Brown called over from her car, "Will someone please get that horse out before she does some damage?"

Sophy grabbed her hat and escaped with a muttered excuse to lead Annie-May down to the school. After a moment the others followed, with Eddy bringing up the rear as Peter explained the incident on the way back from the show last weekend.

Mrs. Kenley listened attentively. Hilda Gordon was seriously impressed and watched Sophy as she mounted with rising respect. Peter went to begin his class, closing the school gate behind him, and the secretary touched her boss on the arm and said something to her which obviously met with approval, as the two of them smiled at each other before turning to watch the horse.

The first half of the lesson went well. In spite of Annie-May as ever showing off to her small audience, Sophy was accustomed now to her extravagant trot with its big, soft, swing through the back and could sit to the stride with comfort and confidence even when she produced her spectacular extensions. Even the instructor's call for the first time for a metre or two of leg yielding from just inside the track to the fence did not phase either of them. It was clearly one of those days when Annie-May had decided that she would perform these strange exercises out of regard for her rider and trainer, and save her explosive gallop for another occasion.

The other occasion was not long in coming. The first request for a medium canter produced a flying, flat stride more suited to the racecourse than a riding arena, and Sophy found herself totally at Annie-May's mercy for three complete circuits of the school.

The watchers by the gate were horrified. Holt stood in the centre with his hands on his hips and watched with a small smile on his face. There was nothing he could do, but all his instincts told him this was Annie-May's last throw of the dice. She was making quite sure everybody knew who was really in charge here before she condescended to pay proper attention to what she was asked.

With another horse, one who was actually running away with his rider rather than just making a point, there might have been the danger of a fall in a corner, but Annie-May was far too athletic and too smart for that. And he had confidence now in Sophy's own instinct and ability to ride out the storm.

Sophy knew in two strides she would not be able to stop her. Once upon a time she would probably have screamed, and hung on to the reins, and fallen off at the first corner. Not today.

Trusting the mare to keep her footing, she slightly lifted her seat, leaned a little forward, and took care to keep her own balance in the turns. It was hair raising, but it was rideable. And she knew that Annie-May would never hurt her on purpose. In a moment of inspiration, she leaned more forward half way down one long side and gently pulled her ear, and immediately Annie-May slowed down and a few yards further on she was able to ride her into a reasonably round working canter and turn on to a circle in the centre of the school.

She looked towards Holt standing in the middle of the circle, out of breath and very relieved that she and Annie-May had survived without a catastrophe. Incredibly, he raised his cap and winked at her. She could not know he was hiding his own relief. He took his pipe out of his pocket. A wide grin creased his face.

"Stop messing about," he said. She eased the mare down into trot and then walk and stared at him. He stared back as Annie-May of her own volition stopped right in front of him and gave a short, loud snort. She put her nose on his chest and pushed him backwards. In the next moment, all three of them were laughing out loud. The spectators were mystified and looked at one another in bemusement.

The instructor lit his pipe.

"Go and ask again for a medium canter," he said to her. "Just a few strides. Then try to collect it with only your seat and no rein at all, just keep the shape. Do it twice on each rein. I'll bet a pound it's magic. Then walk round once on a long rein and then get off and give her a cuddle." He grinned again. "You'll both like that. Don't start until you know you're both relaxed and ready."

For Sophy, and to a lesser degree to the watching 'boss' as well, the following five minutes provided another example of the man's preternatural ability to read and empathise with the horses under his care.

Having stretched herself to her heart's content, and reminded her current guardians she was still without doubt the fastest horse on four legs and not to be trifled with, Annie-May delivered medium canter with grace and aplomb exactly as ordered, and when offered a long rein promptly headed straight for the man in the middle and rubbed her nose on his arm.

Sophy looked down at him from the saddle over the mare's sweat streaked shoulder. Her face was alive with joyous satisfaction.

"I'm still jealous she loves you best," she said, pretending to pout.

"*I'm* jealous you're the one riding her," he said. "Go on, cool her off and then come to the tack room. It's time for a campaign meeting." He patted Annie-May's neck, ran his hand softly over her eye in a gesture of pure affection, and set off towards the gate.

There were just enough chairs and coffee mugs in the tack room to accommodate all the participants and have a mug to spare for Eddy, reading the paper in the Bentley front seat.

When Sophy arrived, with Annie-May's tack over her arm, Peter Holt seemed to have assumed the chairmanship and invited her into the seat next to him. It was evident he had planned the occasion at least to some degree, as unusually there was a packet of chocolate biscuits on the table, which would not have survived Kitty and Jennifer's attentions for ten minutes had it been a regular feature.

Mrs. Kenley picked up her coffee mug and selected a biscuit with a smiling aside to her assistant.

"Not quite the same ambience as the last board meeting we attended," she said to her.

"Sorry about that," Holt said, and they exchanged one of those private glances which tied them together across the huge divide in their separate circumstances.

"Now then," he went on. "I know Annie-May played up this morning, but she's coming on well and I was happy with what happened at Downside. It wasn't perfect, but it was a necessary experience and I don't think we could have expected more. I think it's time we introduced her to the big wide world of proper competition.

"There's a well known equestrian centre outside Winchester which is staging a four day dressage festival in three weeks time to celebrate its fiftieth anniversary, and I think we should start there. There's a Novice and an Elementary class on the same day, the Friday, so you could take Gypsy as well," he turned briefly to Sophy sitting beside him. "It'll be a sort of coming out party for both of them. And for us too, I suppose." He grinned at Sophy.

"As a matter of fact, I went up there and did a recce last week. The arenas are top class, and there's covered stands to watch from, not like some places which don't have any spectator facilities at all."

Sophy felt a flutter of nerves. She knew the venue he was talking about very well. But suppose Annie-May did what she did this morning in the ring? And then she remembered the medium canters which had ended the session. He had to be right. It must be time. They could school for another year, and Annie-May would still be Annie-May.

Mrs. Kenley felt Hilda press her arm. "Whatever you say," she agreed. She looked at Sophy and spoke quietly and earnestly. "You mustn't forget I've ridden myself. That was a very fine thing you did last weekend with that child. And I don't know anybody who could have handled Annie-May better than you did this morning. It's Hilda's suggestion, and I'm a little bit cross with myself that I didn't think of it first, but I'd like to sponsor Gypsy for you, you know, pay the bills for him."

It was a bolt from the blue.

"I couldn't possibly part with Gypsy," Sophy said, alarmed and faintly bewildered by this unprecedented suggestion.

"That's not what I meant," Mrs. Kenley said gently. "I wouldn't dream of trying to buy him. I just thought I could help with entry fees and the livery, that's all. He's your horse and always will be. But if he and Annie-May are going to shows together, and you're riding for me, it does seem to make sense. I know I said I wouldn't pay for him when we started, but we women do change our minds sometimes. And I didn't know you then. If there's one thing business does teach you, it's to be careful who you trust."

The compliment was lost on Sophy, but not on Peter Holt. Sophy still looked a little bemused, and he answered for her.

"We're very grateful," he said, smiling broadly at his pupil's confusion.

"I'll draw up an agreement," Hilda said, smiling in her turn.

Holt had another thought. "What will happen if Gypsy beats Annie-May one day?" he said mischievously.

"He'd better not," Jenny Kenley said severely, and it took a moment for Sophy to realise she was having her leg pulled by serious people who had a growing respect for her. It was a warm feeling of friendship if not family. She reached up to her Dad's medallion. He'd be proud. She swallowed a small lump in her throat and forced herself to pay attention.

"There is one other thing," Jenny Kenley went on. "It seems a long time ago now but I mentioned when we had dinner together I was interested in buying the estate, the house, the farms, the stables, everything. Well, Hilda tells me the negotiations are all progressing very satisfactorily. Tell me," she looked at Peter Holt. "I've been looking into some of your past exploits before the acc...well, before you came south. It's amazing what Hilda can find on the internet. If it all goes through, why don't we acquire a couple of eventers and really make you work for a living?"

Holt regarded her with a quizzical frown and raised a crooked eyebrow.

"The question is," he said, and he and Jenny spoke together before they both broke into laughter, "am I past it?"

Chapter Fifty Six

For the first time since she'd sold her car, when Sophy visited the bank in Chichester the following week she actually paid in more money than she had spent. Obliged by her mother's insistent nagging to record everything, it was a hugely satisfying moment.

Returning to the yard for a lesson on Gypsy, whose work was now so reliable they were working on the beginnings of collection, she said as much to Peter as she dismounted and on the spur of the moment casually offered to buy him a drink in the pub at lunchtime.

He responded with a smile. It was a far cry from their first encounter in this very school, a little over six months ago, when she'd regarded him with anger, confusion and suspicion and she herself had almost no experience of ever visiting a public house.

"You should be careful, inviting strange men to pubs," he said as they walked together back to the yard. He watched over the stable door as she untacked Gypsy and gave him a pat and a hay net.

"You're not a strange man," she said as he stood back to allow her to lift the saddle off the door.

He made a wry face. "Well, not to you I dare say. But most of the world doesn't do horses for a living, or live alone with whippet, so you'd have to say it's all relative."

She wasn't sure how serious he was.

They were sitting in the bar sharing a drink and a snack and talking about Annie-May's prospective lesson that afternoon when Sophy's phone rang. A glance at the screen told her it was Felicity calling.

She made an apologetic face across the table and answered it. Felicity was concerned that now Downside's season had ended, and knowing that she had at least two other horses to ride who were both more advanced than hers, that she and Toby were going to be left out.

Sophy was caught off guard. She hadn't ridden Toby or spoken to Felicity for over a week, he hadn't qualified for the championship show, and if the truth was told she had barely given either of them a thought in recent days.

She took refuge in an excuse, announced she was too busy to talk now and would call her back later.

It was impossible for Peter Holt not to have overheard her half of the conversation. He took a bite of his cheese bap and regarded her with mild amusement.

"What it is to be in demand," he remarked with a smile. "I had a feeling she'd call you. I taught her a couple of days ago, last time I was over there, and she's getting more confident but I don't think she'll ever want to compete again. Another happy hacker. But she does like to watch her horse in the ring, and Downside's summer season will start in a few weeks. Are you going to keep him on?"

Sophy hesitated. "I don't know," she said. "He's a nice little horse, but what would Mrs. Kenley say? And will I have time?"

Briefly, Holt was silent.

He was remembering the spoilt, bitter, selfish girl he'd first seen schooling last August, treating her horse with callous disregard and yet even then showing signs of a rare ability which had excited his interest.

The question then had become not so much whether she possessed the potential talent, but whether she could come to terms with what life had thrown at her and accept the compromises that all apprentice professionals have to make.

He'd made those compromises himself all his professional life. As he well knew, in the course of a week, or even a couple of days, a freelance journeyman horseman could be asked to long rein and back a youngster, teach a seven year old child on a nappy pony, ride a racehorse on the gallops, go hunting on a green pointer and then ride a horse he'd never sat on before over a five barred gate.

In many ways, Sophy had no idea how fortunate her first steps along the road had been, especially when her interest was confined, at least for now, to dressage, a discipline which had been in its infancy all those decades ago when his own career was just beginning.

Even so, from Sophy's point of view, it must seem a far cry from riding Annie-May for a millionaire in a prestigious Elementary class to hacking a cob like Toby for a nervous, middle aged spinster whose sole ambition was to see her horse perform an adequate, unaffiliated Prelim. test. While he well knew that each and every equestrian experience was an opportunity with a value all its own, she would not be the first of his students to wonder if some activities were beneath their dignity or just not worth the effort.

"You don't get to the top without starting at the bottom," he said seriously. "Look what Rufus has already taught you about riding Annie-May. And a little horse like Toby will teach you far more about balance than any fancy warmblood up to twice your weight. If you let him." He paused. "It's got to be your decision, though. Believe me, it's a good one to have to make when you're just starting out. When I first went independent it was ages before I could even think about saying 'no' to anybody."

Sophy looked thoughtful. "But what about……," she started to say, when he stopped her.

"Jenny's paying us handsomely to produce Annie-May," he said. "But she knows and so do we that it's not a full time occupation. The fact that she's chosen to sponsor Gypsy doesn't make any difference. You and me," he grinned at her, "are both freelance. We don't have to have all our eggs in one basket, and it wouldn't be wise either. Suppose Annie-May went lame, or Jenny decided to move her to another yard? How would you manage? You wouldn't be buying me lunch that day."

He regarded her quizzically with his head on one side and a slight smile. It was a shattering thought, and for a long moment there was silence between them.

Holt broke it. "I know," he said. "I don't expect for a minute it's going to happen, but as a self-employed person you have to look out for yourself. Horses are unpredictable and work can vanish in a minute. And there's always someone who puts you up on a dangerous horse and doesn't tell you, or gets you committed to a project and then doesn't pay what they should."

While Sophy could easily imagine a horse not behaving properly, it was harder, with her limited exposure to the vicissitudes of life, to think of someone deliberately endangering a rider through carelessness or worse. It was an aspect of where her career might take her that had never even occurred to her.

Holt saw the doubt cross her face. He spoke quietly then.

"Horses are wonderful," he said to her. "But sometimes people aren't. We just have to stay awake, that's all."

He thought suddenly of Tony Kenley, and the fraught relations he'd observed between him and the girl sitting opposite him. Without knowing what had happened between them, still she might have been finding that out for herself already. For a moment, he was thoughtful on his own account. Anybody'd think I was this kid's father, he reflected, and inevitably then the remembrance came of the last time he was caring for teenagers and the reason why he was here in the first place, trying to remake a life hundreds of miles from home.

He forced himself back to the present and drained his glass.

"Come on," he said. "Enough doom and gloom. It might never happen. And there's a rather lovely grey lady waiting for us just down the road."

Annie-May's acceptance of her new role in life gradually become more established, and while it was never possible to guarantee her responses, still there were times when Sophy could ask her to use her natural advantages to full effect instead of just trying to keep her contained.

Medium canter was also coming together A judicious compromise, which involved allowing her the freedom of the hills to stretch her legs a couple of times a week, had pointed the difference between her new role and her racing days, and she no longer regarded the aid to lengthen in the school as an excuse to take charge of the proceedings for the next five minutes.

Confidence was growing, in both the rider and the trainer, that Annie-May was not going to let them down when the time came for her fully fledged debut at a 'proper' dressage party.

There was much to do on the Tuesday before the big day. Annie-May was scheduled for a ride out on the Down first thing, and later in the morning Peter was coming to give Gypsy a final tune up before he was allowed to relax with only light work for a couple of days before his first affiliated class.

Peter also wanted to discuss transport with her, although there probably wouldn't be time until later this evening. They'd been expecting to hire Downside's box, but it had recently broken down and was still off the road. In addition, neither of them knew how either of the horses would travel, but with the show only two days away a decision was urgent.

Annie-May was well experienced and unlikely to be difficult whether they chose to hire a trailer or engage a carrier, which would be much more expensive, but Gypsy was another question altogether. So far as Sophy knew, he'd only ever been transported twice, and the last time, to come to Fairgate, she'd watched three men take over an hour to load him.

After lunch, she was due at Downside to school Toby in the indoor school for half an hour before Felicity, heart in mouth and greatly daring, took him out for a first brief hack accompanied by one of the students; and in the evening the four girls were due for a lesson ahead of a Pony Club dressage competition that same weekend.

Late in the afternoon, returning from Downside, she parked a little wearily in her usual place and noticed that Joe's car was already here, and Rufus and Blackie's stable doors were open. She wasn't late, but they must be waiting for her in the school. The cup of coffee she'd been anticipating before the lesson started would have to wait.

As she closed the car door there was the sound of another vehicle approaching in the lane and she turned casually to see who it was, expecting the other girls to be arriving.

A pale green, two horse lorry passed the gate, closely followed by a small saloon car. It was odd, because although the lane eventually became a track which returned to the main Chichester road on the other side of the Down, it was barely passable after another hundred yards for motor traffic, and there were certainly no more dwellings on the way.

Then her other two young clients arrived in the same car, leapt out and rushed off to the paddock to collect their mounts, and their single parental escort came towards her to chat. There were other things to think about as they walked together down to the school, where Joe was keeping a watchful eye on the two earlier arrivals.

Kitty saw her and instantly rode over to the gate.

"Have you got your times yet?" she said eagerly. "Me and Jennifer think we might be able to come and watch if you don't go till late. If Dad takes us straight from school."

She looked doubtfully at Joe, who shrugged. "I know it's not feasible," he said, "but you know Kitty. And it's a big show, apparently. She'd love that, they both would."

It was hard to find fault with such devotion, but still it was necessary to create a differential between them. She spoke to the pair of them as Jennifer rode up to join her friend.

"I'd love you to come," she said, and was surprised to find she actually meant it, "but I won't get my times until tomorrow, and in any case it's too far. You need to concentrate on your own tests on Sunday. Why don't I come and watch you instead?"

She turned to Joe, who nodded enthusiastically. "Now that is definitely a deal," he said.

Kitty and Jennifer exchanged a disappointed glance.

"Will you help us before we go in?" Kitty demanded. "Like that posh girl who brings her own instructor?"

Sophy laughed and Joe chuckled to himself. The 'posh' girl had been a source of envy for these two ever since she came into the neighbourhood and joined the local Pony Club a year ago.

The arrival of the other two members of the class, already mounted on hastily brushed ponies and eager to begin, closed the conversation and Sophy followed them through the gate to begin the lesson.

With the experience of a dozen lessons behind her, she was confident enough now to enjoy teaching what Joe was inclined to call her local fan club, and by popular demand she closed the class with some formation riding.

Her four pupils had become familiar with the exercise over the past weeks and today produced a polished and accurate demonstration which was highly satisfying for the participants and even elicited a few hand claps from the spectators by the gate.

As they filed out past him, with Sophy bringing up the rear to close the gate, Joe said to her, "They could do that at the village fête this summer. It would go down a storm, I bet. What do you think?"

Sophy, expecting Peter any minute to make the transport decision for Friday, anxious to get home for her tea and due to meet Terry in the 'Shepherd and Flock' later, paused looking slightly blank.

"I suppose it might work," she said uncertainly. She'd never actually been to a village fête.

Joe laughed at her doubts. "Don't you worry," he said. "It's months away yet. I'll have a chat with the vicar, he does most of the organising."

They followed the ponies into the yard; all four girls were standing in a line still holding their ponies and staring in awe at an immaculate, twin ramp, pale green two horse box parked beside Joe's car. It was clear from the windows it was fitted with day living, it sported the latest number plates, and was obviously brand new.

It was also discreetly sign written on both cab doors with three lines of black lettering, proclaiming *Kenley Industries* DRESSAGE HORSES *Rider: Sophy Taylor*.

Chapter Fifty Seven

Peter Holt had not been to an offically recognised show, or excepting only Downside a show of any of any size or description, since leaving Yorkshire.

At half past ten on that bright Friday morning he drove Mrs. Kenley's new box with its precious cargo through the wide, automatic double gates at the head of Harrison Equestrian Academy's drive suffering a confused maelstrom of emotions, with doubt and an unaccustomed feeling of trepidation chief amongst them.

It was very unlikely to happen today, but in the relatively small world of equestrianism, he had to be prepared for someone, eventually, to recognise him, and what would follow would be out of his hands. While he had finally satisfied his own conscience about that distant event, with the unknowing help of his Fairgate friends, whether an indifferent stranger would believe him culpable or innocent would depend on their own interpretation of the facts.

Sophy, sitting beside him in the cab, with Teddy curled up on the seat beside her, had nerves of her own and did not notice how quiet he had become.

The horses had travelled well. Annie-May, like the old hand she was, had loaded easily with her ears pricked, and Gypsy, trusting the girl now leading him who had been riding him daily for several months, had followed her up the ramp with barely a pause.

The new lorry rode smoothly enough, and Holt was an experienced livestock driver well used to the need to look farther ahead than other road users, whose passengers were safely sitting down, and so were less likely to be unbalanced by sharp braking or a curve taken too quickly.

The lorry park was busy but not full, and he eased the little box to a halt between two much larger vehicles, with plenty of space for the side ramp to be lowered, before he switched off the engine and turned to Sophy.

"So," he said with an encouraging smile. "This is it then. At least you've been here before so you'll know your way around. Let's get organised. I said I'd be your groom today and I meant it. We've got an hour before Gypsy's test so if you want to see if anything's changed and check things out I'll tack him up for you. Go and see if there's anything in the arena he might not like. I think we'll leave Annie-May where she is for now."

He swung round in his seat to survey the lorry park and the car park beyond. "I see no Bentley," he added with a grin. "I don't think the others are here yet, but even if they are we mustn't be distracted, not this first time. Off you go then."

She'd learnt the tests, of course, but she hadn't seen a sixty metre arena for nearly a year. It looked huge compared with the forty metre school at home and Downside's tight indoor arena, but otherwise the venue was unchanged from the last time she'd been here.

Apart from the size, the only thing about the arena that might upset Gypsy was the low grandstand along two sides, canvas covered in case of bad weather, but it was unlikely to be densely populated for the Novice and Elementary classes where she was entered. In any case, having ridden here before, she knew there was always a minute before the bell rang to ride round and get used to things.

It was a strange, different feeling to be here today, when she was riding for a living and not just to please herself. She watched a couple of competitors in the Prelim. class, going full swing in the main arena where she would soon be riding Gypsy, and found herself critiquing their performance with far more perception than she used to have.

A voice behind her said, "We haven't seen you for a while," and she turned and managed to smile briefly at the steward, clipboard in hand, moving to open the gate as the test finished.

"Better get on," she said to her, with an unconscious pun, and made her way back to the lorry.

Gypsy was brushed off and tacked up and Peter Holt was holding him ready for her and chatting to a smart woman in breeches who looked familiar and seemed to belong to the lorry next door. Her brow furrowed as she came closer and recognised Judy Sampson, her rival from Fairgate.

They acknowledged one another warily and without much enthusiasm. Holt was faintly amused but made no comment.

Judy Sampson said, "I'm a bit early. I thought I'd have lunch in the restaurant. I'm only doing the Elementary. I see you've got an entry too. I don't think I've seen your other horse."

Sophy agreed that this was true. "She's still on the lorry, " she said.

"Bit lively, eh?" said Ms Sampson, and Sophy frowned.

"I should warm up," she said to Peter.

"You should," he said. "Come on."

He gave their neighbour a polite glance of disengagement and turned his full attention to Sophy. She buttoned her jacket, put on her hat and gloves, took her whip out of the cab and he legged her easily into the saddle.

"I always mount off the ramp," the watching Ms Sampson remarked in a faintly superior tone.

This time it was Peter Holt who frowned. "We have our reasons," he said to her, but without elaborating.

He had not discussed it with Sophy, but with so many new experiences crowding in on him, there was no need for Gypsy to be exposed to a new method of mounting on top of everything else. It was also entirely possible he would object to standing beside the ramp, which might deter him from loading later, and would certainly not put him in the right frame of mind to give of his best in the ring. It was also true that many years ago he had seen an inexperienced, fidgeting horse badly damage a foreleg on the protruding closure bracket.

Sophy's feet were finding the stirrups when he said suddenly, "Just a minute. We'll do the leg exercise again."

She stared down at him, aghast. Ms Sampson, talking to her groom beside the front of her own lorry, heard him too, and they both turned to see what he meant.

It was *excruciatingly* embarrassing. Quite unashamedly, he put her through the same stretching routine, culminating with her head touching the croup, in full view of anyone who cared to watch, that he had done that first day.

When finally she was allowed to sit up, the first thing she saw was the Sampson woman's expression of disbelieving amusement. She could have killed Peter Holt at that moment, but he was completely unmoved.

"How's it feel?" he asked her, and she was obliged to admit it felt good. Not only was she sitting deeper, the tension had eased out of her.

Out of nowhere, Mrs. Kenley and Hilda Gordon appeared.

Mrs. Kenley looked up at her and said, "Hello, Sophy. We just passed your Mum and your boyfriend in the car park."

She turned to Peter. "All well?" she asked, glancing at the lorry. He chuckled then.

"I might know you wouldn't do things by halves," he said to her and they both laughed. He spoke to Sophy. "You'd better get going," he said. "We'll find our own way."

The Harrison Equestrian Academy featured two full sized outdoor arenas as well as a smaller indoor school, and on dressage show days the indoor school served as the warm up area. Spectator viewing was limited to standing in the doorway, with the constant threat of impeding competitors moving in and out. After a quick glance at Sophy and Gypsy trotting calmly amongst their compeers, at Peter Holt's suggestion they left her to it and went to sit beside the arena, where the Novice class had just begun.

Terry, whose interest in the proceedings was strictly confined to what Sophy might do, volunteered to fetch everyone a cup of coffee.

Sophy was agreeably surprised that Gypsy was behaving with a maturity beyond his experience. He worked steadily into her hand, trusting her to guide him safely through the five or six other horses working within that relatively confined space. It helped, of course, that the other horses and their riders were all well familiar with the routine and seemed to have their own guidance systems which automatically avoided the confrontations an outsider would have believed must have been inevitable.

A girl on a large black horse, at least a hand taller than Gypsy and handsomely plaited and patterned, rode up beside her.

"It's Sophy Taylor," she said, looking down at her with a supercilious smile. "Where have you been? Are you back from the dead? And whatever are you riding? Did you leave the cart at home?"

It had to happen, of course. She probably couldn't attend a dressage show anywhere in the south of England without someone remembering her, and the string of expensive horses she'd had at her disposal. Unluckily, today of all days, it was Vanessa Burton, a bitter rival from those times whose resources had matched her own, but who had never managed to beat her.

She bit back an angry reply. In that moment of pause, the reality of no longer being a horse besotted teenager but a committed horse professional, hit her with a force it never had before. Gypsy was who he was, and she was proud of him, but she would not descend into defending him against silly insults from spoilt children. Peter Holt's mantra came again into her head, that whatever horse you were riding, you rode him with affection and respect and made the best possible use of him.

"Hello, Vanessa," she said. "I've had some difficulties. I dare say you know that very well. It's good to be back."

The other girl smirked, glanced contemptuously down at Gypsy, with his coloured mane pulled and not plaited and his steady but uninspiring stride, put her magnificent Danish warmblood into canter and rode away.

She passed the preceding horse as it left the arena with a nod of greeting, and heard the gate catch close behind her. Gypsy looked about with interest at the unaccustomed size of the arena and the tiers of seating behind the perimeter fence; Sophy herself was surprised by the number of spectators for which was, after all, a run-of-the-mill Novice class usually attended only by the competitors connections, who like Terry would normally watch only the horse they were concerned with.

The establishment had in fact attracted some local trade sponsors for the event in honour of its anniversary, and not unnaturally some of their personnel had been invited to attend with hospitality provided in the cafeteria. With lunchtime approaching but not yet due, the early arrivals had gravitated to the scene of the action they were subsidising, and there must have been thirty or forty people, rather incongruously mostly men in suits, spread about the two small stands.

It was time to concentrate. She allowed Gypsy to walk half way round the arena, crossing on a long rein in front of the judge's box, before picking up a trot to wait for the bell. It was a huge relief that he did not shy at the grandstands. She shot a glance towards Peter Holt as she passed; he was talking to her mother, with Jenny Kenley on his other side, but he met her gaze and winked cheerfully.

The bell rang. It was the re-beginning of real life and her spirits *flew*. Surely *this* was what she was born to do.

She turned down the centre line arrow straight, and her elation was irresistibly infectious; Gypsy caught her mood and surged forward in the big, balanced pace he usually reserved for the top of the Down with the wind beneath his tail and a lively canter in prospect.

Jenny Kenley, whose acquaintance with Gypsy was limited to occasional glimpses of him walking in the distance, gasped. Her impulse to sponsor him had been driven chiefly by a wish to help Sophy, but clearly this horse was better than that. Involuntarily, she squeezed Peter Holt's arm.

"I know," he said, continuing to watch Sophy and without even half looking at her. "They always surprise you."

When Gypsy was in this mood, he was easy to ride. She turned on to the track at C with an elegant, easy bend and lateral balance, kept the rhythm and bend through the ensuing circle and managed to keep his enthusiasm under control when almost at once the medium trot steps were called for, and he responded with alacrity and a striking degree of suspension for his type of horse.

As they changed the rein to repeat the exercises, she took the decision to sit to the trot, feeling that on his less favoured side the impetus was so strong he would fall on to his inside shoulder and become dependent on the contact for balance, a fault already noted on several occasions by the judges at Downside.

She could not know that when she sat to the trot to contain and carry the stride, with the horse's back swinging so freely beneath her, her own movements so blended with his that the picture became one of a coherent whole performing a joyful, expressive demonstration of disciplined obedience.

Gypsy was the only coloured horse in the class, and as such was bound to attract attention from the watching business folk; with a tall, attractive girl on his back who was clearly enjoying herself at least as much as her horse, and who rode with a security, panache, and aplomb not in evidence in the class up until now, one or two who did not know better began to applaud before the canter work had even begun.

Peter Holt frowned as the rattle of clapping pricked up Gypsy's ears and for half a dozen strides he ceased attending to Sophy's aids; it wasn't a catastrophe, but he was late into canter and the balance had shifted; the first medium strides were heavily on the forehand, and the return to working canter was difficult and protracted. Fortunately a loud 'Sshhh' from the steward at the gate allowed Sophy to retrieve the situation for the canter on the opposite rein, and the transitions into walk were both accurate and nicely forward. As she trotted down the centre line to halt and salute, Peter and Jenny exchanged a look of satisfaction and were moved to clap quietly themselves as she walked back to the gate patting Gypsy's shoulder.

One of the smartly suited watchers sitting close to the gate caught her eye as she approached, grinned at her and said, "Good show." And she was quite extraordinarily pleased and blushed.

She passed Vanessa Burton in the gateway, the last to go on her towering, dressage-bred warmblood, and managed to say "Good luck" more or less automatically; the other girl gave her a lofty, indifferent stare, glanced at Gypsy with the same contempt as before, and walked proudly into the arena supremely confident that she was riding the best horse in the class, and the result was a mere formality.

Sophy's satisfaction with her own performance melted a little. It was dented further when she turned to watch Vanessa begin her test, and the quality of the black horse's trot as he moved off became all too evident.

Chapter Fifty Eight

She walked slowly back to the lorry park and dismounted. Peter joined her after a few minutes and together they untacked Gypsy, brushed him down and gave him his hay net.

Sophy deliberately did not ask his opinion of her test, fearful that her canter work had let her down. Instead, she asked him about Vanessa's horse. Presumably he had stayed to watch it.

"Very nice," he observed dryly, "but handsome is as handsome does. I think that young lady is a little over horsed. There were balance problems in the medium work and the transitions. I'd be very surprised if you don't beat her. Is that what you wanted to hear?"

He frowned at her. "Let's not be petty, and we have to face it, whenever you compete Gypsy there'll always be someone with more horse than him. What's more important is that you got the best from him. And you know you did. More than that no one could ask, and you shouldn't ask it of yourself either. Mrs. Kenley, Jenny, was most impressed. Now we have to impress her with her own horse, and that might not be so easy."

They both looked up at Annie-May, watching them with cool anticipation over the partition as they attended to Gypsy at the foot of the ramp.

Annie-May was tied to the lorry being brushed and having her feet picked out when they were interrupted by raised voices from the lorry next door. Ms Sampson and her groom were involved in a loud row of recrimination, and it was impossible not to hear what they were arguing about.

"Damn it, Susan, I told you to check," Judy Sampson was almost beside herself. "You know bloody well I can't ride without it."

"I did check," the groom defended herself. "You must have taken it off the box afterwards."

"Now why would I do that?" the other woman said.

Peter and Sophy exchanged a wry glance of amusement. It seemed something vital had been left behind.

A voice from the front of their own lorry said, "Miss Taylor, you do know there's the prize giving for the Novice in the gallery in five minutes?"

Peter and Sophy exchanged a different kind of glance.

"I haven't looked at the scores yet," Sophy said.

"Please be there," the young woman was most insistent. "For the photographs."

She hurried away, presumably in search of another rosette winner.

"Sounds promising," Peter Holt said to Sophy with a broad smile. "You'd better go and not disappoint your public. I'll sort out her ladyship for when you come back."

She walked into the gallery alongside Vanessa Burton, apparently answering a similar summons, and they regarded each other with mutual antipathy. They were the last of the six prize-winners to arrive, and their host, Mr. Harrison himself, greeted them with a smile of congratulation and invited them to fill the third and sixth places in the line waiting to receive their awards from the sponsor's representative. Perhaps understandably, Vanessa headed for the third place, only to be politely re-directed to the end of the line to make way for Sophy.

It was a moment to savour. As she shook hands with the dark suited man who had applauded her as she left the arena, and accepted her judging sheet, rosette and prize, she glanced quickly down the line at Vanessa and could not suppress a tiny, smug little smile. Vanessa was very deliberately not looking in her direction, and her smile widened slightly. As the man moved on, she glanced down at her marks. Gypsy had scored 72.15%, his best ever. If only those people hadn't clapped, perhaps they might even have won.

But might-have-beens didn't matter. It was impossible not to recall those dark days last summer, when she'd had no horse at all, and how hopeless Gypsy had been, and then there was the shop, and Mrs. Mullins, and Terry, and Mrs. Kenley, and Downside, and the Fairgate kids and that bloody man Tony, and behind it all was her mother's careworn, fretful smile. That smart little rosette for third place in a Novice class at the Harrison Equestrian Academy was worth more at that moment than Olympic gold and world acclaim.

The photo was taken, she suffered the brief exchange of compliments with the other prize-winners, even managing a limp, insincere handshake with Vanessa, and made her way back to Peter and Annie-May.

Everyone was there, waiting for her. The results had been posted almost immediately the class ended, and she and Peter had actually been the last to know. The smiles and congratulations, and Terry's strong hug, made her more emotional than ever. She hugged Gypsy as hard as Terry had hugged her, and he rubbed his big, soft nose on her shoulder before turning back to his hay.

It was left to Peter Holt to get a grip on the proceedings.

"Some of us have work to do," he announced. "Well, one of us anyway."

He untied Annie-May and addressed himself to Sophy.

"We'd better get you up," he said. "You've got forty five minutes, and I've had an idea. There's that big empty field at the end of the car park, and the gate's open. Give her a canter round it before you go to the warm up area. She'll love that, and if you just keep her steady it'll get her nicely relaxed for the serious business."

Sophy looked doubtful.

"Suppose someone objects," she said.

"They won't," he said. "You won't be the first one who's done it today. And someone was lunging in there just now. And I'm going to bring Teddy on the lead for a five minute run out. The poor little beggar's been shut in the cab long enough. I might even light my pipe for five minutes."

She buttoned her jacket and replaced her gloves. Annie-May twitched with excitement as he lifted her into the saddle. The wisdom of a brisk canter before the containment of the dressage arena was suddenly very apparent.

She cantered twice round the field. Annie-May was full of beans but nicely controllable, and she pulled up a few yards from the gate where Holt was smoking his pipe and Teddy was straining at the end of his lead, staring intently towards the hedge; she glanced over her shoulder in time to see a rabbit vanish into the brambles at the edge of the field.

Judy Sampson rode into the field, her white shirt dazzling in the spring sunshine. In spite of appearing disconsolate and annoyed, she stopped to look at Annie-May with interest and slight surprise.

"So this is your secret weapon," she said to Sophy. "You don't see many Arabs doing dressage."

"She used to be a racehorse," Sophy said, feeling obliged to say something. She looked at the woman's bare arms and thin shirt, and buoyed by the confidence of Gypsy's success made an attempt at friendliness.

"Aren't you cold?" she asked her.

"Forgot my jacket," the woman said grimly. "Thought it was Susan's fault, but it wasn't. Dropped it in the straw, took it into the house to brush it, office rang, left it on the hall table." She made a grimace. "I'll have to withdraw, but I saw you come up here and thought at least I'd have a ride before I go home."

Holt puffed on his pipe and looked sympathetic. He looked up at Sophy then, and half raised one eyebrow. It took a moment to realise he was trying to tell her something.

"When are you in?" Sophy asked.

"Half an hour," Ms Sampson said. "Two before you."

She took the plunge.

"You could borrow my jacket," she said, hardly believing she was saying it. "We're roughly the same size."

Ms Sampson was stunned. "You'd really do that?" she said. "You don't even know me."

Holt stepped forward. He took hold of Annie-May's bridle and Sophy unbuttoned her jacket and passed it across. Holt transferred his attentions to Ms Sampson's horse while she put it on. The fit was adequate if not perfect.

Sophy shivered in the slight breeze. The man looked up at the pair of them. "You'd both better go and get warmed up," he said. He chuckled. "Literally." He spoke to Sophy then.

"I'll see you in a bit," he said to her. "I'm going to take the dog round the field. Be good." He walked away, with the familiar wreath of pipe smoke curling round his shoulders, leaving them standing together by the gate.

Judy Sampson watched him go with a particular interest. "I really do want to talk to him," she said. "He trains you, doesn't he? It's so difficult to get anybody who's disinterested and *good*. How good is he? I believe he has some sort of a history, is that right?"

A girl was approaching leading a horse on a lunge line, and they had to get out of the gateway. Walking side by side back towards the show complex, Sophy was careful to answer only the first question.

"I think he's brilliant," she told her. "Every time he gets on one of my horses they do something fantastic. But you can't argue. You have to do what he says."

"That looked painful, what he did to you on your other horse," Ms Sampson said. "I don't think I'd like that much."

"I'm just starting out as a professional," Sophy said without thinking, "so I have to put up with it. It does work, though."

It was the first time she'd ever said that to a stranger, if you didn't count that photographer at the pantomime.

"I thought you might be," the other woman said, offering her a quick sideways glance. "I read what it says on your lorry. I've heard of Kenley Industries. Sounds like a good job to me."

Sophy blushed. "It is," she said. "I just have to live up to it, that's all."

They rode together into the indoor school; Sophy felt a little strange, as the only one warming up without a jacket, but Annie-May was on her toes again and there were quickly other things to think about.

She did not notice when Judy Sampson was called, and then suddenly Peter was there with her jacket over his arm beckoning her to the doorway.

"How did she go?" she asked him.

"It's a damn nice horse," he said. "She did OK. Well, better than OK to say the truth. She was very pleased, and very grateful."

He walked with her to the arena gate and stood beside her as the preceding horse finished its test.

Chapter Fifty Nine

The steward moved to open the gate.

"Hello again, Sophy Taylor," she said cheerfully.

A violent storm of nerves possessed her and she couldn't move. She simply *could not* move. Her hands were trembling. A big chestnut horse passed her on its way out, and she didn't know whether a man, a woman or a monkey was riding it.

The steward, her hand on the gate, was waiting to close it behind her. Holt looked up with the same question in his eyes, saw her face and guessed her mind in an instant. He put his hand on Annie-May's shoulder and she stared down at him, barely aware.

His voice was soft and firm, but he spoke only for her. The steward was six feet away, saw his lips moving, and wanted to hear him but could not.

"Be proud," he said, holding her eyes with his. "Sit tall and deep with soft hands. Only think the aid, and she will answer, for she loves you, and you love her. Go *now* and *be wonderful.*"

He stepped away.

She lifted her eyes to look forward, and Annie-May instantly walked through the gate and then paused to look about her.

The audience had grown since this morning, and now there might have been eighty or even a hundred spectators thinly spread in the two stands. Mr. Harrison's generous invitation to attend his celebrations, extended to any one who had been professionally connected with his establishment in the past fifty years, had been accepted by more old friends, clients, acquaintances and ex-employees than he might have expected.

The gate closed behind her, and in that moment Annie-May realised that she was the star. She hadn't been the focus of attention for so many people since she'd last raced at Fontwell many months ago, and she'd won that day; it had been a breeze. She raised her lovely head high, pricked her ears, and took Sophy completely by surprise.

She strode across the arena to the opposite fence, unasked, imperious, confident, fully aware and totally in charge, in a huge, flamboyant Spanish walk. A loud murmur of astonished approbation brought Sophy to her senses. Whatever was she doing? They reached the fence at F and she turned her left on to the track. Annie-May condescended to pay some attention, came nicely into her hand and adopted a proper medium walk.

Completely bemused, Sophy automatically gave her a pat.

The audience, with the single exception of Peter Holt, assumed she'd done it on purpose. He grimaced slightly. No one could have foreseen that. Where on earth had a racehorse learned Spanish walk? Somebody, somewhere, had something to answer for. On the other hand, Annie-May was Annie-May. Maybe she just knew. At least Sophy had handled it calmly.

He crossed his fingers. Please God she conquered her nerves and had the ride she deserved. He remembered his own feelings the first time he rode for an owner; it did get easier, but the pressure for a professional to perform better than the next man was always there, and was always most intense at the beginning.

There were thirty two horses in the class, and the judge, a highly respected woman with fifteen years experience, had already seen twenty three of them. The standard had been variable, as usual, but the last test in particular had been, well, seriously dire, you would have to say. Ridden by a heavy man who couldn't sit to the trot but tried to, the horse had been hollow and unhappy throughout and finding even a six had stretched her integrity to the limit. Pen in hand, collectives decided, she wracked her brain for something positive to say.

Her teenage writer, one of the Academy students, drew a sharp breath. She looked up in time to see a flashy, grey Arab mare performing a Spanish walk across the far end of the school. Her first thought, that's all we need, was tempered a little by the quality of the medium walk as the horse turned on to the track, but it was not an auspicious first impression.

"What a lovely horse," the girl said.

"Might be alright in a circus," the judge responded dourly. "We'll see." She scribbled something bland about 'potential' on the bottom of the previous man's sheet, put it aside with relief, and rang the bell.

Sophy gathered herself. The nerves were subsiding, Annie-May was expectant, the world was waiting to be conquered. She straightened her back, felt her seat sink deeper in the saddle and wished for the trot she knew Annie-May could deliver if only she wanted to.

And she wanted to. Possessed of all the acumen of her ancient breed, she knew now what all that strange, shape-changing practice in her new home was all about. They turned down the centre line immaculately straight to halt geometrically square for Sophy to salute. As they stepped off to eventually turn right, a mere two metres in front of the judge's window, Peter Holt breathed a sigh of relief and the judge was startled to hear herself say 'nine' to the girl sitting beside her.

Over the next five minutes Annie-May proceeded to explode every preconception the judge, and indeed many of the more knowledgeable spectators, had ever had about Arab horses and their alleged unsuitability for dressage. Superbly soft and through, obedient to invisible aids, with her natural athleticism and lilting paces, and that indefinable, bewitching Annie-May pride and appeal, it was a performance which lingered long in the memory.

Without quite knowing how or why, Sophy knew she was riding better than she had ever ridden. It was only later, talking to Peter, that the answer came to her.

"The horse cannot go better than you ride," he said to her. "But it's a two way street. You cannot ride better than the horse goes. And Annie-May was surely going today."

Dressage tests are usually ridden in an atmosphere of quiet respect; Annie-May and Sophy performed that day to absolute, rapt attention.

The canter tour was stunning. Annie-May's medium canter, reflecting her racing pedigree, and with more room in the long arena, followed by her disciplined return to collection, drew gasps from the stands.

Aware that her marks were already the highest she had ever given, the judge was torn between her reputation and her conscience. That last canter screamed for a ten, and she'd already given two, but did she dare give another? And to an Arab?

Sophy turned down the centre line, asked again for a few strides of that dazzling medium trot, and halted at G with the pinpoint accuracy she had displayed throughout the test.

She had a sense that Annie-May was again saying 'is that all?' as she saluted. It was Peter Holt who broke the silence with a single, quiet handclap, which quickly swelled to a ripple of applause around the arena as Annie-May walked forward and Sophy turned her towards the gate.

As Holt had known, Annie-May was no stranger to applause and knew exactly what it meant. As they passed in front of the stand along the long side she took advantage of her long rein and turned and lifted her head to acknowledge her adoring public.

Holt grinned. He was irresistibly reminded of a royal carriage progressing down the Mall and the regal waving of its occupants. Sitting again between Jenny Kenley and Sophy's mother, he felt their emotion keenly.

"That was terrific," Terry said, sitting the other side of Hilda Gordon and clapping more fiercely than anyone. It was worth taking the day off to see Sophy do so well. He had the wicked thought that perhaps he should have brought his Dad's old football rattle after all.

Jenny Kenley had tears in her eyes, and Holt turned to her and squeezed her arm.

"I know," he said softly. "He would have loved that. And it's only the beginning."

She put her hand on his. "I'm so grateful," she said. "And I'm saying that for both of us."

Terry, two seats away, didn't hear her, but Hilda and Edith assumed she was talking about Sophy and wondered why. It was only the instructor who understood she meant Gerald, the pain of whose absence, in spite of everything, he knew in some measure still never really left her.

The applause was replaced by the murmur of talk as the girl with the clip board opened the gate.

Sophy said, "Thank you," and offered her a smile, and the girl stared up at her awestruck and admiring.

"What a fantastic horse," she said.

"Isn't she ,though?" Sophy said emotionally. She dismounted and gave her a quick hug.

"May I?" the girl said, and she too gave Annie-May a quick pat. Annie-May flicked an ear back, coolly accepting a compliment from a stranger as was only her due.

The next horse was arriving, and Sophy led her away then, through the indifferent crowd to whom she and Annie-May were just another unknown pair of hopefuls, and back towards the lorry park.

With the Elementary class drawing to a close, and only the Medium to follow, the lorry park was less congested than earlier and although Judy Sampson's box was still present, with her horse tied up outside it, the lorry on their other side had departed. Ms Sampson herself wasn't there, but her groom was rolling up bandages and gave her a nod of recognition.

Gypsy greeted Annie-May with a soft whinny of welcome back, and Sophy set about untacking her under the watchful eye of Teddy the whippet, who was keeping tabs on the neighbourhood through the open cab window while waiting for his master to return.

She'd slipped off the bridle and tied the mare to the lorry a safe distance from Gypsy, and was bending down to release the girth, when the sound of a vehicle approaching disturbed her. As she straightened up to lift off the saddle, the Bentley appeared and parked carefully in the vacant space beside her.

Eddy stepped out and put his cap on.

"Good afternoon, Miss Taylor," he said politely. "Have you done well?"

She looked at him in some surprise, the saddle over her arm.

"Er, yes," she said. "I think so." She frowned. "I don't understand. What's happening?"

In the distance behind him she could see Mrs. Kenley and Peter between two trailers coming towards her, with her mother and Terry following. Hilda Gordon was on the phone, bringing up the rear.

Eddy enlightened her.

"It's picnic time," he said with a smile and a wink. "When we came this morning, Mrs. Kenley decided it was such a nice day she sent me back to organise it with the cook." There was a hint of sadness in his eyes as he added, "It's like old times. They always used to picnic at the races. Never missed. We even had a sort of folding marquee in case it rained."

He opened the Bentley's capacious boot to reveal the biggest picnic hamper Sophy had ever seen. Packed on each side of it were half a dozen folding chairs and a collapsible table. Unhurriedly, evidently following a familiar pattern, he began to unload and erected the table.

Mrs. Kenley and Peter were approaching, deep in conversation. Hilda still had the phone in her hand and seemed to be trying to attract her boss's attention.

Peter spoke to her first.

"You should go and look at the scoreboard," he said, grinning hugely.

Judy Sampson appeared from nowhere. She glanced at Peter Holt, but she spoke to Sophy.

"I don't believe it," she said, and her usual air of sophistication had vanished. "I never saw such a score. What did you do? Did you bribe the judge?" Suddenly, she smiled, grabbed her hand and shook it hard. "I saw it," she said. She looked at Annie-May, standing quietly a few feet away. "Bloody marvellous. Never seen a test like it."

She turned to Peter Holt. "You and me, we are definitely going to have to talk. And I won't take no for an answer." She turned back to Sophy.

"And so many thanks for the jacket," she said, with undiminished enthusiasm. "Saved my life."

She turned round and realised she had made herself the centre of attention at a party where she didn't quite belong. "Oops," she said. "Sorry."

With a glance over her shoulder, she vanished back to her own lorry.

Sophy felt as though it wasn't just her hand that had been shaken.

"It looks as though you've won a friend for life there," Mrs. Kenley said.

Her patient PA finally caught her attention, and she allowed herself to be a led a little apart and the phone was put in her hand. She listened for a moment, they all heard her say, "Excellent, we'll talk soon," and she hung up and handed the instrument back to the waiting Hilda.

"It's a day for good news," she said, and there was no doubting the satisfaction in her voice. "That was Agatha. Kenley Industries, or perhaps I should say Mrs. Kenley personally, just became the new owner of the Fairgate Estate."

Holt kissed her on the cheek. "Congratulations," he said.

A champagne cork popped beside the Bentley and Eddy was already pouring it into glasses on a tray on the fully laid table. A moment later he was offering it to them.

Sophy took a sip. She really didn't like champagne, but it would be rude to say so just now. The taste reminded her that the last time she'd sipped champagne Dad had been alive. Automatically, her hand reached for the medallion hidden beneath her blouse. If it hadn't been for his car..... Her mother, familiar with the gesture, saw her and their eyes met for a moment.

"You really should go and check your score," Holt said again.

A rather more sedate Ms Sampson reappeared.

"Excuse me," she said. "I couldn't help overhearing. We'll both be wanted for the prize giving. Shall we go over together?"

"I'll come too," Terry announced. He produced his phone. "I'll take a picture." He grinned at Sophy. "I'll have it framed and put it on the workshop wall."

She stared at the scoreboard in a state of disbelief. Annie-May had won the Elementary class with a score of 88.6%. Nobody she knew had *ever* scored 88%.

Terry and Judy Sampson, standing on each side of her, realised that for just that moment they weren't there, and for Sophy Taylor, dressage rider, only that impossible number existed. Then fear struck cold inside her. It must be a mistake.

She felt a hand on her shoulder, and turned to recognise the judge, also checking the board at the end of the class as she was bound to do, standing behind her.

The judge's stern features split into a smile.

"Remarkable," she said to her. "Every now and then, you see a horse and a rider you won't forget, and it makes the whole job worth doing. And today, you and your Arab mare, you were it." She was turning to go when she caught sight of Judy Sampson, in shirt sleeves again.

"Well done to you too," she said to her, "but you met your match today. You'd better find your own jacket for the prize giving. I did notice, you know." She pointed to the logo on the pocket of Sophy's custom made jacket.

Sophy and Ms Sampson exchanged a half guilty glance and giggled like naughty schoolgirls.

"It's still on the hall table," Judy Sampson explained. Her lawyer's quick wit, and a sharp sense of the ridiculous, prompted her to add, "I can't possibly reach it from here."

She caught Sophy's eye and they both started to giggle again.

Terry was mystified. He could see that Sophy had won by a country mile, and her new friend seemed to have come second. Even so, all this hilarity hardly seemed called for.

"So what's all this about jackets?" he asked in a faintly bemused tone. Was there some strange rule about jackets? According to Sophy, there was some strange rule about just about everything else.

"Never you mind," Sophy said, trying to pull herself together. The prize giving would be on in a minute. They'd be wanting her picture again, and this time it would be her holding high the trophy. It wouldn't do to be giggling.

She grabbed his arm and pulled him closer so she could kiss him on the cheek.

"You wouldn't understand," she told him. "It's a rider thing."

Mr. Harrison appeared.

"There you are," he said. He looked at Sophy with a disbelieving smile. "We haven't seen such a score in fifty years. If you ladies would like to come this way, we can begin the formalities."

Lightning Source UK Ltd.
Milton Keynes UK
UKOW05f0221261116
288598UK00006B/254/P